THE
ANIMAL
UNDER
THE FUR

Published by Four Eyed Owl,
Village Station PO Box 204, New York, NY 10014
Editing by Dori Harrell
Cover Design by E. J. Mellow
Cover Typography by Dan Covert

ISBN (paperback) : 978-0-9981563-3-0

ISBN (ebook) : 978-0-9981563-1-6

For Joy,
whose fire can illuminate galaxies

THE
ANIMAL
UNDER
THE FUR

E.J. MELLOW

The Devil whispered in my ear,
"You're not strong enough to withstand the storm."

Today I whispered in the Devil's ear,
"I am the storm."

—*Unknown*

PROLOGUE

Nashville

I've killed more people than years I've been alive.

And for reference I'm twenty-six.

With a name like Nashville Brown, one might be surprised by this. Well, more surprised than normal when learning someone has taken lives. A woman called Nashville Brown, with her charming red hair and angel blue eyes, sounds like the type of girl who traps intruding spiders in water glasses to free them outside. Someone who might smile as a leaf floats into her lap where she sits under a giant oak, reading a book. A book most likely given to her by some small-town sweetheart or, better yet, borrowed from the quaint bookstore where she works weekends after her shifts are up at the local diner.

This girl deserves my name, deserves to laugh carefree with her head thrown back as the summer sun dances across her vibrant burgundy strands. But life, I've had to learn too early, doesn't quite work out like we expect it to. It can be cruel, a jester, and most always too short.

So I've adapted. Done what the creature I've been born into was made for—I've survived.

And by doing so, I've been able to maintain some semblance of the Nashville I should be, the Nashville that my name was meant for. I've separated her from the other me, from my other life, job, and dark soul that delights in swimming under the surface waiting for prey, a coiled snake ready to bite. This predator has a different name, though just as fake and made up, which might be my two halves only similarities. Both names were given by others. Neither of them what's legally written on some lost and forgotten birth certificate. Neither of them what my parents had called me when I first came into this world.

Which is fine.

I don't want to know that girl. I abandoned her the day they abandoned me.

So I'll take my two invented names and live my two lives and be whoever I want to be, whoever *they* want me to be.

And most of the time that's a killer.

CHAPTER 1

3
Madrid, Spain: 2300 hours

He looks as bad as he smells, a festering wound left out in the heat, and despite the opulent penthouse, he matches it well. It might be the overindulgence of gold fixtures or the mirrors stretched across every surface, but they both reek of tacky European new rich. The oxblood leather couch slumps with exhaustion as he sits in the middle, his belly a balloon about to pop the buttons down his yellow shirt.

"Mmm, where are you going, *cielo*?" the large Spaniard calls as I walk away.

I glance over my shoulder, giving him a heavy-lidded stare. "I think we should take this to a place where you can get me more wet," I purr, deliberately letting a strap of my turquoise gown slip down before slinking backward toward the large bathroom.

"*Gracias a dios!*" he whispers, flicking his gaze to the ceiling before attempting the impossible of pushing his two-hundred-and-forty-pound form from the sofa. His silk suspenders dangle with defeat as he waddles forward, his greased-back black hair, tied low in a ponytail, winks under the dim lights. His pencil-thin mustache shares the same sheen, either from a mutual hair product or from the collection of sweat that seems to always gather on his brown-hued skin. His dark eyes, which roam my body, are polished with a slight coat of intoxication.

"Turn the water on real hot, will you, *amante*?" I murmur as he comes to stand before me, and I run an obsidian shellacked nail over his belly, stopping right above the top of his pants. "I'm going to get something from the bedroom and will join you shortly."

"Join me now." He grabs my wrist with rough insistence, the scent of his recent twenty-five-year-old McCallen scotch and two Cuban cigars wafting from his palate, stale and acidic.

"But, *amante*." I lean into the round man. "Don't you want to make me *more* dirty in the shower than clean? I have some toys that will make me *very* dirty," I whisper into his ear before giving his lobe a lick, tasting salt and his vitamin B, as well as probably X, Y, and Z deficiencies.

He groans, and I can't ignore the heavy cologne mixed with body odor that flows off him like animated stink lines. Having an advanced sense of smell isn't always a plus.

"Oh, *cielo*, you might be my new favorite." He squeezes my bottom before letting me go.

I giggle and playfully swat at him before sauntering toward the bedroom. As soon as I'm out of sight, my smile drops, and I walk to my bag that Señor Bejar's men placed on the silk-sheeted bed after thoroughly checking its contents. This room is another overdecorated space draped in opal-soaked end tables, gold-dipped adornments, and intricate woven rugs. I wait to hear the water run, his bare feet slapping heavily across the bathroom's tiled floor before unzipping the duffel and taking out a purple dildo. Unscrewing the bottom, I remove the battery area and break open the plastic compartment above. A small syringe falls out.

I grin.

Not thorough enough, compadres.

Reaching once more into the bag, I remove a ball gag, twisting it open to find a clear vial of liquid. Rhythmically, I fill the syringe while replacing the objects in my carry-on. Sliding out of my dress, revealing specially made black lingerie underneath, I place the syringe in a safety compartment in the string of my thong.

I turn just as Alanzo calls out, "*Cielo*, you are making me wait too long. You better get in here soon if you don't want to be made *too* dirty."

Stopping at the threshold of the gold, silver, and marble bathroom, I catch a glimpse of myself in one of the large mirrors. My lithe body is moon pale against my inky-black wig, and I know if I looked closer, my natural blue eyes would be covered with brown. Turning from my reflection, I watch the devil himself—dubbed *El Dragón Royo*, The Red Dragon—and kingpin of the European sex trafficking trade stand under the cascading water. It's as if every pound of his evil hugs him with sick pride, every inch of his fat a woman, a body he's easily handed over, stolen, abused for monetary gain. But just as his collection of girls makes him strong, women are also his weakness. Like most men, his lower half is nothing but a divining rod trying to find water, and I just happen to be a giant overflowing lake.

Transforming my face into a feline smile, I concentrate on the back of the fat man's head and desperately ignore the rest of his naked life-size Pillsbury Doughboy form. Quickly and quietly I enter the large standing shower. Steam wafts around his large shoulders, the floor slick from the three working showerheads.

Placing my hands along his pock-scarred back, I say into his ear, "But I wasn't gone too long, *amante*, and I can promise it will be well worth the wait."

He moans in pleasure.

I'm not sure why, but I decide to look him in the eyes as I do it. It might be because this particular man disgusts me to no end, *or* I've grown bored with how easy it's become to sneak up and deliver the eternal card of sleep, or I've just finally become a sick son of bitch. Whatever the reason, at this particular time and place, I don't really give a flying squirrel's derrière, so with an even pulse I gently guide Jabba the Hut around.

He has a quick flicker of hungry appreciation as he takes in my exposed body before his dark eyes widen in shock when he finds my hand jabbing into his flabby neck, dispelling the contents of my syringe.

He stumbles backward, the poison rapidly taking effect.

"*Cielo*?" he whispers in confusion and then "*Puta!*" as he has the brief clarity of the situation.

The room shakes with his weight hitting the tiled floor, and I lean over his corpulent form now slumped in the corner of the shower, the water beating over his pathetically exposed churro. "Yes, I might be a bitch, Señor Alanzo Bejar," I sweetly coo, "but *you*, sir, are a terrible dresser, and...you smell...*bad*."

That'll show him.

His eyes rage as his body groans to react but stays paralyzed to the spot.

"Don't worry, *amante*. It won't be humiliating *at all* when they find your naked"—I flicker my gaze down—"*lacking* self dead in the shower. But I think this is a rather poetic end in comparison to the ones you often deliver, don't you think?"

He grunts in the pitiful way they all do when they can do nothing but stare and listen.

I pat his head. "Shhh, don't try and get up for my sake."

Watching his mouth begin to foam and his gaze lose the lucidness of the present, I turn away. I know what comes next and have no need to see it to confirm it.

After appearing like an airheaded side companion for the past two week (proximity is everything with these particular jobs), I've finally, *finally* located the whereabouts of his cathouses and can truly croon with contentment, those future and current women potentially saved, at least from new nightmares. Their current memories will be a different beast for them to slay.

This thought brings a growl to my throat, and I resist turning back around, exercising my true creativity with *El Dragón Royo*'s corpse. Instead I take in a calming breath and step out of the shower.

I unfortunately don't have time to play.

Running a towel over my wigged hair, I pat dry my undergarments that, after enough of these gigs, the agency has thankfully made waterproof, and wipe the suite of my DNA and fingerprints. Now a ghost in the room, I grab my cell from my bag and press in my code.

"3, is it done already?" A man's voice clicks on.

"Yes, the pig has been slaughtered. I'm sending the coordinates now." I drape my gown back over me.

"Damn, that might be the new record."

"Akoni?"

"Yeah?"

"Stop buttering me up, and inform Axel. I'm going home." I slip into my heels.

"Don't get all pissy, 3. I'm trying to compliment you."

"Yeah, well, if you had to spend the last couple evenings with this slimy blimp of a man, you'd be pissy too. Thank God I was able to dance around his advances until now."

Akoni laughs through the line. "Heavyset men not your thing?"

Opening the balcony door that's on the top level of the hotel, I shine my phone's light three times into the darkness before I duck back inside. "Heavyset perhaps. Swollen, curdled, and rancid *leche fritas*, no thanks."

Akoni chuckles again as a *thwack* hits the exterior of the building. "And here I was jealous of your trip to Spain."

Reopening the balcony, I find the expected grapple buried into the marble facade.

"Yes, by all means, next time take my place," I say, stepping outside. Madrid's summer night breeze dances through my legs, sending my dress fluttering, and I grab the handle attached to the wire.

"Nah, I think I'm good living vicariously through you."

"No surprise there." I test the line with a gentle pull. "Considering your whole life is lived vicariously through your nightly MMO gaming."

"Screw y—"

Clicking off my phone, I place it in my bag now strapped behind me and push off the balcony.

Flying over the unaware Spanish streets below, I don't look back as I zoom toward what awaits me on the other side.

My other self.

CHAPTER 2

Nashville

Her familiar lilac perfume hits me the second she steps out of the elevator. The sound of her juggling the keys out of her purse rang in my ears six minutes before that. The front door opens and then closes.

"I didn't expect you to be home already." Ceci places the groceries by the door and throws her tote on the bench that lines the entryway. Her dark skin has a slight sheen from lugging the parcels up, and she pushes her thick, curly black hair out of her face. Wearing one of her favorite baby-blue short-sleeved blouses with a jean skirt, her delicately defined legs stretch out to slip into low-top sneakers.

"The deal got settled faster than we thought it would." Lounging on the couch in my gray shorts and white tee, I glance back at my tablet—I'm playing my nightly game of Internet

Scrabble.

Turds! Triple-word score. Stupid smart computer.

With a huff I click off the screen as Ceci carries the bags farther into my large loft apartment. Situated in the West Loop of Chicago, it's part of a trendy new condo complex made from once abandoned warehouses. I moved to this neighborhood two years ago after switching to a freelance operative for SI6.

"I hope you bought those groceries with the money I left you." I walk from the living room to the kitchen, where Ceci has started putting things away. My space might be open and modern, but I made sure to cover it with enough wood to make it cozy. A butcher-block island separates me from where she opens rustic but sleek wooden cabinets.

"I didn't touch that money, Nash. It's still on my dresser where you left it, like I was some weekend whore."

"Please, I paid you too high if that was the case."

I easily snatch the package of toilet paper she throws at my head. "You're such a cow sometimes, you know that?" She glowers.

I flash her a smile.

Ceci and I have been friends for as long as I can remember. We both grew up at the Bell Buckle Orphanage in Tennessee, one of the few orphanages left in the States. Later I learned this was because SI6 is the private benefactor of the home—keeping it running fairly decently in comparison to the other foster care houses in the US. Obviously their charity isn't without reason, since they use it as a recruitment center. Orphans make the perfect operatives.

Ceci was there two years before me, and even though she was one of the youngest kids, she was never approached about a future with SI6. Most of the children weren't actually, leaving them oblivious about the real role of the orphanage. I on the other hand was sought out before the end of my first month. Considering my whacked-out genes, it wasn't any great surprise. I'm what's called an A+. Not the curriculum grade, but a genome type—A-positive aggressor. A human born with the gift of heightened senses, above-average strength, and an aggressive streak to survive.

We exist.

We walk among you.

And despite the larger population having no idea about our presence, A+ humans make up about two percent of the world's population. Most aren't functioning in society though. The majority who are still alive are held in high-security prisons around the world. These individuals either weren't found early enough, trained properly, or didn't give a shit even when they were and acted more on their aggressive side than their logical one, condemning them to a life of solitude in a windowless box with five-inch-thick walls. I could've easily ended up like that, bound with a muzzle, sedated daily with horse tranquilizers...a murderer.

Instead, my murders have merit. *Zing*!

But for real, when I end a person's life, I'm allowed. I'm ordered. It's my job. To say I *enjoy* killing would be a bit dramatic, but I won't lie—I like what I do. I like solving problems, catching bad guys, and trying to make this planet a better, safer place. If the price of that outcome is ending someone who never deserved to walk this earth in the first place, then that's the cross I have to bear. Though currently I have no weight on my shoulders.

Of course some Kill Operatives aren't like me. In fact, most aren't. The majority are regular ol' people, but with stellar skill sets. We train together at SI6, and while they put up a good fight, my kind always win—*I* always win.

It's safer for everyone, actually, if I always win, and yes, I'm working on this with my therapist.

Ceci begins to hum a tune as she places food into my fridge, and I settle comfortably onto a stool before grabbing a bag of unopened chips from the island. Normally my skin would be crawling to move, act, do *something*, but thankfully my occupation also helps ease the...emotional build up that occasionally accumulates from being an A+. Let's just say if I don't let out my aggression every so often, I'm like a tank of nitrogen near a flame, highly combustible.

After stuffing a handful of chips into my mouth, Ceci makes a face as I chew. "Want some?" I mumble, tipping the bag toward her.

"Asks the beast to the human," she mutters before turning back to her task. Ceci hates anyone who chews with her mouth open, and by doing so now, it's my subtle way of testing her devotion to me. Considering she hasn't stormed from the room or torn the bag from my hand, I'm satisfied that I'm still the exception in her life. Grinning, I scoop another handful out.

While Ceci might have been ignorant to what was going on at the orphanage, she's no idiot. We couldn't have grown up together without her becoming aware that I have certain abilities that differ from the average Joe. Maybe not to their full extent, but she knows I can lift a car to change a tire and that I can identify everything she's eaten that day with a mere whiff of her breath—another trait she absolutely hates. She asked about it when we were younger, but I merely shrugged and said I wasn't sure why I could do these things, which is true. I don't know why

I was born with these abilities and the rest of humanity wasn't. And even though I've been told numerous times by my superiors that it's a gift, a small part of me can't help wondering if it's the reason I found myself orphaned in the first place. This thought is very short lived though. If my parents didn't love me enough to work with my difference, then I'm better off not having them in my life.

All that's important is that Ceci can handle me—well, what she knows of me at least. She believes I work for a private investigating company, which isn't too far from the truth. Just replace the word *investigating* with *intelligence*, and we're golden. Because of the stack of NDRs I had to sign upon employment, I was saved from having to explain much further. I also had to sign my consent to have another K-Op kill me if I did.

Yeah, heavy stuff.

But Ceci has a wonderful ability to know when not to pry, which is probably the main reason she's the only person I've allowed to get this close. I certainly had no idea I'd be in my twenties procuring a small fortune while taking down bad guys. Especially not when I walked through Bell Buckle's doors all those years ago. I only remember being scared poopless. Of course I realize now that it was them who should have been fearful, considering I did just kill a dog with my bare hands a week prior.

But that's a story for another time.

Ms. Clarice, our headmistress, used to say I came to them skinnier than a farmer's toothpick and as wild looking as a hog. They never knew the exact date of my birth, considering I was found abandoned on the street, but assumed I was around Ceci's age because of my height and build. So they penned in the birthdate of January 1, 1991, on my birth certificate, and that's what I've been going off ever since. I also for some reason didn't remember my name, so they started calling me Nashville because of the city I was found in, and it stuck. As for my last name, well, as Ms. Clarice was filling out my paperwork, she leaned down and said, "Child, what's your favorite color?" And for some stupid reason I looked up into Ms. Clarice's warm dark eyes and said brown. So that's what I got saddled with, Nashville Brown. Made-up birthday and made-up name. In other words, SI6's wet dream.

But if my new name wasn't bad enough, I was also blessed with loud red hair. Obviously I was picked on immediately. That first week, a day wouldn't go by where I wasn't called a ginger or someone would get up the nerve to yell out *Nasty Nash*, to the pleasure of all the snickering kids in the mess hall. Eventually—okay, maybe only like three days in—the taunting pushed me over the edge, and I went crazy. I bit, scratched, and punched any kid who even looked at me funny, giving them all a proper reason to dislike a redheaded girl. They stopped their taunting after that. I might have even created a good ten-yard personal bubble around myself. Which was fine—most of those kids smelled anyway. But I mean *literally* they smelled, and not because of my heightened senses. Have you been around children lately? They stink.

Ceci was the only one who treated me with any kindness and didn't catch any slack for talking to me, all because of one reason—everyone liked Ceci. She has a voice as soothing as a spring breeze and a face of an angel. Her smooth dark skin, unique gray eyes, and then-unruly brown hair would melt all the caretakers as well as the kids. She has a way of making everyone smile, living off the love of others like it's her favorite flavored lollipop—can't get enough.

"So how was Spain?" Ceci asks as she continues to shuffle around my kitchen. "Man, I am *so* friggin' jealous you get to travel so much. If you ever need, like, an assistant or anything..."

She thinks my trip to Spain was to procure a possible new client, which again, it kind of was. Or rather carry out a client's order.

"It was all right." I put aside the bag of chips and reach for a dishrag to wipe off my hands. "I wasn't there for very long, and it was mostly work, so didn't get to see many sites."

I've been to Spain more times than I can count, but these trips are mostly consumed by work. A vacation is definitely in my immediate future.

"Still, that's so cool! Maybe I should've gone to college after all," she jokes.

Oh yeah...I might have lied to her about college too. For the four years I was "in undergrad," I was actually occupied with SI6 training, which had started in high school. My after-school "private tutor"? Yeah, foreign language, weapons, and combat classes.

Before we go much further, I should probably be honest about something. K-Ops—we hardly ever tell the truth.

Leaning against the counter, Ceci reaches up to put a box of cereal away, letting her shirt ride up, and my eyes zero in on a hideously large bruise on her waist. Her beautiful black skin made purple and splotchy. I'm around the kitchen island, pulling up her shirt faster than she has time to lean back down.

"What the crap, Ceci!" I take a whiff of her and catch the subtle scent of cigarettes, body odor, and old cologne that only fits with one individual. *How did I not notice this before*!

"It's nothing, Nash, seriously." She pushes her shirt back down and tries moving out of my iron grip, the sound of her pulse picking up speed filling my ears. "I was being a total klutz and fell."

"*Really*? You fell into a perfect fist print?" I eye her coolly. "Goddammit, Ceci. I'm going to kill Roger. I thought you weren't seeing that genital wart anymore. Jesus, I've only been gone for what? Eight days! What happened?"

"Nothing, *nothing*. Please, Nashville! Calm down!"

"Calm down! I can't *fucking* calm down," I seethe as I pace back and forth. I glance from her waist—now covered, but the bruise no dimmer in my memory—to the refrigerator door back to her waist. I finally settle on the refrigerator door. Honing my rage at the metal surface, wondering if I can tear it off its hinges. I know I can.

He is *so* dead, that piece of filth. I've never met this particular beau of hers, but as soon as she started talking about him, something felt off, wrong, like I wouldn't like him, and I quickly learned why. Glancing back to Ceci, I find tears slipping down her cheeks, and everything in me melts.

"Goddammit." I take her in my arms and hold her. "Please just tell me what happened. I promise I won't blow up again."

She starts to shake in my arms, so tiny, the smaller one of the two of us. I always felt like I needed to watch out for her, though all those years in the orphanage she'd been really looking after me. I restrain a snort at how backward that is.

"I hate when you get like this," she says between sniffles. "You're not you anymore."

"Of course I'm me." I grab the box of tissues from the counter.

"No, you're this...other you. You get so cold and resolved. You know how I hate when people are angry. You especially," she finishes in a whisper.

I look away and play with the extra tissue in my hand.

"Well, can you blame me for getting pissed? Maybe the years of seeing you taken for granted have taken its toll."

She flinches at my words, and I immediately regret saying them. But hell if they aren't true. Once we both hit high school, I watched helplessly as Ceci would go from one train-wreck relationship to the next. Always trying to find the love she desperately craved. I on the other hand, after seeing her go through heartbreak after heartbreak and asshole after asshole, wanted nothing to do with any romantic relationship. Not that my fluffy personality would have landed me in one. But still, if I learned anything by being left on the street by the people who were supposed to love me unconditionally, it's that the only person you can really rely on is you. And even that's pushing it.

We're both quiet for a while.

"I just don't understand," I say more gently. "I told you that you could stay with me as long as it takes for you to get back on your feet again. I know it's hard to find a job right now with the economy and this thing with Roger..." I have to pause, calming the rage that threatens to break free. "I don't mind helping you with money. I just can't have you going back to these dirtbags, not while you're living in my house. I thought you had left all that behind when you moved to Chicago."

She ignores my gaze, so I try a different tactic.

"Listen. I know it's hard." I frown. "Us coming from nothing can make us feel like that's what we deserve, but we don't, Ceci."

I touch her arm. "You, out of everyone, deserve the world."

It takes her a second to respond, and when she does, her voice is small as she struggles to meet my eyes. "I don't want to take your money, Nash. I feel dirty taking it."

"And you feel better getting it the way Roger wants you to?" I say in disgust. "You're better than that." I lean against the counter.

Ceci transforms into her glazed-over look she gets when she's trying to forget the reason she's fighting in the first place. It makes my skin crawl, and I realize I need to do what I should have done a month ago.

"Can you just answer me one thing?" I ask, handing her the extra tissue. She takes it while cautiously meeting my gaze.

"Okay."

"Yes or no, was it Roger?" I know the answer, but I need to hear her say it.

She stares at me for a moment, and I can tell she's deliberating if it's worth trying to lie.

With me, it never is.

Letting out a defeated sigh, she says, "Yes."

I narrow my eyes infinitesimally, reveling in the familiar shiver of adrenaline that runs up my spine anytime I come to a particular decision.

"But he apologized, Nash," she says quickly. "He really did. And he's never done something like this. I swear. I shouldn't have said those things to him. I knew he'd get mad, but I said them anyway. I was just so upset with how we left things. You know me. I can be such a bitch sometimes. Please don't be angry. I can't stand it when you are. I know it was stupid to go see him, and I promise, I *promise*, I won't see him again. Seriously,

I won't." Ceci twists her hands over and over.

Ugh. I hate what this man turns her into. Her usual strong, vibrant flame extinguished.

Forcing a reassuring smile, I take her nervous fingers into mine, calming them. "Yes, Ceci," I say, holding her gray gaze, "that's one thing we can both agree on. You most certainly won't be seeing him again."

CHAPTER 3

Carter
Paris, France: 0130 hours

I give the finest bare bottom I've laid eyes on, at least in the past forty-eight hours, a little slap as it saunters away.

"Oh, Benjamin. You are ze devil." The woman giggles over her shoulder as she makes her way into the bathroom, her blond hair turning to honey under the low candlelight.

"Mademoiselle, I can assure you, I can be much, *much* more wicked." My smile curves to one side as I stretch out on the soft sheets I've found myself entangled in tonight. Glancing down, I catch four long scratch marks on my abs and grin further, bringing to mind the manicured nails that caused them.

I think Paris is my new favorite city.

Not two minutes into my relaxed state does my phone beep from my jeans hidden somewhere on the floor. Rolling my eyes,

I hesitate for a second before retrieving it.

"Yes?"

"It's time."

The line goes dead.

Looking longingly at the closed bathroom door that houses my current favorite naked form, I sigh before quickly redressing and slipping out of the apartment.

I can't complain too much. At least they waited until after and not during.

Leaving my leather jacket open, enjoying the summer night air, I make my way through the small streets of St. Germain toward La Seine River. I wait at the water's edge, watching couples walk by arm in arm. The city crawls by lazily, tourists mixing with the locals as they mutually take in the twinkling lights of open shops and cafés. The occasional clinking of glasses and pleasant chatter fill the air as a young woman in a black shift dress and heels approaches. She leans beside me against the stone wall that runs the length of the river.

"Bonsoir," she says in a smoky voice.

I incline my head. "Bonsoir."

"Do you have a smoke?" she asks in French.

"Only *Gauloises*," I reply in her native language.

She nods, showing a brief smile of understanding.

I shield the flame with my hand as I assist her in lighting her cigarette, watching the orange glow from the match dance over her ruby lips.

"I hear the crowd at La Poison Noir is fine this evening," she continues in French, blowing a line of smoke from the corner of her mouth.

We watch a few pedestrians walk by.

"Is it?"

"*Oui*, it has the most extensive wine cellar. If you go, you *must* have a look." She takes another drag while glancing at me.

I take a moment to enjoy her femme-noir beauty of brown perfectly quaffed hair, shapely form, and dangerously full lips. Giving her a playful grin, one that she returns, I decide on a whim to lean over and whisper the name of a nearby hotel.

Pulling back, her eyes flicker over my body with more interest, and her mouth moves into a deeper smile. Taking one last puff of her cigarette, she drops it, puts it out with the toe of her high heel, and nods ever so slightly.

Tucking my hands into my jeans pockets, I watch her retreating form, keeping my eyes on a certain voluptuous lower half longer than the rest before I turn, more than pleased, and head toward my destination.

Yes, Paris is most definitely my favorite city.

After a nice walk, I come to the brick alley that shares the back door to La Poison Noir. A single bulb rests above a door, shining a yellow spotlight on a suited sumo wrestler of a man standing outside. Seeing me, he flashes the Glock 30 at his waist.

"Can I help you?" he asks gruffly in French.

I stare at his shaved head and robust build, guessing he's got about three inches and ninety pounds on me. Piece of cake.

"As a matter of fact, you can," I answer in English.

Immediately he pulls the gun from his holster, but I quickly jab him in the throat and knee him in the genitals, and when he's falling forward gasping for breath and searching for his manhood, I land a severe elbow to the back of his head, knocking him unconscious.

I stare at the unmoving mammoth of a man and wonder how the hell I'm going to drag him from this area to hide his body.

"Real smart thinking, Carter." I scratch the back of my neck as I search around the barren alley. Settling for filled garbage bags taken out by the kitchen, I pile them on top of him. It's definitely disrespectful, and he'll be extremely pissed and smelly when he wakes up, but as the French say, *c'est la vie.*

Slowly I open the back door, finding the entrance dark and empty. Taking a step in, I remove my subsonic loaded Smith & Wesson 1911S (also known as Minnie) and attach the suppressor, all the while looking around for the door leading to the cellar. I hear the restaurant patrons' chatter through the wall to my right and see the kitchen staff zipping about through the two circular windows in the swinging doors to my left. The threshold I'm in seems to be a mudroom, separating the garbage collection area from the kitchen. On the farthest wall is an unassuming black door.

Bingo.

Opening it, I find wooden stairs leading down to a cellar and catch the echo of men's voices coming up. Quietly I descend, pressing against the stone wall, its surface cold and damp even through my jacket. The stench of cigars and liquor reach my nose, and I stop a couple steps above the floor, still hidden in shadow. Filtering through the sound of things shuffling and plastic hitting plastic, I surmise they are indulging in a game of poker—at least four men are in the room.

"Ah! Gustav, you son of a bitch. If you were not our guest tonight, I would be pissed at you for taking so much of my money," rumbles a deep voice in French.

Hearing the one name I needed assurance of finding down here, I grin and step into the light. "Hello, gentlemen, mind if I join you?"

Pushing aside the glass of fifty-year-old scotch left on the table, I survey my work. In a past life I might have indulged in a sip, but my desire for anything alcoholic died a long time ago, when they did. Now I simply ignore the amber liquid while glancing around the cellar. Gustav Babineau, my target for this evening and now very dead, stares out at nothing, easily put down with the first of my bullets straight to the head. One of his bodyguards, meeting the same end, lies flaccid in a heap next to him, and two more players unfortunately needed to be removed for no other reason than they were going to shoot me if I didn't shoot them first. The last two guests have their hands in the air, and after patting them down for weapons and finding none, I see they are just hapless participants to an unlucky game. I let them live.

"I'm sorry to cut the festivities short, but the business I had with Monsieur Babineau was rather pressing." Straightening my gray T-shirt, I approach the two men staring up at me. One has his mouth pursed in contempt, while the other wobbles with uncertainty. "Now to ensure that none of you steal the pot that seems to have found its way to the floor, I'm going to bind your hands."

One of the French men spits near my shoe.

Spits.

I mean, really? Doesn't he know these are Mezlan exotic

alligator leather?

"There's really no need to be so uncivilized, *mon petit homme*." I place the barrel of my gun against the saliva-happy man's forehead. "Binding your hands is a much better alternative than what I could do instead." I lean in closer. "Or would you prefer that option?"

The man kneeling next to him, whose wire-rim glasses have begun to fog with his nervous perspiration, watches on as his companion shakes his head and lowers his glowering gaze.

"I didn't think so," I say before straightening and smacking the butt of my gun against the spitting man's skull. He hits the stone floor with a thud as the last man lets out a little squeak of surprise.

Glancing to my bifocaled friend, I give him a wink. "Don't worry," I tut. "You're next."

"Body count four. Assets standing two. No crowd drawn. You can send in the Sweep team."

"You couldn't have had body count at one, Carter? Just this once?"

I grin into my cell while fixing my dark hair in the reflection of one of the many wine bottles lining the walls. "And make your job any easier, Jules? Never."

"I shouldn't have even asked," she grumbles through the line. "I just dispatched the team. They should be there shortly."

"Perfect." I check the rounds left in my gun before placing it back into the holder at my back. "Now if you'll excuse me," I glance to my watch while climbing the stairs. "I have a certain French caterpillar hopefully naked in a hotel that I must make sure I cocoon before I leave."

Jules makes a gagging sound. "I can't believe woman mistake that as charm."

"And what would you mistake it as, my darling?"

"Being well endowed."

I stifle a chuckle. "Oh, my dearest Jules, one of these days you're going to let me show you just how well endowed I am."

I can practically hear her eyes rolling, and it makes me smile more.

"Yeah, too bad I like lady parts over boy parts."

"See! We are made for each other." I push through the back door of La Poison Noir, the warm night air wrapping around me fondly. "I like lady parts over boy parts too! Let's make love already."

Jules laughs. "Get your ass home, Carter."

"Yes, ma'am."

"And Carter?"

"Hmm?"

"Do it safely."

I grin. "Yes, ma'am."

Hanging up, I giving the pile of garbage that's in the same place I left it a fleeting glance before I make my way out of the dark alley and into the starlit night, whistling a tune as I go.

CHAPTER 4

3

Chicago, Illinois: 2215 hours

I watch him drunkenly stumble up his apartment complex stairs before he pushes open a faded green door on the fourth floor, disappearing inside. I dial a number into my phone.

"3?"

"I need a favor."

Silence, then, "What kind of favor?"

"A personal one."

Silence again.

"*Akoni*, remember Santiago?"

"Sure, sure, a favor. I can do a favor."

I shake my head, annoyed I needed to bring that up. Talk about gratitude.

"In about an hour I'll be texting you an address. I'm going to need a disappearing act for this one, okay?"

"*Ooookay?*"

"Akoni!"

"Yes! Geez, okay. I got it. Don't worry—you'll be taken care of."

I hear typing on a keyboard.

"I just need to know one thing, 3. For my own peace of mind."

I wait.

"Is this something that will come back to bite me in the ass?"

I stare at the door the man went into. "No, Akoni, I don't think anyone will be sorry to see this package go."

I slap the man lying on the bed hard across the face. "Wake up, sleepyhead."

His eyes blink open before they widen in shock. They grow even larger when he realizes he can't move. He tries to speak, but he can't do that either.

Leaning away, I regard his internal struggle for some sort of external response and take in his appearance. Bad choice of tattoos cover his—I'm very displeased to admit—impressive exposed chest, the black ink standing out against his white skin. A shaved head sits on top of a slightly attractive face but is ruined, in my opinion, by the existence of a soul patch and dirty jeans worn low along his hips. He smells of another woman's cheap perfume and booze. I cock my head to the side, trying to see the appeal.

I find none.

"You know what I think we humans take for granted?" I ask,

moving from the bed, the plastic I placed under him crinkling before I walk around the room. His small apartment is unoriginally
cliché for the type of man who lives here, and I play with random
objects thrown about. Pleather this and faux-fur that, bowls of
discarded cigarettes and joints, fluorescent illuminated fish tank
in the corner serving as our only light source. Douche bag chic.
"The human nervous system," I answer, glancing back to his
slack body lying across his wrapped sheets, his breathing erratic,
his fear pheromones off the charts.

"Yes, it's really never paid attention to." I drag a grungy-look-
ing kitchen chair to the side of his bed and take a seat. "For
example, did you know that every square inch of your nervous
system has a purpose? A job allowing you to blink your eyes." I
flick him in the eye. "To breathe through your nose." I hold his
nose shut for a second, enjoying his panicky intakes of breath
when I let go. "To even take a piss." His gaze bulges, and I can't
help but laugh. "Don't worry. I won't be going there...yet." My
smile is serpentine. "Yes, the human nervous system is quite
fascinating." I lean back, removing a piece of lint from my jeans.
"Like right now. I bet you're asking yourself, 'Now why can't I
move?' Well, I'm sure you're asking a lot more than that, but let's
stick to what's important here, shall we?"

I look to my companion for an answer, watching his veins
pop in anger and confusion, his skin beading with sweat, while
low guttural sounds are desperately trying to escape his mouth.

"Good, agreed. Now I'm sure you're asking yourself this
and didn't think that it could be caused by the slightest tweak of
chemicals mixing along your central nervous system. Did you
think about this? No, I highly doubt you did. But what I find the
most fascinating is how certain parts of the body can be function-

ally shut down yet still be open for stimulation."

I wait a beat.

"To put this in layman's terms," I continue, staring him dead in the eye, "you can't move, but you sure as fuck can feel."

The man seems to produce some wiggling after that, finding his deep-rooted animalistic adrenaline to slightly wear off the paralysis.

"Oh, do you need more fixin'?" I grab the small pouch I placed on his nightstand. "Don't worry. I've got just the thing." Taking out a syringe, I quickly dispel the blue-hued liquid into the base of his neck. He stills.

"There." I return to my seat, crossing my legs. "Now, where was I? Oh yes, not being able to move but still being able to feel. Yes, amazing, isn't it? That things in your body can be controlled like that? But I think you can relate to the appeal of things being in your control. Things being at your *mercy*. Can't you, Roger?"

His eyes lock on to my mouth, transfixed on his name coming from my lips. I give him my most feral smile.

"Yes, unfortunately, I know you very well, Roger." I snap on latex gloves before unrolling a large collection of surgical equipment. Choosing one of my favorite knives from the middle, I let the metal wink in the dark, a devil's promise. "And I think you're about to know me very well too."

CHAPTER 5

Nashville

I shuffle into the kitchen, searching for the pot of coffee whose smell got me out of bed.

"Morning," Ceci greets me from where she's perched on the kitchen island, eating cereal and reading the paper. She's in light-washed jeans and a pink blouse looking just as fresh and perky as she always does.

"Morning," I grumble.

I hate morning.

"Man, you look beat. Did you not sleep well?"

"I had some work to do until late." I pour myself a cup and lean against the counter.

Ceci drops the paper by her side. "I'm going to check out some waitressing jobs today. Are you going into the office?"

"Not if I can help it." Taking a sip of my coffee, I glance out the large windows that run the length of my loft apartment. It's too bright outside for its own good. My eyes are always more sensitive in the daylight.

After an overseas job, one that was successful, and rather clean I might add, the agency usually leaves me alone for a while. Since I already debriefed in the Madrid headquarters before heading home, there's no reason for me to get called in for at least a couple weeks. Vacation bells sound in my head again.

"Listen—about yesterday..." Ceci plays with her spoon in her bowl.

"Don't worry about it."

"No. Let me finish." She hops off the island. "You're right. I don't know why I..." She pauses, searching for the right words. "I'm not going back to those bars. I've decided to only look for jobs in safer places, maybe some of those fancy five-star establishments downtown." She tips her chin up, meeting my eyes with a look of resolution. "I think that will solve a lot of the messes I've found myself in...in the past."

"That's great." I put my mug on the counter. "I never understood why you worked in those cesspools anyway. A hot, smart girl like you? You could work anywhere."

She perks up at my approval, before frowning. "Yeah, but those places were all we've ever known."

"Well, lucky for you I also know a number of people in the downtown area that owe me some favors. I can make some calls—"

Ceci wrapping her arms around me cuts me off. "Nashville Brown, that would be *amazing*! Do you really know people?"

I smile and hug her back. "Of course. I know lots of people. I could even try and get you a position as an assistant—"

"No! No nine to fives. You know how much I *loathe* the corporate system. Though given how much you travel, I might be changing my mind." She nudges me with her hip. "But I like the atmosphere of restaurants and bars. I get to meet all kinds of people and basically get paid to talk all day. Not to mention in the right place, the tips *certainly* don't hurt."

I shake my head at her weird love for the food industry. It repels me. Having to cater to people's beck and calls. Deal with pompous assholes on a daily basis who get upset if their goat cheese isn't sprinkled on their salads just right. Yeah, no thanks. Restaurants, to me, are usually loud, crowded, smelly places. Talk about unnecessary sensory overload.

"Okay," I concede, refilling my cup. "But don't get mad at me for trying to make an honest woman out of you."

"Darlin'," Ceci says, using her Tennessee swagger voice, "that ain't neva gonna happen."

After a long run and shower, I sit in my living room indulging in an afternoon Scrabble game while searching possible vacation destinations. The island bells chimed their final toll, and I answered. Maybe I'll take Ceci with me this time. I usually like to vacation alone, but with the drama she's had to deal with lately, she deserves a beach and an overabundance of fruity cocktails.

I'm about to click on an extremely indulgent villa in the Caribbean, when my work phone buzzes.

Seeing the name flash across the screen, I curse before answering. "David, please tell me you're only calling to sing my praises for the job I did in Madrid."

"I can certainly tack that on to the reason," rumbles my group director's deep voice through the line.

I close my laptop with a sigh. "What's up?"

"Come into the office, and I can answer all your questions."

"This better be worth it. I was about to book a vacation."

"After this job you'll be able to book six."

I hold back a snort. "Dangle the carrot much?"

"More like the three commas."

Damn.

"I'll be there in twenty."

"I'll see you in ten."

CHAPTER 6

Carter
COA Headquarters
Manhattan, New York: 0900 hours

I stare at the man's photograph that's attached to his profile. Very unthreatening brown eyes and an unimpressive face stare back.

"*This* is Chenglei Kam?" I ask with raised brows.

"What exactly were you expecting? He's a businessman, not a mob boss. A very dangerous businessman, but a businessman nonetheless." Anthony Ploom, my group director at COA, takes a seat across from me in one of the many glass-walled conference rooms in our building. His small gut, which has promise for growth, pushes out of his wrinkled gray jacket as he leans back in his chair, his thinning brown hair looking more ashen under the fluorescent lights.

I was back in New York City no less than two days before the agency had another "dire" assignment that called me into the office.

"Still, he looks nothing like a man running one of the world's most notorious underground biochemical weaponry distributions."

"I'm glad you're not entirely ignorant of our situation," a woman's voice chimes in.

Jules enters the conference room and takes a seat across from Anthony and me. Her blond hair sits thick around her shoulders, covered in a black blazer. Her hazel eyes are a little too wide to be called conventionally pretty, since they make her seem like she's in a constant state of wonder, but where she hates that, I've always found it endearing, like she's a walking Disney princess.

"I'm glad you haven't lost any of your breathtaking beauty, Jules." I smile.

She merely shoots me a forced grin before launching into the briefing, the tablet in front of me filling with new images. "Chenglei Kam is the son of successful Hong Kong tech businessman Chen Kam and is in line to take over the family business. But until then he's been a rather busy boy building his own legacy. As you so accurately put it, Carter, he is well versed and deeply involved in the manufacturing of biochemical weaponry. His father knows about this side of Chenglei but is playing the ignorant card and turning the other cheek with all of his dealings. This operation is one hundred percent Chenglei's. He's already made very lucrative and successful transactions with some of our friends in the Middle East and Russia, but we have recent intelligence that he's about to make a new friend with some very powerful men in

North Korea."

I snort as I skim through the information that Jules is recapping. "Making new friends by doing trades on the playground?"

"Something like that," she says. "It's been whispered that Chenglei has a new toy in his arsenal. A very precarious new toy that he's willing to sell to the highest bidder. He's stepped out of his usual safer governmental trading routes and is taking this one digitally underground to a silent auction."

I glance between Anthony and Jules. "Okay, so where does that leave me? This sounds like a much bigger job than a step in and take down."

"Our client and main informant on this assignment have knowledge that the code to obtain the formula for this weapon is held with our dear Mr. Kam," Anthony explains. "The code unlocks an insanely secure digital diary where the formula is stored."

"What about the techs who created the digital lock? The scientists?" I ask. They both look at me without answering. "Ah, he got rid of them. Well played."

"Call it what you will," Anthony says. "But what we're being paid to do is retrieve the code from Mr. Kam before discarding of him. We can't chance this formula getting into the hands of possible terrorists."

"Do we know what the BCW is? What it particularly does?"

"No." Ploom shakes his head. "Just that it's something that has garnered a lot of chatter and desire amongst the less favorable groups."

"And what of our client? Are they to be trusted with this information once we get it?"

"Leave the morality of our client's intentions to me, Carter, and I'll leave the killing of multiple people to you."

I cock an eyebrow at Anthony but otherwise stay silent on the matter.

"Okay, so I go in, persuade Chenglei to share the coveted password that will unlock the how-tos in creating this biochemical weapon, and then put him down. Sounds easy enough."

"This all needs to be accomplished before Sunday. Sunday is the day of the silent auction."

I gape at my group director.

"You do realize today is Tuesday?" I ask. "And it takes a full day to get to Hong Kong from here. What about recon? Getting the lay of the land? Possible habits to use as points of contact? Why did you wait until now to call me in for this assignment?"

"Still sound easy?" Jules slips me a grin, and I give her a piercing glare.

"Don't worry," Anthony says. "We've got that all taken care of. Eu-fùnh Li"—he pauses for effect—"will meet you when you arrive in Hong Kong. She happens to be our current local specialist dealing with Kam."

My face lights up hearing my dear friend's name.

"Geez, try to hide your sexual excitement a little better, will you?" Jules tightens her lips.

Anthony merely shakes his head. "Thought that would make you more cooperative."

Okay, so Eu-fùnh might be, on occasion, a little more than a dear friend.

"When do I leave?"

CHAPTER 7

3
SI6 Headquarters
Chicago, Illinois: 1030 hours

"Does that sound doable?" David Axel asks as he absently spins his pen on the conference table. Around and around.

I glance from my tablet to my boss. At forty-three Axel has always been one of the better-looking older men I've come in contact with. His easygoing blue eyes and thick golden hair don't fit the job description of group director here at SI6. Most of the other men and women in his position wear the stress of the job on their clammy skin and gaunt demeanor. Axel, on the other hand, still maintains his military physique and has a lively, gentler face than a man should for dealing with what he does daily. Especially after working with me for the past six years.

"Yeah, sounds fine." I lean back, drumming my fingers on

glass table. "I've done recon on Chenglei before and am familiar with his day-to-day schedule."

"Leave it to you, 3, to be ahead of the game."

I give David a small smile and, not for the first time, find myself getting caught up in his appraising eyes.

Akoni clears his throat from the other side of the room, and we both glance his way. Like Axel, Akoni breaks the mold for a stereotypical intelligent tech assistant. With his Hawaiian descent and burly build, he appears more like a man who should be taking up space on a pro football field than slouched behind a computer screen. The only things that pigeonhole him are his thick black-rimmed glasses and his limited wardrobe of geeky shirts. His current choice is a gray tee that reads *Come to the nerd side. We have π*. He has the same one in green and red, something I've made sure to make fun of over the past three years we've worked together.

I've been trying to keep eye contact with Akoni to a minimum today. Ever since the favor he did for me the other night, he's acting a little skittish. And I'll admit, I might have been a little more...*creative* than I needed to be, but I was swept up in the moment. What can I say? I'm a passionate individual. The thought of that creature being able to break any future Cecis sent me over the edge more than once, but I felt much better afterward, which is really all that matters. Now the next time I go out of town, I'll have a calm mind knowing Ceci won't be in contact with that ingrown hair of a man anymore. The way I see it, it's a win-win. So really, Akoni can just grow a pair.

"It's about to get a whole lot easier too," Akoni says, pushing another file to light up the screen in front of me. "Chenglei is holding a gala on Friday, two days before the silent auction, at one of his family's hotels and where he's a regular resident. He most likely will be staying there the night of the gala."

I study the pictures of where the party will be held, the ornate invitation along with blueprints of the building.

"Perfect. So I fly in Wednesday, look around, attend the gala Friday, and if an earlier opportunity doesn't present itself, find our dear Mr. Chenglei Kam alone in his suite. What about the code that only he has?" I glance between Akoni and Axel. "I happen to know he won't be susceptible to torturing it out of him. He's engaged in some brutal training for such occasions."

Axel nods. "Yes, slightly unconventional actions for a businessman, but for the secrets he holds, very proactive."

"A man after your own heart, David." My group director tends to be a zealot for dramatic preparations in the name of a job, which is probably why he's the only boss here that I've been able to work with successfully. A+ can be a handful, or so I've been told.

David laughs. "Yes, if it weren't for the extremely terrifying biochemical weapons he invests in, we could have been great friends." He clicks on a hologram screen, which rises above us with more images of schematics, and Chenglei's profile floats between us as he continues the briefing. "Our client has a two-part request. In the event that you're unable to get the code, which will most likely be the case, we'll need a full DNA sampling taken instead."

"How will that help in retrieving the formula?"

"I'm not sure, but for the money they are paying, I'm not going to ask too many questions."

I silently agree. When David showed me the numbers for this assignment, I had to sit down. I've never been too curious as to who our private clients are, considering all the targets I've had to take down are deserving of their ends, but the sum for this job definitely raised my brows. Usually with a backing like that the government is a silent conspirator in the case.

"And guess what?" Akoni perks up at the other end of the table. "I'll be going with you, and I've got some fun new tech toys to show you."

"Dork." I cough into my hand.

"Psychopath." He glares at me while coughing back.

"Blow-up. Doll. Lover." I loudly enunciate every word.

"Dog killer." He matches my tone.

Damn, he's got me there. But again, a story for another time.

CHAPTER 8

Nashville

I've just finished packing when the apartment door opens and closes. Lilac and the tapping of familiar heels against the wooden floor reach me. Ceci's home.

Carrying my bag to the open area of my apartment, I catch her studying her phone with a frown as she leans against the kitchen island, the afternoon sun streaming through my windows warming her dark complexion. I have no doubt she's wondering why a certain someone hasn't reached out, and thankfully never will. She's the only person who can make me feel bad when she's upset, but in regard to this particular reason, I feel completely fine. Happy even. It's for her benefit even if she will absolutely never know.

"Hey."

Ceci glances up, and her frown deepens when she sees my

bag. "Going somewhere?"

"An emergency called me back into the office right after you left. I have to go to Hong Kong for a couple days."

"Holy shit!" She straightens. "Hong Kong. Okay, now I'm *really* jealous of your life."

I place my suitcase by the door. "You going to be okay alone here for a little bit? I know I just got back—"

She waves a hand. "Of course I will. Now I can keep walking around naked like I did when you were in Spain."

I wrinkle my nose. "Please tell me you refrained from sitting on any of the furniture."

Her answer is to avoid eye contact.

"Ceci!"

"Don't worry about all that." She clucks while opening the fridge and retrieving a soda. "When will you be back?"

I glance at all my furniture questioningly. "Hopefully by Monday, if everything goes well."

"Big client?"

"Something like that." I grab the opened can from her and take a sip. "So did you hear from my friend Christopher from Turquoise Waters?"

"Oh! Yes." Her pink blouse twirls as she swivels toward me. "I completely forgot to tell you. I'm going to talk with him tomorrow. Thank you so much for calling him. That restaurant is the hottest spot in town. I had no idea you knew Christopher Walters. Geez, Nash..." She studies me shrewdly for a moment. "Wait...*how* do you know him?"

It's my turn to avoid eye contact.

"Nashville Brown!" She screeches. "You *better* explain!"

Never going to happen.

"Oh. Look at the time." I glance at my watchless wrist. "I have a plane to catch."

"No you don't! You better not leave before—"

"See you in a couple days." I blow her a kiss and dash for the door, scooping up my suitcase. Christopher Walters and I have a slightly nonconventional relationship. When urges call, we're both there for each other, no questions asked and no complications afterward. Perfect for him to continue his notoriety for being one of Chicago's most eligible bachelors and for my constantly shifting schedule and lack of interest in anything serious with a man.

"If you think I'll let this go, Nashville, then you don't know me!" Ceci calls out as I step into the hallway.

I peek my head back into my apartment. "On the contrary, I know you better than I'd like. And now so does my furniture!"

Keys *thump* against the door right after I swing it closed.

I shake my head.

How I'm friends with someone so violent is beyond me.

CHAPTER 9

Carter
Hong Kong: 2148 hours

She slaps me hard across the face, and I growl at the assault. Throwing her against the wall, I feel down her smooth thighs and guide them to wrap around my waist. Pinning her supple form with my hips, I push into her, her gasps making me move faster, rock harder. Her nails dig into my back, and I moan in pleasure. She bites down on my lip, and the flavor of blood trickles across my taste buds. I whirl her around, laying her on the small table that sits in the entryway. A vase of flowers crashes to the floor, but we ignore it as she pulls my hair to force me to meet her mouth again, and we both explore each other as I continually pump into her.

"Ah, Carter!" she screams as I feel her climax around me, setting my own release loose. Slowly I move a couple more times before I drag us to the ground to pant and recover.

I touch my lip gingerly. "You bit me."

Eu-fùnh laughs beside me, the sound rumbly but unmistakably female. "Wouldn't be the first time."

"No, I suppose not," I say as I roll on top of her again, securing my arms on either side of her face, the marble floor cool against my skin. Eu-fùnh has a face, and body for that matter, that promises a man a good—yet probably painful—romp in the sheets. Her eyes are as black as her waist-length hair, her lips pink and full and edged with a constant tilt, as if she's ready to whisper something sinfully delicious into your ear. It makes a person want to lean in, pay attention to her next purr. Over the years, we've worked together in various cities, and no matter what our personal situations are at home, we always end up naked, sweaty, and satiated. Given that I don't have anything serious back in New York and never plan to, I have absolutely nothing to feel guilty about.

"So are you ready to be filled in on our target for tomorrow?" she asks as she rakes her nails up my chest and down my back.

"I'd rather fill *you* in a bit more," I say, letting her feel that I'm ready for round two. The side of her mouth slides up, a vision of tangled bedsheets at midnight, before she grabs my ass invitingly.

This time, I bite back.

—◼

"Okay, so you've secured us tickets to the gala tomorrow"—I filter through the papers—"and we know he's most likely going to retire early given his usual early morning regimen."

Eu-fùnh drapes my tux on the back of the couch and comes

to sit beside me. Our penthouse has two master suites, one for each of us, situated on opposite sides of the large space with a communal dining and sitting area in the middle. Floor-to-ceiling windows stretch its length and currently reflect the afternoon light of Hong Kong's skyscrapers with shimmering sharpness.

"Yes. He never stays up past midnight if he can help it," she says, smoothing a hand over her black pencil skirt. "He's heavily watched on a regular basis, but because of the upcoming auction, he's taking no chances and has tripled his security."

"Okay, so what do we have planned?"

Eu-fùnh smiles and pulls out a tablet from a leather attaché, illuminating a blueprint. We discuss possible points of entry, examine the security features that are set around the entrance to his suite, and look through a folder of reports that she has put together regarding Kam. We're able to maintain a business demeanor for a couple more hours until we've secured a decent plan for tomorrow. Once that's set, let's just say our attention turns to something a little less fully clothed for the rest of the night and well into the morning.

I think Hong Kong is my new favorite.

CHAPTER 10

3

Hong Kong: 2300 hours

The wind whips through my hair as I take in the expanded city around me, a bird perched on a skyscraper. I'm too high up to hear any noise from the busy streets of Hong Kong below, and I soak in the peace. It's rare I get to experience this kind of quiet.

"How's it look, 3?" Akoni's voice bursts through my earbud, and I let out a frustrated sigh. *Two minutes is better than no minutes.* Glancing down from where I stand poised at the edge of the roof, I can barely make out the miniature world bustling eighty floors below.

"I think this is our best bet. Entering his suite from the inside will require too many passcodes and silent removal of guards for it to be quick and effective. Approaching from the outside eliminates all those tedious obstacles."

"Not to mention you get to try out our new toys," Akoni adds.

I hold back a laugh but allow a smile since he can't see me. "Yes, there's that too."

"Were you able to access the roof easily through the service elevator?"

"Yeah, like we saw in the blueprints, there's minor security to reach this point, but I'm sure during the gala there will be more. There's only two locked doors that require a passcode, and the ones we've acquired worked."

"Stellar."

"Akoni, you may be from Hawaii, but you don't surf. You can't use that word."

"That's totally bogus, brah. I surf the web all day."

I groan.

"So how far down is the balcony?" he asks.

I measure the distance to the only terrace that juts out of the luxury hotel, marking the treasure that's buried inside like a giant X.

"Two generous stories, not too far. Must be a three-story suite."

Akoni whistles, accosting my eardrum. "Sounds nice."

"Sure does." I massage my ear.

"I see that you tagged the security cameras on your way up. Nice work. I've got the eyes going. Do you want to come back and talk about possible exits?"

I take in a large breath, cataloguing the barrage of information it brings me while letting the wind push against my skin. It's so strong it almost shoves me over. It's perfect.

"No, Akoni, I think I've already got mine."

The following night I regard my reflection in the bathroom mirror of my hotel suite, running a hand down my floor-length emerald-green Lanvin dress. I must say, the costume department at work certainly treats me well. The color combined with the slight cowl neck and *very* low scoop back compliments my normally frighteningly pale skin. My natural blue eyes appear brighter with this green and are thankfully left uncovered. No matter how hard our scientists work at it, the colored contacts still have a tendency to stifle my advanced eyesight, something the regular Ops have no issues with. Playing with the ends of my copper hair that flow past my shoulders, I think how it's almost a shame I have to hide it. Taking one last glance at the girl in the glass, I begin to pin up my long tresses, enabling me to secure the dark-brown wig over the top.

Thirty-four minutes later I step out of the bedroom and into the modern dining room of my suite. Akoni is there, his large form hunched over, reading his camp of monitors and laptops while he rocks a gray hoodie with an image of a USB drive with the words *I pull out* under it. His eyes flicker up with my approach, and he immediately stops typing.

"Holy…"

I raise an eyebrow at his gaping mouth. "Really? I look ethereal to you? How kind."

"Sorry." He fumbles to recover. "I've just never seen you all dolled up in person before. It's…well, it's something."

I place my gold clutch down and survey the table of gadgets. "All right, what am I going to be packing?"

Thankfully, my preferred tool when disposing of a target is not something metal detectors can detect. Even if they could, after Akoni and I secured our plan, I made sure to stash most of my arsenal in the hotel and on the roof. Early bird gets the worm and all that.

"Okay, here's your two-way transmitter mic." He hands me a skin-colored sticker to place behind my ear. "And eyes for me." He opens a velvet box to reveal a ruby-encrusted gold necklace, absolutely no sign of the miniature camera that hides within.

As I clasp it on, the metal gives my skin a chilled kiss.

"I've also got some sleepers in case someone is bothering you." He drops three small sheer sheets in my hand. They look like I'm about to drop acid. "You can hide those in your purse. They only dissolve in liquid. Otherwise they are as durable as rubber."

"Nice."

"I know, right?" Looking like a nerd who just won the gadget lottery, Akoni slides over to type something on his keyboard. "Okay, well, that's really it," he says, leaning his large form back in his chair, pushing up his glasses. "Everything else is already at the hotel."

I nod just as a beep comes from his phone. "That'll be your car." He reads the screen. "You should make your way down."

Grabbing my clutch, I pat down my body for the sixth time, making sure all my hidden flexible plastic blades are contained in my lingerie underneath. I shouldn't need these at the gala, but a girl can never have too many knives.

"You'll do great," Akoni says.

"I know." I turn toward the door.

"3?"

Glancing back, I find Akoni's brown magnified gaze on me. "You really do look lovely."

If I were a woman who blushed, I would be now. Thankfully, I'm not.

"I'll be in touch," I say.

"I'll hear and see every word," he returns with a smile.

And with that I make my way down to yet another night on the job.

CHAPTER 11

Carter
Pearl River Hotel
Hong Kong: 2240 hours

Eu-fùnh moves around the elegantly decorated room in her graceful alluring strides, a goddess descending to mix with mortals. Her formfitting red gown only heightens her demanding presence, and it took all my strength not to tear it off her the moment she stepped out of her bedroom. If all goes smoothly, I'll get the opportunity later tonight.

From my spot in the corner, I watch her turn, twist, and bow to greet various businessmen and their dates, creating the illusion that she's the woman who connects them all. Eu-fùnh has always been better at working a room, where I'm more inclined to sit back and take in the proceedings undisturbed.

Skimming over the different participants of this evening's

event, I catalogue the bankers and traders, government officials and their adversaries, billionaires and their mistresses of the night, all mingling with delight at the expense of another's dime. My gaze travels lazily around the opulence, passing over tall white columns and the sleek couched area, wondering when the man of the hour will show, when I stop on a young woman sitting alone across the room at the other bar. Her shoulder-length brown hair is cut in a style reminiscent of Cleopatra, and its angled severity shockingly contradicts the voluptuous but lean body that flows out from it, which is delicately wrapped by an emerald-green floor-length gown. Without knowing it, I find myself moving through the crowd toward her.

As I draw closer, she fleetingly looks my way, and I almost stop in my tracks. Her eyes are extraordinarily blue, the purest glacial waters, and rest in a porcelain-smooth face. I steal a glance at the fatter gentlemen next to her as he tries to engage her in conversation, and I get a flutter of pleasure when she rebukes his attempts.

Stepping in front of Fatso, I smile and make room for myself beside her at the bar. She gives me an uninterested glance before moving her gaze somewhere else, and if I'm not mistaken...yes, I did see it. A flicker of annoyance passed across her features before she covered it up with practiced indifference.

Interesting.

"What will you have, sir?" the bartender asks, and without moving my eyes from the woman, I reply, "Tonic with lemon peel, please."

She's intentionally not looking my way, which for some reason delights me.

I'm never ignored.

Continuing to admire her features, I take in the delicate structure of her face, her small, slightly upturned nose and deep-red lips that set off her milky-white skin. Everything about her seems poised and graceful, and she hasn't done anything more than take a sip from her martini. I have a deep urge to see what she looks like sweaty and in pleasure on top of me.

If I wasn't trained to notice details, I might have missed her tiny exasperated breath before she turns to meet my gaze. "Can I help you?" she asks in a lyrically pleasant voice I can tell she only uses in public.

My grin widens.

"Hello." I extend a hand. "I'm Simon."

CHAPTER 12

3
Pearl River Hotel
Hong Kong: 2245 hours

I saw him coming a mile away. Mr. Rich-Kid-Suave. Tall, ob-vious impressive build hidden under a Gucci tailored tux with thick, swept-back brown hair and green eyes that practically match my dress. Out to bag-and-shag a lady who, most likely, one of his father's business partners is married to, or better yet, escorting as his mistress. I can easily detect a woman's rose-scented perfume hugging him, and there's no mistaking his heightened testosterone levels from either just getting—or soon expecting—some nooky. Good luck trying to get it from me, sir.

I knew I had no time for this man before I even saw his face. One that I hate to admit, on a nonworking night might have made its way into my sheets for an only-once roll around. He has the appeal that some might say is devilishly good looking, with his smooth, angular jaw and tanned skin. I'm more inclined to package such features with a disappointing conversation and proof that beauty really is only skin deep.

I stare at the hand he's held out for an awkwardly long time, even though he's pulling it off with confidence, and instead of shaking it, take another sip of my drink. He chuckles, the sound rich and thick, a cashmere blanket, before curling his fingers back around his glass.

"Not one for introductions?" he asks, keeping those annoyingly cocksure green eyes pinned to me. He's probably used to having woman immediately swoon over him. Too bad I don't swoon, unless I'm able to kill the man who makes me.

"Only if I see the benefit in it," I reply while perusing the room. Using my senses, I pick through useless conversations, an overabundance of peaked hormones, expensive colognes, and a few radio blips from the earpieces of security guards, who are peppered along the wall. The only man I care about tonight has yet to arrive, which I hope changes soon. The faster I get this done, the faster I can get home, collect my money, and fall asleep on a private beach.

Mmm, beach.

"Looking for someone?"

Turning back, I find Simon's easy smile now mixed with a darker gaze, an examining one. Immediately, I hone in on him: Heart rate 42 beats per minute, blood pressure 120/80, no contacts or evidence of nervous perspiration. Last meal—I subtly inhale—nuts, specifically cashews from one of the bars. I hold back an annoyed curl of my lip. Nothing out of the ordinary. Just a horny man in prime physical condition completely at ease beside me.

"Not particularly," I mutter before taking another fake sip of my martini. "And what brings you here this evening, Simon, was it?"

He inclines his head. "I'm sure for similar reasons as you."

I'm bored already.

"So you're also organizing Mr. Kam's escort service for the rest of the month?" I ask.

His eyes spark, delighted. "Next month," he answers without missing a beat before leaning in to add, "and I'm tempted to recruit you."

It takes all my strength not to break the stem of my glass and jab it into his mirth-filled gaze.

"Simon, darling. Who's your friend?" A sensual voice breaks into our moment, the floral perfume I smelled on him earlier curling around us. Simon returns to his full height of six feet three as he turns to our new guest.

A striking Chinese woman drapes herself against his side. Her deep-brown eyes are rimmed dark and smoky, allowing her red dress to appear theatrical in representing fire, but in a tasteful, deliberate way. Her long black hair is stick straight and comes down to her waist, which is made cartoonishly small by a hidden corset. Her heartbeat is as steady as her companion's, and her pupils dilate as they study me.

I have just met someone who would serve an introduction.

"Victoria," I say, holding out my hand, and catch Simon's look of understanding. I'm not sure I like how acute his sensibilities are turning out to be.

The Chinese woman smiles and takes my hand. "Jia." Her grip is strong.

"Your name is certainly fitting." I smile. *Jia* means beautiful.

Her face brightens. "You know Cantonese?"

"I know enough," I respond in her native tongue, and she briefly catches Simon's eye.

I also steal a glance at him. He appears to be dancing around a thousand questions, and I know I'll soon have to take my leave. Despite my initial belief that only air filled this particular gentlemen's head, I'm quickly realizing these two are no beginners in the subtleties of conversational interrogation.

"How lovely," Jia continues in Cantonese. "It's so rare to find an American that is well versed in our language."

"Your own accent is barely recognizable in English," I compliment in return before continuing our verbal tango as Simon watches on. Even though I'm not looking, I zero in on Jia's long red nail that's making circles along his neck. *Yes, I get it. You two have bumped uglies. No need for a show.*

My internal eye roll is interrupted by the sound of a voice I've memorized piercing me from across the room. Quickly I flicker through the crowd to find a familiar middle-aged man moving about the opulent space. He's wearing an immaculately tailored gray tux with a red pocket square, and what's left of his thinning black hair is parted and swept to the side. Chenglei Kam slides through the gala followed by three giant bodyguards, stopping every few feet to greet guests. How long has he been here? I hold in a growl. If it weren't for these two distracting me, I would have known.

Tracking Chenglei as he stops to talk with one of his personal advisers, I listen as he mentions retiring to his suite and to send the files from their earlier board meeting. The same three bodyguards surround him as he takes his leave through a side door.

In and out. Just like that.

A man with little need for parties and pleasantries. In an alternate universe, we might have been friends.

As the door closes over Chenglei's small form, a dusting of goose bumps settles over my skin, and my shoulders stiffen. As if carried by the low music filling the room, a feeling of someone watching me vibrates across my nerve endings. Particularly someone who doesn't want me to *know* they are watching me. With new alertness I scan the gala. Hundreds of finely dressed people fill the high ceiling-glass ballroom, mingling, talking, and laughing. I lock on to all of them, but their scents begin to mix into one. *Where are you, little perv?* A ghost of a shadow rests behind one of the room's giant columns, but when I return my gaze, it's gone.

I clench my jaw, wanting nothing more than to cross the space to investigate, but I don't have time, so instead I shake off the feeling and return my attention to my companions.

"If you'll excuse me," I say to Jia and Simon.

"Leaving us so soon?" Simon glances at my drink. "You haven't even finished your martini."

"Yes, how rude of me, but I find myself in need of the ladies' room."

"Another time then, Victoria," Simon says as I slide off the stool.

I don't mistake the promise in his voice, and I almost laugh at his failure to catch any form of my intrigue.

"It was a pleasure to meet you, Jia." I smile at the woman, who flashes her pearly whites. As I walk toward the powder room, I can feel her clever brown eyes remaining pinned to me and have no doubt her gaze isn't the only one that lingers.

CHAPTER 13

Carter
Pearl River Hotel
Hong Kong: 2306 hours

I'm still staring at the space where Victoria's delicious form rounded the corner. I might have only met her for a moment, but there's something about this one...

Damn.

Why did Eu-fùnh have to come over and scare her off? I have no doubt her interrogation, though subtle, was the reason for Victoria's quick exit. A woman who avoids questions about herself is an alluring specimen indeed, and I'm nothing if not a man of allure.

"Okay, *Simon*," Eu-fùnh says by my side. "Let's talk with Li and see if Kam has indeed left for the night."

We both noticed **Chenglei** make his brief appearance, and

while Victoria's departure was disappointing, it was rather well timed. Glancing once more in the direction she left, I let out a subtle sigh before gesturing to Eu-fùnh to lead the way.

Maneuvering through the crowd, we approach a middle-age Chinese man who's sitting on one of the gray sofas with a woman who's a thousand points above him in attraction. She's curled to his side, playing with the lapels of his suit, whispering something in his ear, which causes his lips to curve into a devilish grin.

"Director Li," Eu-fùnh begins in her native tongue, bringing his attention to us as we give respectful bows. "I was wondering if you could inform Chairman Kam that I have an important potential business partner that wishes to speak with him."

Chenglei's adviser looks me over, appraising the cost of my designer suit to the style of my hair to the gleam of my gold cuff links before he returns his attention to Eu-fùnh.

"My lovely Jia, I wish I could help you with an introduction, but I'm afraid Chairman Kam has already retired for the evening. I suggest you set up an appointment with my assistant for a time that is convenient for both parties." He snaps his fingers, and a small, older woman standing behind him quickly steps closer, bowing to us.

Eu-fùnh graciously inclines her head. "As always, Director Li, I thank you for your advisement. I will talk with my companion for his availability and will discuss it with your people. I also look forward to being able to discuss more than just work at some point with you this evening." She finishes with a clever smile.

The woman beside him glowers, while Director Li merely preens in pleasure before we walk away, me not having uttered a single word.

"You wicked girl," I say once we're behind a column. "You'll have every man eating out of your palms before the night's up."

"Who says I don't already?"

A low chuckle escapes me. How much Eu-fùnh reminds me of someone...oh yes, me.

"So Kam's gone to his room," she says. "Are you ready?"

I adjust one of my cuff links that's already perfect. "Of course."

"You have my cell and know where we're regrouping." She absently cleans nonexistent lint off my shoulder, a small crease between her brows—the only sign of her worry. While friends, both of us know better than to form any real attachments, and not only because of our line of work. Feelings lead to loss, to hurt, and my ability to accept such things died a long time ago. Now I make a point to keep everything casual. Casual is safe. Casual doesn't rip your heart out and force you to watch it be buried six feet under.

So claiming Eu-fùnh's hand, I wait for her to look me in the eyes before sliding her a playful grin. "I'll be warming our bed in an hour."

Picking the security card off the sixth guard I've had to knock out, I make my way through the last door in the labyrinth of henchmen Kam has leading to his suite. The hotel's hallway is peppered with low-glowing modern light fixtures set against silver wallpaper and a patterned red carpet. It's taken me seventeen minutes to reach the top floor from the gala, and when I press up against the last bend in the hall before reaching my target's door, I let out a relieved sigh. I'm not nervous, just hungry. Literally.

I was an idiot and skipped the dinner portion of tonight, having settled for nuts at the bar. The faster I get this done, the faster I can find a street vendor and feed the growl growing in my stomach.

Using the mirror finish in my cuff links, I peer around the corner, catching two guards standing outside Kam's door. The bulk in their jackets outlines their short-barrel shotguns, a favorite of Kam's men and a not-too-favorable outcome for myself if I get shot by one. Talk about a mess.

Crouched in the security cameras' blind spot, I point my scrambler at the lens and count to five before moving to the next one, closer to where the guards stand. After I'm confident they're both down, I remove my tranquilizer gun and, leaning my head against the wall, take in three steadying breaths before quickly whipping around and shooting the first, then second, guard in the neck. They both let out surprised grunts before dropping to the floor, unconscious.

Reaching the bodies, I prop both men against the wall, checking that they're properly knocked out before binding their arms and legs.

"Now you two just relax out here," I say, removing one of their key cards to swipe the lock before raising the same guard's hand to press against the finger scanner. There's a small beep, a flash of green, and the door pops open.

I smile before pocketing the card and walking in.

CHAPTER 14

3
Pearl River Hotel
Hong Kong: 2336 hours

The relentless Hong Kong wind pushes me against the glass
surface of the hotel as I silently propel down to the balcony.
Dressed in black flexible outerwear, I'm hidden from anyone
looking out and shielded from the brutal gusts that accompanies
being eighty flights up. My dress is safely tucked in my small
sleek backpack, along with the other equipment I'll need tonight. My face is completely covered by a tight hood and mask
that I've attached my thermal eyes to.

I might have better than 20/20 vision, but I never said I
could see through walls.

Reaching the safety of the balcony, I detach my cord, retract
it, and place it in my bag before padding over to the sliding glass

doors to survey the interior.

There are two warm orange-red forms on the floor below and one in the room directly in front of me. A dimmer shape is deeper into the second floor behind many walls, and from the blueprints, it's most likely Kam in his upstairs office.

"How's the place look on your end?" Akoni asks in my ear. With him able to key in to the hallway security cameras, I left off wearing eyes inside the suite. I'm more than capable of locating the targets here myself.

"There are two hounds downstairs and one near my entrance on the second," I say quietly. "From the size of the man farthest in, I think Kam's in his office."

"Perfect. Well, all's quiet outside. This should be an easy one." The sound of Akoni's fingers flying over his keyboard patters in the background.

Making quick work of the locked balcony door that, not surprisingly, doesn't have an alarm system (because who would be crazy enough to approach from the outside), I slide into the dark threshold of the upstairs sitting room. With a barely audible *whoosh*, I close it behind me and creep to the corner, hiding in the shadows.

"3, wait," alerts Akoni. "We have malfunctions on the cameras leading up to Kam's suite. It's subtle, but I can tell they're frozen. I won't be able to see if anyone new is entering." The sound of typing. "Something doesn't look right...maybe we should hold for a second to see if I can get them back online."

"No, I'm already in. I'll proceed."

"But, 3—"

"Don't make me mute you," I whisper.

Thankfully, that shuts him up.

Putting the guard on the second floor in my sights, I turn off my thermals. A low yellow light illuminates the upstairs, the décor simple and modern, while an ornate chandelier hangs high in the ceiling and paints a set of stairs golden that wind down to the first floor. The five-foot-ten man stands fifteen yards away from me, down one of the hallways leading to Kam's study, his black clothes a darker spot in the dimly lit space. Taking a subtle intake of breath, I pick up his recent cigarette break and slight body odor from not showering in two days. He's turned away from me, looking at his cell phone as he leans against the wall, the blue glow from the screen washing out part of his face. His shoulders are slouched, tired, overworked—easy.

Slinking forward, a spider against the floor, I concentrate on the soon-to-be-stung fly. Soundlessly I remove one of my syringes from an inside pocket, the clear liquid dancing in the light, and then stop, crouched directly behind him. I remain invisible, mute, nothing but the inky shadows stretching across the walls as I slowly stand. And then I become the nightmares children pray aren't under their beds. Like a whip, I wrap around the man and inject his neck, muffling his short surprised moan and quieting his fall.

I wait a beat, my ears opening to my surroundings, but the suite remains still, unknowing. Switching my thermals back on, I glance to the door to my **right, finding no body heat. Opening it, I look upon an empty bathroom and stash the guard inside.**

"**Upstairs babysitter** down. Approaching target's office," I whisper to Akoni, making my way through the hallway and passing a few rooms along the way before I come to a break in the wall. Once I turn right and take fifteen more steps, I'll come to Kam's office, but the sound of soft approaching footsteps stop me. They float forward from the other side of the hallway, which stretches unlit and circles back to where I just was on the second floor's threshold. From the careful tread, it's obvious the owner doesn't want to be detected. I sniff the air—male, young, a hint of rose. It's familiar, but I can't place why. Behind my mask I wet my lips and grow small again, disappearing into my veiled surroundings.

Eight seconds.

Three.

The outline of a large man steps forward, and I immediately strike, but in a rare moment of surprise, my fist is deflected with a low grunt, and I barely miss my opponent's right hook before twisting out of the way and elbowing him in the face.

This also is dodged.

Interesting.

Continuing to attack, I also find myself annoyingly defending as we move back and forth down the hallway. The space is too small and dark to make out anything more than a tall man in a tux, who knows how to fight and smells familiar.

His quick reflexes and attention to hitting my weaker points shows his Krav Maga training, while the way he blocks hints to an advanced background in Muay Thai. He doesn't favor either side, revealing he's ambidextrous, but having the same ability leaves this intriguing rather than threatening. His skills are impressive, for a normal human, but my interest quickly dissolves to impatience the longer the tango lasts.

I don't have the time to play.

Landing a successful kick to his side, he lessens the blow by grabbing my leg and twisting me to the ground.

I let out a growl.

Kicking to a standing position, I'm about to reach for one of my knives, when he locks me in a choke hold. Grabbing my facemask, he pushes us into a lit portion of the corridor and rips it off. My bare skin hits against the central air blasting into the apartment, and I blink, adjusting my eyesight.

That's it. I'm so over this!

Reverse head butting him, relishing his muttered curse of pain, I quickly drop and spin out of his grasp. In a single move I have one of my knives at the ready, the titanium flashing a forewarning as I lock eyes with a familiarly attractive yet slightly-less-put-together, dark-haired, green-eyed man.

We both freeze.

Simon?

CHAPTER 15

Carter
Pearl River Hotel
Hong Kong: 2342 hours

I blink and then blink again.

"Victoria?" I stand paralyzed, staring at a slight but impressive figure that looks like a ninja with the face of an angel. The same angel I recently admired downstairs. While the majority of her head remains tucked inside a tight black hood, her exposed blue eyes and pale skin are impossible to mistake.

What the devil?

Still in shock, I almost miss her coming at me again, barely dodging a slice of her blade to my throat as I struggle to regain my ability to strike back. A thousand questions swirl in my mind as I momentarily resign myself to merely defend.

How is this the same **woman whom** moments ago I was

imagining taking to bed and now find myself trying not to be killed by? Because that's *exactly* what her moves intend to do. Kill me.

"Hey, maybe"—I block her fist—"we should"—I knock away her knifed hand again—"talk about this."

She ignores me, just keeps pushing forward, eventually getting a clean roundhouse to the side of my face.

Holy bitch slap, that hurt.

Tasting blood, flames flicker on.

Now before I go much further, let me state that I am not a man who would ever hit a woman...normally. I even go out of my way to avoid being paired with them during training, because no matter how skilled they are, I always have a deep sense of guilt for physically harming them in any way. I'm a gentleman like that. But flexing my now loose jaw and seeing that this little angel is more of a devil, all those rules go out the window.

She wants to play? Okay, let's play.

As she moves to land a punch to my throat, I see my next in. With a dodge I grab and twist her arm, making her drop her blade, and swing her around. But she merely leaps into my movement, running along the wall to land behind me.

Crap.

She kicks me from behind, and I grunt as I fall forward.

With a snarl I turn to face her, but before either of us can charge the other, a new form steps between us, snagging our attention. Chenglei Kam stands in utter shock in the entryway of his office. Somehow our scuffle landed us near his room.

Before Kam can so much as scream or grab for his U22 Neos I know he has stashed on his person, Victoria and I simultaneously hit him in the larynx. Falling forward, he grasps his neck while wheezing for oxygen. With the power from both of our hits, I wonder if he'll ever be able to regain it. *Double crap.* Not wanting to deal with any more obstacles, I pull out my trusty Minnie to knock him unconscious, but not a second after Kam hits the ground, my gun is kicked out of my hand and caught by the woman I decide I now hate more than blue balls. And *that's* saying something.

Looking up, I find Victoria pointing my own weapon at me with a steady hand and, if it wasn't for the uncoiling disdain dripping from her icy-blue eyes, a rather impressively blank face.

It's in this moment, with her a millisecond away from trying to shoot me, that I realize why I found her so intriguing before.

Leave it to me to be attracted to the craziest chick in the room.

CHAPTER 16

3
Pearl River Hotel
Hong Kong: 2347 hours

My finger pulses on the trigger as I stare at a man I wouldn't have guessed in a million years would be standing in front of me. *Where the deuce were my senses downstairs?*

If it weren't for him putting down Kam, I would have shot him already, but it appears we both might have the same intentions. Making that the *only* reason I'm hesitating.

"3? What's going on? I can hear you fighting? Is everything okay? Do I need to get you out of there?" Akoni says in my ear.

I ignore him.

"Who do you work for?" I ask Simon, or whatever his real name is. Obviously being in the same line of business, he can't be dumb enough to use his real name.

Glancing over his uncovered face and the same outfit he wore at the gala, I retract that thought.

Yeah, he's probably dumb enough.

His green eyes narrow before he relaxes his stance, seeming to come to the conclusion that I'm not going to shoot him. It makes me want to all the more.

"Probably for a similar employer as you," he says while straightening his perfectly tailored tux.

His vanity in this moment bristles along every one of my nerves, but I push the sensation down as I quickly run through the other agencies. It wouldn't be unheard of for Kam to have more than one price on his head, especially with the upcoming events.

"You're American?"

"Your powers of observation are uncanny," he says dryly. "Yes, I'm *American*, and this man's Chinese, and that chair's red, and you're a crazy woman pointing my own gun at me. Don't you know it's rude to hold another man's gun?" His gaze rakes the length of my body. "But if you need the security of holding something of mine, I may have another option."

My finger twitches on the trigger again.

"What agency?" I bite out. "PIA? SI6? COA?" His eyes dilate slightly on the last name. *Gotcha.*

"Uh...3?" Akoni's nervous voice filters through. "I fixed the cameras, and there's a trail of knocked-out guards leading up to Kam's suite."

I curse, lowering my—Simon's—weapon.

"*Idiot*," I hiss. "You're really that stupid to leave a path of bodies for anyone to see?"

He scowls, annoyed by my accusation but only slightly surprised that I knew of his way in.

"Well, I would have already *killed* this guy and been gone if you didn't get in my way, so it wouldn't have mattered."

I watch him closely. "You're here to kill Kam?"

"And you're not?" he counters.

Ignoring answering his question like he's ignoring mine, I glance to the door, listening for the guards downstairs. Simon seems to know my intentions, for he says, "Don't worry. I took care of them. Yeah, you're welcome, sweetheart."

Sweetheart!

My eyes dart back to his, and I catch him sizing me up, searching for what foot I favor, which arm might be stronger, any weaknesses in my stance.

Good luck finding any.

We stand there for a moment, trying to gauge how much we might trust the other, and I know we both reach the same conclusion—we don't. If I wasn't fairly certain that he works for a sister company to SI6, I would have shut him up already. A part of me still wants to if it wouldn't come with a mountain of paperwork.

"Don't move, and this will all go smoothly," I say in warning as I lower to the ground, making a show of placing his gun to my side. He casually watches my every move.

Leaning over Kam, I check that he's breathing before placing a chloroform cloth over his mouth and nose, ensuring he'll stay unconscious for the remainder of my stay.

"What are you're doing?" Simon asks.

I ignore him as I take out my DNA-collecting kit and get to work. Lifting Kam's lips, I swab the saliva and place the wet Q-tip in a container. Drawing from an artery at the inside of his elbow, I take four vials of blood.

"You're collecting DNA samples?" Simon moves closer, and I quickly raise his weapon again.

"I have a feeling you're too vain to enjoy being known as an Op that got shot with his own gun."

He stops, but his lips purse smugly. "I hate to break it to you, but that's biometric." He nods to what's in my hands. "You can threaten me all you like with it, but it won't go off unless I'm holding it."

My grip tightens as I realize he's right. *Goddammit.* My senses are *not* up to par tonight.

"I don't need a bullet to shut you up," I say icily as I drop the useless gun to my side, still making sure it's out of his reach. "Do *not* get in the way of my operation."

"*Your* operation!" He barks a laugh. "Honey, we've *both* obviously been put on the same assignment."

HONEY!

Taking in a steadying breath, I reel in the red that's tinging my vision and continue with what I need to collect—hair samples, nail clippings, fingerprints, retina scans.

My companion checks his watch, letting out an annoyed huff. "Are you almost done? I'd like to have some time with him as well."

I begin to remove Kam's pants.

"Whoa!" Simon steps back, hands in the air, as I grab Kam's penis and press on certain pressure points. "*Ugh.* Why am I not surprised that you'd have a thing for flaccid guys?"

I hold a container to his urethra, and urine flows into it. I glance to Simon and grin sweetly. "What? You not comfortable enough with your own sexuality to see another man's genitals? Maybe you need to do some sexual exploration and sort all that out."

"As long as I can start with you, sweetheart." He flashes a thin smile.

I swear steam funnels out of my ears. *Nope. Na-uh. No way.* If I don't leave now, I'll do something I'll regret. *Paperwork, think of all the paperwork.*

Packing up my supplies, I pull out my trusty stinger and fill it with the final blow of poison, but before I get too far, Simon grabs my wrist.

I didn't even see him move forward.

Which is unlike me. *Very* unlike me.

My gaze follows the path of his strong hand wrapping my wrist up to his eyes. His face hovers close to mine, and the nearness unsettles me, but not in the way that I'm used to. At this distance I catch the flecks of gold in his green irises and two faint scars along the left side of his jaw. Besides the rose scent of Jia I got off him earlier, I now detect something else, something uniquely male that's coating my nostrils pleasingly—a musky cinnamon.

I switch to breathing out of my mouth.

"If you know what's good for you, you will remove your hand." I pour as much venom as I can into my voice.

He leans back but keeps his grip firm. "Listen. I don't know who the hell you are or who the hell you work for, but there are some things I need this guy to tell me. So why don't you go on your merry way and leave the rest to me."

I narrow my eyes. *Things that Kam needs to tell him?* When I realize what he must be talking about, I actually start laughing. "Are you serious?"

His brows furrow.

"Is this your first assignment or something?" I ask and then add more to myself, "Seeing how you entered, it must be. Such amateur brazen moves."

"What are you *talking about*?" He squeezes my wrist harder, and I immediately see four fatal spots he's leaving open.

Not yet. Not yet.

"If you're trying to get the code, you're shit out of luck."

This brings some clarity into his eyes, and I smile smugly, pulling my arm free.

"What do you mean?"

Whomever he's working for obviously is lacking in the intelligence department, and it's not my job to clean up their mess.

"This isn't a *game*," he growls. "If you have reason to believe that the code is unattainable through Kam, I need to know, or you won't be leaving this room until I've gotten it from him."

The fact he thinks he has the ability to carry out that threat is almost cute. If I had the time, I'd let him try, but I've already been here too long. Simon's jaw clenches in silent frustration as he waits for an explanation.

"Chenglei Kam is unsusceptible to torture," I say. "He's been training over the past five years to withstand any method all the way up to death. Take off his shirt and see for yourself." I wave to the unconscious man. "He has plenty of scars for proof."

Simon glances from me to Kam, then back to me, searching my face for any indication that my words might be false before kneeling down and ripping open Kam's shirt. A storybook worth of torture scars splays across his otherwise defined chest.

Simon curses.

"Happy?" I impatiently flick the liquid potassium chloride in my syringe. He scowls but doesn't stop me as I bend down, ending this mess. Sticking Kam in one of his puckered scars near his heart, I release his permanent slumber and listen to his pulse weaken before it completely stops, assuring me that my assignment is now complete.

Swiftly repacking my supplies, I stand, regarding the only man now alive in the room, and find myself shaking my head.

"What?"

"Are you really that cocky that you'd show your enemy your face like that? I mean, you didn't even change your clothes from the gala."

"What? Am I supposed to take my cues from the ninja movies you obviously watch?"

That's it. *I'm going to kill him.* But before I can reach for another blade, Akoni's voice halts me. "3, the first set of guards have been found."

Touching my ear, I keep my hateful stare on Simon. "Copy that. I'm done here."

CHAPTER 17

Carter

Pearl River Hotel
Hong Kong: 2402 hours

"Who are you talking to?" I ask, knowing she would never tell me but desperate to find clarity in this turd pile of a situation. Ploom will *definitely* be hearing from me.

"You better get out of here if you value your ass as much as I imagine you do,"
she says as she moves to a computer in the corner, which appears to be a receptionist's. "Your little paper trail has been found." Her gloved fingers flutter rapidly over keys, bringing up video surveillance from cameras in this office. Quickly and easily she clears the memory. Damn, she's smarter than I wanted her to be. Without looking back, she runs from the room.

Flickering a last glance at Kam's body, I let out a frustrated huff before grabbing my abandoned gun from the carpet (ammo removed by the detail-oriented wench) and follow her out.

We both silently maneuver our way down the hallway and back to the open sitting room on the second floor. She approaches the balcony doors and throws them open. Hong Kong's dark wind bursts in with a howl, the air cool as it slaps across my skin and filters through my suit jacket.

"Oh yeah?" I laugh. "And how the hell are you going to get out that way?"

She doesn't say a word as she steps out, gracefully hopping onto one of the tables butting up to the banister. She's an inky silhouette against the glittering skyscrapers, and I can't help admiring her lean, muscular body that more than hints through her black cat suit. She unzips and attaches two sections under her arms and between her legs—gliders.

Twisting to look down at me, her blue eyes spark in the night. "Like this, *honey.*" Then replacing her face mask, she flexes one long gloved middle finger my way, before opening her arms and leaping off the ledge.

Disappearing into the night.

Well, fuck me.

It was a close call traversing my way down and out of Kam's hotel before his security stopped anyone else from entering or exiting the building. I might have even needed to utilize a laundry chute, much to a few maids' shrieks of surprise and my annoyance for getting my designer tux dirty, but despite all that I made it safely onto the Hong Kong streets. I know that shrew of a woman's warning saved my ass, but I will absolutely not bring myself to internally thank her.

Goddammit!

Punching a metal security gate covering a shop's entrance, I let out a growl, catching more than one nervous glance from pedestrians walking by. I resist growling again. I can't believe I completely failed my mission. I've *never* failed before. Well, Kam *is* dead, but I didn't even do it, for Christ's sake! Shoving my hands into my front pants pockets, I continue stomping toward my hotel. Even at this late hour, downtown is bustling, lit advertisements flashing against the asphalt and illuminating the people as they shuffle about. But I take notice of none of it, my mind a gray storm of frustration, forcing those in my way to move first.

How did she know that Kam couldn't be tortured? How did she know and COA not? And Eu-fùnh! How did she not know? *Local expert my ass.* They made me look like an idiot in there. I would have been torturing Kam for hours with no results if she hadn't shown up and told me.

Nope. Don't go there, Carter. Don't give her an *ounce* of credit. Even if she did help, did warn me of the bodies being found. An image of her patronizing sneer flashes before me. *Shit.* I don't think I've ever hated someone of the opposite sex so much. And I thought she was an angel. I snort, gaining more stares from passing strangers. *Angel my ass. More like Satan's spawn.*

Running a hand through my hair, which must be in all kinds of directions by now, I replay what I've been able to deduce so far. She's definitely no rookie, with her fighting capabilities and the way she methodically took those DNA samples. If I didn't want to hate her, I'd actually be impressed, maybe even a little turned on.

Gross, Carter, gross. Satan's spawn, remember?

I will not let any sort of reverence blossom for that woman. I mean, look at the way she killed Kam...with *poison*. Like a slimy reptile, a creepy bug.

Needles.

I shiver.

I've always hated needles. I can watch a man's head explode from a bullet without blinking, but needles...yeah, she's psycho for sure.

Memories of her completely in her zone, undeterred by both of us getting assigned the same target, swim before me. She made it perfectly clear she was getting her check in the box, and in the bank, one way or another. Which leaves me walking the streets of Hong Kong with *nothing* to show. Why didn't I demand she give me a copy of his DNA too?

Shit. How did this happen?

I've never been so riled after a mission. And I've been out-numbered, cornered, standing on a ledge with nowhere to go, but in all those instances it was still *me* calling the shots, *me* getting my butt out of there. Not another Op telling me how inept I was at my job.

Is this your first target?

Holy crap sandwich, do I hate her.

Turning a corner, I catch sight of my hotel a few blocks away, the fifty-story sleek building shining white and blending in with the rest of the steel structures.

Drawing closer, I pull my phone from my pocket.

"Hello, darling." Eu-fùnh answers on the first ring. "I ordered us champagne to celebrate."

I let out a breath. "Well, I hope you haven't uncorked it, because we have a problem."

CHAPTER 18

3

39,000 feet somewhere over Alaska
Singapore Airlines

Sitting in first class, Akoni snores in the separated bed next to me as I study a file. A file attached with a man's face that will forever set my blood to boil in a mere instant. I've never met someone who has gotten under my skin so quickly and easily. And I've met *a lot* of really horrible and annoying people. Maybe because I've always been able to end their pathetic lives, I've been able to move on with mine. No such luck here.

Glancing back over the legend, I read an Ops-claimed background, one that Akoni was able to procure before we left. Getting a facial scan on him was all too easy.

Name: Carter James Smith.

Alias: Benjamin Nickels. Simon Andrews.

A.K.A: The Bull.

Age: Thirty-Two.

Height: 6' 3".

Hair/Eyes: Brown hair / Green eyes.

Family: Deceased. Father, Christopher
                Andreoli. Mother, Sophia James
                Andreoli. Brother, Simon James
                Andreoli.

Nationality: American. Italian descent.

Company: Covert Operations Agency (COA).

Status: K-Op. 8 yrs active.

Training: Navy SEAL, tae kwon do, Krav
                Maga, Muay Thai, karate, boxing,
                kickboxing, mixed martial arts,
                archery, advanced armed
                weaponry, bomb disposal and
                detonation, diving, pilot
                license, advanced speed driver.

**Weapon of
Choice** :   Custom S&W 1911s, Beretta 92.

Languages: English, French, Spanish,
                Italian, German, Mandarin,
                Cantonese, Portuguese.

**General
background:** Born in Maryland Presbyterian
Hospital as Carter James Andreoli. Son of
Christopher Andreoli and Sophia James
Andreoli. Joined army after high school. 2 yr
active duty in Iraq. Same outpost as older
brother, Simon James Andreoli. Brother to die
in combat while Carter was posted in
Iraq. Parents to die in car accident later
that same year. Carter granted short leave

> of duty due to mental instability diagnosed
> by military psychiatrist, Dr. Peter Collins.
> Later funneled into special operations
> program where he showed remarkable abilities
> and quick growth. Recruited into COA August
> 2005. Been known to show slight reckless
> behavior and contempt for authority. Noted to
> be extremely dedicated and loyal.

I read over the part about his family again. It's not surprising he has no surviving kin. People recruited into this business rarely do. The fact that one of his aliases is his brother's name shows that he still holds those emotions close. At least I never knew my family to have to mourn them. I don't remember anything of my parents, and I know I'm better for it. Less baggage.

As much as it pains me, I have to admit that his skill sets are impressive. Not as impressive as mine, *obviously*, but still nothing to ignore.

Akoni lets out a sleepy mumble, and I glance to his askew eye mask and drooling mouth, his dark hair standing cowlicked against his pillow. His current relaxed state is a far cry from how he was when I stormed into our hotel, demanding we find a picture of Mr. Lack-of-Tact and use it to gain whatever information we could on him. Now thirty thousand miles in the air, I'm looking down at a friggin' colleague. His nickname, The Bull, is comically accurate after Akoni showed me the surveillance of knocked-out bodyguards left in his wake.

What a joke.

COA is a sister company to SI6, so as tempted, and close, as I was to killing him, I thankfully didn't. That would have been a mess of meetings and debriefs that I absolutely have no patience for. COA and SI6 have been great public allies for years, though they privately compete vehemently. I wanted to scream at Axel when I called him for our status update. Our line wasn't one hundred percent secure, so I had to hold a lot back, but I have a feeling he's more than aware of my impending wrath since I made sure to slip in words like decapitation, castration, and bamboo rods.

I mean, *come on*. How could the companies be so stupid? To put us on the same target unknowingly. Aren't they supposed to be the leaders in intelligence? Thinking back to meeting Carter at the gala, I should have known better. That woman, Jia, was too smart, too keen to be just another aristocratic woman in the world of Chinese businessmen and their egos. Who was she to Carter? Whoever she was, it was too obvious they were playing hide the cannoli. I'm sure he needs to be in someone every second of the day. No wonder his actions reflected a lack of blood to the head.

I let out an annoyed breath. *The Bull indeed*. Shutting the folder on Carter's smug and annoyingly symmetrical face, I tuck it back into my bag. Reclining my seat, I try to relax by switching on a game of Scrabble. Eventually I cool down enough to close my eyes and get some sleep, but even as I'm about to drift into the dark, I can't help the slithering feeling that all this is merely the calm before the proverbial cataclysmic, earth-ending storm.

CHAPTER 19

Carter
Hong Kong: 0100 hours

Name:	Nashville Brown.
Agency Name:	3.
Alias:	Victoria O'Hera. Stephanie Keller.
A.K.A:	The Wasp.
Age:	Twenty-six (disputable).
Height:	5' 7".
Hair/Eyes:	Red hair / Blue eyes.
Parents:	Unknown.
Nationality:	American. Scottish. Mexican Descent (obtained from DNA swab).
Company:	Special Intelligence 6 (SI6).

Status: A+ genome. K-Op. 6 yrs active.

Training: Basic US Army combat training, cyber intelligence, Surma stick fighting, tae kwon do, Pencak Silat,Krav Maga, Muay Thai, mixed martial arts, archery, armed weaponry, bomb disposal and detonation, diving, pilot license.

Weapon of
Choice :   Various poisons, hand-to-hand combat, Glock 17 w/ silencer, FN Five-Seven, tranquilizer pistol.

Languages: English, French, Spanish, Italian, German, Mandarin, Cantonese, Japanese, Russian, Hindi.

General
background: Place of birth unknown. Found at the assumed age of four outside Nashville Police Department near James Robertson Pkwy, Nashville, TN. A+ Genome acquired. Parents unknown. Original name unknown. Given the name Nashville Brown at Bell Buckle Orphanage along with date of birth, January 1, 1991. Recruited into SI6 at the age of 16. Skill set advanced. Spotless assignment completion expedited her to early freelance position within SI6. Freelance for past 2 yrs. Specializes in silent kills. Notes of being short tempered, which usually accompanies A+ specimens. Otherwise considered a perfect operative.

The lights of downtown Hong Kong cut dramatic shadows across the dark and quiet penthouse as I sit on a couch glancing over her file.

Nashville Brown? What kind of honky-tonk name is that? I stare down at the picture of her annoyingly beautiful face and, *screw me*, natural apricot hair. I've always had a thing for red-heads. Why did *she* have to be one?

I glance back to her status. So she's an A+. A lot clicks into place now. I've only met two A+ humans, and both had similar hot demeanors. Neither had been so young though, or female. For some reason there are higher male mutations than female. As soon as I learned of their species when joining COA, I was immediately intrigued. They're the closest thing we have to super-heroes, and if the rest of the world knew of them, I can imagine the field day they'd have. An image of Nashville as an action figure flashes in my mind, and I grunt my annoyance.

Skimming back over her skill set and training, I hate that I'm impressed. Even with her genetic advantage, it's still extensive, and at her age no less. I was just getting started in this business at twenty-six.

Flipping the file closed, I curl my hands into fists as I sit back against the leather couch, taking in the pixilated city glowing on the other side of my hotel's tall windows.

I'd been lying in bed earlier trying to force myself asleep, but after unsuccessfully clearing my mind of this girl and the file that Eu-fùnh gathered, I got up to take another look. It took longer than I would have liked to get a visual for a face scan, another reason why she's good at what she does, but we eventually found one of the Op entering the gala.

My mind constantly flips through images of the dark-haired woman at the party, her sensually wrapped body and intelligent blue eyes, to the woman in Kam's suite. Stealthy as a cat, ruining my assignment, ruining *my* kill.

But of course she would.

She has the *spotless* record to uphold.

The title of a *perfect operative* to maintain.

I scrub a frustrated hand over my face as footsteps pad softly across the marble floor. Familiar fingers run through my hair, and I close my eyes.

"You have an early flight. Why are you up?" Eu-fùnh slides beside me on the couch, her deep-purple silk robe falling off one shoulder alluringly. Half of her face is cast in shadows, while the other is lit by the white glow of the city outside.

Her eyes roam my bare chest and then drift to the folder on the coffee table. She smiles knowingly. "It all worked out in the end," she says. "We practically work for the same company, plus Ploom assured the information gathered would be shared."

I glance back at the file and frown. Sure the information *she* gathered would be shared. It all worked out in the end because *she* killed Kam. *She* did everything. *She* even knew more about Chenglei.

"Did you really not know that he couldn't be broken?" I ask, laying my head on the back of the couch, staring at the dark glass chandelier above.

Eu-fùnh shifts over to straddle me. Her long nails graze along my arms, and I move my hands to feel up her smooth thighs. She watches me with an amused gleam in her eyes.

"Like I said the last time you asked, I didn't know. I had extensive knowledge on Kam and never encountered such intelligence. I'm impressed our little girl did." She continues to stroke her hands down my chest. "I knew there was *something* about her when we met at the gala," Eu-fùnh muses. "She seemed... different."

I scoff. "Different, as in an evil shrew."

Eu-fùnh's husky laugh fills the space. "I like her," she says before lowering her face inches away from mine. "And I like her even more because she's gotten under your skin, something not easily done."

My fingers flex on her thighs. "I don't know about my skin," I say, "but I'd certainly like to get under yours." Grabbing her hips, I guide her to grind against me. Our only separation are my boxer briefs and her thin silk bottoms. I need something to distract me, and by Eu-fùnh's movements, she knows it. Bringing her lips to mine, I hungrily taste every inch while she moans against me, but before I can slip off her robe, she pulls away.

Her dark eyes are endless in the dim lighting, her drape of black hair a waterfall of onyx as it falls forward. "I like this girl," she says as she tugs my head back by the root of my hair. "But I don't like her enough for you to be thinking of her while having sex with me."

I certainly don't want that either.

"Then make me forget," I say with a crooked grin.

She cocks an eyebrow at the challenge before forming a sensual smile.

"My pleasure."

CHAPTER 20

Carter

Manhattan, New York: 1735 hours

I swirl the amber liquid in my glass and hate how the color reminds me of a certain person's hair. Tipping the glass back, I finish my apple juice in one swallow, for the first time in a long time wanting it to be something stronger, something numbing.

"Need another?"

"Yeah, thanks, Matt." I slide the glass over to where a thin tattooed man stands behind the bar. "But this time make it tonic with lemon peel." Anything to not look at that color again, be reminded of *her* again.

I've been back in the city for a week now and still feel like I'm being haunted. Despite my desperation to forget, everything seems to remind me of the woman I met in Hong Kong, specifically anything blue or orange. Which means I can pretty much kiss enjoying any Mets or Knicks game goodbye.

Awesome.

The meeting yesterday with COA didn't help either. It was the first time in a long time I had to call in a spade. **Sure I've left big messes for COA to clean up from time to time, but never without a positive completion of my assignment. A positive that *I* made happen, not someone else.**

Ploom told me to go easy on myself, that it still counts as a Complete because we got what we needed and more.

Yeah, thanks to *her*.

After my disappointing debrief with my team, the longest work out of my life, and a fitful night's sleep, I came straight to my local bar, Uncorked. It's attached to a swanky hotel on my block, and its dark lighting and worn wood is perfect for wanting to blend in and be left alone. Even if I don't indulge myself with a stiff drink, I still find such establishments soothing. Well, sometimes. Thoughts of my parents' deaths, the images of their mangled car, flash through my mind, and I swallow down a lump in my throat as Matt places my new beverage in front of me.

Grunting my thanks, I take down half the glass. The liquid is cool and refreshing. *Damn, how I wish this was filled with whiskey instead*.

Echoes of Jules gushing over Nashville's records still play in my ear, and my resolve drops. I'm suddenly desperate to lean over and grab one of the bottles behind the bar.

Jesus, get a hold of yourself.

Instead I crunch the ice from my drink between my teeth.

What I really need is a new assignment, anything to help remove this past one. Even with Eu-fùnh's *very* skilled talents, I still found myself thinking of Nashville immediately afterward.

Pfft.

Nashville.

What a name.

Under different circumstances I might have found it cute, but there's nothing *cute* in this situation. I just don't understand why I'm still wasting mental energy on this chick. This isn't like me. I let things go. Walk forward without looking back. Especially when it comes to women. But this is more than that. This is my reputation being messed with, and in my line of work, that's all K-Ops have.

When I pressed Ploom about why we didn't have the same intelligence on Kam, he assured me he would look into it, but this is how the business goes. The sister companies are notorious for withholding information from one another, and some things get lost in the shuffle. I almost punched him in his muffin top when he said that. How can I trust my department, or any future assignment, if that's the case?

Taking another drag from my drink, I notice someone approaching from my left. Glancing over, I watch an attractive blonde slip onto the stool beside me.

"Hi there," she says with a flirty smile.

I assess her bleached-blond hair instead of red, her tanned skin instead of milky white, and her dark-brown eyes instead of daylight blue.

She's perfect.

"Hey." I grin.

We stumble into her hotel room, and she giggles when we knock over picture frames that line the walls. She tastes like the last tequila shot she took before telling me she had a room at the connecting hotel. *Didn't have to tell me twice, Kristy...or was it Misty?*

Pushing me against the other wall, she explores down my body while I feel up her thin frame to her breasts.

Man, I'm so happy not to be thinking about someone else right now.

Kristy or Misty takes off both our shirts before continuing to kiss me, moving us toward the bed.

Because she really doesn't deserve another minute of my time.

Misty unbuckles my belt.

I mean, it was too obvious she thought she was better than everyone with her A+ genes and Spider-Man moves.

My pants hit the floor, freeing me, and Kristy moans with pleasure.

I hope I never see that dragon-woman's face again.

Pushing me onto the sheets, Misty licks her way down my abs, and I lay my head back, taking in the white ceiling above.

So empty.

Blank.

God, how I envy it.

Warmness from Kristy's mouth envelops me, and I suck in a breath, my mind finally zeroing in on what's taking place.

I tangle my fingers into Misty's hair just as a shrill ringing of a phone fills the room.

We both ignore it, Kristy's attention occupied by bigger, more important things.

The ringing continues.

And continues.

And continues.

Goddammit.

I glance around the room.

Is that my cell?

As soon as the buzzing stops, it starts up again.

That's definitely mine.

I don't know what causes me to stop what's going on at this very moment, but I'm obviously not sane anymore, because I sit up and pull Kristy away from me. She whines as I roll off the bed to grab my pants. Fishing out my phone, I resist chucking it against the wall when I see the caller ID.

"Ploom," I answer with a growl, "what do you want now?"

CHAPTER 21

3
SI6 Headquarters
Chicago, Illinois: 0930 hours

I can't believe I'm walking through these doors. David *promised* I could get my vacation after the Hong Kong assignment, yet here I am, back at SI6 only a week after coming home from China. David caught me in a weird sense of déjà vu, as I was scrolling through vacation resorts this morning and saw his name pop up on my phone. Just like last time. Except *this* time, I really could use that vacation.

It took me three days, running twenty-two miles, six hours at the gun range, five intense sessions with my combat trainer, two with my therapist, and a healthy dose of yelling at Axel and Akoni to rid myself of the anger I had from the tête-à-tête with COA operative Carter Smith. I'm a short-tempered person. I know it doesn't take a lot to get on my nerves, and despite the rigorous meditation classes SI6 mandates I take, I'm a short fuse. But even with all this, no one has lingered in my heart's hate box as long as this guy, and I barely met him.

I even confided to Ceci, something I rarely do when it comes to work situations, but as soon as I got back, she knew something was up. I of course left out the part about us both being assigned to kill the same person, saying instead that we got the same client to investigate. After word vomiting for a good hour, Ceci looked at me with the biggest grin and told me she thinks my problem is that I finally met my match, someone who "can volley back what I serve," as she put it. Basically, someone like her.

I laughed so hard I peed a little.

Ceci's one thing, but if Carter and I are playing in the same game, I think it's only too obvious who's winning. Sure, he held his own in our small combative run-in, but in the end *I* killed the target, *I* got the DNA samples, and I finished my assignment— and his. What did he do? Fix his tux?

That's the only silver lining in all this, imagining him reporting back to his team. How did he explain what happened? How did he take getting an *INCOMPLETE* stamped on his folder? A grin slides onto my face. Yeah, call me vindictive or immature, but you don't get a perfect record by being nice to your competitors. *Especially* if your competitors turn out to be your colleagues.

But all that's in the past now. I have emotionally and mentally rid myself of Carter Smith, Simon, Ben, *The Bull*. Whatever stupid name he wants to give himself. I will never see him again, and that fact right there allowed me to wake up this morning with a smile and look for vacation destinations. Now I just have to decline whatever assignment David thinks he's giving me, get home, and finally, *finally* book this thing.

"3!" Akoni jogs down the hall toward me, his broad shoulders pulling at his T-shirt, which has an image of a computer with the words *I have a harder drive than you* underneath.

"Hey, Akoni, did you get called in for this thing with Axel too?"

"Uh, yeah...I did." We walk in step as we pass this floor's open floor plan. It's covered in neat rows of desks, **where the newbie operatives sit. The more advanced associates and directors have offices that ring the second floor, with windows peering down into the pit—mob bosses looking at their factory floor.**

Hearing the unease in Akoni's voice, I stop at the base of the ascending stairs. "What?"

He glances around before asking, "Do you know why we're talking with Axel today?"

"No." I pucker my brows. "He didn't elaborate on the phone. Why?"

He scratches his bicep while pressing his lips together. "Well, whatever you do, just don't blame me, okay?" And before I can answer, he takes the stairs up two at a time.

"Akoni!" *What has he done now?* Letting out a frustrated huff, I continue my way to David's, but as I reach the second-floor landing, I find myself hesitating when a light fragrance of cinnamon and male wafts under my nose. The scent is barely there, but it immediately raises the hairs on the back of my neck.

Turning left, I peer down the hallway to my group director's office, which rests at the end. Akoni slips in, past David Axel, who's standing by the door, dressed in his usual black slacks and light-blue button-down, chatting to three strangers. My attention slides to a young blond woman, high bun in place, directly opposite him, and I quickly take in her profile. About five eight, late twenties, tan skin, quarter-sized birthmark under her right ear, and sharpened features that seem on a constant verge of slipping into an easy grin. Her white buttoned-down shirt and black pant-suit fits her perfectly, but from the way she stands with her legs slightly apart and one hand fluttering at her hip, as if searching for more to grab, I can tell she has a police background.

An older gentleman is beside her and shares the same age as David, but that's where the similarities stop. Where my group director is tall with a muscular build and broad shoulders, this man's height is only an inch taller than myself, with a gut that hangs over his khaki pants, exposing his pleasure in never skipping the dessert menu. He skin has a pasty sheen from not getting enough vitamin D, and his hair is styled in the way of a newborn's, barely there. He's blocking another man sitting at the conference table, but as I draw closer, he shifts away, revealing the third stranger.

I nearly trip over my feet as the blood rushes from my head and settles in a whirling motion of chaos in my chest.

As if sensing someone watching, the man, who's slouched comfortably back in his chair, moves his green gaze from David's and locks on to mine. His body instantly tenses, and the same surprise washes over his features before it's gone, replaced with his brows slamming down and his jaw tightening in silent fury.

This isn't happening. This isn't happening. THIS ISN'T HAPPENING.

Carter, almost-ruin-my-mission-in-China, I-will-stab-him-in-the-eyes-with-thumbtacks, Smith sits a hundred feet away looking out at me from *my* group director's office.

In *my* agency.

In *my* city.

What. The. Fuuuuuck.

CHAPTER 22

3
SI6 Headquarters
Chicago, Illinois: 0938 hours

The Rapture is about to pour out of me as I continue forward. I can practically feel it erupting from every cell to sweep through the room in an acid wash, peeling, burning, and gleefully devouring each person's gurgling screams. As it leaps forward to take and claim, I'd hold it back from David though. I would pull on its chains, ordering it to heel as I'd walk over Carter's melting corpse, not giving him a second glance, and make my way to Axel's cowering body. I'd smile as his large form kneels and begs for mercy, taking in his words of remorse for his deception, for lying, tricking. I'd let him desperately babble, apologize, before laying a gentle hand to his cheek, shushing him, giving him a glimmer of hope, allowing him one tear of relief to fall, seeing my mercy right before I dropped the leash and let the devil shred him to pieces.

The hallway snaps back into a focus as the last of my rage dream subsides, and I work hard to keep my face impassive as I step into David's office. A large, sleek conference table stretches in front of me, parallel to the windowed wall to the left, which has a view to the downstairs pit. His oak desk, with additional low seating, rests in the far right, and I wonder which object he'd miss most when I throw it through the glass pane.

"3." David addresses me with a smile, and my brain nearly short-circuits as my fury doubles. *How can he even* think *to smile at me!* "I'd like to introduce you to a few people."

I don't move my gaze from his, ignoring the raised heart rates of the others in the room.

I will murder you in front of all the people, I silently glower to Axel.

And have to fill out all that paperwork? he counters with a raised brow.

It'd be worth it.

But then who would you blame for random things tomorrow?

There's always someone.

David's lips twitch, but he smartly refrains from grinning again as he turns to the quiet onlookers. "This **is Anthony Ploom, group director from COA." He gestures to the thin-haired** man, who extends a reluctant hand, as though it might come back severed.

I feed off his fear like an afternoon snack and give him my most feral smile.

"It's a pleasure." He practically squeaks as I grip him firmly, cataloguing the scent of his three cats, breakfast of a single cup of coffee, and the skin discoloration on his ring finger. Recently divorced or separated.

"Julie Hockins, his tech and intelligent assistant," David continues, gesturing to the blonde in the room. Her hazel eyes quickly flicker over my body before slipping back to my face, a flush of attraction.

Interesting.

"I was very impressed with your file, 3." Julie's handshake is steady, her gaze uncowering. "And please, call me Jules."

Even in my current temper, I know I'll like this one.

Still not having uttered a word, I watch David motion to the final newcomer. "And considering you two have already met..." He lets the words momentarily hang, a body swaying in its noose. "I don't think we need to introduce Carter Smith."

The monster inside me rumbles, pushes against my skin to be freed as my impassive face meets Carter's dark storm.

He remains seated at the conference table as neither of us nod an acknowledgment, speak, or move to shake the other's hand.

We stay separate.

Two icebergs claiming separate oceans.

The mood grows tense, quiet, scared.

And all I can think is, *Good. You all should be terrified.*

In a charcoal buttoned-down shirt with the sleeves rolled up, Carter sits with steepled fingers, elbows resting on either armrest, showing off strong forearms. His brown hair is swept lazily out of his face, and a shadow of stubble brushes across his jawline. Something that wasn't present in China and brings out his actual age of thirty-two. His green gaze is a mad wizard's fire as it meets mine, a rolling tsunami about to crash down, and for the first time I think how we have something in common—our fury. His rapid heartbeat of *thud thud thud* fills my ears as that disturbingly pleasing scent of cinnamon and male flows off him.

My senses feel skittish taking him in. *What is he doing here? What does this mean?*

It's a rare moment that I'm not in control. Whatever's about to happen is at the whim of someone else. Someone who's not me.

The world becomes a red whirlpool. *You could do it*, the beast purrs. *You could take them all out so quickly, so easily. End what's about to happen before it begins.*

David clears his throat, and I slam down the monster's cage, ignoring its displeased preen.

"Okay, now that we've done introductions, let's get to why we're all here, shall we?" he says.

Everyone moves to a seat, and even though I walk with grace, every one of my movements feels jerky, tense, and I roll out a chair next to Akoni, the farthest one from Carter.

"I'm sure you're all wondering why a team from COA is meeting with a team from SI6," David begins, sitting at the front with Ploom. The two look like caricatures of the adjectives *big* and *small*. "To put it simply, the sister companies are trying to cross-pollinate their resources, and it was brought to the attention of both boards that we recently had a successful, though unplanned, group assignment take place."

His words drip into my brain slowly, building a throb of unease at the base of my skull.

"And I don't think I need to explain which recent assignment I'm talking about." He and Ploom share a look. "Because of this success, and also due to the nature of this next assignment, the companies feel that having the same two teams brought together would be the perfect first test of cross-pollination."

The animal's cage rattles. *No no no no no no—*

"3, Carter"—David glances between the two of us—"you're to join forces."

CHAPTER 23

Carter
S16 Headquarters
Chicago, Illinois: 0952 hours

I wonder for a moment if I actually died in China. That I never
made it into Kam's suite that night but instead got my chest
blown out by one of his henchmen's short-barrel shotguns.
I'm not really sitting in this office in Chicago, but back in Hong
Kong, lying with my guts hanging out and staining the hotel's
red carpet redder. Yes, that must be it, and this—here, now—is
merely the devil's doing, the price for all my sins. For everything
about this moment screams my personal hell, and I'm not delu-
sional enough to think heaven would consider even for a second
about taking me. I grow slightly relieved at this thought. Being
dead is a world better than being alive and sitting across from
Medusa's ugly stepsister.

When I was told I had to go to Chicago, Ploom said it was to meet with SI6 on what happened in Hong Kong and for us to file an official complaint about the mismatched intelligence. I wasn't entirely sure why *I* needed to be present for this, but when he mumbled something about protocol and paying for my entire weekend no matter what I decided to "get into," I stopped asking questions.

I should have smelled *trap* then and there.

Instead I flew like a dumb little gnat into my team's web of deception. What a little slimy worm, that Ploom.

Cracking my knuckles under the table, I imagine all the things I could do to him if there weren't witnesses. My gaze goes to the few wisps of hair desperately clinging to his head. I'd shave those off first. Make him watch in a mirror as I take away the last thing I know makes him feel young.

And then there's Jules...

Loveable, quick-mouthed, no-reason-not-to-trust-her Jules. I can't even bring myself to look at her. She's my right-hand lady. The person I depend on to provide me with all my information. She's *supposed* to be the one truth in my life. Did she know about this?

I hold back a disgusted snort.

I should have known better.

I work in an industry of lies, and even if I didn't, relying on anyone is a fool's mistake, which currently makes me a big fat buffoon.

David Axel's voice continues to fill the room, but I can't concentrate on his words, my attention distracted by the sensation of being watched, or more specifically hunted. With my nerves set to buzz, I glance up, not surprised to find 3's eerily composed face pinned to mine, but even with her mask, there's no hiding the malice swirling in those sapphire eyes.

Yeah, well, feeling's mutual, sweetheart.

My gaze drifts over the top half of her that rests above the table, memories of her walking into Axel's office replaying like a shameful dirty dream. The first thing I'd seen were long, toned legs fitted in dark-washed jeans, before traveling over a tight gray T-shirt hugging hills and valleys that teased under a black leather jacket. My body went rigid, pleased, before my gaze continued up to find gleaming copper hair framing a delicate familiar face. And just as quickly as my blood heated, it got doused in ice-cold grandma bathwater. Nashville poop Brown had made her way toward me, and everything in me recoiled.

Despite how my body initially reacted, I *hate* her.

Hate this agency.

Hate every single sentence being said in this stupid room.

I've spent days trying to clear my head of this witch, and now...now I'm being forced to *work* with her.

Yeah, this isn't going to happen.

"No," I state flatly, interrupting Ploom muttering on about how this will be good for our records.

"What do you mean, *no?*" Ploom asks, all eyes landing on me, and I want to strangle him for looking surprised by my reaction. He knows how mad I was after Hong Kong. He was on the receiving end, for Christ's sake.

"No. As in, no, I'm not doing this."

There's a pregnant pause as Axel and Ploom share a glance.

"I'm afraid declining this assignment isn't an option," Axel says.

"Well, I just did," I say. "Sorry to have wasted your time, but

I think we can all agree this is not going to happen, *nor* will it have any sort of successful ending."

"Carter." Ploom clears his throat while smoothing down his lopsided silver tie. "To explain further what David said, the companies are *mandating* this. They already have most of it planned, and it's going forward with or without your full cooperation."

The room grows out of focus. A blinding flash of a bulb.

With or without... What the f—

"I'm a little confused why our previous assignment wasn't considered a success for the companies to apply with other SI6 and COA operatives," 3 pipes in. "Carter and I proved that it can work. Why do we need to prove it again?"

I'm pissed that I'm both grateful and impressed with her argument.

"While that's a valid point," Axel agrees, "this next assignment is an extension of the one you completed in Hong Kong, making it rather time sensitive. It wouldn't make sense to brief a new team."

"Well, considering I'm no longer full time with the agency, and have in my contract the right to refuse assignments..." She drums her nails on the table. "I'm going to have to turn this one down."

For the first time since all this started, Axel shifts uncomfortably, and the movement makes me realize how much she has the men on her team by the balls. I hold back an eye roll. *Good luck trying to grab mine, honey.*

"I'm sorry, 3," he says, "but for this specific assignment, that option has been withdrawn. If you remember, there's also a clause in your contract that overrules agents if the board of directors get involved."

The energy in the room plummets to freezing as 3 grows deathly still. Akoni inches slightly away from her while I bite back a grin. Despite both of our predicaments, I can't help feeling smug that little Miss Freelance-Special-Pants isn't so special after all.

"You're going to have to work together on this." Axel holds her sharpened stare. "We *all* will."

"This is absurd," 3 grinds out, her fury finally showing. "Don't you see you're already sabotaging the mission? Carter and I *can't* work together. It's impossible."

"Nothing's impossible where you're concerned." Her group director looks at her with a soft smile.

I think I just vomited in my mouth.

"As much as it pains me to admit this," I chime in, "I agree with 3. We are *solo* Ops."

"Who both have had partner training," Ploom adds.

"Years ago," I counter. "And that was with people who could be cooperative. No offense, darling." I glance to 3, catching her fingers curling into a fist on the table. "But I have a feeling you wouldn't use my hand if it was extended to help you out of a burning tar pit."

Akoni snorts next to her, and she flashes him a steely glare, quickly having him swallowing back the sound.

I shake my head. This chick needs to unclench a little.

"Despite you two starting off on a rocky foot," Axel cuts in, "I'm confident in each of your abilities to get this done. You're both the top Ops in your agencies and know how to put personal issues aside for the sake of a job. Or am I mistaken?" He pointedly looks at 3.

Her nostrils flare once, twice, before giving the smallest nod.

"Carter?" Ploom glances to me, and the room hangs in a deafening silence waiting for my answers.

Say no. Say it. Tell them all to go to hell, and then get up and leave. No, run! Run far away and never look back. Do absolutely anything, but say—

"Fine," I grunt. "It's not like it can get any worse."

Famous last words.

CHAPTER 24

Carter
S16 Headquarters
Chicago, Illinois: 1035 hours

"*What!*" 3 and I both blurt out.

Jules pauses, flipping through the files that are lit up in the center of the darkened conference room. "Newlyweds," she repeats in an I'm-so-innocent-I'm-guilty tone. "You'll be paired up as newlyweds."

"No fucking way."

"Carter." Ploom sighs. "Please let Jules finish the debrief."

"But—"

"It's done," he cuts in. "Everything you're about to hear is happening whether you curse and throw punches the whole time, so I suggest you let us finish so we all can get out of here quicker. No offense." He glances to David Axel, who raises his hands as if to say *We understand each other*.

Crossing my arms, I slouch farther into my seat, ignoring the fact I've just mirrored 3's exact movements. Instead I glare daggers at Jules. It might be dark in here, but there's enough glow from the hovering projection to make out the twinkle of pleasure in her hazel eyes.

You're dead, I mouth to her.

She merely winks before allowing David Axel and Ploom to go through the broader part of our assignment. As Akoni stands to hand out the briefing tablets, they each take turns explaining that we'll have to do most of our own recon on site for this mission, making it a longer trip than usual.

I mean really, they should just pull off my fingernails one at a time. It would be less painful.

"As we're all aware," Axel says, clicking to display an image of Kam, "our last target, Chenglei Kam, was successfully put down. We didn't get the code to retrieve the formula, but the Sunday auction was momentarily cancelled, and the DNA samples that 3 swiped were enough for our client to gain access to certain information. It helped us to move forward and bring us to our current assignment." A new image of data lights up, matching what's on the tablet in my hand. "There seems to be a silent partner aiding Kam's biochemical weapon."

Swiping through my screen, I study the multitude of pictures and articles, a little astonished with what's on them.

"I can see you're all a bit surprised at the name connected to this," Axel continues. "Which is understandable since a group like this is rarely involved in such business, but we believe that's why they saw the benefit in it. The silent partner is the Oculto Cartel in Mexico."

Surprised is putting it mildly. I've never heard of a drug cartel, especially such a notorious one, that has *ever* been attached to biochemical before. Physical weaponry sure, but *biochemical*? A picture of Manuel Mendoza, the current leader of the Oculto, is featured at the top. His square-jawed face and weathered brown skin would almost be warming if not for the mangled scar on his neck and his hardened gaze. Even with his bright-blue eyes you can tell he's a man whose soul has long since been sucked away.

"Our intelligence found that the Oculto have been responsible for perfecting the formula and has been working on manufacturing the weapon locally." Ploom pushes up his wire-rimmed glasses and continues where Axel left off. "If this is indeed the case, what we need to find is the lab it's being created in, acquire a sample before shutting it down, and take out this second-party threat. The fact that we're only finding out about them now shows we're not going up against amateurs. They are known for their abilities to stay hidden and keep quiet, and with Kam's death, the Oculto will be lying even lower until things cool down. Which is where we come in. Their stillness buys us time to find their lab before they move or sell off the product at another silent auction. Kam and his company were the face of this business, had the connection to traders. The Oculto were behind-the-scenes research and manufacturing. This will be their first time handling this side of things, and we're hoping their greenness causes them to drop trails, leading us straight to them."

"Questions so far?" Axel leans back in his chair.

"Why would a drug cartel switch to biochemical?" 3 asks.

"We're not too sure, but ever since Mendoza took over from the long-ruling Vicente Rios, the business of the Oculto has slowly shifted away from drugs and into this territory," Axel explains.

3 looks back at her tablet, her eyes slightly unfocused, as if she's trying to piece something together. "Do we know what form this weapon is active in or what it exactly does?"

"Unfortunately, we're still unclear on these details. We just know it's being marketed as something to advance the power of armies by tenfold," Axel says.

3 frowns. "Advance the power of armies...and we're sure it's biochemical?"

He nods. "Yes, that we know for certain. From what was pieced together from the few files we were able to retrieve of Kam's, it has something to do with DNA mutation. There's been talk of a possible virus, but again, we're not one hundred percent certain. This will be up to you and Carter to go in and finish filling in the pieces."

"Can we get access to the acquired Kam files?" I ask.

"Yes, of course." Axel nods to his tech guy. "Akoni, can you gather that for 3 and Carter?"

"Sure thing." Akoni types something on his tablet.

"Are there any more questions regarding the Oculto?" Axel asks.

3 and I shake our heads.

"Great." He nods to Jules. "If you wouldn't mind."

"Of course." She sits up straighter, covering the center of the room with new images as she launches into the specifics of the mission. "The Oculto's operation is said to be located near a small town set high in the Mexican hills, called Cuetzalan, which resides in the state of Puebla. It's about a hundred and twenty miles outside of Mexico City. Perfect for them to have access to airports and deliveries, but far enough away to be secluded and aware when visitors come to town. It's also close to the ocean for port access."

Images of a small, quaint town lights up the room. It looks like a place, on a different occasion, I would love to spend days exploring. The narrow streets are filled with cobblestone paths that wind around whitewashed houses and red-tiled roofs. The whole city of sixteen thousand residents is surrounded by lush green mountains, making it hard to imagine the Oculto being a resident.

"We don't know exactly where in the mountains the lab is." Jules flips to a map of an expansive jungle terrain. "But we'll be starting in Cuetzalan and taking expeditions to a few different suspect locations." Six red dots light up the areas. "Cuetzalan is known to have a few tourists throughout the year, especially of the honeymoon variety. Which is why"—Jules slips me a quick grin—"as I mentioned previously, you'll be going as newlyweds."

I swallow down a bit of bile as Jules explains that she and Akoni will be traveling with us but staying at a different hotel in town. They will be there under the guise of photographic journalists, and we'll have a backup team standing by in Puebla for when, or if, we need to call them in.

This is when I start to drown her out as thoughts of how exactly I'll get through this undisclosed amount of time with 3, *as my wife*, fill my head.

How will we survive the first night without one of us stabbing the other in our sleep?

With 3's attention on her tablet, I steal another moment to study her. In the muted lights, her hair has turned a darker maroon, and the glow from her screen highlights a scattering of freckles that are normally hidden. On first appearance she looks like a girl who should be laughing more than she frowns, and I find myself wondering if she ever does. What's she like when she leaves this place? Does she have friends? The capability to *keep* them?

Following her graceful neck down to her exposed skin that's framed by her T-shirt's collar, I glide over the hint of cleavage peeking out and am brought back to my initial attraction to her at the gala.

Maybe we just misunderstood each other.

Maybe she's not that big of a beast.

Maybe we actually might get along and have some fun on this assignment.

Looking back up, I find a cold blue glare stabbing into mine, 3 more than aware of where my attention was just resting.

I don't know what makes me do it, but there's something about this girl that provokes my worst self, because before I can stop, I slide her a crooked half smile and wink.

And I gotta say, the dripping disdain that pools in her eyes afterward made it completely worth it.

With the room's lights brightening, our debrief ends, each of us instructed to meet in Mexico City in four days' time before heading to Cuetzalan. Standing with a stretch, I make my way to talk to Jules, but before I can utter a word, 3 stomps toward me.

"Just so we're clear," she says, her voice barbed wire. "I don't like you. I don't like your methods, and if you get in the way of me completing this mission, I will not hesitate to remove the one thing from your body that I know gives you your sole reason for existing."

I cock a brow. "I'm flattered you're even thinking about my *thing*, sweetheart."

My head being slammed to the conference table and my arm being twisted to a near breaking point catches me off guard.

"And whatever you do," 3 hisses in my ear, her impressively strong grip tightening and making me grunt against the pain. "Do *not* call me sweetheart, honey, or babe *ever* again." With a final push, she lets go and stalks from the room.

Pushing myself up, I calmly straighten my shirt and smooth back my hair. "Right," I say, turning to the shocked-silent audience. "Who do I see about getting a divorce?"

CHAPTER 25

Nashville

Sitting on my couch in a white T-shirt and yoga pants, I flip through the files on my tablet that outline our undercover profiles. They assigned me one of my usual aliases, but now my Ms. Stephanie Keller will be Mrs. Stephanie Keller *Nickels*. Can I get a million barf bags, please? Carter is Benjamin Nickels, owner of a small Internet startup based out of Paulo Alto, and I'm his lovely new bride trying to make it as an interior decorator. I'm playing someone a bit older, like usual, and Carter someone a bit younger. We're twenty-eight and have been together for four years. The quaint and vanilla couple met in college in San Francisco and tied the knot this past month. It sounds like a happy, peaceful life.

I hate it.

I've never been one for white picket fences, two-point-five

kids, and flowers on my birthday. Considering it isn't even the real date, I never saw the point in celebrating. Ceci of course never misses the day, but I suspect it's because she revels in any chance to sing loudly off key, embarrassing me in a public. A lesser mortal wouldn't stay alive to croon the second verse, but Ceci's different, and she unfortunately knows it. **I've worked hard to limit close relationships in my life, a**nd considering how much of a handful she is, I was right to do so. I don't know how anyone has mental or emotional space for more. No wonder my parents couldn't handle raising a kid.

Pushing my new profile aside, I look back at the information on the Oculto cartel. Manuel Mendoza's image stares out. With pitch-black hair, weathered olive skin, and a low brow that seems to rest in a permanent scowl, he seems every bit the mob boss. But what's more unnerving are the piercing blue eyes inside his shadowed features. The contrast of light to dark make them that much more focal, and as I stare into them, I find myself unable to look away.

Like a bulb breaking, I get a flash of similar eyes, but warmer. They are filled with love and awe, and I blink, startled, dropping the tablet.

My skin erupts in a chill as I stand, having no idea where that memory came from. Fervently glancing back at the screen that rests innocently on my couch, I hesitate to pick it back up. Whatever that was, I don't want it to happen again.

The sound of keys clanking fills my ears—Ceci coming home—and I'm rocked out of my paralysis to quickly scoop my briefing materials into my satchel and flop back onto the couch.

"Hey," she calls as she drops her bag onto the kitchen counter. She's dressed in a smart gray pencil skirt and white top that complements her dark skin, her hair pulled into a tight ponytail. She looks absolutely fierce and not surprisingly got the job at Turquoise Waters. She's been working the brunch shifts as the maître d', coming back for a small break before changing and returning to waitress dinner. She says she's been loving it and that Christopher sounds like my biggest fan. I've refrained from acknowledging her latter comment.

"Hey," I call back just as I turn my screen to my last Scrabble game.

"What did they need you for at the office today?" she asks as she carries two oranges over and hands me one.

I find myself tearing into the fruit like it's a certain person's face.

"Whoa." Ceci raises her brows as she falls into the couch beside me. "That bad, huh?"

"They put me on a project with Carter Smith."

She's silent for a moment, blinking once, twice, before keeling over with laughter.

"I do *not* find this funny."

She snorts as she tries to compose herself. "I'm sorry, Nash— I'm sorry—I just—" She breaks down again, and I'm about to leave, when she holds up a hand, telling me to stay. "I'm sorry," she repeats again, breathing out a few final chuckles while wiping a tear away, "but this is amazing. Karma really handed you one this time." She doesn't try to remove the smile plastered to her face.

I scowl. "What do you mean?"

"I *mean* that you, Nashville Brown, have to actually work with someone you don't get along with instead of run away from them."

"What the hell are you talking about?"

"Nash, come on. Don't be obtuse."

"Obtuse? Why, Cecilia Williams, did you finally download that word of the day app?"

She throws an orange slice at me, her gray eyes narrowing. "Don't be a hag."

I give her a syrupy smile while popping her ammo fruit into my mouth.

"What I'm trying to say," Ceci begins again, "is that you only have two modes of dealing with something you don't want to. You either A"—she holds up a finger—"turn and run as fast as you can in the other direction, or B"—she holds up another finger—"make *it* run as fast as it can in the other direction."

I give her a bored look. "I fail to see your point."

"That's not dealing with something."

"Actually it is."

She rolls her eyes. "Okay, let me clarify. It's not a *healthy* way of dealing with something."

"What do you know about being healthy? You use peanut butter as dip for Cool Ranch Doritos."

"Don't try and use your evasion tactics with me." Ceci waves a hand. "Besides, the only ones who need to understand my relationship with peanut butter and Cool Ranch Doritos are me and my peanut butter and Cool Ranch Doritos."

"You are so gross."

"And *you* finally need to learn to work through your people issues. I understand it's hard. Don't forget. I was right there with you at Bell Buckle and all through high school, but we're grownups now. We need to move on from why we were there, *who* we were, and like you told me, need to start making some healthy changes."

"Well aren't you little Miss Dr. Phil today."

"Nash," Ceci says with a resigned sigh. "I'm not trying to get all Oprah on your ass. I just love you and know how sweet—yes, sweet!" she repeats when I make a face, "you can be. Not to mention loyal, funny, and a blessing to have in a person's life. I want other people to see that too."

"Why?"

"Because"—Ceci smiles—"I think it's a sin to keep you all to myself."

"Ugh, you're such a Hallmark card." I shove a pillow over my face. Suffocating seems really appealing right now.

My couch cushions shift. "I can be a great teddy bear too!" Ceci squeals before latching on to me with one of her vicelike hugs.

"No, Ceci! *Don't.* I hate 'Bear Hug Time'!" I squirm under her grasp, but it's too late. She's already started to sing.

"Bear Hugs! Bear Hugs! When you get hugged like a bear, you forget all your cares! So open your arms, and let's get to huggin' so we can feel all the lovin'!" she croons.

I try not to vomit on the both of us. "Bear Hug Time" is a devil-worshiping song they taught us at the orphanage. Once the words are spoken, you can't get them out of your head for days.

"I hate you," I pant as the song begins to spin on repeat in my brain.

"Aw, I love you too." She grins.

Like trying to hold in a fart, it proves too painful, and I let out a laugh. Ceci beams before hugging me tighter.

And this time, I hug back.

That night I dream of something I've conditioned my mind to never dream of, so when she materializes, it takes me a second to remember who she is.

But of course I know her, for how can someone forget their mother?

The images aren't like a picture though. I can never see her eyes or nose or mouth. Her whole face is a smudge in a painting. But that's okay, because the things I can bring up are more important. Like her scent, lilac with lemon; her laughter, light and ever-flowing; and her touch, calming and soft.

These dreams terrify me, for I know they won't last. Even in my current peace within her arms, I know the next part is coming. For when I'm with her, so is he, and the darkness is quick to follow.

At first the man's just a shadow that hovers close by, watching us smile and play, and at first I'm not scared of him. The three of us are happy. He's strong and lifts me high in the air until I giggle and squeal. We laugh, she, he, and I, because again, we're happy. But then I sense my mother's worry. Her heartbeat gets louder, thump, thump. *Gets faster,* thump, thump, thump. *And we run and run and run before we hide. Stay quiet, my little flower, she whispers. Be very quiet. More shadows dart by.* Quiet, little flower, *she says again.* Quiet.

And I do.

I stay quiet.

So quiet.

Quiet for the both of us.

Quiet until I can't hear or see anyone because I'm alone.

And she's gone.
But don't worry, Mommy. I'll keep quiet.
Always and forever quiet.
Until you come back.

Choking on a breath, I snap my eyes open. It's the middle of the night, my apartment dark, with Ceci's soft snoring filtering in from across the hall. I listen to her rhythmic breathing as my own slows, and my fingers loosen from where they're clenching my sheets. The ceiling fades in and out of focus as I stare up at it. It's been years since I've been plagued with that dream, and with a decisive twist of a deadbolt, I keep my mind from exploring why. Instead I throw off my comforter and get dressed. Even though I still have three more hours of rest, I know I won't be going back to sleep. For when it comes to dealing with what might be waiting for me if I do, Ceci was one hundred percent right—I will not hesitate in turning and running as fast as I can in the other direction.

CHAPTER 26

3
Undisclosed Location
Mexico City, Mexico: 0800 hours

The flight to Mexico City went by quickly, and the drive to our base to meet Jules and Carter went by even quicker. Time enjoys playing cruel jokes like that. When you dread starting something, it bends the space-time continuum to get you there faster.

The base is connected to an American bank that's on the west end of Paseo de la Reforma, a wide avenue that runs diagonally across the heart of Mexico City. The larger portion of headquarters resides underground, like most do. It makes it easier to muffle sound when testing equipment, and even simpler to eradicate the building if necessary by collapsing it in and flooding it. Intelligence agencies are big on those types of insurance plans: learn everything, share nothing. My own personal motto.

Akoni and I split up when we get there. Him going to gather his Inspector Gadget trench coat of items while I make my way into the weapons warehouse. It's a large gray hangar that sits ten floors below ground level. Entering, I immediately spot Carter on the far side of the room, his tall form dressed in dark jeans and a black T-shirt as he and a specialist look over a few tables lined with guns. Upon seeing him, I immediately do an about face, deciding to check out the toxins they've made for me first, which thankfully are contained in an airtight glass lab on the complete opposite side.

Introducing myself to the resident scientists standing by, I'm led into a disinfectant chamber to be blasted clean before entering the lab. There's something about being in a Clean Room that gives me a weird tickle of joy. With everything contaminant-free, quiet and contained in their petri dishes and freezers, my oversensitive senses feel normalized. I pick things up easier, and my concentration comes more naturally, not having to block out all the superfluous noise. It's the one time I get a glimpse of what it must be like to be a normal human, and while somewhat boring, the simplicity is almost breathtaking, the constant buzz in my ears gone.

"We're very excited to share what we've prepared for you today," Dr. Falto Pérez says, a tiny bald man with wide brown eyes. Nodding for me to follow, he shows me to an area filled with vials. "It's rare we get an Op with such an extensive portfolio in toxicology," he chitters exuberantly as he pulls forward a silver case, his white lab coat shifting stiffly under the fluorescent lights as he clicks it open. I give him a small smile. Out of all the specialists in the intelligence field, I've always respected the scientists the most. Not only because of their obvious cognitive advancement compared to everyone else, but also because when SI6 first brought me in as a child, they were the kindest people there. When they could have easily made me feel like a lab rat during the DNA tests to determine my A+ abilities, they never did. They always addressed me by my first name, played games with me, and made a point to explain exactly what they were doing and how it would work. It's what got me initially interested in the human body and how to manipulate it. As technology and science advanced, I only became more obsessed. The things we've learned we can do are absolutely beautiful and completely terrifying.

My ideal combo.

So it's no surprise that I find myself raptly watching a video MRI of a brain with its prefrontal lobe being clouded, inducing short-term memory loss.

"Amazing," I say as I turn to read the listed details of the toxin Dr. Pérez just showcased. "And this can be transferred into spray form?"

"Oh yes." He nods, picking up a can that looks like traveling hairspray. "We actually prefer it that way. Less painful for the recipient, and you won't need to get as close. You'll have to wear a breathing mask though, but that comes standard. See here." He pulls off a small cylinder stuck to the side. "Just bite on this piece, and the face mask will expand around your nose and mouth."

I graze my fingers along the ridges of the collapsed mask. "And how long has it been recorded to last?"

"The canisters you'll be provided have TML, temporary memory loss, for up to three hours. We feel this is sufficient in getting you out of the situation you're in and far enough away so that you can go dark before anyone starts looking."

"Wonderful."

The doctor beams before showing me a couple more serums they've customized for me, mainly involving temporary paralysis, hallucinogens, tracking liquids, and of course, extermination. Christmas came early this year.

Eventually I have to do weapons because I've exhausted every other option waiting for Carter to leave that area, but I see he's still cleaning a gun, bent over the range table where four target dummies rest in the distance. My fingers curl into fists at my sides as I stomp forward knowing he's purposefully been taking his sweet-ass time. Stepping beside him, I'm unable to ignore the scent of a woman's day-old perfume that lingers on his black T-shirt. It mixes aggressively with his male and cinnamon scent, as if to say *I was here. Remember me?* I'm guessing flight attendant, and I sneer in disgust before taking in what's in front of him.

"Jesus, what are you preparing for? Armageddon?" I glance over his pile of semiautomatics, handguns, and a submachine gun.

"Funny, I've been using the same nickname for you too," he says while continuing to wipe down the chamber of a Chiappa Rhino, a revolver known for its accuracy due to its ability to recoil straight back.

Suppressing the desire to show him how truly apocalyptic I can be, I start collecting my standard arsenal from the nearby racks. An assistant steps over to help, but I wave her off. My needs in this field are minimal; I grab only two **Glock 17s with** silencers, a Beretta LTLX7000 shotgun, and by far my favorite, an FN Five-Seven, all of which are biometric. Though I appreciate and respect them, I'm not big on guns. I feel less in control with them. I prefer hand-to-hand combat given that the closer I am to my opponents, the easier I can pick up on their temperaments and determine their next moves. There's no life in a gun, and your target is often too far away to read. Unless I'm standing downwind. If that's the case, then game on.

Guns obviously make my job easier though, so when I do engage, I love the FN Five-Seven. With its ambidextrous controls, low recoil, large magazine capacity, and ability to penetrate body armor, it's quite the busy bee.

Looking back at Carter's plethora of weapons, I pick up a Corner Shot Grenade Launcher. "Seriously?"

His green gaze goes from what's in my hand up to my face. "Trust me. You'll thank me later."

"Don't hold your breath."

"If it will end my misery of your presence faster, I just might," he says before lifting his Rhino, aiming down the sight and hitting one of the far targets right between the brows.

He flashes me a cocky grin.

Without losing a beat, I pick up a standard handgun, turn off the safety, and, not removing my eyes from his, take three shots at the target. From the way his gaze narrows and his jaw clenches, I don't have to check to know I hit precisely where he shot. Three times precisely.

My turn to smile.

Sucking on the front of his teeth, Carter snatches up a grenade launcher and, barely giving me time to take hurried steps back, lets loose a shell. It barrels forward, rocketing toward the other side of the room before a loud BANG shakes the walls. All four targets explode in a barrage of flames, the warehouse plummeting into shocked silence while the fire crackles and smokes its final destruction.

"I win," Carter singsongs before dropping the launcher onto the table and returning to cleaning his gun.

If my eyes had the power to pierce, the whole side of his stupidly defined face would be filled with holes.

Grinding my teeth to near dust, I shove my weapons to the wide-eyed assistant and leave. Neither of us acknowledge the other's presence for the remainder of the time we're at base.

A behavior, I'm hoping, we can maintain for the entirety of the trip.

CHAPTER 27

Carter
Undisclosed Location
Mexico City, Mexico: 1135 hours

The prop assistant backs up like a cornered rabbit, and I take in a calming breath, telling him for the tenth time what to do.

"Give me the keys." I hold out my hand to him.

"If you give him the keys, you'll regret coming to work today," 3 says through clenched teeth.

We've been having a standoff for the last ten minutes about who'll be driving to Cuetzalan, and I'm on my last nerve.

"Benny, was it?" I ask the assistant. He nods while glancing at 3 nervously. "Listen, Benny. Let me ask you a question. If a couple were on their honeymoon, who do you think would be driving them around? The husband or the wife?"

"Don't *even* play that sexist card," 3 cuts in.

"Benny, who do you think would drive?" I repeat. The man opens and closes his mouth. "That's it. Just say it," I goad. "I know you have an opinion. You wouldn't be working here if you didn't."

He swallows. "El marido, señor."

I smile triumphantly, snatching the keys from him. "Exactly, the *husband*," I pointedly say to 3, who if she were a cartoon character, would have steam pouring from her ears in this moment. Dressed in a smart black leather jacket, gray T-shirt, dark jeans, and boots, with her fiery-red hair pulled into a high ponytail, she appears every bit the hard-ass she's trying to come across as. I'm almost curious as to what depraved torture fantasy she's conjuring up for me as I take in her icy-blue gaze.

"You know," I say, walking to our assigned car located in the garage. "I specifically remember someone threatening me about not messing up the assignment. I would think not appearing like an *authentic* married couple would be a threat, don't you?" I ask sweetly as I load my bags into the back of the small two-door Nissan Sunny. Cuetzalan's streets are teeny tiny and often abruptly become stairs, so anything larger than a thimble would be worthless there.

"*Fine*," she growls. "But I'm controlling the music." She nearly smacks my head when throwing her duffel into the trunk.

"Whatever will keep your trap shut, swe—" Seeing her fingers twitch at her sides has me stopping short, memories of my head slamming onto a conference table replaying in front of me. "You've got problems. You know that?" I shut the trunk.

"Yeah, and I'm looking at my biggest one."

"Oh *snap*! Where'd you learn that one? Elementary school?"

3 takes a threatening step forward, but I remain still, daring her to try what she did at SI6 again, but before either of us can do much of anything, Akoni and Jules walk up, interrupting our

super-enjoyable, fun conversation.

"All right." Jules shoulders her bag, her jean jacket riding up a bit. "You guys able to hold off killing each other until we arrive in Cuetzalan?"

She and Akoni will be traveling separately in their own car. Lucky fucks.

"I think that question's directed at *you*, wife." I flash a syrupy smile.

"And I think the answer depends on whether *you're* going to magically transform into a completely different person on the ride there."

"I don't know about the ride there," I say, "but we can certainly satiate your desire for role-playing when we get to the hotel."

Her eyes pinch to slits before her demeanor quickly melts and shifts into something foreign, heated, and I warily watch her slide closer to me, a snake approaching in high grass.

Every muscle tenses.

"That's a great idea," she purrs, her voice a trickle of warm blood as she presses her breasts against my chest. This close I can smell her subtle scent of coconut shampoo, and the hairs on the back of my neck stand tall, unsure if it's from fear or arousal. *What the crap is going on?*

"You can be my patient." She runs a finger up my bicep, a trail of fire. "And pretend like it doesn't hurt when I *cut out your intestines and hang you from them*." With a sharp poke of her nail, her gaze turns from dripping honey back to sleet, and I watch stunned as she turns, stomping back the car before slamming the door shut.

What the—

I blink to the space she just occupied, trying to straighten out my confused male libido that her creepy-smooth mood change just stirred.

"Yeah." Akoni steps next to me. "I'd stay away from any sort of role-playing games if I were you. It didn't end well for the last guy."

I glance to him, trying to gauge if that was a joke or not, but he merely gives me a sympathetic pat on the back before walking to his own vehicle, backpack snug against his large gray hoodie. Jules flashes me a thumbs-up before following him, leaving me once again wondering how the hell I can get out of this marriage.

***

The *only* positive thing so far on this trip is that 3 likes jazz, something that caught me by surprise when she set up the music for our ride. Living in New York for as long as I have, I think it's impossible not to feel an affinity for the genre. Its calming and mellow notes are something I always tend to crave after returning from a rather intense assignment. So when 3 clicked on Duke Ellington, it appeared both of our moods thawed a bit.

Despite this one commonality though, we haven't exchanged more than eight words in the past thirty minutes. 3's gaze has been plastered to the view beyond her side of the car since escaping the city limits, and I slide her a fervent glance, watching her red hair, made copper in the sunlight, flutter around her face from the wind slipping through her cracked window. Her usually pale skin is made a shade warmer in the morning light, and I hate to admit that she really is quite pretty when she's not sneering and gnashing her teeth.

"So, 3, hunh?" I try starting a conversation because I'm either a masochist or my ADD for sitting still has kicked in. "Are all the Ops at SI6 numbers?"

She continues to study the passing scenery of farmlands and

sloping hills.

"Listen." I let out a resigned sigh. "I know we don't like each other. It's painfully obvious we'd both rather be getting Chinese water tortured than confined in this car, but here we are, and we're about to be stuck with each other for God knows how long. Can we at least call a truce for this mission? Then I promise we can go back to plotting each other's demise."

She keeps her eyes glued forward, like she didn't hear a word.

"Fine. Whatever." I grip the wheel tighter, concentrating on the curve of the road as it winds into small mountainous terrain.

"No."

I glance her way.

"The SI6 Ops aren't numbered." She plays with her phone in her lap.

"So why do they call you 3?"

"It's a nickname."

I snort. "Yeah, no *shit* it's a nickname. I'm asking how you got it. Are you sure you passed the entry IQ—"

3 shooting me a murderous glare cuts me off.

"Sorry." I hold up a hand. "Truce mode. I promise."

Flicking a glance at the roof of the car, like she's asking for help from a higher being, she lets out a huff. "It's how many mission targets I completed in a day."

"Like, you had to take down three in one assignment?" I ask to clarify.

"No. Separate assignments. Separate locales."

The sound of Duke Ellington's fluid piano playing is the only sound for a moment as I let the improbability of this sink in. "How is that even *possible*?"

She shrugs. "It was just one of those days."

"*Just one of those—*" I glance at her wide eyed, taking in

her bored expression, right before I fall into my wheel laughing. It's one of those laughs that has me slowing the car so as not to crash, one that aches against my stomach and lasts until little tears build in the corners of my eyes. "Oh, hon—3," I quickly correct. "We might get along after all."

She merely purses her lips in distaste before sliding her gaze back out the window, returning our drive to its edgy silence.

Then again, maybe not.

We arrive in Cuetzalan in the evening and head straight to our hotel, Flor Tranquila. It's located in the north central part of the small town and has a tiny stone entrance that leads to an open courtyard, where five floors of balconies stretch up to a cloudless blue sky. The entire infrastructure is made from a variety of stone: red bricks tile the floor, crude cut rocks make up the walls, and uneven slate steps lead from one door to the next, creating a charming, lost-in-time, secluded atmosphere—a perfect honeymoon destination.

3 checks us in while I handle the bags like a good hubby. She speaks fluently in Spanish to the cutest little old lady sitting behind the concierge desk. She's wrapped in a colorful textile shawl and introduces herself as Señora Flores. Taking us up to our suite on the fourth floor, she explains how she's the third-generation owner of the quaint establishment and that the rooms are more like little apartments, meaning we'll be left alone unless we request otherwise. 3 and I share a glance, knowing this eradicates the issue of stashing our gear from room cleaning. Again, making this a perfect retreat for newlyweds to get randy. It's almost a crime that all these consummating conveniences will be wasted on us.

Stopping at a door at the end of the hall, Señora Flores uses a vintage iron key to show us into our room. The small sitting area, kitchen, and bedroom are all laid out together in an open space with a tucked-away bathroom in the corner. The floor is decorated with a beautiful rust-colored tile leading to white painted walls with yellow, blue, and red mosaic crown molding.

Dropping the key into my hand, she gives me a knowing smile, telling us to enjoy ourselves before leaving us standing awkwardly alone, staring at the one piece of furniture that's obviously placed as the main attraction. A four-poster bed with a soft white draped canopy sits in the center of the far wall, beside the bathroom and near an open balcony door. The fabric sways lightly in the breeze drifting in and shines translucent from the setting sun.

I'm not one to be emotionally moved, but even I'm taken aback by the romantic wistfulness and become painfully aware of 3's presence beside me, all her hard edges mixing with the soft slope of her undeniably female curves. I almost want to laugh. This might be the only time in my life where I'm in a hotel room with a woman and have no idea what to do.

Another beat passes, our quiet deafening, before we each talk at once—3 saying she should take a quick shower and me explaining that I should unpack.

"Right." 3's brows furrow as she picks up one of her bags. "We can explore the town when we're done."

"Sounds good." I scratch my neck, watching the back of her leather jacket disappear into the bathroom.

Looking down at myself, I realize for the first time in the hours we've been together that we match.

Shit.

I try not to think about what that might imply.

CHAPTER 28

3
Cuetzalan, Mexico: 1726 hours

The sun casts the village in a warm yellow glow as we walk the cobblestone streets. Cuetzalan is also known as Pueblo Mágico, or Magic Town, for the mist that tends to descend from the surrounding mountains. It also retains the name from the ancestral legacy that still lives so vibrantly among the people and the ever-changing winding footpaths that beg to be explored. A few indigenous men and women pass by wearing traditional garb while carrying goods, and just like their clothing, the buildings feel untouched. The mix of raw stone facades and whitewashed walls accented with vibrant colors gives away the richness of history. Cuetzalan is easily one of the most peacefully beautiful places I've ever been to on assignment, and I've been to *a lot* of really amazing locations. Too bad they're always stained red from work.

The air is warm but still crisp from the nearby foothills, and I pull my sheer cardigan closer as we pick our way along shops that are slowly closing down to get ready for the night. The owners watch fleetingly as we pass, seemingly used to the occasional tourists. And I *definitely* feel like a tourist with my hair down, flowing freely around my shoulders, and my dark-navy summer dress. Stephanie Nickels, interior decorator, at your service.

Gag.

"Hold my hand," Carter says as I turn away from taking a photo of a doorway lined with potted plants.

"*What*?" I recoil.

"Don't look so excited," he says dryly as he grabs my palm, which I remove at once.

"What are you *doing*?"

"We're on our *honeymoon*, remember?" he says in a low voice. "I'm not exactly lighting fireworks about this either, but we have to start acting like we're in love."

Ick. Love.

I study him for a moment, taking in the way his normally neatly swept-back dark hair is currently tousled, his two days' worth of scruff shadows his jaw, and his gray T-shirt and jeans give off the vibe of a man on vacation. His mouth is set in a thin line revealing that he *does* seem rather butt hurt about the idea.

"Fine." I take his hand, despising the sensation of having his warm, strong fingers entwined with mine. "But don't get any ideas about needing to consummate it as well."

He snorts a laugh. "Trust me. I'd rather hug a cactus naked."

"Good."

"Great."

"*Fine*," I bite out.

"*Perfect*," he volleys.

"*Stop it!*" I forcefully tug on his arm.

He fights a grin as we walk on, and I internally count down from ten. I don't know who came up with this method of relaxation, but it's friggin' idiotic and currently not working. Usually I can fix my annoyance by getting rid of the thing that caused it, but glancing at Carter as he smiles down at a little girl who shyly peers up at him from behind her mother's legs, I unfortunately don't have the option of getting rid of this one.

Eventually we make our way to the Church of San Francisco, the town's big tourist attraction that sits in an open square and whose bell tower can be seen from practically any point in the village. Letting out my senses, I poke around for anything that might be out of the ordinary, but there's almost a startling vacancy of elevated heart rates or fear pheromones—merely a village wrapped in soft breezes and, although a Wednesday, bars and restaurants humming with content patrons.

Walking through the center, I wish I could say holding Carter's hand for this long has been a miserable experience, but I've surprisingly been able to do it without upsetting my gag reflex. Maybe because he's not half bad looking and knows what a shower is, I'm able to bear it longer than with the other slimeballs I've needed to drape myself over in the past.

Still, I do mind getting any sort of cozy with him. So indicating that I need to put my camera away, I hastily remove my hand from his.

"This looks good." He gestures to a small café that's close to the church square.

Taking a seat at an outside table, Carter leans back, draping an arm across my chair, and I instinctually straighten away.

"I'm not going to bite," he says with a quirk of his lips. "Of course, unless you want me to."

"God. You can't help yourself." I scrunch my nose but manage to relax a bit.

Newlyweds in love. Newlyweds in love...

This part of the job should come easily to me—pretending to care, pretending to be someone I'm not—but for some reason it's proving more difficult than normal, and I'm starting to get really pissed by that.

I'm better than this.

If Carter can so flawlessly transition into this role, so can I. With his other hand resting on the table, I place mine on top, nestling into his side. He shoots me a surprised glance, and I give him a smile like a woman head over heels. He blinks, empty headed, before flashing his own grin, and in this light I hate to admit it, but he *is* sort of attractive. His moss-green eyes are by far his best feature and are made brighter against his olive skin. His nose has obviously been broken a few times, but it gives him character, which he clearly could use.

"See, that wasn't so hard." He leans over to whisper in my ear, and I resist, tilting my head away from the warmth of his breath grazing my skin. A ticklish feeling flutters in my stomach, and I frown. Maybe I'm coming down with something, except I never get sick.

A waitress walks over to take our order, and Carter and I ask for coffees. Not only do we need something to pick us up from our drive, but Cuetzalan is known for this beverage. It's the village's main trade.

Sipping the frothy drink, my taste buds explode with richness. Normally, I don't like too many spices or sweets, given my oversensitivity to them, but this is like heaven wrapped in a dream cloud.

"Oh God," I groan.

Carter shifts next to me. "There are a lot of indecent comments you just set me up with, but seeing that we're in truce mode, I'll refrain. But you should know"—he smooths his palm up my arm—"it's taking a great deal of effort."

The skin feels too hot where his fingers traced, and I stiffen while saying, "With the nickname *The Bull*, I'm impressed you have any kind of wiring for restraint."

"Wire, rope, handcuffs." He flashes me a mirthful look. "I'm a fan of restraining in all sorts of ways."

I roll my eyes. "Well, that lasted two seconds."

He chuckles, the vibration of it running along my rib cage. "What can I say? I'm a mere mortal."

I don't comment but turn to watch a group of old men jabbering nearby.

"It's crazy," Carter muses.

"What?" I take another sip of my coffee.

"This place." He nods to our surroundings. "It's hard to imagine it has any connection to our friends."

"Actually, the older the family, the more they tend to reside in places like these."

"Of course you'd know that."

I fight a grin at his annoyed tone before catching sight of Jules and Akoni walking out from a small alley, Akoni excitedly snapping pictures of practically everything he sees. I shake my head. His tendency to be overly exuberant in taking on his undercover profiles is one of the reasons he's rarely given one on our assignments. He's more useful hidden in a room behind computers, especially since his height and bulk make him stand out just about anywhere.

Carter sees them too and lets out a low chuckle, the sound throaty and warm, while watching Akoni's theatrics before they notice us and slowly make their way to our café.

"We should figure out where to eat tonight." Carter traces lines with his finger on my exposed shoulder again just as Jules and Akoni take a seat at a nearby table. "I'll go ask the barista if they have any suggestions."

I merely nod as he leaves, rubbing away the flush of my skin where he just touched. Maybe I have a fever, except I never get fevers. While I'm busy stewing on my discomfort, I almost miss the change in the air, an electric current sent through the wind that only ever means one thing.

We're being watched.

And not the glimpses-of-strangers watched, but purposefully studied.

Taking a slow sip of my drink, I flicker my gaze to anywhere I would choose to observe someone unnoticed. I glance at every darkened window, deep alley, and shadowed doorway. There are too many spots to be able to pinpoint which one holds my admirer, but I know they are there, somewhere.

Thump, thu-thunk. I shuffle through the heartbeats in the surrounding area, trying to find any that would give them away, but besides a few locals that suffer heart arrhythmias, the scene is calm. I'd use scent, but it would currently do little help given our proximity to so many restaurants and that most of the people here have an overwhelming amount of body odor. Deodorant seems to be a novelty for the town's folks.

I catch Carter walking out of the café wearing a grin. "I've got the perfect place for us," he says, wrapping an arm back around my chair.

"We're being watched." I smile over to him like I'm telling

him something funny.

His jaw muscles jump before he does a casual sweep. "You sure?"

"I'm never wrong with these things."

"Of course, *dear*," he drolls, knowing he can finally call me a pet name in public while enjoying my attempt at keeping my smile plastered in place. "You should see yourself," he says with a grin. "You look crazy."

"Maybe because someone is *making* me crazy," I say through clenched teeth.

"Crazy in *love*."

As he leans in playfully, I grab his chin and bring him closer, as if for a kiss, and he immediately tenses, his quickened heartbeat filling my ears. "If you keep this up," I whisper, my grip tightening, "I'll make you regret it when we're back in the hotel room. I have something that will keep you from screaming, but not because you won't want to."

His lips pucker in distaste as he pulls away. "You really know how to kill a mood."

"I know how to kill lots of things."

"Right," he says with an eye roll. "So where's this stalker of ours?"

Letting out my senses again, I scrunch my nose. "They're gone."

Crap. How did I miss them leaving?

"Hunh." Carter lifts his coffee cup.

"They were there though." I glance around quickly. "I could feel it."

"Maybe they were just intrigued by a pretty girl sitting alone, and seeing me come out scared them away."

"Maybe," I say, ignoring Carter calling me *pretty*.

I can't get distracted like that again.

While I'm not certain if the person watching is from the Oculto, the energy they sent my way was definitely dangerous, and in a small, quiet town like this, there's only a few possibilities of whom that danger could be.

CHAPTER 29

Carter
Cuetzalan, Mexico: 2115 hours

To find where we should dine tonight, I did the classic trick of retaining the right information by asking for the exact opposite. I feigned a worried, protective husband and asked what parts of the city we should stay away from, so as not to unknowingly stumble there with my new blushing bride.

Now 3 and I head straight to the area of forewarning after leaving Jules and Akoni. They will be doing their own exploration before we regroup in the morning.

The streets are less populated in the southeast part of town and darker closer to the outskirts, where a bit of the historical charm falls away. Simple whitewashed buildings with red painted bases fill our surroundings, giving off the vibe of housing the local villagers rather than the tourists, especially after a few ask if we're lost.

Holding 3's hand again, which feels deceptively small and fragile considering it's more lethal and constricting than a cobra, we come to a small square that appears to be this neighborhood's local watering hole. There are a couple bars and restaurants lining its perimeter, and 3 and I catch eyes when we spot the name of one of the drinking establishments. *Búho Oculto* (Hidden Owl) reads the wooden carved sign above a bar that's tucked into the corner of the open rotunda. The front is dimly lit save for a single gas lamp, and a few gentlemen stand outside talking to a man who sits on a stool smoking a cigarette and resembles an MMA fighter. It definitely looks like the type of joint disreputable individuals would inhabit, almost in a cliché way.

We pick a tiny place to eat directly across from it, and our table has a perfect view of our headlining establishment, but to say our presence goes unnoticed would be the biggest lie of the century. Everyone seems to watch us as we sit down, stupid gringos encroaching on the locals' haven. I sigh. So much for stealth. We'll need to put on an Oscar-worthy honeymooners act now, and while that thought turns my stomach, I know 3 probably despises it even more, which makes it a little less intolerable.

"It seems your information was correct," 3 says quietly in German while perusing the list of food a waitress brought over.

Smart girl. Even in small, secluded towns like this, English-speaking individuals can be found, and with the few prying eyes, it's better to be safe than sorry.

"Da." I nod my agreement.

"We'll need to figure out how to get in," she continues in the foreign tongue.

"Da."

"But we won't be able to tonight."

"Da."

Her eyes narrow at me from above her menu. "Is that all you know?"

"Nicht," I reply.

She presses her lips together, as if in discomfort, and I sit up straighter. "Oh my God. Are you about to *smile*?"

She clears her throat and looks away. "Nicht."

She might hate smiling, but I certainly don't, and I can't help the one that forms. I'm about to push this further when our waitress walks up to take our order, breaking the moment.

As the food arrives, 3 and I continue to talk quietly in German while furtively keeping tabs on the bar. Mostly men walk in and out with a few above-average women wrapped to their sides, most of which, I'm sure, are getting compensated. The patrons all seem to know each other and clap the gorilla bouncer on the shoulder before walking in.

"I'll have to go in alone tomorrow night," 3 says, leaning back in her chair, her gaze sweeping over the door again.

I tilt my head. "And why alone?"

"Because if we both went, it would look suspicious compared to a single lost college chick exploring the town and stumbling in."

"What about a lost college *guy*?" I counter, not liking where her mind is going. This is *our* assignment, and I won't be sidelined.

"A girl is less threatening." She takes a swig of her drink. "Plus, men are easier to seduce and appeal to their softer side."

I barely contain my recently sipped soda from coming out of my nose with my snort. "*Really*?" I splutter. "You think a man has an easier-tapped emotional side than a woman?"

"When it comes to a pretty girl letting down her guard and

appearing vulnerable, of course. Men like to conquer. Like to feel the predator. When they sense something weak, particularly in a female, they see an easy meal and little threat in allowing them to get close. Especially when their basic desire is always sex."

I study her impassive expression. "And where, exactly, are you pulling this psychobabble from?"

"Evolutionary biology."

I laugh. "*Right.*"

Her brows pinch in as she studies her plate, playing with her food as if suddenly upset about something.

"What?" I ask.

"Nothing."

"No, what is it?"

She peers at me from behind her lashes. "Well...I also know because I made it my life's work to understand human nature."

I remain silent, unsure what to make of the way her features have gone all soft, no longer clenched with her internal frustration when in my presence.

"Do you want to know how I came into this field of work?" she asks.

"Uh...sure."

Taking in a deep breath, as if to prepare herself, she says, "I was abandoned as a child." Pausing for a moment, she lets the words hang in the night air as she watches an older woman walk by. "I was practically a baby when I was left on the streets."

I knew this from her file, but to hear this admittance in person, and from her own lips, makes the reality of her beginning life hit home. It's also apparent from the thickness in her voice that she's still very affected by it, which *might* prove she's human after all.

"Don't get me wrong," she goes on. "My life wasn't as bad as it could have been if different people had found me...or not found me at all. And while I tried to get past my beginnings, to move on, there was one thing that I couldn't let go of. That I needed to find the answer to."

She goes quiet, worrying her bottom lip.

I can't help myself. I reach over and place my hand on top of hers. A silent reassurance that she can keep going, not wanting to talk in case it scares away this unexpected openness. I watch as her blue eyes shimmer with emotion, holding me still. The flame from the table's candle sets her hair in a golden glow and smooths her already silky skin. I'm once again reminded of the angel I saw that first night at the gala. Unknowingly I find myself caressing her palm with my thumb.

"I needed to know..." She stops, taking a swallow, and I gently squeeze her hand before she squeezes back. "I needed to know just how quickly you would prove my point." Her mouth tips up at the side, a sneer of a cat that caught a mouse, and I watch, stunned, as all the delicate emotion she just poured out gets sucked away, vanishing without a trace.

"You're crazy," I breathe, snatching my hand away like it'd been burned.

3 calmly settles into her chair. "Don't get your panties in a twist. Like I said before, men are pretty simple creatures."

I wrinkle my nose, suddenly feeling dirty, and not in the way I prefer. "I can't believe you pulled the orphan card."

"It worked, didn't it?"

I study her replaced mask of indifference, not even a hint of the emotion she let flow so freely present. Yet I can't help wondering if there was any truth in her admission of her past or if she truly is as cold and heartless as I previously concluded her to be. A piece of me wants to believe she's still nursing those wounds, but I'm not sure if it's because I'm still nursing mine.

⸻

We make it back to the hotel a little before midnight. Not much interesting happened outside Búho Oculto while we were there, so we called it quits for the night. Señora Flores smiles as we walk into Flor Tranquila, still set up in her colorful shawl behind the front counter and, so far, the only person we've seen at the hotel.

Up in our room, 3 heads to the bathroom while I dig through my bag for my toothbrush. We've both been skirting around the subject of our sleeping arrangements since checking in, and if the long standoff regarding who would be driving is any indication of how successfully we compromise, this conversation won't go well.

Laying my jacket over a chair, I glance up as 3 steps back into the room in small gray jersey shorts and a white tee, her red hair resting over one shoulder in a messy braid. Even though her clothes are meant to be modest and frumpy, glancing at her exposed toned legs and the fact that she's one hundred percent not wearing a bra has my stomach plummeting.

Screw me.

But seriously, I want her to screw me. *Crap.* This isn't good. Why does she have to be psycho *and* gorgeous?

Without uttering a word, I walk past her into the bathroom, her familiar scent of coconut following me the whole way.

My hand curls into a fist.

This *really* isn't good.

Just when I thought I had my bearings around her, she goes and puts on pajamas. I *love* women in pajamas. Even volatile, murderous, schizophrenic, hide-your-children-from-them women in pajamas. Pj's remind me of beds and tangled sheets and what can happen between them.

Quickly washing up—with *cold* water—I shut off the bathroom light and step out, finding 3 standing by the open balcony doors. She's looking into the courtyard, the gray glow from the moon gently flowing over the curves of her body.

Running a hand through my hair, I stand there, unsure what to do now that we're here.

"You can take the bed," she says without turning around.

I glance to the hard stone floor. "Neither of us will be sleeping on the ground."

She peers over her shoulder about to reply, but stops as her gaze flickers over my body. "Really?"

"What?" I look down at myself.

"Put a shirt on, Carter."

"It's *Benjamin*," I remind her, pulling back the duvet, "and this is how I sleep. You should feel lucky I made the effort to keep on my briefs. I usually go commando."

"Gross."

"On the contrary," I say, slipping into the cool sheets. "God created us naked for a reason, because it feels fucking fantastic."

"Well, I'm definitely not getting in there with you like that." She crosses her arms.

"Why? You scared you won't be able to resist such an Adonis?" I drape myself suggestively over the mattress, enjoying the way her small nose scrunches in disgust.

"Don't flatter yourself."

"But it's so much fun." I flash her a grin. "You should try it."

"I don't need constant reassurance like you do." She walks over and grabs a pillow.

"You're *not* sleeping on the ground." I sit up as she pulls a blanket from one of the chairs in the room.

"Watch me." She begins to set up a sad floor nest.

"You're going to wake up with a stiff neck, and then what use will you be?"

She pauses from fluffing her pillow.

"You know I'm right, 3." I go on. "If there was a couch in here, I'd be the first one on it, but there's nothing but hard stone and wooden chairs. We both need to be in the best shape for this assignment. Neither one of us should risk that because we're too stubborn to share a bed. Plus, it's not like either of us are going to make a move."

I watch as she internally struggles to keep from agreeing.

"First, it's *Stephanie*," she says as she stands, throwing my own reprimand back at me. "And fine, we'll both sleep in the bed." She walks over and gets in. "But if I find you draped over me with your morning wood poking into my side, I'll turn you into a eunuch without a hesitation."

"Got it. No morning wood poking you in the side." I snuggle into the sheets and close my eyes. "I'll make sure it's poking you in the back or butt instead."

A pillow whips so hard against my face that if I were a lesser man, I'd have squeaked, but instead I merely gather it under my head and say, "Sweet dreams to you too, Wife." And though a slow smile lingers on my lips as I drift off to sleep, I still curl a thankful hand around Minnie tucked under my pillow, hoping I don't have to use it.

CHAPTER 30

Nashville

I can't fall asleep.

I've been faking it for an hour while Carter is dead to the world beside me. I've *never* slept in the same bed as someone my entire life. Not at the orphanage, not with Ceci, and *especially* not a man. Even with Christopher Waters I've always left right when we were done, and he never asked me to stay. Mainly because he knew I wouldn't.

Yet it's not the unfamiliarity that's keeping me up. It's the noise. Carter doesn't snore, thankfully, but he's still *incredibly* loud. His light breathing sounds more like giant puffs of air from a steamship, his slow heartbeat claps of thunder in my head, and the sounds his stomach makes—don't even get me started. How do people sleep next to one another with all this racket?

I shift onto my back and stare at the ceiling, thinking about how much my life has changed since Hong Kong. I've done *a lot* of firsts lately. Agreeing to an assignment with another K-Op, allowing someone else to drive when I could have, holding someone's hand and being *kind of* okay with it, and let's not forget my Mother Theresa's worth of patience. It's a miracle I haven't maimed anyone yet, especially considering how close Carter's gun is under his pillow.

You know... I can hear Ceci's voice in this moment. *Cactuses actually taste quite sweet under all those prickles.*

I let out a sigh, glancing at Carter spread out on his stomach. It's not lost on me that all these firsts have been with him, and taking in his unconscious form, I allow myself to linger on his body. Slivers of moonlight streaming through the balcony doors highlight his back muscles and play across his solid arms that hook around his pillow. I know from earlier that his stomach is nothing but definition and abs, and as emotionally hollow as I often come across, I'm not completely inhuman and can appreciate a nice body when I see one.

I just have better control over my desires than most, something I was trained to master since I was a child. The intense simulations and exercises I went through allowed me the proper restraint needed to manage my quickly violent tendencies. A side effect of this just happens to be losing a bit of my other emotions, including empathy toward others, but it's a loss I'm willing to sacrifice. I've witnessed the irreversible consequences of A+ humans losing control, and I refuse to let that happen to me.

People who know about us can often be envious of our abilities, but what they don't know is how much of a burden it can be. To constantly keep tabs on the bubble of energy that simmers under the surface is almost excruciating, hence needing to let it out every so often. There have definitely been moments when I've wished to be like everyone else, that I could experience the peacefulness of a park without being bombarded by the swirling, chaotic sounds of birds, insects, leaves rustling, and every person's conversation or bodily noise. Their breathing, their heartbeats, their chewing, the chains on their bikes clanking as they ride by, the thousands of notes blaring from their earbuds, the dogs they walk panting and barking. If I didn't work for two decades to learn how to block it all out, I would surely have gone crazy, like others have.

That's something regular humans take for granted, being blessed with a quiet life.

Because my life...has always been brutally loud.

CHAPTER 31

3

Cuetzalan, Mexico: 0920 hours

The population of the town must double on market day, for as we make our way through the stalls of goods, waiting to "run into" Jules and Akoni, I have to take a moment to adjust to the overstimulus of activity.

People barter enthusiastically over produce, while venders hold up colorful woven tapestries or pottery to the passing buyers. Clutching my purse strap, I peruse the various goods on display, all shining with life under the morning sun, and look for something to pick up for Ceci. She loves this kind of stuff—trinkets.

Carter walks beside me, his face relaxed under his sunglasses, his scruff a little thicker today as his constant easy grin plays along his lips. He stops at a leather-goods booth to look at wallets, and I watch him speak Spanish to the owner. With his back turned, my gaze runs over his tall form that's dressed in a seafoam-green T-shirt and dark jeans.

After another hour of staring up at nothing last night, I slipped out of bed to quickly call Ceci. On my shorter assignments, I don't usually reach out until I'm on my way home, but something about this mission left me craving her calming voice. I tried not to think about why this was as I called her in the bathroom.

"Nash?" Her groggy voice answered. "Everything okay?"

"Yeah." I tucked my knees under my chin as I leaned against the tub's side, sitting on the cool tile floor. "I wanted to let you know I got to Mexico safely."

I heard shifting on a bed. "It's almost midnight. Are you feeling okay?"

"Yeah, why?"

"It's just..." Her yawning cut her off. "It's just you never call to tell me this sort of thing."

"Yeesh, and I guess I won't again."

"Oh stop," she chided. "You're always so dramatic. I'm glad you called. How's Mexico? Have you exploded in the bathroom from drinking the water yet?"

I smiled and leaned my head against the lip of the tub. "Not yet, but that definitely gives me an idea for Carter."

"Oh God." Ceci laughed. "The poor guy. Is it that bad already?"

"It never *stopped* being bad."

She snorted. "Again, dramatic."

I picked at a piece of dirt on the floor, suddenly growing uncomfortable with how much this—chatting casually—had already made me feel better.

"Right, well..." I cleared my throat. "I just wanted to let you know my plane didn't crash or anything. I should go."

"Excuse me? No *How are you doing, Ceci? Tell me about your day, Ceci,*" she scoffed. "Talk about self-involved."

My lips pressed down a smile. "How was your day, Ceci?"

"Well, I'm not going to tell you now. You'll just have to call me again and ask without being reminded."

"Ceci—"

"Nope. I've already paid a fortune for this long-distance phone call. I should go."

"I called *you.*"

"Yes, well, my cell plan double charges. It's horrible like that."

"Right, then by all means, let's hang up quickly."

"You first."

"Nope, I will not play that disgusting phone game with you."

"Can't get mad at me for trying." She laughed before yawning again. "Okay, you really should go. We all know how you need your beauty sleep."

"Are you calling me ugly?"

"Your words, not mine."

"Remind me again whose house you're staying at for free?"

"The most beautiful, gorgeous person I know."

"And don't forget it. *Good night,* Ceci."

"Good night, lovey. Oh, and Nash?"

"Yeah?"

"Sneak a little in his coffee."

"What?"

"The tap water."

Even though we were a country away, I know we shared crooked grins as we hung up.

The morning market snaps back into focus when Carter slips his hand into mine and gives me a small smile. "Peso for your thoughts?"

"I was thinking about toilets."

One brow lifts. "Man, you're weird."

"I'll take that as a compliment."

"As only a weirdo would."

Biting my lower lip, I keep back a grin as we walk on. Something I've had to do more than once lately, and whether from talking to Ceci or us actually giving this truce thing a go, the tenseness I felt yesterday when holding hands isn't as great today. Though my gut still twists a weird vibration of unease anytime his strong fingers play between mine, which I'm convinced is from the spectacle of it all.

PDA might as well stand for *public display of assholes* in my book.

"Let's go look at that cart over there." Carter points to a merchant selling local pottery, and I catch sight of the other half of our team.

As we walk over to "bump" into Jules and Akoni, my turquoise dress flutters up from a sudden breeze, and I mutter a curse as I clutch it to keep from exposing my lady bits.

"You look like Marilyn Monroe." Carter chuckles, and I try yanking my hand free, but he holds tight. "*Which means* I just compared you to America's most iconic babe. That's a compliment, not an insult."

"And yet it still sounded like you were making fun of me." My eyes remain narrowed.

"That's because you have a very warped perception of the world, my dove. Funhouse-mirror warped." And before I can comment on the use of his newest nickname, he tugs us forward to talk with Jules and Akoni.

After exchanging pleasantries, we **get breakfast together** under the facade of uniting as Americans in a foreign town.

"You're definitely going to need to do something about your hair," Akoni mumbles through a mouthful of rice and beans after I finish explaining what I have planned for tonight. "Redheads are few and far between in these parts. You'll be too recognizable."

"Exactly why I don't think she should go in alone." Carter takes a couple bites from Jules's plate. He quickly devoured his own breakfast, and when he attempted to pick from mine, I almost stabbed him with my fork.

"I already plan on wearing the wig I used in South Africa and thought about putting those brown contacts in," I say to Akoni, ignoring Carter.

He nods. "Yeah, that'll work."

"Bad idea," Carter chimes in again.

"*Good* idea." I glare at him. "It's not like any of them are an actual threat to me."

"One against a bar full of thugs?" Carter raises his brows. "Even *you* couldn't take them all on at once."

"Care to put a wager on that?" I sit back while crossing my arms.

"Children, please," Jules interrupts, shoving away a strand of blond hair that escaped her ponytail. "Let's not get sidetracked with your pissing contest. Ben, Stephanie is right." She smartly addresses us by our cover names. "If you went in together, it would call too much attention. Let Stephanie play the weak lost duckling to get information. We can wait close by in case she needs help."

"I won't need help."

"Of course." Jules flashes me a placating grin. "I'm saying in the *slight*, probably-will-never-happen possibility that you do."

I nod, satisfied.

"Okay." Akoni wipes his mouth with his napkin. "Then we're in agreement."

"I don't remember *agreeing* to anything," Carter grinds out.

"Listen, *Ben*." I place my hand on his. "I'll be fine, and you'll be close by. You need to remember this is what I do for a living."

He stares at where I'm touching before sliding his hand away. "Considering it's what we *both* do for a living, it's a little hard to forget."

"Yes, but who does it best?"

Carter bulks, about to respond, when Jules raises her coffee. "To the three seconds you both lasted without reengaging in your pissing contest."

"To three seconds." Akoni smiles, clinking his mug with hers.

"You better enjoy those drinks now," Carter says, his voice oily slick. "You never know where our piss might land next."

And that's when it happens, another first—I laugh genuinely while on a job.

CHAPTER 32

3
Búho Oculto
Cuetzalan, Mexico: 2030 hours

The gorilla-sized doorman eyes me as I walk up, lingering on my exposed legs and staying even longer on my cleavage. I'm wearing cutoff jean shorts and a gray V-neck T-shirt. A casual outfit that will do just fine in gaining the attention of the men here while also screaming American college chick on holiday.

With my dark-brown wavy wig clipped in place and my blue eyes hidden behind brown contacts, I slip him a friendly smile. "¡Buenas noches!"

He merely nods in response and indicates I can go in, but not before letting his amused sympathy show as I pass.

When I step through the door, away from the eyes but not ears of Jules, Akoni, and Carter, who are set up on a nearby roof,

I'm pleasantly surprised by what I find. From the outside the bar appears to be run down, a classic dive, but inside it's none of those things. Sections are dark, but tastefully dim rather than from a broken bulb. Low-burning Victorian lamps are patterned along the raw exposed rock walls, and sleek wooden tables stagger the space. It's a weird mix of old and new, the layout reminding me of a western-styled saloon, with a first floor that opens up to a second that has a wraparound balcony. Five doors run along the perimeter of the top, and by the women who stand up there with overdosed perfume and slinky clothes, along with the subtle sounds of moaning coming from some rooms, I don't have to guess as to what they're used for. But even with this sleaze factor, Búho Oculto is well maintained, especially for a place that appears to mainly serve a rough-looking group of middle-aged men. I count a total of twenty-three spread throughout the bar, and I scratch the side of my ear in quick Morse code to let Akoni know.

"Twenty-three," his voice filters through. "Copy that."

Slowly walking to the bar that sits in the back, I smile naively at the patrons as I pass. Everyone noticed my entrance, but only a few stare me down hungrily. The others shake their heads at my apparent stupidity and turn back to their drinks.

Three men sit at the bar, one with a female companion, and they watch, curiously, as I saddle up next to them.

"I'll have whatever you've got on tap," I say to the bartender in Spanish.

He peers at me while wiping his hands on a dishrag. "We only do bottles," he responds gruffly.

I giggle at my slipup. "Oh, then I'll have..." I glance to my neighbor. "Whatever he's having."

"Tequila."

"Sounds perfect."

The thick-bearded bartender scrutinizes me for a moment more before placing a glass down and pouring my drink.

"Gracias." I take a fake a sip.

While I'd like nothing more than to indulge in this nation's liquor, I need all my senses tonight.

"Ay, *culona*." The man next to me leans in. "What gives us the pleasure of you visiting this fine establishment?"

I turn to my neighbor. Age approximately forty-three, height five nine, brown hair, brown eyes—the left showing early signs of glaucoma. Breath indicates three tequilas and a beer in the past two hours. Works outdoors, from the drastic skin contrast where his shirt's unbuttoned, showing a paler complexion underneath. Plus his earthy scent is a dead giveaway. No wedding ring or mark from taking it off while working. Overall possible threat: minimal.

I smile. "I'm on tour through the country and am set up here for a few days. *Mi abuela* would talk about Cuetzalan and its beauty growing up, so I wanted to finally see it." I chitter away as the men close by listen.

"Your grandmother from here?" my new friend asks.

"Not Cuetzalan specifically, but Peubla. She said she would visit here often though. But between you and I"—I lean in con-spiratorially—"I think she was harboring a secret romance."

"I wouldn't doubt it." He chuckles. "If your *abuela* was anything like you..." His gaze lands on my cleavage for the third time. "I'm sure she had her fair share of admirers."

I sit back with a cluck of my tongue. "You're a smooth one, aren't you? I'll have to keep my eye on you."

He puffs out his chest, pleased that his Don Juan behavior amuses me.

"Your boyfriend meeting you here?" he asks, quick to get to the point.

"Oh, I have no boyfriend."

His brows rise. "I don't believe it."

I open my mouth to respond, but stop short, bombarded with a tingling along my spine.

I sense the same heightened chill I got the first day in the square—the watcher...they're here. Peering over my left shoulder, I take in a large man sitting in a booth in one of the purpose-fully dim alcoves. He brings a cigarette to his lips, and when he inhales, the red embers glow bright, momentarily illuminating his features against the dark. He's the youngest guy here, prob-ably late twenties, and has the facial ruggedness of one used to a hard life. He's tan with pronounced cheekbones covered in rough stubble. His thick black hair is a bit long for my taste, inching over the tops of his ears and forehead, but other than that he's quite attractive, in a street rat sort of way. The one thing that contradicts his unrefined appearance is his outfit. It's nice, *really* nice. Black slacks and a black buttoned-down shirt that fits per-fectly around his wide shoulders. While his clothes are tailored to his size, I still sense his discomfort in them, like he's wearing another person's skin.

He watches me watching him and eventually inclines his head, inviting me to join his table, where he sits alone.

"Ah, I see Ramie's caught your eye," my companion says be-side me. "All hope is lost for me then." Taking a sip of his tequila, he nods toward the booth. "If Ramie requests for you to sit with him, *cielito mío*, you sit with him."

"Um, Okay," I say meekly before grabbing my drink and sliding off my stool.

The room grows tense as I make my way forward, a field of insects grown warily silent, and while outwardly I feign a bit of fright, walking toward the lion in his den, internally I'm yelling *Jackpot*.

CHAPTER 33

3
Búho Oculto
Cuetzalan, Mexico: 2045 hours

Taking a seat across from Ramie, I smile nervously. "Hi."

He leans casually against the corner of the booth, one leg propped on the bench as he holds a cigarette, his other hand lazily wrapped around his beer on the table.

"What's your name?" he asks in Spanish, his voice deep and soothing, the stillness at the bottom of the ocean. I let it roll through me, cataloguing his lack of accent that would place him in a region and watch as he studies my appearance before flicking his gaze back to mine. His eyes are endlessly black, and his lashes are almost femininely thick.

I quickly try taking down his profile, but besides what I gathered earlier from a distance and now seeing a few scars on his neck and jaw—indicating his regular brawling—he's proving hard to read. Which is weird. No one is hard for me to read. His heartbeat is steady, his breathing relaxed, and other than the sweet, pungent smell of tobacco from his cigarette, he doesn't even have a scent I can detect.

Everything goes on alert.

"Abilia," I reply.

"Abilia." He rolls the name around on his tongue. "That's a beautiful name."

"Thanks." I induce a blush. "And I take it you're Ramie?"

He nods, sipping his beer.

Oy, this guy is laying on the dark and mysterious rather thick.

"So your grandmother grew up in Puebla?" he asks, keeping his gaze locked to mine. A normal person would squirm under such a look, so I shift in my seat.

"You heard that?"

The side of his mouth tips up. "When someone like you walks into a place like this, you pay attention."

I laugh nervously. "Oh." Glancing around, I note the other patrons furtively watching us. Ramie is obviously someone important, and by the collective raised pulses in the room, possibly dangerous.

Just my type.

"Yes, she grew up there, but has lived with my family since I was born."

"And by your accent, I'd say your home is the US."

Important, dangerous, *and* keen.

"Is it that bad?" I grow smaller, embarrassed.

"No. I'd say it's rather perfect."

"Perfect?"

"And cute," he adds, flashing me a crooked smile.

I tuck my short brown hair behind my ear. "So, uh, do you live around here?"

"I live close by."

"In town?"

He takes another drag of his cigarette. "Sometimes."

I laugh lightly. "You don't like questions, do you?"

"What man does?"

Oh, good Lord.

"Well, this will be a very short and rather awkward conversation if that's the case." I grin, leaning against the leather-back seat. *It's time to move this thing along.*

"I'm sure we can find other ways to pass the time that's agreeable for both of us," he says, tapping ash onto the table, and I resist pointing out there's an ashtray to his left.

"And what ways would those be?" I raise a brow.

A slow smile spreads across his lips, showcasing very white teeth. "I'd rather show you than tell you."

I think back to my conversation with Carter, about men being simple creatures, and almost laugh at how quickly I'm, once again, proven right. "How very forward of you, Ramie." I flirt. "But my *abuela* taught me to keep away from men like you."

His eyes light with amusement. "And what sort of man am I?"

"I'd think it was obvious." I play with the rim of my glass as I steal a glance at him from under my lashes. "The cuddly kind."

His bark of his laughter fills the room, and I sense everyone flinch before relaxing with the sound, finally returning to their own conversations.

"I can't fight your *abuela* on that point." He keeps grinning over his beer, and the expression changes his features to rather breathtaking, like a setting sun right before it slips below the horizon. I catch a glimpse of a younger Ramie before whatever life he's now a part of took over. "Cuddly men *are* usually the most dangerous."

"So you're dangerous then?"

He rakes his eyes up my body, not in the assessing manner he did earlier, but now with a bit of heated intrigue. "Mostly."

I bite my bottom lip, a little too hard, when I hear a familiar male voice outside the bar. My surroundings get doused in a chill before erupting in flames, realizing what's about to happen.

That son of a—

The door swings open, and in walks Carter Smith, an arm around a local chica. He's wearing black jeans, a white buttoned-down shirt with a navy Yankee baseball cap, and—I. Kid. You. Not.—a mustache. The dark-haired girl giggles at something he whispers in her ear before his gaze sweeps the room, only colliding with mine for a second before continuing on. As he settles into a table along the far wall, his companion slides onto his lap, playing with the hair at the nape of his neck while her deep-purple dress rides up her thigh.

"Something wrong?" Ramie asks, glancing from me to the new additions to the bar.

"No." I smile before sipping my drink. "Just thought that girl looked familiar for a second, but I was wrong."

"That's Clara." Ramie studies her trailing kisses along Carter's jaw. "I wouldn't doubt if you've seen her before."

"Why's that?"

"Let's just say, she gets around."

I don't have to pretend to be grossed out to make my next face.

Of course. Leave it to Carter to find *that* type of woman so quickly.

I force my heart rate to stay even, but it's like trying to keep a soda can from bursting open after shaking it. *Friggin' Carter.* He's compromising this whole goddamn operation by being here, and the fact that he doesn't trust me to handle this part on my own does little to silence the rage monster growing inside.

"So." I return my attention to my companion, ignoring the whispering laughs coming from the other side of the room. "Has Clara gotten around with you?"

Ramie's eyes light up with pleasure from my question. "Would it hurt my chances if she has?"

"And what makes you think you had a chance to begin with?"

Ramie leans forward, laying a large hand on mine. "When you sat down, *mi rosa.*"

My heart stutters. *Mi rosa. Mi rosa. A dark face smiles down at me. Come here, mi rosa.* I blink away the memory, my skin exploding with goose bumps. *What was that?*

Schooling my features into another blush, I try settling my jumping heart rate. "That was very smooth," I chasten.

He doesn't comment or remove his hand from mine. "Do you want another drink?" He nods to my full glass. "You don't seem to like that one very much."

The sound of Carter's low chuckle hits against my eardrum again. "No." I lean back, slipping my hand from his. "I should be going actually." Something about this situation, now that Carter's here, is raising every red flag.

"Are you sure?"

"Yes." I paint on a coy smile. "I'm not one who usually stays long in the company of mostly dangerous men."

"Then let me walk you home." He stubs out his cigarette on the table and stands. "I wouldn't want you to run into any other such men on your way back."

Sometimes it's too easy.

"Really?" I say with raised brows. "You don't have to do that."

"Abilia." He grabs my hand, helping me up, and I take in his six-foot-plus height. "It would be good for you to remember I never *have* to do anything."

"Oh." I breathe out, feigning a fluster. "Then by all means, walk me home."

He hooks my arm into his. "I intend to."

As we pass the bar heading to the exit, he tells me to wait at the end while he has a word with the bartender. Getting ready to eavesdrop, I keep from frowning when I see Ramie writing a note instead.

My mind races as to what that could mean, when Carter stands in my periphery, making his way toward me.

My hackles raise. *Breathe*, I tell myself. *Just breathe. Don't remove the small blade strapped to your spine and stab him with it.*

As Carter reaches my side, casually leaning on the bar, I stand seething, while remaining calm, but wanting to murder, while breathing evenly. The overwhelming amount of Clara's perfume that clings to him makes me want to gag. *Jesus, how can he stand it?* Glancing to his heavy-bosomed companion, I find my answer.

"You've got some nice stems coming out of those shorts,

beautiful," he says with a slight New York accent.

Wrapping my hand around the edge of a stool, I ignore the light *crunch* as the wood splinters. "And that's a nice rat that died on your upper lip," I say in Spanish.

Carter merely wiggles his ridiculous mustache and gives me a wink.

I'm.

Going.

To.

Kill.

Him.

But before I get the chance, Ramie hands his finished note to the bartender, telling him he'll be back later, forcing Carter and I to turn away from each other.

"Was he bothering you?" Ramie asks, returning to my side and watching Carter order his drinks.

"No, just some stupid gringo thinking I didn't understand English."

Ramie's eyes stay pinned on Carter as he walks away, smoothly sliding back into his booth and handing Clara her beer. She puts it down with disinterest while taking his hand to glide up her thigh.

Gross.

"Do you want me to speak to him?" Ramie asks, and I actually hesitate because the temptation to find out how quickly Carter's stupid mustache would fall off is *really* enticing.

"No." I loop my arm into Ramie's again. "I'd just like to get that walk home now."

He studies me a moment more before the shadow in his gaze lightens. "Then that's what you'll get."

Gliding us to the exit, he returns his attention to Carter one last time, allowing me the opportunity to glare as well.

But if my K-Op partner feels either of our stares, he ignores it, too busy listening to what Clara wants to do to him when they're alone. And from the crude and rather complex descriptions, I know they won't be in public much longer.

Yeah, the floor's all his tonight.

Leading Ramie to Jules's and Akoni's hotel, because no way would I show him where I was staying, we weave through a fair number of people still out on the winding village streets. I caught a glimpse of our tech Ops as we left the square, having moved from their position on the roof to pass us on the street. As Akoni and I caught eyes, he gave me a small headshake, letting me know he wasn't aware of Carter's plan to go rogue.

I suck the side of my cheek in silent frustration. All of this is just another reason why I work alone.

"So." I glance to Ramie as we walk side by side, his hands now resting casually in his pockets. "What do you do in Cuetzalan?"

"What makes you think I do anything in Cuetzalan?"

I laugh. "Ramie, you'll have to answer some of my questions."

"I already told you, Abilia." He peers down at me. "I never *have* to do anything."

I allow myself one eye roll before continuing in Spanish. "Okay, how about this. For every one of my questions, you can ask one in return?" I know this is entering dangerous territory, but I don't see any other way. Plus, I lie for a living. I think I can handle this.

He stops to take out another cigarette, regarding me with lidded eyes as he lights up and takes a drag. "Okay," he says, blowing smoke to the side. "I work for my family's business."

"Their business is in Cuetzalan?"

"Is that your second question?"

"Whoops." I play innocent. "No, ignore that one."

His eyes dance playfully as we start forward again. "Okay, while you think of your next question, here's mine. What's a pretty girl like you doing traveling alone?"

I frown. "What's wrong with traveling alone?"

"Ah, ah," Ramie tsks. "That's answering a question with a question. That's not allowed."

"Seeing as I made up the game, I'm saying it is."

An amused rumble escapes his throat. "No, Abilia, it isn't."

"Bien." *All right.* "I'm the only child, and my parents aren't fit enough to travel with me. Plus, I don't mind being alone." First rule in lying successfully: stay close to the truth.

"No," he says, watching me from the side. "I don't suppose you do."

Pushing the conversation along, I continue to ask in his native tongue. "What's your family's business?"

"We work in coffee," he answers, like he's had to say this line a thousand times.

"Ah, well that makes sense."

He raises a brow in question.

"Your clothes." I gesture to his outfit.

"What about them?"

"They're really nice. If you're family works in coffee, especially in Cuetzalan, you're obviously doing well for yourselves."

"Perceptive *and* beautiful," he says as we keep pace up a small hill. I watch an older lady almost bow at the waist as we pass. She's the fourth person who's shown Ramie such respect—respect with a touch of fear. If his family truly is in coffee, they would almost certainly have a connection with the Oculto. Any business as big as a coffee distributor in a town that's famous for its brew wouldn't be able to get out of a partnership with them. Now I just have to figure out which "family" he's really the prince of.

"And yes, we do okay," he continues before taking another puff of his cigarette. His heartbeat remains steady, his features calm.

"How much longer do you have in town?" he asks.

"Second question?" I hold up two fingers.

He nods.

"I'm here for about two weeks, traveling around the area, but can make the stay longer if needed."

He catches my meaning with a dark grin. "Good to know."

"It is, isn't it?"

I almost forgot how nice it is to flirt with someone who's worthy of it. Even if he might be a murderous, biochemical weapon–trafficking mobster or a spoiled child of a coffee empire. A girl's gotta find the perks in her job somewhere.

"We're here." I nod to the small hotel on the corner. Ramie sweeps his gaze over the stone building before turning back to me, regarding me.

"What are you doing tomorrow?" He steps closer, brushing a brown lock of my hair from my shoulder and playing with the end before letting it go.

"I still have a question before you can ask another one," I point out.

He shakes his head. "We've stopped playing that game."

"We have?"

He nods.

"Well, that's not fair." I pout. "I didn't get to ask my last question."

"Didn't anyone ever tell you, Abilia, life's never fair?"

I give a humorless laugh and without thinking say, "We don't need people to tell us that. Life shows us all on its own."

His gaze grows intense at my words, penetrating but with a rim of softness, a lens focusing on what it was trying to capture all night. And as our eyes remain locked, everything in me is yelling *idiot* for talking so freely, but before I can turn away or make light of the situation, like a ripple in the air I catch an odd wave of compassion from him, the shadowed energy of a shared soul even though we are perfect lying strangers. In a blink it's gone, but I'm still left with the residual haze of it. *What the hell?* Stepping back, I shake off the sensation.

"Yes." Ramie's voice comes out in a deep rumble. "Life certainly does."

I give him a wobbly smile, repainting the face of the girl he thinks he's talking to while my skin grows warm against the blade I have hidden along my spine.

"You never answered my question though." Ramie drops his cigarette and stubs it out on the cobblestones. "What are you doing tomorrow?"

"Um, I wanted to hike some trails in the mountains."

"The mountains?"

"Yes."

"They can be dangerous." He pushes his hands into his front pockets again. "Do you have a guide?"

I nod. "But what do you mean by dangerous? A lot of wild animals?"

"I've just heard that it's best to go with someone who knows the area. Easier not to get lost."

"Are there any specific areas I should stay away from?"

He smiles. "I'm sure your guide will know if there are. I don't go into the mountains enough to know."

Nice deflection.

"It was a pleasure seeing you safely home, Abilia." He takes my hand and places a gentle kiss against the knuckles. "I've got to get back to the bar. I promised a few friends a card game, but I think fate had a part in us running into each other tonight. I hope it works its magic again soon."

I look into Ramie's jet-black eyes, taking in his unreadable expression with his indiscernible scent and steady pulse, an invisible man standing in a world of color.

"Yes," I say. "I hope so too."

CHAPTER 34

3
Cuetzalan, Mexico: 2205 hours

He steps out of a small bodega, and I watch crouched on a shadowed roof as his tall form slides around a corner. Ramie is not going back to the bar, and I wet my lips in anticipation as I follow him from above, slinking silently from building to building, another spot of dark in the night. I made quick work of changing into the black durable leotard I had stashed in my purse, before catching up with Ramie's trail. He might not have a scent, but his hand-rolled cigarettes do, and every whiff of that vanilla-and-spice puff brought me straight to him.

He turns left, descending down crooked stairs, and I balance beam across a ledge, staying a few feet behind. An older gentleman greets him at the bottom, and I duck into a covered windowsill. I'm nothing but a moonless night as I listen to him talk about the last football game and the final score. I resist a yawn.

Come on, friend. Tell me something good.

After patting the man's shoulder, Ramie sets off again, his pace quickening, and I twist, crawl, and twirl from one roof to the next, never removing him for long from my sights.

He enters the main town square, the church bell a sleeping giant at the other end as he crosses over the empty cobblestone space, the surrounding storefronts and restaurants closed and dark.

I internally curse as I look for the quickest path across from where I am above, but the only way is to go around. Even though night, with no one else out, I'd most certainly be seen making my way through the center.

I pounce forward, the sound of my tread nonexistent as I carefully navigate the delicately tiled terracotta roofs. Ramie enters an alley on the other side, and I speed up, but when I round the square and leap across the gap of buildings, made by a street below, I slink to a stop.

The narrow ally he walked into is quiet, and peering down, I catch no sign of life. I sniff the air. There's a hint of his sweet smoke, but in the direction from which we came. He hasn't lit up again.

Where'd you go, little fly?

Hooking my leg over the ledge, I drop from three balconies to land crouched on the ground. A dog barks in the distance, and I slide against the wall, looking left and then right down the inky cobblestone path.

Dark...stillness...nothing.

Crap.

Opening my senses as wide as I can, I listen while tasting

the air, but besides the sounds of a few TVs, animals skittering about, and late-night meals being prepared, there's nothing identifiably him.

Leaning my head against the stone facade, I close my eyes, resisting a frustrated growl.

I rarely lose a target, even in streets like these that bend and turn in unexpected places. Rolling my shoulders, I let out a short breath before swinging back onto the nearest roof, determined to spend a few more minutes searching. But as my time ticks down without so much as a crumb to follow, I finally let out the growl I held in earlier and head home. As I pass the last place I saw Ramie, the alley still empty and quiet, my skin prickles with a fortune-teller's promise.

Even though I might have lost him tonight, I have a feeling he'll appear again, but not a second before he wants to be seen.

CHAPTER 35

Nashville

My phone reads 1:00 a.m., and Carter still hasn't returned to our hotel. Part of me wants him to stay out, but the other part, the slowly simmering one, wants him to show up so I can finally let out my rage from earlier at the bar. Plus, losing Ramie didn't help.

Tonight feels like a total botch, and curling my fingers into my sheets, I stare up at the bed's soft white canopy. We have to meet Jules and Akoni early tomorrow—well, technically today— to trek into the mountains and visit one of the locales marked as a possible Oculto operational territory. I could lie awake for a few more hours, wait on his ass, or I could get some sleep and not be a complete grump in the morning.

As if Ceci were in the room, her voice fills my head. *It's not so much that you're not a morning person. It's that you're more like a morning monster.*

With a frustrated huff, I slap off my bedside lamp and settle further into my sheets, because in all honesty, whether or not Carter comes home tonight makes little difference in him escaping my wrath.

I play with the white lace on the bottom of her dress as she sits at our kitchen table humming a tune.

She's in my dreams again, my mother, and like always, we start out happy.

I glance up at her, her face nothing but a sunspot reflecting in my eyes. The blurred edges of her features are silhouetted by bright-orange wisps of hair, a similar shade to my own, and her laughter fills the room. My little flower, are you fixing my dress? *She reaches down, and I reach up, but then she's gone, and a dark form grabs me instead. Slight panic, then I relax, for I know this man.* Mi rosa, *he says in a deep voice.* Come here, mi rosa. *And I go to him willingly. His scent is of the earth, and his face is rough under my hand.* Mi rosa, *he whispers again and kisses my cheek. I giggle at how it tickles my skin. The three of us are happy, but like always it lasts only a moment. For then it's the* thump thump *of my mother's heartbeat and the* thump thump *of her feet fast against the ground.* You can't take her! *The deep voice bellows all around.* Stop! *It calls again. But we don't stop. Until we are forced to. Until I fall and fall and fall. And then I'm crying and scared and there's so much noise and so many people—a high-pitched scream and a* thwack *and another loud* thump. Don't you dare touch her! *A man's voice roars. More scuffling. Then I'm flying. Wind whips past my ears, muffling all noise, all except my mother's heartbeat.* Thump thump, *it pounds into my head.* Thump thump, *it carries us away. I want to scream* Mama! *But I can't. I want to scream* Stay here! *But I don't know how.*

"Nashville." A hand caresses my shoulder. "Nashville, wake up."

I blink to a figure above me in the dark, green eyes peering down. "You were having a nightmare," he says softly, and my breathing hitches as I twirl away, pinning him to the bed.

"It's me!" he chokes out. "It's Carter!"

"Carter," I whisper, confused, before his features come into focus.

Black mussed hair, stubble-filled chin, sharp jaw with slightly crooked nose, and that strangely pleasant musk of cinnamon and male under all the other scents from his evening.

"Yes, Carter," he wheezes under my vice grip before I let up.

"Why were you touching me?" I move from the bed.

He rubs his throat, still dressed in his outfit from earlier tonight, but without the hideous mustache. I glance out the window to the sliver of moon—3:00 a.m.

"You were having a nightmare and weren't waking up when I called your name." He sits up, straightening his white buttoned-down shirt.

"You called me Nashville," I accuse.

"Yeah, well, you weren't responding to 3." His eyes flicker up my body, making me realize my tank top is askew, my stomach partially exposed. I quickly fix it.

"What were you dreaming about?" he asks.

"Why would I ever tell *you* that?"

"Jesus, never mind." He stands, making his way into the bathroom.

I follow, the floor tiles cool under my bare feet. "What the hell was that at the bar tonight?" I ask while he bends over the sink, splashing water on his face. "You could have compromised this whole operation."

Carter snaps a hand towel off the hook, drying himself. "But I didn't, did I?" He walks past me, returning to the open room and removing his shirt in one pull. His back muscles shine against the soft night light streaming in through the windows, tiny scars from his past like a splatter of an artist's paintbrush across his skin. If we were both standing naked, we'd have mirrored history to compare.

"That's not the point!"

"Then what *is* the point?" He faces me in a challenge.

"The point," I seethe, "is that we agreed on something, and you disobeyed that agreement. Went rogue on our mission, because why? Because you felt left out? Because you're still sorting through your childhood bruised ego from being picked last on the kickball team?"

Carter folds his shirt and places it neatly on a chair. "Can I ask you something?" He slowly turns back around. "Do you come in any other model besides sandy vagina?"

I punch him square in the jaw.

"What the fuck!" he yells before spitting out blood.

We hold each other's glares, his furiously annoyed, mine, no doubt, murderously out of patience, and in that moment we both know exactly what's about to go down.

But he's ready for me this time. With my fist aimed for the

other side of his face, he grabs it and pins it behind my back, pressing me tightly against his bare chest. I head butt him and spin away, kicking his feet out from under him. He goes down with a grunt and a curse before I throw myself on him, knocking over a low coffee table in the process, but he rolls away, standing.

We stalk each other, two animals in the small apartment.

"You know," he says, "there's other ways to work through issues than with violence."

I cock my head to the side. "But so much less fun."

"And here I thought you were allergic to fun."

"Not this kind," I say before going for his throat, but he knocks away my arm. We trade blow after blow, circling and circling. He gets a solid punch to my ribs, knocking the wind out of me and crashing me into a nearby chair. But I spin with the drop, taking out his legs again and jump on top of him. We're both breathing heavy as I pin him to the floor, my knee to his neck, my other leg draped across his torso, holding him down. My fist pauses midprojection to his left eye when the sound of small footsteps patter toward our room.

A knock at the door. "Señor? Señorita?" A meek voice calls. "Everything okay?"

"Si," we both shout in unison. Well, Carter wheezes more than shouts, given that I'm currently cutting off his air supply.

"Are you sure?" she asks again.

Carter gurgles while trying to buck me off. I stand, allowing him to snap to his feet and attempt to straighten himself before going to the door.

I stop him.

"*What*?" He turns with a glower.

"You have blood on your face." I look him over. "And some

on your chest."

"Gee, I wonder how *that* got there."

I ignore his caustic tone and shove past him. "Let me talk to her." Removing my hair from its braid, I muss it up while stripping off my shirt. Holding it against my chest, I crack open the door.

Señora Flores stands in the dim hallway in a floor-length linen negligée, wrinkled face pinched with worry.

"I'm so sorry," I say in Spanish, hiding a blush while trying to fix my hair. "Were we being too loud?"

As she takes me in, her concern melts into a knowing grin. "Just a little my dear."

I give her a shy smile. "Sorry. We'll be quieter."

"Yes, well..." She tries peeking into the room. "It's okay if it's a *little* loud."

I laugh nervously. "Okay."

She nods good naturedly before I shut the door.

Carter is still standing in the middle of the room in his dark jeans and no shirt. His hair is a mess, and his chest rises and falls from our recent exertion. The hazy moonlight coming in plays across his defined abs, and he pins me with a gaze that does weird things to my stomach before it lowers to where my hand presses my shirt against my bare breasts.

"Do you mind?" I narrow my eyes.

"Not at all," he says, staying exactly where he is.

"*Turn around.*"

"Thanks, but I'm good."

I grind my teeth and swivel around instead, slipping my tank back on.

"If that's what gets you naked," he says, "I'll gladly fight with you again."

Lord. Does he ever turn it off?

"You don't always have to be like that, you know." I walk toward the bathroom.

"Like what?" He follows.

"Sarcastic. Not show that you're bothered by something."

"Oh, so you think it's better to be a raging lunatic like you?"

"Sometimes." I wash the speckles of Carter's blood from my hands, hoping Señora Flores missed this detail. "At least I don't keep things bottled inside."

Glancing into the mirror's reflection, I watch Carter snort and lean against the doorframe, crossing his arms. I try not to notice the way his biceps bulge with the movement and instead concentrate on his lower lip, which is already starting to swell from where I got in a right hook. Something in me preens with satisfaction.

"Yeah, I wouldn't label you the bottling type," he says. "At least not when it comes to your anger."

"You don't know the half of it," I mumble and start to rebraid my hair.

"Don't." Carter steps into the bathroom.

I frown, glancing at him in the mirror again. He's right behind me now, his broad shoulders framing my smaller form. Looking at us like this, one wouldn't believe I had almost double his strength.

He reaches for my hands paused in my work, but I step forward, bumping into the edge of the sink. He sighs and tries again. "You've got beautiful hair," he says and lets my partial braid fall free. My red locks fan in gentle waves around my shoulders.

We both gaze at one another in the glass, blue to green, green to blue, the gap from his chest to my back growing way too hot as neither of us speak for a moment.

And then we both talk at once.

Him saying he should shower, me saying I should get to bed, and with an awkward sidestep tango, I leave him in the bathroom and climb into the sheets.

Pulling them up to my neck, it's not until I close my eyes that I realize I left my hair down.

CHAPTER 36

Carter
Sierra Madres Mountains, Mexico: 0722 hours

The jungle is cool this early in the morning, and a fine mist teasingly covers the dense green foliage like a bride's veil. Shrugging my pack more securely onto my back, I wipe dew from my forehead and continue up the dirt path. Jules and Akoni lead the way, their brown and gray-clothed forms blending in, the only sounds our booted feet crunching the fallen debris and the constant buzz from birds and bugs echoing in the trees.

3 walks behind me and has been uncharacteristically quiet. Not that she's talkative to begin with, but her silence isn't filled with the usual cloud of outward hostility. Instead it seems wholly self-reflective this morning. Peering over my shoulder, I watch her graceful body, which moves a lot quieter than any of ours, glide forward as she takes in our surroundings. Her red hair is

pulled into a low ponytail and tucked under a black baseball cap, while the rest of her is encased in a forest-green long-sleeve shirt and durable gray yoga pants.

Because Cuetzalan is within the foothills of the Sierra Madres mountain range, it didn't take us long to get to our starting location. After driving to the end of a dirt road, we gathered our packs and followed a trail through the jungle toward La Cascada de las Brisas, a waterfall and one of the main attractions outside of town. From there we'll head northwest into unmarked territory to a spot Jules says is deeper in the mountains and slopes into a hidden valley. If we don't find anything today, we'll resort to plan B, and after my tussle with 3 last night, I'm really praying it won't come to that. Being trapped alone with her in the middle of the wild for a week sounds as enjoyable as taking a nap on top of fire ants.

Stealing another glance her way, I catch her sniffing the air, and slow my pace. "Got anything?"

She shakes her head as she walks to my side. "Just that we'll be the only ones at the waterfall when we get there."

"You can really tell that from here?"

She nods. "Humans give off the loudest scents."

"Loudest?"

"Yeah, not subtle. Like getting smacked in the face. Loud."

"Hunh," I say, watching Akoni gather over Jules's tablet up ahead before indicating for us to turn right. "So that must have been weird with Ramie then."

3's brows pinch in again, her features sliding into their previously contemplative state. "Yes."

Though not a very long debrief, when the four of us regrouped this morning, we each went over our intel from last night. Jules and Akoni learned of a few more potential areas to visit on our jungle trek, and I explained that the bar we visited last night is indeed a place some of the Oculto have been known to visit (thank you, Clara). 3 told us about this Ramie guy, who, much to my surprised annoyance, I watched her leave with.

"So why do you think that was?" I ask.

"What?"

"That he didn't have a distinguishable scent."

She presses her lips together, studying the ground. "I don't know."

Even I know this is big for her to admit. 3 seems like the type who rarely finds herself at a loss for answers or solutions. Just like...well, me.

"Maybe there are humans that genetically don't smell," I suggest. "Kind of like how some people don't produce body hair or sweat or have their pee smell normal after they've eaten asparagus."

She gives me a dry glance at my last point.

"Come on." I arch a brow. "Even *you* have to admit those people are weirdos."

"Complete circus freaks," she says with an eye roll.

Despite last night's row, and maybe because of it, there's slightly less hostility that hangs in the air between us now. It's still charged, but our knives seem momentarily sheathed. Trading hits seems to be our messed-up way to blow off steam, and even though I usually prefer a different, more...grinding way of getting a release, sparring with 3 and having her meet my strength with her own has become a weird sort of foreplay.

Glancing to my K-Op partner as we crest a hill, I can't help wondering if there's any part of her that feels the same.

"So..." 3's voice interrupts my thoughts. "Clara said Ramie visits that bar once a week?"

"At least," I answer.

"And she never said if he had a connection to the Oculto?"

"Well, I couldn't exactly come out and ask, could I? It's apparent the townsfolk know better than to blab about the Oculto."

"She didn't seem to mind blabbing other things," 3 mumbles, and I cock my head while looking down at her.

"Did Clara's colorful words bother you?"

Her cap is hiding her eyes, and while I know she has to keep it on to cover her beacon of red hair, I wish I could tear it off and brighten our surroundings with her flicker of flame. Waking up to it fanned across her pillow this morning was a weird sort of torture. I've never wanted to touch and look away from something so badly in my life, the feelings it provoked more confusing than when I glimpsed my first nudie mag handed to me by my brother.

"I think it *bothered* everyone in that bar."

"I don't know about that," I say. "They seemed rather familiar with it."

She recoils. "And that turns you on, does it? Being with someone who's..."

"Who's what?"

"So *liberal* with their affections."

"Why, 3, how archaic of you. There's nothing wrong with a woman finding pleasure with more than one partner."

She snorts. "You don't have to tell me that."

I blink. I always painted 3 as someone whose level of intimacy went as far as her sticking pins in her macramé voodoo dolls.

"But there *is* something unappealing," she goes on, "with

someone, male or female, that's so public about it."

"Maybe if Ramie was as public with you, you wouldn't have been jealous."

"*I was not jealous.*" Her blue gaze swings to stab into mine.

"My mistake." I raise a hand. "Bitter, then."

Her face grows a shade redder.

"Envious?" I cock a brow.

Her fingers flash out to pinch my chest, hard.

"Ow!" I palm my smarting nipple as I stare at her wide eyed. "3...did you just...did you just *purple nurple* me?"

"You should be lucky that's all I did." She turns away, but I grab her wrist, pulling her back.

Like silk threading through my fingers, she twists out of my grip, and I suddenly find us both at the ready. Knees bent, weight even, just like last night. Except there's no old lady to stop us, only the caws of the surrounding jungle cheering us on.

So much for sheathed knives.

"I think it's only fair that I get you back." I slide her a syrupy grin, not attempting to hide that my eyes are zeroed in on her breasts.

Her hands fly to cover her cotton-clad chest. "Just try it," she growls.

"Everything okay back there?" Akoni calls to us.

Neither of us answers, holding each other's death stare before 3 eventually straightens and says "Just peachy" before pointing a finger at me. "If you come within a *foot* of me today—"

"With your body odor, I'll be happy to give you *yards*."

Her lips angle into a sneer before she turns and strides toward our tech assistants.

And to think I was about to admit that besides paying for a

few more of Clara's drinks, I headed back to the hotel, leaving Clara and all her "liberals" well alone.

"You good?" Akoni asks, waiting behind for me as the girls walk ahead.

"Extremely," I say, rubbing my sore pec again. I'll definitely have a bruise, which is perfect since it will match the one on my jaw. The one Akoni is currently staring at, that neither he nor Jules asked about this morning. "She did this to me, you know." I point to my chin.

He nods, pushing his dark-rimmed glasses up on his nose. "Figured."

"Your overwhelming concern is touching."

Akoni chuckles. "If I didn't think you could handle her, I would be. Concerned, that is."

I eye the large man as he keeps step beside me. We're the same six foot three, but he's got about thirty more pounds of bulking muscle. How a guy that spends most of his time in front of a computer can be in such shape is beyond me.

"How can you stand it?"

"What?"

"Working with someone so..."

"Passionate?"

"Feral."

He laughs. "Yes, I suppose she's that too."

"There's no *supposing* about it."

"She can be pretty wild." He looks to where 3 and Jules hike ahead, the tall trees swallowing their tiny forms. "But she's also pretty amazing."

"Because she's an A plus."

"That, but also because she's the most loyal person I know."

I snort.

"It's true," he says. "She might be all hard edges and steel skin on the outside, but I've never met someone that's had my back the way she has." He glances my way. "Even after everything she's been through, which has given her plenty of reason to be full-on psycho, she still has the capability to...well, care."

"We all have our sob stories," I counter.

"Sure." Akoni tugs on his backpack straps. "But I'm surprised she's as normal as she is with how she was brought into this world...or rather abandoned in it. Her idea of family is a bunch of scientists and weapons trainers, a room full of suits figuring out how to make the most profit from a young girl with a gift and explaining that killing is good before she's even a teenager. I don't know about you, but I'd certainly be a little prickly around the edges if that was my beginning."

I'm silent at that. Even though I no longer have a family, I know it's a very different beast to have never known what a parent is in the first place, to be raised and feel the unconditional love that comes with it. Who held her when she had nightmares? When she got scared?

Anyone?

"I was terrified of her when we first got partnered," Akoni admits as we watch her snap off a leaf and taste it. "Still am at times," he adds with a smile. "And up until Santiago, I would have put all my chips on her hating me."

"What happened in Santiago?"

His eyes cloud with a memory before he rubs the back of his neck. "I—we were stationed there for a longer mission. Similar to this one, but after it was done, I didn't go back to the States with 3. It was my first assignment abroad, and I wanted to enjoy it a little longer. I got bit with the gambling bug and decided to try my luck at a few casinos. I won a lot of money"—he clears his throat—"and when I say a lot, I mean a few million."

"Jesus."

"Yeah." Akoni grins meekly. "But my excitement was short lived when I learned a million was the magic number to draw the attention of the owners...one in particular that also happened to be the head of El Anillo de Serpiente."

"Shit." My eyes grow wide. El Anillo de Serpiente, or The Snake Ring, was one of the most lethal South American gangs spreading throughout most of the continent before it got broken up when their leader vanished.

"Exactly." Akoni puffs out his cheeks before blowing out a breath. "It was bad. I didn't realize how angry people get when they learn you're particularly good at math."

"You were caught counting cards?!"

"Hey"—he holds up his hands—"is it my fault I have an advanced brain?"

"Apparently not advanced enough." I shake my head. "What happened?"

"You mean after I pissed and pooped my pants when they held me in a warehouse preparing to kill me? 3 showed up and saved my ass."

I blink.

"When I wasn't back at work the following week and no one could locate me, 3 did some digging, found out about the gambling, and knowing me, put it all together from there. First time I didn't mind being predictably stupid." He laughs dryly. "I wasn't even her assignment," he goes on. "David told me later that it was given to another Op, but she left to come get me before they were even done debriefing him. And boy"—Akoni lets out a low whistle—"you should have seen her when she showed up. It was like the Grim Reaper fell over that warehouse, men getting yanked into shadows one by one, gurgles and screams filling the space. It would have been beautiful if I wasn't terrified that I was next. But then there she was, gliding out of the dark to slice open Antonio and carry me home."

"*3* killed El Anillo de Serpiente's leader?"

"Yeah, but *shhh*." Akoni glances around the empty forest. "The agency spun it as a disappearance. No one wants that powerhouse of thugs coming at them."

"She saved your life." I don't know if it's a statement or a question.

"Yes." Akoni nods. "So while she might be short tempered, a bit scary, okay, *a lot* scary, and intense at times, she still has the capability to care and to love. She just has a...unique way of showing it." He glances to me. "She saved my ass that night, and as hard as it might be to believe, I think she'd save yours too."

I don't respond, just mix this new information in with all the other things already painting a complicated picture of the person I thought 3 to be.

"The question is," Akoni says, watching me steadily, "would you save hers?"

I look to where 3 climbs down the last slope to a rocky ledge that has a wide view of the waterfall. Her lithe form stands at the lip overlooking the powerhouse of water crashing into the pool below, one majestic beast regarding another. We've been at each other's throats since our first meeting in China, terse, cutting words flung back and forth, not to mention our overwhelming need to compete, but a locked-up part of me has almost enjoyed it. I've never felt more alive and awake than I have in these past few weeks, even if it's been peppered with white-hot frustration and anger. She's done this to me, gotten under my skin and un-hinged my apathy that has been a strange security blanket since that year, so long ago, when I lost everything. And even though I'm currently trying to sift through whether or not I'm glad for this change, there's still no ignoring that it's happening.

So reluctantly I find myself saying, "Yes," my voice oddly gruff. "I would."

"Good." Akoni claps me on the shoulder. "Because whether she wanted to or not, she's heard every one of our words."

I whip around to face him, completely forgetting about her advanced hearing in this moment.

Shit.

But Akoni looks the opposite of worried as he tips his ball cap, shooting me a coy grin before joining the girls. One of which is no longer facing forward, but regarding me with clear blue eyes and a shrouded frown, telling me that yes, she heard every one of my words and is just as confused as I am that I uttered them.

CHAPTER 37

3
Sierra Madres Mountains, Mexico: 0845 hours

The wind barrels against my face as I duck under a low branch, scrambling up a boulder-strewn hill and leaping over a fallen log. The early morning jungle is nothing but a green blur in my periphery, and I listen to his footsteps fifty yards behind mine, quick, just like his heartbeat. My lungs take in greedy gulps of crisp air, tasting the barrage of information it provides. The plant life is healthy, the animals safely secluded this thick into the jungle, and I revel in the wild of it all, the oasis. Bursting through a tangle of dense foliage, I come to the edge of a cliff with a breathtaking view of a deep valley. Slowing to a stop, I rest my hands on my hips, my bag securely strapped to my back, and take it all in. The treetops go on for miles before me, the Sierra Madres cresting the skyline like layered sound waves, and

I take solace in the small moment of peace before he catches me.

"I didn't think you were going to run the whole way," Carter pants as he reaches my side. Pulling up the bottom of his shirt to wipe his face, he gives me a quick blink of his tan abs.

Our group split up yesterday after finding two of the locales closer to the waterfall empty. Now it's on to plan B, with Carter and me continuing deeper into the mountains as Akoni and Jules return to Cuetzalan to visit some of the surrounding coffee plantations to see what they can find.

"I want to get as close to the next location as we can before the sun goes down," I say, removing a water canister and taking a swig.

"Seeing as the sun just *rose*, we should be good."

"I wasn't sure how slow you'd be running with your bag."

He shoots me a dry glance. "You're only *slightly* stronger than me, 3."

"Whatever you need to tell yourself," I say, following the cliff's ledge east.

"You want to test it?" He catches up to me in four long strides. "We never do seem to finish our one on ones."

"I'm good." I break off a leaf from a low-growing bush, tasting the rough surface with my tongue. I peer into the woods. A mountain lion came through approximately five hours ago—night hunting.

"Because you're scared you'd lose," Carter taunts, causing me to glance back at him.

His eyes are bright against the morning sun, matching his forest-green T-shirt that stretches across his broad shoulders. It's damp from his run, making his unique aroma of cinnamon and male come off stronger, and I frown at how someone's body odor can actually smell good.

"More like hurt your ego," I say.

"All right." He stops, undoing his pack. "Let's do this. Right now, right here."

"Carter, we don't have time for this."

"Sounds awfully like an excuse someone would give who knows they're about to lose."

I glare at him while biting the inside of my cheek. "*Fine*. You want to go, let's—"

The echo of an off-road vehicle revs in my ears.

I snap to attention and peer across the treetops. A cluster of birds take flight a mile off.

"Carter—"

"I hear it." He's right next to me, his pack back in place.

We glance at each other, a moment hanging in stillness right before it erupts in movement as we run.

"You think they're with the Oculto?" Carter whispers as we lay on the forest floor hidden behind a tangle of leaves. He has a pair of binoculars pressed to his face, while I use my advanced eyesight to take in the group of men standing in a small clearing around two jeeps a hundred yards away.

"Hard to tell. They could also be hunters." I study their M&P10 sporting rifles casually draped over their shoulders. They rock camouflaged jackets and pants while talking and laughing around a packed breakfast.

"Can you hear what they're saying?"

"Nothing of interest. Just about some girl their friend had sex with recently."

"Typical," Carter mumbles, and it sounds so like something

I'd say that, with him not looking, I let a grin form.

A radio crackles from inside one of the cars, and a man bends over to retrieve it.

"Wait." I angle my head, listening. "Someone just told them they can make their way over now."

"Did they say where?"

"No."

"Shit."

We both watch as they repack their things and huddle into their jeeps.

"Can you keep up with them?" Carter asks, shifting to a low crouch.

"Yeah, but I'll lose you."

"Turn on your tracker, and I'll follow behind as quickly as I can."

I stand, glancing to where the men set off down a small dirt path, barely visible, meaning it's not often used.

"Okay," I say and without a backward glance become the wind.

It takes two hours for Carter to regroup with me, and I turn when I hear his approach, watching as he climbs the slope to a small flat ledge where I stand, overlooking a lake. His scruff has turned slightly beardish from our time away from civilization, and his dark-brown hair is disheveled from the run. His shirt's completely damp with sweat now, hugging the ridges of his chest and abs like a second skin, and his fitted outdoor pants make little sound as his tall form marches to my side.

"Enjoying the view?" he asks with a sly grin.

"Was," I say. "Then you showed up."

He muffles a snort. "What happened with our friends?"

"They stopped down there." I point to a section of the lake that turns into a beach. The afternoon sun streams through the surrounding trees while throwing a dramatic spotlight on the flat turquoise water. "And met with another car that had a boat. They used it to drop two black crates into the middle of the lake, then left. I followed them up until I saw they were heading back towards a main road that leads out of the mountains to the east."

"Hunh." Carter keeps his attention pinned to the middle of the water. "And the crates?"

"Still down there." Removing my cap, I wipe away a bit of sweat and enjoy the small breeze combing through my hair's wet strands. While I kept up with the cars, I haven't run like that in a while, and even though it was invigorating, it's left me extremely hungry.

"Are you thinking what I'm thinking?" Carter asks as he shrugs out of his pack.

"Unfortunately, yes."

"Come on." He grins, kicking off his boots. "What better way to end an exercise like that than with a nice swim in the middle of the jungle?"

"How about sitting in a hot tub overlooking the Swiss Alps with a plateful of chocolate strawberries?"

He blinks at me, pausing in the middle of taking off his shirt. "Yeah, okay, that sounds fucking fantastic, but this has to be a close second." Then with him stripping down to nothing but his boxer briefs, showcasing a chest rippling in all the annoyingly perfect places, he shoots me a wink and jogs down to the lake.

Letting out a resigned sigh, I wait ten more seconds before shimmying down to my sports bra and underwear and following.

"How do you want to do this?" I ask as we stand on the beach looking out at the water. The sand is warm under my toes, and I wiggle them, wishing I was on one of my tropical vacations instead.

"Well, normally you walk in until you need to start swimming."

I narrow my eyes, unamused, and Carter smiles.

"I think we'll need to determine how deep it is before we dive," he says.

"Yeah," I agree, bending down to my pack. "I've got string in here, and we can tie it to a rock."

"Look at you being a resourceful spy."

"Basic math and science is *really* impressive."

"Hey, don't sell yourself short." Carter frowns. "We all know the basic stuff is the most challenging for you."

"Har-har. Now shut up and help me with this."

A few minutes later we're both treading water in the middle of the lake, the temperature just a touch cold, and I try not to pay attention to all the animals I can hear swimming around us.

Ick.

"Okay, I think I hit the bottom," Carter says as he bobs in front of me. Lifting part of the rope, he reads the marking. "Not bad. Fifteen feet."

"I'll go."

"No, I can. My lungs are bigger than yours."

"But are you strong enough to lift the crate?"

"Are you calling me weak?"

"I'm calling you human."

"I hate to break it to you, *wife*, but you're human too."

"Yeah, an *advanced* one."

"God, we'll be here all day." He floats onto his back, gazing up at the blue sky. "How about this? We *both* go. We might need each other anyway, to lug one of those things up."

I hover in the water for a moment. "Fine."

"Wow." He returns to treading, meeting my eyes. "Did the perfect operative just compromise without getting violent?" Carter grins, and I hate that it looks somewhat adorable in this moment with his hair wet and sticking in every direction.

Wait. What? No. Carter is *not* adorable.

"Don't make me change my mind," I say, ignoring the small stroke I obviously just experienced.

He merely chuckles. "Ready?"

I nod right before we both take giant intakes of air and dive.

The water is murky, and I can only see a few feet in front of me even with my advanced eyesight and flashlight. Carter swims at a quick pace beside me, his own light hitting small schools of fish, floating algae, and a few turtles as we move deeper. Right when my lungs begin to feel the first twinge of burn, the floor of the lake comes into view, and sitting like a dark spot are four black plastic crates. Kicking down to them, I dig my feet into the muddy bottom, testing one of their weights.

Turds. It will definitely take both of us.

Seeing this, Carter swims to me, and with each of us letting out gurgling bubbles of air, we push off the ground and head back up.

We break the surface with a gasp and one-arm breaststroke to the beach, the crate dragging between us.

"There are rocks in here," Carter says as we haul it onto land. "Millions of rocks."

"Let's hope not." I wipe a bit of water from my eyes and crouch to the opening, taking a generous whiff.

Nothing.

"It's airtight." I stand. "I can't detect anything without opening it."

"The lock's digital." Carter runs a hand through his damp hair. "We can use a scanner."

"I'll grab mine." After retrieving the lockpick from my bag, I twist my wet hair into a messy bun and head back to the beach. I'm busy preparing the device so am caught off guard when I glance up to find Carter watching me with a strange intensity. He looks annoyed as his eyes sweep over my body, and I check to see if I've got something stuck on me from the lake, but there's nothing but my soaked black sports bra, underwear, and a complexion that looks frighteningly pale in these sunny surroundings.

"What?" I ask, but Carter remains silent, his gaze finding mine as a flicker of heat flashes behind their green depths, sending a chill along my spine. We both stand there motionless, barely listening to the rustle of the surrounding jungle as we each seem to suddenly realize we're in nothing but our underwear. Our wet, sticking-to-every-curve underwear, and Carter's lips thin, as if he can't decide if he likes it or hates it.

Under his unwavering stare, my skin shifts from cool to way too warm, deciding for itself how it feels about the tall, well-built man in front of me. "Um..." I frown and turn away, bending to attach the device. "This might take me a few minutes."

Carter clears his throat. "I'll just...I'll get our clothes."

Fifteen minutes later we're both standing—with a sizeable gap now between us—redressed, dry, and staring into the open crate.

"Well, shit," Carter says.

Stacked to the top are bags and bags of cocaine and methamphetamine.

"At least we know they're cartel." He scratches the back of his neck.

"Goddammit." I kick the side of the box, and it tips over, the drugs spilling out.

"Feel better?"

"No."

"They still could be Oculto," he says.

"Even if they are, it doesn't matter. Mendoza would never put the same men on the biochemical weapon."

"How do you know?"

"He's been able to keep his involvement in the business quiet. He wouldn't risk spreading his people out like that. I have a feeling very few members of his family are even aware of what he's doing. The guards at the location we're trying to find probably have no idea what they're guarding."

"Still, couldn't these same men take us there unknowingly?"

I chew my bottom lip, glancing down at the bags covering the sand.

"This is our only lead so far," Carter goes on. "Might as well wait for them to come back to grab the crates and then follow."

"They wouldn't store them in the same compound."

"But maybe we'll pick up something new along the way."

It's a risk, with possible little reward, but so would continuing to walk around aimlessly in the jungle searching the other locations. We can always check them later. I sigh.

"Okay."

"Okay?"

"Do I need to say it louder?"

He raises an appeasing hand, his dark hair curling slightly as it dries in the sun-soaked air. "No, just taking in the fact that this is the third time you've agreed with me today. Are you sure you're not coming down with something?"

I punch him in the arm.

"There she is." He grins while rubbing his bicep.

"We have to get this back into the lake."

Carter frowns down at the crates. "And we just got dry."

"I'll do it. It's not as heavy once it's in the water." I move to take off my shirt, but he stops me.

"No, no. I will. Lord knows we can't have you getting wet again."

"And what the hell does *that* mean?" I cross my arms over my chest as he bends to scoop the bags into the crate. "I don't mind getting wet."

"Jesus, 3." His features pinch in an odd mixture of pain and amusement. "Just...don't say anything else."

"But—"

"No." He holds up a hand. "Trust me. We'll be able to get through this if you don't talk anymore."

"Screw you." I stomp back to my bag, and even though his voice is low, still hear his quick response.

"Promise?"

Normally I'd ignore such a comment, but now as I watch Carter strip off his clothes, once again baring his broad shoulders and tan skin, to slip back into the water, that one little question sends a new twister of confusion through me.

It waves like a staked flag in the sand, and I'm not sure when or why I've begun to take notice.

But I have.

CHAPTER 38

Carter
Sierra Madres Mountains, Mexico: 1826 hours

They never come back.

It's been three days, and besides the two of us, no other humans make their appearance at the lake. 3 and I are both frustrated from gaining no new intel, sore from sleeping on the ground, and impatient for a standing shower and decent meal. Well, at least I am impatient for those things. 3 has a knack for not complaining about anything unless it has to do with me. It's both a blessing and a curse that our time is almost up to head back to town. A curse because so far we have nothing to show for it besides a drug drop point, and a blessing because despite our usual barbed banter, an almost dizzying heated thickness has seeped into our time together since that strange moment out on the lake, and I'm desperate to escape it.

I've always been attracted to 3. I'll never deny that, and I don't think any man could. Her body is the epitome of perfection, and as she stood there, soaked, luscious, and firm after stepping out of the lake, I nearly collapsed on the spot. Taking in her full breasts, flat stomach, and long legs, my attraction went from an unrealistic fantasy and harmless way to nag her to a painful desire to consume. Now I can hardly look at her, watch her tie her apricot hair into a braid or catch a glimpse of her toned form slipping from the water after a wash, without feeling a deep ache in my chest and...much lower regions. I've been telling myself that I've been in the jungle too long, that it's because she's the only woman I've been around lately and my usual...frequency of release has been put on hold since this assignment, but even I can hear the desperate lie in these thoughts. The truth is the longer I spend with 3, the more I reluctantly see how similar we are, and in what we differ, I only find myself appreciating her more for.

There's no denying Akoni's statement of her being fiercely loyal. In rare breaks of her carefully walled persona, she lets slip details of her life back in Chicago, specifically about what seems to be her one and only friend, Ceci. If 3 were ever to admit she had a family, Ceci would be there front and center, and I'm more than curious to meet the girl who has allowed a lone wolf like 3 to form such an attachment.

In quick snippets of us eating our miniscule breakfasts of dried fruit, nuts, and protein bars, I also learn 3's not a morning person, coming awake when the sun begins to set. As if the bright light of day offends her in some way and only in the warm orange haze of the afternoon can she truly relax into the talents she was born with. I learn she has a weakness for Scrabble, that she would drink orange juice over water if she could, that the only pet she's ever had was a goldfish that lived for twelve years and whose memory she'll never replace with another, and that she has thirty-two scars on her body, none of which she'll explain, but from the few she showed, I found myself desperately wanting to trace them with the tips of my fingers.

These rare moments of openness are like seeing a shooting star in the sky, quick, mesmerizing, and as soon as it's gone, I remain awake for hours, eyes fixed, unblinking, into the darkness, desperate to catch another. This is when 3 becomes Nashville, when the genetically heightened K-Op becomes human, a girl with the same emotions and secret desire for connecting to another soul as I have. And just like me, as soon as she realizes she's let them rise to the surface, have them peek through the safely hidden depths of uncaring, she's quick to push them down, to drown them in the depths from which they came. After this she goes from a light switch of warm and bright to cold and closed off. I never press her when this happens though, allowing her to turn away, and forgive her curt gruffness that follows. Because not only do I understand such a reaction, but I'm just as scared that I may have opened up about something. For despite me being more
alert with her near, I also have never felt more relaxed. A dangerous combination.

So as we currently distance ourselves from the lake, finally deciding to leave what
became our temporary home to check what remaining locales we can in our final days in the jungle, I make a point to jog the last few miles before breaking camp. When we run we can't talk, and when we can't talk there's no threat of me sharing or learn-

ing more about the woman in front of me, who's unknowingly resurrecting a man I had buried a long time ago, left to decay and disappear.

"This looks good." 3 slows as we approach a small shallow alcove in a rocky wall. She sniffs the air at the entrance of the cave. "There were some foxes using it, but they're long gone."

"As long as there's none of their scat that I'll end up laying on, I'm fine with it."

"But it might improve your smell." 3 slides me a side smile.

I merely grunt and drop my pack, trying to ignore the way her rare playfulness warms my skin. The first time I saw her smile genuinely, I forgot to breathe for a moment, it was that radiant, and I've done my best to suppress the desire to make her grin like that every second of the day.

Rifling through my bag, I choose between eating an energy bar, an energy bar, oh, and an energy bar! "God." I throw them all back into my pack. "I can't wait to binge on all the food when we get to town."

"There's a decent-sized river a half mile that way." 3 nods west. "I can see if I can grab us fish instead of this hamster food."

"Really?" I'm a bit dubious at her generosity.

"You're not the only one sick of eating these things," she says. "I was going to find something else tonight anyway and it'll only be a little inconvenient to get something for you too."

"Well, only if it's *little*..." I cut her a wry glance.

"I'll be back in about an hour." She unstraps her bag and pulls out a small switchblade, holstering it to her thigh. "You won't be scared out here alone, right?"

"With you gone, it'll practically be warm and cozy."

She gives me one long sardonic glare before turning and

sprinting into the tall yawning trees, the streak of her red hair the last thing I make out before the slowly approaching night swallows her whole.

I keep from moaning in ecstasy as I bite into the tenderly cooked trout 3 caught. Two more rest skewered through the center over a low fire, which special kindle—thanks to SI6 and COA scientists—burns dim and produces no smoke, saving us from easy detection.

"Do you like the seasoning?" I ask 3, who sits on a small rock on the other side of the flames. She's in a black long-sleeved thermal and pants, no doubt fighting against the slight nip that's crept into our night. Her braided hair glows golden against the fire while the rest of her is hugged in the inky blackness of the surrounding forest.

"It's okay." She shrugs, using her knife to pop a sliver of meat into her mouth.

"*Okay?*" My eyes widen in offense. It took me a good twenty minutes of scouring the jungle to find the right plants to take our meal from camping to glamping. "I don't believe you. I was conceived in a spice shop, so I think I know a thing or two about adding flavor."

She chokes on her swallow. "You were *not.*"

"I was."

Her gaze narrows. "How?"

"Well, it happens when a man puts his pe—"

"*Carter.*" She throws a fish bone at me, which I easily dodge. "You know what I'm asking."

"When it comes to this particular topic, I can never be too sure."

"Never mind." She goes back to carving out her fish, now a little too aggressively.

"It was my grandmother's," I say. "My mother's mother. When my parents would visit, they would take over her afternoon shift until close. I guess being around all those smells is a natural aphrodisiac or something."

"And your parents actually told you this?" she asks with a frown. "Where they..."

"Bumped uglies?"

"Had sex." She cuts me a glare.

"Yeah, they did."

"But why?"

"Why what?"

"Would they tell you this?"

"Um...I don't know. Because it's funny?"

The fire snaps softly between us as her attention moves to it, her eyes fogging over with some thought.

"What?" I ask.

"Nothing."

"No, what is it?" I sit up from leaning against my log.

"I guess I just...didn't know they could be like that."

"Who?"

Blue eyes find mine. "Parents."

It's like someone reaches in and knocks my heart loose. There it is again, another shooting star, and my throat burns from holding back a swallow, desperate to figure out how to keep this 3, this Nashville, with me a little longer.

"Parents can be like a lot of things," I find myself saying, surprised I'm even able to talk about this, a subject I swore to never discuss or bring myself to think about again. But seeing the hesitant curiosity in 3's gaze, the hidden yearning to understand, leaves me with little strength in stopping. Something about this woman has me reacting in ways I can't predict. Even when a part of me is warning that this might be another one of her games, another ploy to prove just how malleable and easily manipulated humans, specifically men, are, I still can't help myself.

"And yours?" She tilts her head. "What were they like?"

I take in a deep breath, feeling an odd pressure in my gut. Do I do it? Do I say what I've locked away for so long? Is she worth it? Is she sincere? She certainly looks it, her eyes penetrating as they gaze at me over the flames, her features soft without their usual scowl. Is this the price of learning more about her? A piece of my soul for a piece of hers? At least from what little scraps we each have left.

She shakes her head, her demeanor rapidly changing. "Never mind. Forget I asked."

"No," I find myself saying. "It's okay." Which is odd, since it certainly wasn't before. Running a hand through my hair, I lay my fish over our makeshift grate and search for the words I've tried to remove from my memory. I barely have time to brace myself from the acute pain that floods in when I find them.

"My parents..." My voice comes out rough. "Were good people. Understanding and funny. My dad especially, you couldn't leave a conversation with him without having laughed at least once. My mom was quieter but saw everything. I don't think my brother and I got away with a single lie growing up." I smile, staring into the flames. "She patiently listened to whatever tale we wove after getting caught doing something we weren't supposed to, never showing her frustration or anger, just stared like she knew exactly what we were hiding and letting us word vomit until we cracked under the pressure and confessed everything. She would've been an amazing interrogator." I feel something in my chest thaw at the same moment it prickles in sorrow.

"You were happy," 3 says, and I glance up, trying to see if there's any teasing in her eyes, anything to show that she's laughing at me, but there's not, only a weird confusion, like she's trying to picture the past I'm painting but coming up short.

And this is when I fully realize just how different her upbringing was from mine, from most, and though I know she doesn't want my pity, I can't help feeling just that—sad. How different would she have been if her parents stayed in her life?

I barely hold in a dry laugh, realizing how pointless such a question is. It's the same as asking how different I'd be if mine stayed. The answer's inconsequential because they didn't.

Happy.

Was I?

"Yes," I say. "I was."

"And now?"

"Now...now I'm here."

She nods. This she understands, agrees with. All we ever have is the present. The past and future are nothing but intangible stretches in time. One we can't change. The other we can't touch.

"Carter." 3's soft voice brings my attention back to her, and I take in the way her body sits rigid, her eyes boring into mine like she's trying to speak straight into my mind.

"Yes?" I ask gruffly, feeling a mix of every emotion in this suddenly tense moment.

"Don't move, but we have an audience."

My cells jump in awareness, a ripple of gooseflesh as I barrel back to reality.

Who? Where?

"Five men, armed, approaching quickly on foot from half a click away." She answers my silent question while cutting out one last piece of meat before placing her fish down. She chews slowly as she cleans her blade. "They've just split up to surround us."

My fingers inch to Minnie strapped to my thigh, screwing on her silencer. "And they're definitely a problem?"

As if to answer my question, I hear a light echo of a gun's safety being switched off.

I sigh. "And we didn't even get to have dessert."

"Who says it didn't just arrive?" Her mouth curves viciously.

Goddamn if she's not smoking hot right now.

"There's two at my six o'clock, aren't there?" I ask, sensing the telltale twinge in the air of approaching company.

She nods. "And three at mine. From the sounds of it, they have rifles. When you move, go left and low."

"Just tell me when." I grip my gun in one hand while twirling my newly removed dagger in the other.

3's gaze grows out of focus like it does anytime she taps into her senses. She becomes something else in these moments, more animal than human, and I can't help feeling terrified and in awe watching her.

The forest grows quiet, as if it too knows what's coming, before 3's blue eyes collide with mine. I catch them dilate with a hunter's pleasure as she whispers "when," and like a gust of wind blowing out a flame, we both vanish into the dark.

The bullets whiz past my jacket as I dash behind a tree, placing my night vision goggles firmly in place before taking in the forest now painted in hues of green. The two men were closer than I thought, and I barely made out their location before I dove for cover. They each carry a SBR tactical rifle with suppressor, a gun popularly used for hog hunting, and I don't know if I should be offended or amused to be considered similar prey. Not far off there's a gurgle of a man's scream before it's silenced—3.

With my heart pounding, I block out all noise except the close treading of feet to my left.

Gotcha.

Swiveling around, I get two clean shots straight into one man's forehead fifty yards away, his body dropping before his companion lets rain more bullets in my direction. Wood splinters near my cheek as I duck back behind the tree before sprinting to another location, finding a thick, moss-covered boulder. Sweeping my gaze over the surrounding forest, I catch sight of a dark spot in the distance. Another one of our friends has his back to me, crouched in the brush. He carries a different gun from the rest, small, but with his hand covering its length, I can't make out the model. I watch as he prepares to stand and shoot in the direction 3 must be. Raising Minnie, I'm about to take him out, when a splash of night passes over my sights. To anyone else it would appear like nothing more than a starlit shadow, but because I know what to look for, I see it.

I see her.

Ever so slightly she appears and disappears on her approach to the man, slipping from tree, to rock, to bush, the jungle's huntress, its ghost. And before he even has a second to realize what's upon him, I watch her turn from black liquid and mist to solid as she rises behind him, and the poor soul of the man goes from his to hers before the slice of her blade to his neck sets it free.

In a blink she's gone, the only evidence of her existence the corpse left in her wake, and my heart ricochets in my ears.

Dear God she's exquisite.

"There's only one man left," 3 says beside me, and I barely contain jumping out of my skin and giving away our location.

"*Jesus*," I hiss. "Give a guy a little warning before you slither up next to him."

She looks the opposite of sorry as she leans against the boulder. Wisps of her hair have come loose from her braid, and the softness juxtaposes against her sharp features as her breaths come out labored, but more in excited bursts than from any real exhaustion.

"We should keep him alive for questioning," I say.

She nods, and before 3 can pull another vanishing act, I tug her back.

"This one's mine," I say. "You've had more than your share of fun tonight."

Her eyes spark silver with her night vision. "Fine." There's a slight lilt to her lips. "But don't say I never gave you anything."

"Wouldn't dream of it." I cut her a smile before peering over our rock and dashing into the jungle.

The butt of my gun connects with the side of the man's face as he slumps onto the leaf-covered ground. "I'll ask you again nicely before I let her have a turn," I say in Spanish while gesturing to 3, who watches on, arms crossed, behind me. "And trust me when I say that I'm the good cop in this situation. Why are you here?"

It was almost disappointingly easy to find, corner, and disarm the last gunman.

Given that he appears no older than eighteen, he's green with missions such as this, and I have yet to decide if we'll let him live to chance another. If we don't put him down, the cartel he's associated with most likely will. And there's no denying these men were part of a family. Their weapons, black stealth uniforms, and lack of identification documents were enough to pin them to something nefarious. Now the question is, which one?

The kid moans on the ground, clutching his buzzed head, which gleams with a

streak of ruby from where my gun slashed into his skull. We've turned on a low-glowing

lamp that rests by our feet and throws a soft haze on our interrogation, the hiss of bugs in the dense jungle our only witnesses.

A mumbled grunt escapes the boy's hunched form, and I lean closer.

"What was that?" I ask.

"*Jódete!*" *Fuck you.* He spits the words.

"An entertaining prospect." I wipe a bit of his flung saliva from my cheek. "But you're not really my type. Now"—fish hooking his nostrils with my fingers, I pull him toward me—"let's be more cooperative this time, yes?"

He grunts in pain.

"Why. Are. You. *Here*?"

His eyes have turned a bit wild as they travel from me to 3, where they stay.

Peering over my shoulder, I glance at my partner. Encased in black, her features are angular, sharp, under the moonlight as she stares transfixed on our captive, and despite the vibrancy of her hair, she looks every bit like a creature born from the underworld in this moment.

"Do you have a fascination with my wife?" I return to study the boy. "I can't blame you. She is quite pretty, no?"

He remains silent, and I sigh before landing another crack to the side of his face. He groans, blood dripping from his mouth. "Despite what you might think, I don't enjoy getting information this way," I say. "So why don't you help me skip this step and answer us. We all know you will eventually."

Still nothing.

"It's your pain, kid," I continue in his native tongue before grasping one of his hands. He tries to wriggle free, but I straddle and pin him more firmly to the ground, taking off one of his gloves. Very slowly I pull his pinky finger back toward his wrist until there's a snap.

His howl echoes through the trees.

"We have nine more tries to get this right."

"No, no," he gasps, tears slipping down his cheek, and I wait. His tough act has quickly vanished. "*Yo no sé,*" he chokes, his brown eyes wide, desperate.

"Don't know what?" I ask.

The boy begins to shake his head, his whole body seizing in fear. "*No puedo. No puedo.*" *I can't. I can't,* he keeps mumbling.

3 steps over and crouches down. "Shh." She gently lays a hand on his forehead, wiping away a few beads of sweat and dirt. "Don't work yourself up," she coos. "It looks like we've got a long night ahead of us, and your tears should be saved for what I have planned for you."

A wetness seeps out from his pants.

"Shit." I jump up. "That better not have gotten on me."

I glance to his now urine-soaked clothes. This kid obviously doesn't have what it takes for such a life. He probably didn't even want to be a part of this mission. I've seen it many times before. Young boys forced into corrupt roles because of their family's lineage and made to suffer worse fates.

It makes me sick, though 3 looks less than affected by our captor's display of weakness. In fact, she looks completely apathetic to it. To her an enemy is an enemy.

I'm about to suggest we possibly work out a way to let him go, when something pinned to his black fatigues catches her eye.

"What's this?" she asks, reaching for it. "A camera." Her tone is almost delighted, as if now she'll have no issues with what she'll do next. "And who might be on the other end?"

As I study the small black pin in her hand and the wire that connects from it to the inside of the boy's pocket, something in me thrums with déjà vu. Where have I seen this before?

"Whoever it is"—she begins to curl the wire around her fingers, slowly pulling its length from the inside of his jacket—"I hope they saw enough, because while their show is over, yours has only just begun."

And with that she snaps the cord, right when I yell, "*Wait!*"

There's a barely audible beep from inside his clothes as I hook an arm around 3 and drag her away as fast as I can. In the next second we're both thrown to the ground as an explosion fills the jungle, my body covering hers as dirt and wet debris of blood and the young man's flesh smack across my back.

In the reverberation of noise that fills my head, the only thought I was too late in getting out hits up against all sides of my mind.

Oh yeah, the camera, it's also a bomb.

CHAPTER 39

3
Cuetzalan, Mexico: 0722 hours

The room holds the sharp aroma of electricity and plastic. A combination made by an overabundance of tech equipment that has always wrapped around the base of my skull in a painful twinge. It's a similar sensation to staring into a flash of a bulb, but more lasting. Akoni sits on one side of his hotel suite, his wicker chair creaking in protest against his large form with every tap of his fingers against his laptop. Jules leans, arm crossed, against their open balcony door that gives way to a view of a tiny cobblestone ally, the cool air rolling in with the mist that always covers the town this early in the morning. Carter, clean shaven, rests on a small love seat beside her, leather jacket over gray T-shirt and dark jeans, chewing on a toothpick while his feet are kicked up on a coffee table whose ornate carvings are as offended as I to see his muddy boots draped across it. I stand on the opposite side of all of them, resting a hip against a wall peppered with a few framed watercolor paintings from local artists.

As soon as Carter and I gathered ourselves from the explosion, we headed straight back to town, hardly washing the grime from the jungle off, and that poor sod of a man, before coming to Jules and Akoni's hotel.

"The area where you were attacked is pretty desolate. The closest town, besides Cuetzalan, is Ecatlán." Akoni swivels his computer around, showing pictures of a slightly derelict village on a hill. Unlike Cuetzalan, whose buildings stand separate and proud from the surrounding jungle, Ecatlán is almost completely covered in green. Nature threatening to reclaim the territory as it creeps through the streets and climbs over rooftops. "They could have come from there or here or been stationed in the jungle like you were, doing a sweep, and merely happened on you guys."

"I don't think so," Carter says, dropping his feet to the ground. "They had no camping gear. No car waiting nearby. Their mission had a purpose, and one of those was to keep from being retraced."

My grip tightens around my bicep as I glance his way. Ever since returning, I've felt on edge, and it's not because someone tried to kill me.

People try to kill me all the time.

No, it's that someone *saved* me that has me walking around like I have a permanent wedgie. And not just any someone, but Carter, smug-ass bastard, Smith. It's almost too painful to accept. He's of course said nothing about what he did, how he shielded me with his body, leaving me with barely a scratch while he suffered the entirety of the blow. But I know he wants to. I can see it in his twinkling green gaze every time we catch eyes. Can practically hear his voice in my head right now—*You're welcome, sweetheart*. It's enough to make a girl crazy, and though it might be unreasonable, crazy is preferred compared the other emotion that's pressing against my chest. The one that feels a hell of a lot like...gratitude.

Good God, that's the last thing I want to feel toward Carter.

Gratitude means owing someone, means being indebted to him. And despite what I overheard him admit to Akoni about being willing to save my life, I *refuse* to be locked to anyone like that. *I* hold all the favors, all the cards. No one else, *especially* not him.

"3?" Jules's voice brings me back to the room. "What do you think?"

Quickly I shift through the last snippet of conversation, them discussing who could have been responsible for last night.

"Ramie," I say.

"Ramie?" Carter frowns. "Why would you think that?"

"Because I told him I'd be in the mountains the night he walked me home."

Silence, before...

"*What*?" Carter throws his toothpick onto the coffee table. "You never told—"

"I was fishing for information."

"By giving away your own?"

I shrug. "Now we have a lead."

"How?" Carter rest his elbows on his knees, his leather jacket stretching with the movement. "It makes more sense if it were the men from the lake."

"But they were wearing different clothes."

"Weird." Carter raises a brow. "I wonder how they managed that? Oh yeah, *they changed*."

I glower.

"Think about this for a second," he goes on. "I get that Ramie is a giant question mark, but just because you told him doesn't mean it *was* him. You were under disguise, remember? Why would he send armed men after a doe-eyed college graduate, or better yet, know she was actually a redheaded spy traveling with a dashingly good-looking man?"

Jules lets out a groaning eye roll before I can.

"Unless you think you were compromised?" Carter ignores his tech Op while watching me carefully. "Were you?"

I want to immediately say no, but everything is all backward and upside down now. I want to scream. Carter's right. Last night's attack was no random security sweep, the way they ran straight for us, like they knew where we'd be...

"No, I wasn't compromised," I finally say, flexing my fingers on my bicep again. "It just makes no sense. They came at us like they knew exactly where to look. It was fast. But..." I glance to my booted feet. "You're right. We were much farther out than the waterfall or any tourist trail. Ramie couldn't have known. But I'm telling you—something doesn't sit right with that guy."

"You said he mentioned his family owning a coffee plantation?" Jules asks, her blond hair glowing around the edges from the slowly rising sun outside.

I nod and watch her and Akoni share a look. "What?"

"Well, his alibi might be true," she says. "On a visit to one of the nearby plantations, Akoni and I are pretty sure we saw him."

"What do you mean, pretty sure?" I push up from leaning against the wall.

"As part of the tour, they take you out to the fields," Akoni says. "When we were heading back to the main house, we saw a few men walk out and get into cars. One looked similar to Ramie, but we were too far away to be certain."

My nerves buzz. "Which plantation? How long ago was this?"

"Three days, at Viento del Este." Akoni types quickly on his computer before showing us pictures of a quaint tourist-friendly coffee plantation. Brown villas for guests are constructed next to a main house nestled atop a hill within the edge of the jungle. "It's an hour east of Cuetzalan, roughly three hours from where you and Carter were attacked."

"I'm going there," I say.

"*Ehem.*" Carter clears his throat.

"*We're* going there," I correct through clenched teeth.

"What a lovely idea." Carter leans back into the couch. "I knew I married you for a reason."

"Then that makes one of us."

"Don't be too down and out, 3," he says. "At least there's one good thing we can take away from all this."

"And that is..."

"Whether it's Ramie, the men from the lake, or another family, the fact that they're trying to kill us at all means only one thing." His lips curve into an annoyingly charming grin. "We're close."

***

Wind rustles through the flowers in the dark courtyard below as the soft buzz and chirps of the surrounding moonlit mountains filter through our balcony door. The muffled voices of new guests at Flor Tranquila can be heard a few floors below, and I take in the rare peacefulness of it all before my bed squeaks for the fifth time tonight, causing me to bite the inside of my cheek.

He's doing it on purpose, but I refuse to acknowledge his sophomoric attempt at getting under my skin. Doesn't he know he achieves that just by breathing?

Squeak.

A trickle of blood oozes across my tongue. I bit down too hard.

Squeak. Squeak.

My grip tightens on the tablet that rests on my knees, the glass seconds away from breaking.

SQUEAK.

"Stop!" I throw a pillow at him.

"What?" Carter blocks his face with his forearm. "What was I doing?" He presses his lips together to keep from grinning.

I don't know how he's a successful operative. He can't act for cat poop.

"You know *exactly* what you were doing. If you're going to read, *read*, but stop shifting."

"Oh, was that bothering you?"

I don't respond, merely take a deep breath and go back to looking at my Scrabble game.

We're leaving early tomorrow for Viento del Este, with Jules and Akoni following a bit later, and all I wanted after a week of camping and almost getting blown apart was a relaxing, comfortable night in. So when Carter crawled into bed beside me and, instead of immediately passing out like usual, pulled out a worn copy of a Spanish romance novel, I was more than a little annoyed. His book is wrapped in one of those humorously cliché

covers featuring a luscious woman draped in a half-torn gown
across a bare-chested man. I'm pretty certain he got it from
Señora Flores, but the idea that it's from his personal stash, particularly one that he's read so many times it looks like it got hit
by a truck, has my body clenching in painful fits from resisting to
laugh. A reaction, I'm sure, he was going for.

Even though he won't get it, his creative effort I can't help
but appreciate.

In fact, the longer the two of us sit nestled under the covers
side by side, me in a tank and shorts, Carter (of course) bare
chested, reading, it begins to feel oddly domesticated. Our roles
of a married couple couldn't be more believable in this moment.

My turn to shift.

"Ejaculate."

"*Excuse me*?" I snap my eyes to Carter, seeing him peering at
my tablet.

"Ejaculate," he says again. "Triple word, double letter. Right
here." He points to the lower left corner of my board. "E-J-A-C-U
attached to your opponent's *late*. Sixty points."

I stare at the screen. I'd be able to replace more than half my
tiles with that move, take a clear lead...

"Go on." Carter nudges me with his elbow. "I won't judge you
for using it."

I narrow my gaze, and he laughs softly.

"Does accepting my help *really* pain you that much that
you'd chance losing?"

"I won't lose."

"You are right now."

I glance at my score, my lips pursing.

"Who are you playing against anyway?"

"The computer."

He snorts. "Of course."

"What does that mean?"

"Nothing." He waves a hand. "Go back to playing against your doppelganger."

"Clever." I roll my eyes. "How long have you been waiting to use that one?"

"An excruciating few seconds."

"How fitting, since that's exactly how I've heard women describe having sex with you."

Carter makes a choking sound beside me, and I lean away, wondering if a fly suddenly flew into his mouth, the tiny hero of a bug now jamming his windpipe, but instead of falling over dead, a burst of air barrels out of him as he keels over laughing. I watch, slightly stunned, as he grips the white sheets around his stomach, his tanned muscles rippling under each loud guffaw. The deep sound rumbles through the bed and straight into my chest, a feeling of thawing.

"Oh...my...Nashville," he gasps, placing a large hand on my arm. "That was...too perfect." He lets out a few more chuckles while wiping his eyes. "You win that round. You win."

I stare down at his hand still on my wrist, the warmth spreading out, up and down. While we've traded blows, kicks, and punches, we've never really touched, not like this, not without the facade of being a married couple while in public. After a moment more I realize Carter is looking at it too, his amusement silenced, replaced by the sound of our individual breathing as it tangles in the space between us.

"You called me Nashville." It's not a question or an accusation, only a statement, words to fill the silence.

"It's your name."

His voice is softer than usual, and I make the mistake of glancing at him, finding his face close, precariously so, those bright flecks of gold dancing across his green irises. A *thump thump thump* of his pulse against his neck, while his dark, still-damp hair from his recent shower elevates his scent of male and cinnamon. I want to take in a lungful, stay still to see which way this spinning coin will fall, but as his gaze drops to my lips, flashing the telltale signs of what will happen next, what must, is when reality bursts back into the room, a winter's wind.

This is Carter.

We're on assignment.

We hate each other.

Slowly I slip my arm from under his fingers, leaning away while rubbing the skin that now feels sunburned, branded. Carter blinks, pupils shifting from hazy to focused, and with a swallow, carefully returns to his side of the bed.

I've never hated my senses more than in this moment. Carter's heartbeat is a locomotive in my ears, his pheromones blanketing the sheets like an alluring aroma from a lit candle. How long has it been since I've enjoyed the touch of another? Allowed myself to experience pleasure rather than pain? The hairs on the back of my neck stand tall as my muscles tense from the terrifying desire to grab him and pull him back while also wanting to run from the room, escape. Both reactions would only make whatever just happened, *is happening*, worse. So instead I force myself to remain, to pretend like I can't hear, see, or smell the man next to me. Which is a lot harder than it used to be.

Distract. Distract. Distract.

"Do you like word games?" In this moment it's a ridiculous

question, random, but I'm desperate.

"What?" Carter glances back my way, forehead crinkled.

"Scrabble." I nod to my screen. "You seemed like you knew what you were doing."

He studies the forgotten book in his lap. "My mother," he says quietly. "She loved playing."

I wait, but he doesn't elaborate, and I don't pry. I know better than most how the smallest detail of someone's past can often be the most painful to share, the most important to keep for oneself. And Carter's family, their stories, belong to a different man than the one who's currently sitting beside me. They are owned by the Carter I was with in the jungle, saw glimpses of over the fire's light. And as much as a deep hidden part of me wants to see more of him, I also really, *really* don't. For it's not just him that slips into a different person in those moments.

With a nod I turn back to what's in my hands, the air around us shifting from crackles of flames to a humid summer's day. The heat may be different, but it's still unbearable.

We remain separate, the tangle of sheets a divider as we feign being engrossed with tiles on a screen, words on a page. And the longer we sit, silence stretching out endlessly as I finally play the word Carter suggested, my points adding up to me now winning, something in my chest tightens and screams for release, demands to be voiced, and despite my best efforts to choke it back, it streams from my lips anyway.

"Thank you," I say. It's barely a whisper, but those two words fill the room, paint the walls, and take up all the air. Carter turns to find my gaze, but I can't meet his, my eyes stay locked on to my screen, waiting for him to respond, but he doesn't, and immediately I regret saying them. I want to take them back, want to rewind time and force myself out of bed so I never get the chance to utter what I just did. Because what is a simple exchange between most is a world of complication for people like him and me, especially when neither of us know if my thanks was in regard to more than just the game.

CHAPTER 40

Carter
En route to Viento del Este Plantación
Mexico: 0812 hours

Setting out early, we left behind a mist-covered Cuetzalan, where past spirits still wandered the cobblestone streets before the sun rose to burn them away. Now heading east toward the plantation, we drive through lush, green, and windy roads, our views just as beautiful as all our trips along this region. With the windows rolled down, a warm breeze filters into the car and mixes with the low music of Miles Davis pouring from the speakers. 3 drives (yes, pigs must be flying) with one hand on the wheel, the other dancing through the wind as wisps of her braided hair play around her face. She's in a summer green dress, her shoulders exposed to show a speckling of freckles recently acquired from being out in the sun, while I wear one of my gray T-shirts and black jeans. We haven't said much since the incident last night, which is what I'm now calling it, an "incident." One that needs to be logged, placed into a folder, stamped *CONFIDENTIAL*, and never talked about again. Which I'm more than happy to oblige and have no doubt 3 is too.

Forcing it from my mind like every other painful or confusing thing I've experienced, I look back at the pamphlet in my hand and read about the plantation we're about to visit for the weekend.

"Though some beans are sold in North America," I read out loud, "Viento del Este's main place of business is here, in its homeland of Mexico." I turn the paper over. "It also says it's still owned by the family that founded it in 1918. Pretty cool."

"Sure," 3 says. "Especially since that means they definitely have a connection with the Oculto, being as old as they are."

I glance her way, watch as she studies the road, her face masked in its usual impassive state. "Do you ever see beyond your job when on a mission?"

Her brows crinkle. "What do you mean?"

"Do you take time to enjoy yourself? Go to a restaurant to merely taste the food rather than because a potential mark eats there?"

She's quiet for a moment, Miles Davis's trumpet filling the space before her answer. "No."

I huff my displeasure. "How many countries have you been to on assignment? Fifteen?"

"Twenty-one."

I shake my head. "Yeah, no. Tonight, on this trip, we're fixing that."

"I don't need—"

"Yes, you really do."

Her lips clamp. "We're not here to enjoy ourselves, Carter."

"Would we have stuck with this career if we didn't?"

"That's not what I mean."

"Then what did you?"

She inhales deeply. "These missions...what we ultimately have to do on them is not meant to act like a holiday wrapped in a few hours of work. Every second our targets stay alive is another second they could be harming others, selling weapons that could kill thousands. So if I don't stop to smell the roses while I'm on a job, it's because I'm too busy making sure the rest of the world continues to have that luxury, even if I never get to."

The car dips into quiet, the wind and subtle jazz the only sounds as I study her porcelain profile. "Bullshit."

"What?" She swings a narrowed gaze my way.

"Bullshit," I say again. "Sure, we're here to make the world safer, kill villains, be the silent heroes by committing the ultimate mortal sin, blah, blah, blah, but our jobs are ninety-nine percent of our lives. Even God, if you believe in Him, wouldn't expect us to keep from enjoying the beauties of this world because of that. We see and carry out carnage practically every day. If we didn't 'stop to smell the roses,' as you put it, what would be the poultice to our souls? What would stop us from becoming the monsters we seek to kill? If we can no longer find or appreciate the joy in the things we are trying to protect, why continue to do any of this? I respect your duty to the job, 3, I really do, but there is such a thing as too much."

"And too late?" Her blue eyes bore into mine.

"Too late can wait." I wave a hand. "We'll work this weekend, we'll do what we were sent here for, but you *will* enjoy at least one thing while at Viento del Este, or we won't leave until you do."

"Why?"

"Why what?"

"Why do you care if I...find something to enjoy?"

Good question.

"Because then maybe you'd smile more."

3 frowns. "I smile."

"Like you are right now?" I laugh, making her pout deepen. "Just trust me on this one. Can you do that?"

She turns away, back to studying the road that stretches out before us, and though we remain quiet, I know we're both flipping over the word that has become so blasphemous in our lives.

Trust.

I don't know why I said it, why I asked her in that phrasing, but I did. It's done, and while she doesn't answer me with a yes, she doesn't say no either.

Reaching the plantation a little before lunch, we check in under Mr. and Mrs. Nickels before dropping our bags in our private bungalow that's part of a row of nine others. Each is a couple dwelling, constructed of teak stained wood with white-framed windows and a small porch that overlooks the lush green hills of Viento del Este's property. Purple flowers grow along the perimeter, and a manicured stone path leads from our small village to the main house. The setup reminds me of a kid's summer camp, except for the large king-sized bed that greets us as we enter, and the full modern bath off to the side. There's no kitchen, which is a gentle nudge to visit the plantation's restaurant and enjoy mingling with the other guests.

After grabbing a quick bite in the café, we head out with a tour group to learn about the art of coffee making. Because Akoni and Jules have already visited here, they'll be checking in later and meeting us for dinner.

Our guide, Dominique, a sturdy old man with bright hazel eyes and a weathered complexion, leads us down a path through the jungle to an uncovered slope where rows of green coffee shrubs stagger down a hill. In accented English he explains how Viento del Este grow their coffee facing east so the sun shines on it only in the morning, which keeps it from drying out, and how the iconic beans we all love so much are actually the pits of coffee cherries. He encourages us to pluck any dark-red or black ones we find tangled in the leaves as we walk along the rows, for those are rotten. Bright green or pink are what eventually gets harvested. As I snap off a few, I sweep a glance around the expansive land and lush foliage. The sun is high with few clouds stroking the blue sky, and workers down various strips collect baskets, with large-brimmed hats shielding their faces. It's peaceful here, almost in a meditative way, and I try seeing where the Oculto would plot their operation among such hard-working innocents.

3 is a few steps ahead of me, her rose-tinted hair vibrant under the afternoon light, talking with Dominique about how big of a territory Viento del Este covers and if we'll see all the buildings involved with making their delicious coffee. To anyone else it would sound like she's an enthralled tourist, but knowing her as I do, I understand that not one of her words are wasted. I let out a sigh. This might be harder than I thought, getting her to switch off. How do you rewire a person who's been molded since birth

to put her job first and herself last?

As Dominique gets pulled away by another guest, I watch 3 roll a black cherry between her fingers. She gives it a gentle sniff, jerking back at the apparent sour scent before chucking it to the ground, annoyed, and I hold back a chuckle.

Yes, I'm not sure how I'll do it, but I have no doubt that I will, for I'm nothing if not up for a challenge.

And 3, she's the very definition.

Later that evening we step through patio doors into Colina, the restaurant at Viento del Este. The room buzzes with life, and the smell of fine cooking surrounds us like a grandmother's hug as we leave behind the cool mountain air that followed us on the walk from our bungalow. 3 slips the maroon shawl from her shoulders, revealing toned arms that are gracefully wrapped in a loosely fitted cobalt dress, while her apricot hair pours down her back in gentle waves. No matter how many times I try for it not to, her beauty still takes my breath away, and to distract myself from it, I roll up the sleeves of my charcoal oxford that's tucked into my simple black slacks and peer around the quaint establishment.

Warm candlelight halos across each rustic table that's laid with modern furnishings, patrons leaning forward to enjoy each other's conversations while dipping forks into their meals. Viento del Este might be famous for its coffee, but Colina has been rated one of the best restaurants in the region. Add on its exclusivity with only allowing those staying at the plantation to score reservations, and it makes the whole compound a much-sought-after experience, leaving me little doubt that hacking was involved to get us in on such short notice.

Speaking of our computer whizzes, I quickly find Jules and Akoni sitting toward the back of the room by large bay windows that showcase a breathtaking view of the dusk-covered Sierra Madre mountains. Seeing us, they wave us over to where they're accompanied by two blond strangers who appear in their midthirties. As we sit we're introduced to Olivia and Liam, a Swedish couple they met as they were checking in. Jules explains how they know 3 and me, or rather Ben and Stephanie, from running into us in Cuetzalan. Liam has a thick beard and an easy smile, while his wife matches with her quick fluttering laughter.

"It's so fun meeting other groups when traveling." Olivia beams, placing a hand on 3's shoulder.

She stiffens.

"Yes," I agree, biting back a grin. "I was just telling Stephie how it would be fun to find people we could meet up with in different places once a year."

"Oh." Olivia claps. "Yes, wouldn't that be amazing?"

With her short blond pixie cut and cherub blushed cheeks, Olivia exudes cheery innocence, and I can practically feel 3's displeasure with having sat next to her.

"How long have you been in Mexico?" Liam asks.

"Almost a month now," I say before diving into the breadbasket.

"So long." His brows rise. "Olivia and I can't sit still in one place for more than a few days."

"There's just too much world to see," his wife adds with a nod.

"Yes, well, Stephie and I have just been really *enjoying* ourselves." I glance to 3 with a knowing smile. "And when you find *enjoyment*, why run from it? Right, dear?"

Her lips tighten before she copies my grin. "Oh yes, especially when *Benjie* here is usually such a bore everywhere else."

Akoni snorts into his beer as Liam and Olivia bark out laughs. Jules merely shakes her head, her blond hair winking honey in the warm light, while motioning to the waiter for another drink.

As 3 and I lock eyes, my chest flutters in excitement. *Oh, it's so on.*

But before either of us can play our next move, a tall, well-groomed man with salt-and-pepper short hair and sharp brown eyes floats over to our table.

"*Buenas tardes, damas y caballeros.*" He greets us with a smile. "My name is Rodrigo, and I am one of the owners of Viento del Este—"

"Oh!" Olivia squeals, interrupting whatever he was about to say next. "What an honor! We *love* your coffee. My cousin brought a bag back to Sweden a little over a year ago, and ever since we've been dying to make a trip here. It's become our favorite, hasn't it, Liam?"

"Let's just say we might have an issue with customs on the way back." He laughs good naturedly.

Rodrigo's grin widens, and he gives a little bow. "This makes me very happy. We're always pleased to receive visitors from all over the world. Are you traveling together in our lovely Mexico?" He glances to our group.

"No." Akoni pushes up his black-rimmed glasses. "We actually all met recently, while traveling here."

"*Maravilloso*, wonderful." Rodrigo interlocks his fingers over his stomach. "Well, I do hope you enjoy your meal and the rest of your stay."

As he says the word *enjoy*, I make a point to nudge 3 under the table, to which she responds by stomping my foot. I grunt against the pain before covering it up with a tight smile when Olivia glances my way.

"Rodrigo." 3 addresses the man before he turns to greet the other guests. "I was wondering if you knew whether Ramie was here?"

Jules, Akoni, and I all stiffen.

What are you doing? I eye her from the side, but she ignores me.

"Ramie?" Rodrigo frowns.

"Yes, a friend of mine met him in Cuetzalan a while ago and told me he was family to one of the local coffee growers. If I ever visited they said I should try to meet him."

Rodrigo's gaze travels over the table before locking back on 3. "I'm sorry, *señorita*, but I know of no Ramie. There are a few other plantations surrounding Cuetzalan. Perhaps it is one of those your friend meant."

My K-Op partner only studies the man for a millisecond, but from the quick dilation of her eyes, I know she took down his profile. Whatever information she gathered, her face reveals none of it. "Ah, my mistake then," she says while producing the prettiest blush. "I feel silly for asking now."

Rodrigo tuts, easily charmed. "I don't think you could ever be considered silly," he says while lifting her fingers from the table and gently kissing her knuckles. "Now if you'll excuse me, I'll make the other diners jealous if I stay here too long." And with a playful grin he disappears from our side.

Olivia sighs, watching his retreating form. "What I'd do if I weren't married…"

"Not be in Mexico, that's for sure." Liam raises his brows. "Remind me again who booked our tickets?"

She pushes her husband's shoulder, her eyes dancing with amusement as a waiter comes to take our order.

The dinner progresses with Liam and Olivia leading most of the conversation while Akoni, Jules, 3, and I fill in where we can with our various lies that deal with our cover profiles. While our Swedish friends are a nice change of pace, after catching 3, on more than one occasion, staring into her meal with a clouded expression, I wish they could vanish so we could discuss whatever she's flipping over in her mind.

Does she think Rodrigo was lying about Ramie? He didn't appear to be. There was no stiffening or stuttering or pause at her question, only a man at ease with whoever this stranger was that she mentioned. It was a ballsy move she pulled, asking like that, but I have to say, I'm impressed. That's a tactic I would have used…our techniques seem to be rubbing off on each other.

"So…" Liam's deep voice cuts into my thoughts. "How long have the two of you been married?"

"A little over two months," I say, draping an arm around 3's chair. "This is our honeymoon."

A pleased breath escapes Olivia. "Ah, how exciting. I remember when we were first married." She glances to her husband. "Couldn't take our hands off each other."

"*You* couldn't take your hands off *me*," he corrects. "She's a randy one, this girl." He nods to his wife, and we all laugh, well, except 3. She merely sits up straighter.

"We remember how it was though," he goes on. "You two

don't have to be polite for our sake."

My forehead wrinkles. "What do you mean?"

"I know you want to be draped across one another right now," Liam explains. "I see the way you've been eyeing your wife throughout the meal." He shoots me a knowing wink, and my frown deepens.

Have I?

"Yes, don't mind us," Olivia chimes in.

"We're fine," 3 says evenly. "We're not that kind of couple."

"Pshh, stop." Olivia waves a hand. "Everyone is that kind of couple in the beginning. Go on. Kiss each other already."

3 and I flinch, the words ice to my balls.

"Yes." Liam nods. "Get it out of your systems. We won't mind."

"Like I said," 3 tries again, her voice now edged with a bit of frost, "we're *fine.*"

But neither of our blond friends seem to catch on, for they begin to quietly chant "kiss, kiss, kiss" until it feels like the entire restaurant is turning our way.

I want to yell shut up, possibly punch Liam in the face, but both options would cause a scene, so instead I look to Akoni and Jules for help.

But I should have known I'd find none there, for Jules has joined in on the chant, a Jack Frost mischief grin spread across her face, while Akoni bounces his gaze between 3 and me, wide eyed and at a loss.

Breathing heavy, my blood swirls a havoc in my veins while I claw for a way out of this, of what to do next, and chancing a glance at 3, find equal terror on her face. She turns to me, blue eyes round and saying *don't you dare.*

I'm frozen for a moment, the chanting only growing louder. "Kiss, kiss, kiss."

Do I...dare?

I know they won't stop until we concede, and to save ourselves from this humiliation, we must act upon another. So even though I might get stabbed for doing it, I go for the ripping-off-of-a-Band-Aid approach and grab the back of 3's neck, bringing her forward. There's an instant of resistance before her soft lips collide with mine, but then it's gone because I'm already pulling away, leaning back in my chair, a gasp of air escaping me like a drowned man breaking the surface.

It was an instant, not even a second of time, hardly felt the contact, but my heart still pounds like a jackrabbit's foot, my skin sweaty, and I refuse to turn to 3, too fearful of what expression, or weapon, I might find pointing my way.

"Aw, boo," Liam moans. "That was rubbish. Kiss her like you love her, Ben." He pounds on the table.

Jesus, where are we? On a fucking Viking ship?

"Yeah," Jules says, mimicking his table slap. "Let's consummate this thing!"

I've never wished to be a Jedi more than in this moment, for I would throw Jules straight across the—

Cool hands grasping my cheeks and jerking my face to the right cut off my thoughts as I collide with 3's blue gaze again. She holds me still for a moment, her eyes playing through a multitude of thoughts as, time slowing, she leans in. And it's in this instant, this small gap between her and me, that I get a glimpse of what it must be like to have her senses, for whether it's her heartbeat or mine, a loud thump has filled my ears, and her subtle scent of female and coconut overwhelms my lungs on a deep inhale. A distant part of me thinks that if this is to be my last breath, I'm okay with that, drawing it out, savoring it, right before her eyes flutter close, and she kisses me.

And this time neither of us pulls away.

Feeling her invite, her allowance, my hand grazes up her smooth neck to hold her in place and tangle in her thick mane. I inch closer as my body hums with energy, overflows with the desires I've been locking up for so many days, too many nights. Her mouth opens to mine, the soft prodding of her tongue setting more kindle to this pyre of flames, and I completely forget that we're in public because 3, for as prude and cold as she comes across, can kiss. Good forest nymphs, can she kiss, and I greedily take in whatever she gives, her plump lips molding to mine. More, I silently demand. Give me everything, I encourage with my tightening grip.

But right as I'm on the precipice of a moan, I'm dropped back to earth, 3 loosening her hold and moving away. With a blink, the world goes from a deep midnight of touch and sighs to a bright cold day, and I sit frozen, watching as the room comes back into focus even though I remain a pixelated blown-apart mess.

3 kissed me.

I kissed 3.

And I liked it.

CHAPTER 41

Nashville

The cool night air can't filter into my lungs fast enough as I push outside. The darkness is loud, the surrounding mountains alive as my overactive senses try separating the buzz of insects from the rustling of leaves and chatter of the guests in the restaurant. After I held it together for a full five minutes, I made the excuse that I needed to use the bathroom.

As I stood, each step slow, controlled, my body screamed to run, escape from what Carter and I...

I can't even bring myself to think it, my brain wanting to skip over the moment while my skin still surges from the memory.

What's happening?

It was just a kiss.

A stupid kiss while on the job.

I've had to unfortunately do that countless times, sometimes the allure of a woman the only weapon against men. But this... this felt different. *Was* different.

After Carter grabbed me for a quick, chaste peck, I sat there, stunned for a hanging second, barely hearing our companions whining, saying how horrible that was, that they won't accept it. And something in me snapped, something cornered, desperate to silence them without resorting to stabbing anyone in the neck, so with hardly a thought I took it upon myself to give them what they wanted.

And then...

And then it all went to shit.

Because now I'm here *feeling*. And I am not a woman accustom to feeling anything besides the lick of anger, of rage that constantly swims in my veins.

That I know.

That I can work with.

Was born with.

But this other thing...even with Christopher Waters it was like I was experiencing it buried deep within the earth. But with Carter...I've never felt closer to the sun.

Fuck.

I run a hand down my face as I pace to the end of the stone patio, my night vision painting the cresting mountains in front of me in shades of silver.

How could I have known I'd react in such a way, when for so long nothing but detached blood has pumped through my heart?

Where's my apathy? My ability to shut everything down? To keep my emotions, which are so dangerous to set free, suppressed?

I don't have to glance back to the warm glow of the restaurant to know it was left in a smattered mess across our dining table.

"Stephanie," a man calls behind me, and though I stiffen at the sound, I don't stop from striding away. "Nashville."

Nashville.

A name for someone else, a name for the woman not meant to be here.

"Don't call me that." I turn with a glare.

Carter peers around the empty hillside. "No one heard me."

"I did."

A frown before, "Okay." Taking hesitant steps forward, his tall, broad-shouldered form blocks out some of the stars. "Are you...are you okay?"

"Are you?" I throw the question back with an arch of my brow.

He lets out a deep sigh, raking a hand through his thick brown hair, his charcoal shirt growing tight across his chest with the movement. "What happened in there—"

"Didn't matter," I finish for the both of us.

His green gaze flickers my way, a small dip to the side of his mouth, the same mouth I can still feel against mine.

"We had to keep up our profiles," I find myself saying. "We're married. It was going to happen sooner or later."

It. Not the kiss. Not the seconds where my chest filled with warm pleasure. Just it.

"Yes..." Carter says after a moment.

"We don't have to talk about it," I go on. "In fact, it's probably best if we didn't. We know how we feel about each other. No need to rub in our disgust."

Carter doesn't respond, merely watches me, his expression shuttering over with a blankness.

Good, I think. *This is better.* This is how we get back to how we were.

"I'm going to search the compound," I say, glancing over my shoulder into the dimly lit path that leads back to our bungalow. "Rodrigo, he was smooth, but he's definitely hiding something. You can join...or not, whatever, but I just...I have to go."

"Did you enjoy it?"

"What?" I turn to find Carter's green firestorm pinned to me, his darkly handsome planes and angles heightened in the night.

"Did you enjoy it?"

"Enjoy..." My voice dies out as his earlier words float forward... *You will enjoy at least one thing while at Viento del Este.*

I let out a small gasp. "Screw you. This isn't some game!"

But before I can move away, Carter pulls me flush against him, keeping my arms secured to my sides so I can't strike out, his cinnamon and male hugging me closer. "I'm not making a joke," he says, his voice gruff, firm, as he peers down. "I want to know. And if it makes it easier for you, I did. I enjoyed the fuck out of it."

It.

His gaze dips to my mouth, eyes hungry, and my stomach drops out, melts into a puddle.

No. No. No. He can't. *I* can't.

"Let me go," I say, knowing I could easily escape with one bone-breaking head butt to his nose, but seeing the way he's looking at me, a canister of oil precariously close to a flame, has me realizing he won't stop unless it's of his own volition.

"Please," I add, barely a whisper, and as if that word is a rainstorm on his head, he instantly releases me, taking a step back.

Running two hands through his hair this time, he faces the shadows, hiding whatever expression mars his features. "Go."

One word, not a demand or a plea, just...go.

So I do, quickly. I run, sprint, until my sandaled feet begin to blister and I'm off the lit path, deep in the jungle where only predators dare to roam at night.

My family.

Leaning on my knees, I gasp for air, not because I'm out of breath, but because it feels like the other version of myself, the only one meant for this assignment, is being drowned, taken over, and replaced by something else. Something new.

Something that *enjoys*.

And only for the second time in my life—the first when I was left to fend for myself on the streets, a baby—I become truly terrified.

CHAPTER 42

3
Viento del Este Plantación, Mexico: 0230 hours

The bungalow is quiet as I enter, the sun not set to rise for another four hours. I silently maneuver around the dimly lit space. Carter's bedside lamp has been left on, throwing half the room in a warm yellow while his large form lies motionless tucked under the covers, his back to my side of the bed. Peeling off my black durable outerwear and unhooking my knives, I slip into my pajamas and then into the cool sheets, where I stare up at the wooden slatted ceiling.

I wasn't planning on coming back here tonight, intending to keep searching the compound until the sun rose. But as each warehouse and outpost within a five-mile radius proved empty, innocuous, my resolve turned to fatigue, and I realized how ridiculous it would be if I didn't return. It would only prove how truly affected I was. So with muscles sore from climbing, run-ning, and lifting, I headed back.

We have one more day here, but I have a feeling it will prove just as useless. Despite the unease I felt in Rodrigo's answer about Ramie, this plantation appears to be exactly as it's adver-tised—a coffee plantation, and I huff my frustration. The lack of leads we've run into on this assignment are record breaking.

"Find anything?" Carter's deep voice rumbles from his side of the bed.

I turn against my pillow, taking in his large, strong back, the peppered scars pale against his tanned skin. "No. You?"

I know he went out. Could smell the sweet scent of the jungle on his clothes hanging in the bathroom. Caught hints of his cin-namon as I crisscrossed through the trees.

"No," he says, and as the room slowly dips back into silence, he reaches up and snaps off the light, a wordless close to any further conversation, and I feel slight relief.

We won't be talking about *it* then, which is good. Despite what therapists spout, ignoring something long enough *does* in fact make it disappear. I should know. I've done more than my fair share of avoidance.

Yet as I lie awake, my darkness bright, always lit by sounds, shadows, and scents, I find myself grazing a finger over my bot-tom lip, wondering how to ignore something when, at the end of each day, you find it lying next to you.

CHAPTER 43

3
Cuetzalan, Mexico: 1936 hours

It's been another week of nothing. No blips of nefarious activity, glimpses of a certain tall, dark, and handsome coffee prince, or tip-offs that we're close to finding anything.

It's also been a week of Carter and I remaining professionally indifferent, what happened at Viento del Este never mentioned again, *never* tried again. Even Jules and Akoni have developed amnesia to that night. Probably because after taking one look at us the following day, with our shuttered gazes and stiff postures, knew certain lines had been drawn, and not even they were allowed to cross them. So as the four of us sit in their hotel room back in Cuetzalan, recently ending a call with Ploom and Axel, in which they updated us on the board's impatience for us to make some headway, it almost appears like everything has gone back to the way it was.

Except it hasn't.

What once came as easy digs and banter between Carter and I have now dissolved into thick silences and platitudes. If he says something, I wait for another to comment before I do. If I say something he disagrees with, he leaves it at that, that he disagrees. No snarky retort or filthy innuendos.

I should be happy. Should be relieved. For isn't this how I wanted our operation to be since the beginning? Isn't this how my assignments usually go? In and out. No pleasantries or how are yous. Just a target to be found, finished, so I can get home fast.

But now that I know how it could be different, how *we* were different—this here, him and I not looking at one another since stepping into the room, feels faker than the name written on my passport.

How many versions of a person can be maintained? Work 3. Home Nash. Victoria O'Hera. Stephanie Keller. *Married* Stephanie Keller *Nickels*. And now this other me, the one changing while trying to remain the same. It's exhausting, and this is coming from a person with superhuman stamina.

Where's my friggin' vacation when I need it?

"Where are you going?" Akoni lifts his head from his computer as I walk to the door, his blue shirt that reads $i > u$ stretching across his large chest. We've been preparing a camping expedition to head back to the lake where we saw the drug drop. Out of everything, that's the one grain of constructive intel we've been able to gather since coming here.

"A walk," I say.

"Want one of us to come with?" Jules asks from where she's sitting cross-legged on one of their twin beds, thin cream sweater and yoga pants in place. I don't miss her steal a glance toward Carter.

He's been standing by the balcony window since we ended our call, staring out to the dark alley below. His legs are encased in black jeans, and a gray thermal shirt hugs over his torso and arms that are crossed at his chest. If he's heard any of us speak, he doesn't show it.

"No," I say. "Feel like being alone for a bit."

A mumbled grunt, which sounded like "Surprise, surprise," comes from Carter.

I frown. "Mind saying that a bit louder?"

He slowly turns his head, a bored expression marking his features as he meets my gaze. "Say what louder?"

I pin my eyes to his green ones.

Ten seconds pass.

Twenty.

Say what you want to say, I silently invite.

You first, sweetheart.

Akoni clears his throat, and I blink back to the room.

"Anyone want anything?" I ask, my voice tight. Jules and Akoni shake their heads. Carter wordlessly returns to gazing out the window.

With one hand curling into a fist, I swing open the door and all too easily leave.

The mango juice flows across my tongue as I bite into the fruit that's set up like a popsicle on a stick, the delicious tangy flavors caressing my taste buds.

Walking through the lantern-lit cobblestone streets, I visited one of my favorite produce stands before setting out toward the main square. I have a desire to sit by the tall clock tower connected to the Church of San Francisco and people watch. The night is cool and sleepy, so I take the longer route, traveling down the narrow and winding alleys filled with old ladies and men standing in doorways, talking to one another, a few watering vibrant flowers and plants that mark each of their stone homes.

I smile at a few as I pass, realizing by the third that I'm doing something I would never have done before. I'm taking a moment for me...while on a job. My steps slow as I realize this. No part of the assignment had filled my head as I left Jules and Akoni's hotel, no plan that included finding new information, searching a new location. I merely wanted to walk...relax.

I frown, staring at the half-eaten fruit in my hands before finding a nearby garbage bin and tossing it in.

It's not supposed to be like this. *I'm* not.

Jamming my hands into my jeans pockets, I walk with new purpose toward the clock tower. Once there I'll see if there's anything amiss, anything different.

But as I turn down another set of narrow stairs, passing a dark alley, I catch the scent of something familiar.

My scalp prickles as a spicy caress of a hand-rolled cigarette wafts toward me from the blackness. I turn to look down the alley, the end bending away from my view, and every muscle goes on alert, the hairs on my neck rising.

Finally, *something*.

Peering behind and in front of me, seeing no one, I dip my head low and enter the barren backstreet. No windows or doors mark this path, as if the two buildings were once jutted together before being pried apart, leaving a thin stone space for absolutely nothing.

My fingers twitch at my side as a steady heartbeat reaches out to me from the shadows, the sound of an inhale, then long exhale, smoke being blown away. I lick my lips at what I know I will soon find, soon overpower, for I'm in no mood for any more games. Wigs, disguises, and a wallflower college girl no longer have room here. This assignment has dragged on for too long, and I'm going to end it, here, tonight.

Cracking my neck from side to side, I can only see a few feet ahead as I keep an even pace, the walls bending in a constant curve. But that's no matter. I work just as well in small spaces as large, and after only a minute more I see him.

He leans casually against a worn wooden door that ends my path, a single orange bulb casting him in a dramatic draping of light. The red embers of his cigarette illuminate his dark face as he inhales again, shadows and angles, soot lashes and thick hair highlighted for a quick moment. He doesn't look up, merely picks at his nails with one hand while holding his smoke with the other.

"I hear you've been looking for me." Ramie's deep Spanish words float forward, red wine in candlelight, before his dark eyes peer up to meet mine. The corner of his mouth tilts, taking me in. "Hello, 3."

My K-Op name barely escapes his lips as I launch myself at him, lightning escaping a bottle, and reach for the sharpened blade strapped to my spine, but my fingers barely graze the warm handle before he lashes out with speed that matches my own, snatching me from the air. Hard, unrelenting muscle surrounds me, and I hiss, barely getting an elbow to his rib cage before there's a prick at my neck, cool, icy liquid to my veins. I blink, stunned, surprised, *pissed*, right before I go from every emotion to none as the walls of the alley collapse in, swallowing me whole.

CHAPTER 44

3

Somewhere, hopefully, in Mexico

Soft classical music pushes through the blackness, curling around my conscious, slowly stirring it awake.

Open your eyes, it whispers. *Come look.*

But as my mind floats back to me, a boat reaching land, I keep them closed.

The first thing I notice is the smell—dirt, earth. I'm underground. The second, I absolutely cannot move. My ankles are bound to legs of a chair, hands tied by the wrists behind my back as a solid wire of some sort hugs my chest and arms to their sides. The material is strong, stronger than I, and my curiosity purrs, for there are few things in this world that are. A low whirring of a machine mixes with the sound of people moving about beyond whatever room I'm currently in, and I can feel a pinching at the inside elbow of my right arm, a Band-Aid over a cotton ball—blood drawn. My skin prickles at what this could mean, thoughts of what happened before I found myself here playing in my darkened mind.

Ramie...his speed, his strength. There's no doubting he's an A+, but why couldn't I smell it? A+ are even easier to detect than average humans. We have a scent completely distinct, floral with a metallic copper brushing. When we're gazed upon, it's like we have a halo of energy surrounding us, fireflies in the night. But not Ramie.

A door opening and closing sounds at my back, churning of machinery louder for a hairsbreadth before it's gone again, muffled with a locking of a bolt. Footsteps to my left, then in front, and the way they move, confidently, cleverly, I know it's him. I can also taste him now. What he was able to keep dormant is now awake, and the metal tang of his A+ abilities twists along my nostrils. With the monster inside me stirring, I blink my eyes open, my equilibrium tilting for a quick second as the chloroform he most likely stuck me with wears off.

Ramie half stands, half sits on a mahogany desk in front of me, his large form draped in the same black shirt, jeans, and boots he wore in the alley, while his arms rest on either side of him, gripping the ledge. His energy comes off him in waves now, a shimmering of gold that cages the internal beast he and I both share.

"Have a nice nap?" he asks in slightly accented English, his gaze as unrelenting as my binds, and my wrists pull against them in habit.

Ramie grins. "You might as well not try," he says. "They are meant to hold such creatures as you."

Creatures like us, I want to reply, but in these situations it's best to stay back, to take in, so I continue to keep quiet while moving my gaze around the room. I'm in some sort of office, the walls covered end to end with brown worn bookshelves, while antique rugs of various styles drape the ground, no doubt hiding a dirt or cement floor. Warm yellow tracking lights run along the ceiling's edge, illuminating this caved enclosure for the hiding place that it is, a fortress not meant to be found. The desk Ramie rests on looks old, passed down, and there's a leather maroon writing cover resting across the center, where a white folder lies. Three gold pens sit in a neat row on the left, while two picture frames stand, backs to me, on the right. A record player, the source of the music, turns behind it in one corner, while a rhythmic ticking has me peering over to a grandfather clock tucked into the other, the hands at nine and twenty. I've been unconscious for two hours, which means I can't be far from Cuetzalan. I gather this into the rest of the information. How many times have we walked past this hideout unknowingly? Were we ever close? I inhale a sweet vanillin scent that wafts from my clothes, a flower that holds onto me from the outside, and I file this away too, my attention moving on to the sandalwood aroma that fills the air, pushing against the dustiness of the earth, which stirs something distant in my memory, something forgotten. But before I can dig for what that might be, the door behind me opens and closes again. Ramie pushes to his feet and steps respectfully to one side as an older gentleman files past to sit behind the desk, that familiar sandalwood fragrance now stronger. Lowering himself, his white button-down stretches across broad shoulders and shifts as he leans back in his leather chair, interlocking his fingers across his stomach. His thick black hair is swept purposefully from his face, with a brush of gray by the ears, highlighting the icy-blue eyes that meet mine and distract from the mangled scar on his neck. It takes all my effort to remain composed and not charge the man with gnashing teeth.

Manuel Mendoza, the leader of the Oculto, keeper of our biochemical weapon, and whom I have been sent to kill, sits seven feet away, studying me.

My calm fissures.

"I'm sorry we have to keep you like this." He nods to my binds, speaking in Spanish, his voice gruff, tired, as if he's had to say, and see, many things in his lifetime. It swirls a strangeness in my chest, a...longing. "But I'm sure you understand why."

I glance to Ramie, who shoots me a wink, and my fingers curl into fists at my back.

"He's tested them himself," Mendoza explains, seeing where my attention drifts. "Ramie and his gifts have helped me with a great many things, actually."

So Mendoza knows of our kind, yet it's not this that has my brows pinching in, but in the way he speaks to my mutated brethren, with an affection, a...fondness.

Who are they to one another?

The record player switches to a new song, something I recognize, *Impromptus D.899*, by Franz Schubert. I have no idea why I know this. I have no affinity for classical music, yet there it is.

My skin begins to crawl, a clamminess breaking across the surface as Mendoza leans forward, head tilting to one side as he drinks in my appearance. His heartbeat is a bit quick but healthy, while his features are hard in their weathered skin with more wrinkles between his brows than creasing his eyes. A man that experiences few reasons to smile, and Carter's words on our drive to Viento del Este come back in a wave of understanding. *What would stop us from becoming the monsters we seek to kill if we can no longer find or appreciate the joy in the things we are trying to protect?* Mendoza is such a creature, with a twisted, tar-filled soul. Being on the other side of his scrutiny is a cowering thing, yet I don't whither into myself, but keep shoulders back, jaw tight, my gaze glued to his. Predators such as he, even with his normal human abilities, feed from a person's fear, and I'm only in the mood for him to starve.

After a moment longer of us staring at one another, a small grunt—maybe even a laugh—escapes him, and he slouches back in his chair, his eyes flickering to one of the pictures on his desk before returning to me.

"There's so much of her in you," he says.

Her?

A shiver runs down my spine, but I remain mute, motionless.

"Same hair, same skin, but those eyes...so blue." He holds my gaze. "You didn't get those from her."

Her.

Her.

I take the bait.

"Who?"

His face lights up, pleased, upon hearing my voice. "Why, your mother, of course."

Everything disappears. The room, the music, the constant churning of the machines outside, the two men and their beating hearts, it all fades away, gets blown into the void of white-hot flames erupting around me.

"I don't have a mother." I keep my voice flat.

Mendoza's lips press together, grim. "We all have a mother."

Tick, tick, tick of the clock.

"Okay..." I begin slowly, shuffling the cards I've been dealt and carefully choosing the next to play. "Let's say I do. How would *you* have known her?"

A sad smile barely touches his lips. "Because, *mi pequeña rosa*, I'm your father."

CHAPTER 45

Nashville

Someone is laughing, a loud, bone-shaking laugh as the room tilts left and then right, a Mad Hatter come to tea. This person sounds deranged, unhinged, and it causes a giggle of my own to bubble up in my chest, until I realize it mixes with the rest streaming from my mouth.

For I'm the one with the dipped head, chuckling into my chest. "Oh, you can do better than that," I gasp.

Mendoza watches me from under hooded brows, fingers steepled in front of him, elbows on his armrest. Ramie frowns beside him, a guard dog displeased with my blatant disrespect for his master.

"I understand your skepticism," Mendoza says after a moment. "I was similarly shocked, though didn't quite react as you have." He pinches his lips together as he nods to the folder on his desk.

Ramie scoops it up and rounds the corner to flip it open in front of me.

A duo DNA test is clipped inside. Two columns with numbers running its length, one with *CHILD* written on the top, the other with *FATHER*.

"Do you know how to read one of these?" Mendoza asks, causing my gaze to snap to his, offended by his gentle tone.

"Of course."

He nods. "While you were...asleep, we took it upon ourselves to run a DNA test, to confirm. These are the results."

The Band-Aid across my inner elbow pinches again as my eyes dart back to the DNA alleles, seeing the matching numbers from *CHILD* to *FATHER*, the confirmation.

I tumble out of my seat as I stay firmly rooted to it, strapped to this shit storm of a moment. *No. No. NO!* My breaths come out uneven, the creature in my blood straining against its cage as my body begins to shake. "No," I say in a burst, pressing against my binds. "No, this is faked."

"And why would I do such a thing?" Mendoza asks, leaning back. "Risk bringing you here"—he gestures to his office and what lies beyond—"all for a silly head game?"

My mind races for an answer, gaze darting about before it returns to the paper still held in front of me. The alleles numbers—fourteen matching another fourteen, sixteen with sixteen, so forth and so on. The disputable facts.

No. It's not real. This isn't real!

"How the fuck should I know why your kind does any of the things it does?" I bite out.

"*My kind.*" Mendoza almost smiles at that, while Ramie

snaps the file closed.

"Can't you smell it?" The guard dog demands, his dark eyes pressing me into my chair. He inhales deeply, lids fluttering close for a moment. "It's so obvious when you know what to look for. Your energies are even similar."

"Shut up," I sneer. "We are *nothing* alike because we are not—"

"Do it." Ramie grips me by the root of my hair, whipping my head back, my neck aching at the severe angle.

I gnash my teeth at him. "Try it," he says again, still holding me tight. "And then you can deny. Try it. Unless"—his gaze rakes over my face—"you're too scared."

"Ramie." Mendoza's words come out firm yet soft. "That's enough."

Slowly his mutt lets go, the front of my chair tipping back to the ground, wooden legs creaking.

I glare death into the two men, the blood that will soon pool from their necks once I slit their throats manifesting vividly in my mind. I'd cut deep enough to be fatal, but shallow enough for their lives to drip from them like painful molasses.

"So wild," Mendoza purrs, fascinated, taking in my ragged breathing and wide, flashing eyes.

I know I appear more monster than woman in this moment, but his features only alight with a sick pride.

"She's so like you were in the beginning." He glances to Ramie, and I swear my heart is about to punch out of my chest.

What the fuck is going on?

Nausea swarms me, and I inhale deeply, trying to calm myself, but as I do, everything Ramie mentioned slaps me in the face. Now that I'm looking for it, aware, it's indeed there, clear as day, more validating than any DNA test, any birth certificate, and my eyes roll back in my head as the information drowns me, takes over. The smell of citrus, summer, and earth, the vibrating energy of a mirrored reflection and gooseflesh-inducing pheromones that scream familiar, shout that we are one and the same. It's a subtle musk that sends my mind diving backward to a small living room, sun streaming through floral curtains as a young woman sits reading on a couch. Red hair, the same shade as my own, playing in wisps around her fair features. Features that no longer remain blurred, covered, but finally come into focus. Green eyes and a dusting of freckles play along her pert upturned nose, a wide smile as a man comes to her side, sandalwood, and kisses her cheek. Her light laughter as he whispers something into her ear. Where the woman is morning, daylight, the man is dark, midnight, and as he leans back, I take in his face, olive skin, a rough beard, and blue eyes, the same blue eyes as mine. The same as a man's picture in a file handed to me at SI6. Citrus, summer, and earth, my kin, my family, my parents.

The room snaps back into focus as my head droops, exhausted, and it's not until something wet hits my jean-clad knee that I realize I'm crying. My breaths come out raspy, uneven. I am everywhere in the room, pounding for a way out, a way backward, while gazing down at my body strapped in the chair. I have a father. He's alive and he's...I rush back to myself, slam into my shattering soul as I peer up to the man who once had meant so much to me, so very long ago, and now...

Now...

I pop to my tiptoes and then slam down, splintering the legs and seat of my wooden chair before barreling toward the desk. My arms remain cemented to my side, but I can move now, and that's all I've ever needed. With a blood-tinged shriek, I launch myself over the ledge, aiming my teeth to the man's jugular, when a vice grip wrenches me back, throwing me to the floor.

I let out an *oof* as my wind is knocked from me, the back of my head smacking against the ground as my tied arms twist painfully under my body's weight.

I see stars from the impact, but I still manage to thrash out, growl, and kick before there's another prick, this time at the base of my spine, and everything slows, becoming heavy.

I internally curse. My own methods thrown into my face.

Ramie grasps my shoulders and hefts me against him, his touch now careful compared to the storm of force it was a second ago, and I wonder if it's from his own desire or for that of the man who watches on.

He lowers my useless body into another chair that he drags from the side of the room, forcing me to face Mendoza again. My form hunches, slack, as I stare up at him, and I would spit in his face if it wouldn't end up dribbling down my chin instead.

"Why?" I croak out, slurred. "Why now?"

"Isn't that obvious?" Mendoza says, straightening his shirt before returning his attention to me. If he's angry about my attempt to maim him, he doesn't show it. "Fate has brought us back together. Or was I misinformed that you were sent here for the very reason of finding me?" His brows rise. "Yes, I know exactly what you do for a living, *mi pequeña rosa*, and I must say, I'm rather proud."

My monster erupts again, momentarily fighting the paralysis. "*I am not your little rose!*"

"But of course you are," Mendoza says, a placating father undisturbed by his child's outburst. "Don't you remember your own na—"

"*Stop*." It comes out in a panting plea, which only makes me hate myself more. I feel reduced to dust. "Don't say it. Don't you dare say it."

As long as I live, I will never know that girl. I already have a name, more names than I need, and whether he's dead or alive, this man will *never* be my father. I am still the orphan, still alone.

Blue eyes set in darkness tether to mine. "Okay," he says. "We have plenty of time to get to all that."

Time.

My chest pulls and twists, my heart a bloody mess on the carpet. "You...you abandoned me." It's not what I meant to say, but some broken piece of me, the little girl left in an alley, forces her way through.

"*No*," Mendoza snaps, face hardening. "Never. I thought you had died, or I would have never stopped looking for you."

My eyebrows pinch in, and I can't seem to get enough oxygen to my lungs. "What happened?"

The leader of the Oculto lets out a large breath, settling into his chair. "Your file said you have amnesia from your earlier years, from before...Bell Buckle. Is this true?"

I bite the inside of my cheek, hating that he knows of my life, of what I went through after he left, but I nod.

Mendoza holds my gaze for a moment, a blink of sadness washing over his features before it's gone, replaced by the mask of indifference, the one I wear all too often.

"I think I should begin a little further back," he says. "To when I first met...Isabelle, your mother." He pauses with a swallow. While saying the name obviously causes him pain, it does a brutal number on me to hear, slicing blades along my chest. Over and over.

My mother. My mother. *Isabelle.*

"Your grandfather," Mendoza continues, "my father, was the right-hand man to Vicente Rios, who ruled the Oculto before me, and as part of the upper-elite family, all children were sent to the United States to acquire their college education. Vincente believed education was the key to setting our family apart from the rest, which might have been the *only* thing he and I agreed on." A darkness looms in his voice before he goes on. "I got in to Vanderbilt University and met your mother. It was only the first semester, but I instantly knew. She was so alive, so filled with good and happiness, that I became spellbound. She was like nothing I had ever known could exist." His gaze grows unfocused for a moment, and my throat tightens to hear a memory of a woman whose face I can hardly recall. "Once I saw the other life I could have, with Isabelle, I wanted out of my family and their business. I didn't want her anywhere near that sinful, deprived side of my life, but my father wasn't having it. Once I graduated, I was to come straight back, or my *brothers* would come get me and drag me home. I was a Mendoza, cousin to the Oculto royalty, and we did what we were told. We honored our title, our heritage. I was going to end things with your mother, for it was the only way to keep her from it, but then we found out she was pregnant, with you."

His cerulean gaze bores into mine, and what was once icy cold is now warm, and I want to shout at him to turn away, to not look at me like that, for he has no reason to show me any kindness, nor I him. We might be kin, but we will never be family.

"Once you were born, I became even more desperate to keep

you and her a secret," he continues. "For you quickly showed signs of your...abilities, and we in Mexico knew of your kind, *Los Portafuegos*."

The Fire Holders.

"Others had been born in our village in the decades previous, and all had been dealt with the same." His gaze grows dark. "They were killed."

My muscles stiffen as I steal a glance at Ramie, who stands expressionless, leaning against a bookshelf, staring at a nondescript point in the room. The small scars along his neck and jaw shimmer against his energy. *What led him to be spared?*

"Because of the family's fear of being overrun, overpowered, the Oculto exterminated any sign of a threat as quickly as they saw it coming, and *Los Portafuegos* might have been the only thing Vincente had ever feared. So while I visited home between semesters, keeping up appearances, I never once mentioned Isabelle, never you, and I never told your mother about my other side. You were each my untouched angels, and I would do everything in my powers to keep it that way."

"But you didn't." It slips from my lips, hard and unforgiving.

A haunted expression sits heavy under Mendoza's eyes. "But I didn't," he echoes. "Members of my family surprised me with a visit, saw Isabelle, you, and immediately knew. We tried to go into hiding, but with Isabelle finally finding out about what I was, a liar, a...monster, she ran, taking you with her. She had no idea that she was signing your death warrants by leaving my side, that even though she saw me as a beast, I was nothing compared to my family. You can't run from them. Even separated by a country, I couldn't." His fingers graze over one of pictures on his desk, bringing it closer. "It was raining the day they brought her body to me, threw it by my feet. Her hair, so beautifully red, looked gray against her pale skin, against all that blood. They told me the details as I sobbed over her, how she screamed while they slit her throat, told me how this was my doing, my payment for my betrayal. I had two choices now—my own death or to forget this fantasy life and come home. My Isabelle was dead, my child was dead, and I wasn't sure if I was grateful that they kept your body from me or not. I must have been, for it gave me the sliver of strength I needed to plan what I did next."

He places the frame back into its rightful place beside the other before turning to me. "I came home, showing my penance, my understanding, and became exactly who they wanted me to be. For months I sat behind a shadow of myself as I bid my time until the moment I could step out. And then finally"—his fists curl on his desk—"I killed Vicente Rios while my father watched and then slit his throat as he let them slit hers."

The office fills with silence, the record player having finished its final turn minutes ago, leaving the ticking of the grandfather clock the only echoing rhythm.

Red, red everywhere. I was born into it, so must I die.

The words turn a phrase in my head, devil children chatting as they spin in a circle.

There it is...my story. My past summed up in a few moments, a grouping of words, while I've spent years dreaming to remember and fighting nightmares to forget.

"And me?" I ask. "When did you know I was alive?"

"China." Steady blue eyes hold mine. "We knew of your possible existence then, but not until this DNA test were we for certain."

"China," I whisper, glancing to Ramie. "That was you who I

felt at that gala, watching."

A nod. "I was there for the auction, but I knew Manuel's story and your mother's face. When I saw you, smelled you... I didn't want to jump to any conclusions, but there are only so many female A pluses in the world, and your scent...so like his. Once we gathered a file on you, saw your true hair color and that you were found in Nashville around the same age—"

"It allowed us to hope," Mendoza cuts in.

Hope.

What a silly human invention to rest faith on.

"But you tried to kill me in the jungle."

There's no doubt it was them now.

"If you paid attention, you'd have noticed none of my men were shooting at you, just that little partner of yours. They had tranquilizers for you."

"But...the bomb?"

Mendoza waves his hand. "Insurance. If we couldn't bring you in on our terms, I wasn't about to let you find us through my men. We weren't going to let it go off until you were a safe distance away, but as you know...some things can't be planned. How were we to know you'd end up activating the backup trigger?"

A chime fills the room, our spell broken as the clock in the corner counts to ten. Almost an hour has past.

"Ah," Mendoza says, checking his own watch before standing. "As they say, where has the time gone?" Rounding his desk, his mountainous form grows near, and I find myself leaning away, the familiar energy coming off him even more suffocating this close. "This has gone better than expected, don't you agree?"

I don't answer, merely blink, at a loss for how to respond, how to process any of this. As if he understands my plight, Mendoza gives me what must be one of his rare smiles, changing his face so completely from devil to friend, sending a dozen quick memories flashing behind my eyelids, a dam set free. *The same smile waking me up in the morning, lifting me into a swing, nuzzled into a woman's neck.*

"You have no idea what joy it gives me to see you here," he says softly. "My daughter."

My lips wobble, from rage or sadness or both I'm not certain, but I manage to hold back the tears I feel pressing against my eyes.

"We have much to learn of one another," he goes on. "Much to plan, but that must wait until next time, for I have a few things that need to be seen to."

"Like your biochemical weapon?" I force through clenched teeth.

His smile doesn't even waver. "I will see you soon, *mi pequeña rosa,*" he says, and with the back of his finger, lays a gentle graze to my cheek, stopping my heart—what's left of it—before walking from the room.

Leaving me feeling just as broken as when he left me the first time.

"You're letting me go?" I ask Ramie as he pulls out a syringe kit, picking up the metal tang of the liquid chloroform.

"We're letting you go." He prowls toward me.

"But why?" I frown. "I can tell them about you, about meeting Mendoza."

"But you won't."

I scoff. "And why the hell not?"

"Because"—he leans down, grabbing my chin, a lover asking for a kiss—"you'd have to tell them how you came to us and why you didn't kill Manuel on the spot. How do you think your bosses would take the news that one of their operatives is the daughter of the drug lord they have been targeting? We have the DNA results to prove it now, easily shared with a mere press of a button."

As his words sink in, I hiss and pull from his grip.

He stands, a pleased grin stretching across his beautiful features, a Dorian Gray blocking his wickedly deformed portrait. "Are you really on their side?" he asks, shooting a bit of the chloroform from the needle's tip, the liquid splashing the carpet. "Or have you been a double agent this whole time? You've had a surprising loss of leads, no? Is it because of your purposeful misdirection?" Deep-brown eyes peer down, a child winning a game. "So many questions," he croons, "yet only one true answer—you're a liability now, and we all know what happens to those."

My skin is washed in a cold chill, taking this in, the reality of it.

"They're terminated," he finishes.

Before I get the chance to respond, to ask how he benefits from all this, he pricks the needle into my neck, and for the second time tonight, my world is blanketed in nothingness, the shadow of calm before the category-five hurricane.

I awake, alone, in the same dark alley back in Cuetzalan. From the sliver of stars peeking through the two buildings, I know it's almost midnight, and my head aches from the chloroform still swimming in my veins, my arms sore from where the binds dug in. Sitting up with a grunt, I wonder for a moment if it was all a dream, half of me wishing it was, the other half...of a different mind. But as I stand, a sound of something crinkling in my jeans pocket has me reaching in and removing a glossy photo.

Peering down, my heart races in what seems like its new rhythm, for the blue eyes that regarded me from behind his desk, that spun me a story, my history, my fate, stare out at me again. But this time they're accompanied by two other pairs, one green, another blue. My father, my mother, and a redheaded little girl sit together on a bench under the Tennessee sun.

Looking straight at me.

Smiling.

CHAPTER 46

Carter
Cuetzalan, Mexico: 2215 hours

I gave her until midnight to come home, but now that it's fifteen past, I have no choice but to hunt her down. And I am *less* than pleased by this. I just got to the steamy part in the book Señora Flores gave me.

I mean, how selfish can 3 be? Not answering any of my calls. At first I thought it was because she saw my name on her caller ID, which I'm sure she renamed to *Asshat* or *Tiny Pecker*, but when she didn't pick up for Jules or Akoni either is when my temper really hit the ceiling. Especially when I checked her phone's GPS tracker and saw she switched it off. I get her need to be alone. I haven't exactly been doing jumping jacks of joy from being around the same group of humans day in and day out either.

She above all knows we have a job to do though. She's re-minded me enough times, for Christ's sake. Doesn't she under-stand she can't go strolling for hours on end without checking in? Maybe she's throwing my "enjoy yourself" lecture in my face. It *would* be something she'd do. Especially after...everything. But still, she understands we need to get up early to head back into the jungle, that we have things we still need to discuss. And no, not *that* thing, not the thing that managed to pull something deep within my heart forward, that left me a terrified, confused mess and whose memory still sets my very *not*-tiny pecker to stand at attention while setting my blood to steam.

That *thing*, I'm sure, will never be mentioned because Lord knows 3 is the last person who would ever confront something with words. Why talk when you have superhuman fists to punch it away?

Tugging on my boots with a curse, I continue to grumble as I pull my arms through my leather jacket and head for the door to our room. But just as I'm about to wrench it open, it swings forward on its own, and 3 practically stumbles inside.

I reach out to steady her, my heart in my throat, worried she's hurt, until I see the bottle of tequila in her hand, as well as the bag that holds two more. For once the smell of her doesn't send flames of desire across my skin. She wreaks of a bar's floor, and a very different sort of heat engulfs me.

Mangled metal around a tree, one body thrown through the windshield, another strapped in and covered in blood. Dead.

I blink the pictures from my mind, shaking away a shiver.

"You're wasted." I all but growl, letting go of her, more than okay watching her knock into tables and chairs as she kicks off her boots.

"And you're not," she says, turning dramatically and shoving the bottle into my chest. "Have a drink, hubby. The night's young."

With a scowl, I push the tequila away, and she shrugs before taking a swig herself.

"Where have you been?" I demand. "I've been calling you for hours."

"Walking, remember?"

My hands fist at my side. "Yes, but *where*?"

"You wouldn't believe me if I told you," she slurs, lurching her way into the bathroom and quickly emerging with a glass from the sink. She throws the bag of bottles and herself onto the bed.

"Why don't you try me," I say, stepping over to her. Even pissed out of her gourd, 3's still able to pour herself a drink without spilling a drop.

She takes a hearty gulp before leaning forward, blue eyes glazed as she looks my way. "I've been with the devil," she whispers.

I narrow my gaze as she sits back, fumbling to open another bottle. Her vibrant hair is pulled into a messy bun, her black leather jacket, matching mine, over a tight gray T-shirt and jeans. She might be dressed like her usual self, but she's anything but. She's ruffled, wrinkled, and I wonder how long she's been in her cups.

"What's happened?"

She doesn't respond, merely stops what she's doing to shove out of her jacket before yelling "Aha!" as she finally gets the cork of the tequila to come loose with a *pop*. "I shattered two of these buggers trying to get them open earlier."

"3." I take the bottle from her hands. "Stop this."

"Hey! That's mine."

"Not anymore." I stomp to the bathroom and begin draining it down the toilet.

"What are you doing!" she shrieks, running in and trying to snatch it back. But while she might be stronger, I'm taller, and I hold it out of her reach, pushing against her claws and elbows until the last drop falls.

"You asshole!" she whines. "You owe me forty pesos."

"*I owe you* nothing." Stepping around her, I go for the next bottle.

"No!" She pounces like a bat out of hell, knocking me onto the bed and sending the liquor shattering against the wall. We both watch as the clear liquid slides down the surface, mixing with the glass shards spilled across the floor.

"*I'm going to kill you.*" 3 hisses as she lunges for my throat, and maybe the only good thing about her intoxication is that while she still has strength, it's not as lasting, and I easily pry her hands loose, rolling her below me.

"You still have half a bottle," I grunt, my chest pressing firmly against hers. "*That* I'll let you drink, since you seem so determined to drown yourself in this poison."

"Oh, you'll *let* me, will you?" She lowers her voice mockingly. "You're not my *father*, Carter. *No one is*! I can do whatever I want."

I frown, searching her face, her delicate features set in such scorn. We're close, as close as we were so many nights ago, and like a magnet pulling, always pulling, I move an inch farther. Her lips are right there, parted, panting, wanting. Something in her energy, a lick of a flame, telling me that she'd let me if I tried.

But then the sweetness of her breath, the liquor so obviously coating her resolve to languid, floats forward, and I grip the sheets on either side of her head before pushing myself up.

Not like this.

Muttering a curse, I sit on the edge of the bed, running a hand through my hair. She remains lying there, staring up at the bed's canopy. "What's happened, 3? You're acting crazy, and not your normal crazy."

"Nashville."

"What?"

"Nashville," she repeats. "I'm Nashville right now."

I don't say anything, just...wait.

"Do you remember your first kill?" She twists her head to look at me.

I draw my brows together, caught off guard by her random question.

"I do," she says. "It was a dog."

"Nashville—"

"It was before they found me." She turns her gaze back to the drape of cloth above. "So I was probably around four of five. I've never been too sure of my age." She shrugs. "And while I don't remember much before Bell Buckle, I remember that alley." Her hand moves to play with strands of her hair, pulling it free from its bun to fan around her head. "I shouldn't have been able to do it," she goes on. "Kill that dog. Any other child would have been easily taken by it, its canines straight to their throat. But not me. I was *special*," she says with a slight sneer. "It found me there, in the place I refused to move from, looking just as starved as I was, just as desperate. And I think a part of my little child brain understood this and didn't hate the animal for it. We were

merely two forgotten creatures trying to survive in this world.
So when it ran for me, I made sure to make it quick, breaking its
neck. I was terrified of course, not really understanding what I
was doing, why I knew where to place my hands, how to dodge
its bite as I twisted, but I did. It yipped once. Only once. A short
high-pitched sound. The real fear that was behind all that rage. It
rang in my ears for hours and eventually forced me to leave that
alley. I couldn't stay there anymore, not with that dog's corpse,
its whine continuing to echo across those brick walls."

Her blue eyes collide with mine, and I know she can hear my
quickly beating heart, but for once I don't care.

"I was found an hour later," she continues. "It turned out I
was only a few blocks from a police station and had no idea. Killing that dog...it ended up saving my life, twice."

Silence floods the space where we sit, my chest aching for
the young girl Nashville was then. Born with abilities she did not
understand and forced to test them too soon, too violently.

"Want to know the really messed-up part?" she says after a
moment more. "I remember the dirty gray coat of that mutt, its
hazel eyes and the way its wiry hair felt between my fingers, but I
can't remember anything about my first human kill. I can't even
recall if it was a man or a woman."

I look down at the hands in my lap, the rough callouses
marking my history, my sins. How much death we've both tangled with.

A memory for a memory, I think.

"Mine was a man." My voice comes out scratchy, heavy.
"An Iraqi soldier ended with one snipe through my scope to his
head." Curling my fingers into a fist, I look up, staring at a watercolor hung on the wall directly in front of me, flowers growing

on a hillside. "It was so goddamn hot that day. And I mean balls sticking to skin, suffocating. But in that moment, after pulling the trigger, all I remember is feeling cold. Like a layer of ice enveloped me, freezing whatever aftershock normally follows. I was told it was normal. That it was the mind and body trying to protect itself from such an unnatural act." I hold my gaze to the painting so long it starts to blur, its meaning lost. "At the time I hated it. I thought my penance should at least be to feel remorse for what I did. But I never did. Never felt the guilt. And later... when my brother was killed and then my parents, my father driving drunk with grief, I was glad for it. That coating of numbness. It was easy to call back then. To let it permanently fix to my heart. My special ice barrier to the world," I say with a scoff, shaking my head. "I thought, if life liked to play such violent games, why shouldn't we build a shield from it?"

Only the sound of two people breathing fills the hotel room, the soft breeze from the open balcony fluttering in the cool mountain air as my words fade away.

Words that I held in for so long, let twist in my gut, my atonement.

Now free.

Because of her.

"That's why you don't drink." It's not a question.

I glance to Nashville, finding her steady cerulean gaze pinned to me. "That's why I don't drink."

Slowly her arm tracks across the bed, stopping palm up, by my side. I look down at it, the way the delicate pale skin matches the white sheets, and a painful knot works up my throat before I rest my hand in hers, our fingers curling together. Strong to thin, cool to warm.

"Aren't we the pair?" she says.

Pair. Not separated like usual, but together, just this once.

"Aren't we," I echo and, after holding each other's stares for a moment longer, slide to lie beside her. She follows every one of my movements as our connected limbs come to rest between us.

"Will you tell me?" It's the gentlest I've ever spoken to her, and though it's a vague question, I know she understands what I'm asking. Her eyes peer into mine, so sky blue, bright, and at odds with the soul I know she thinks is black inside. If only she knew I now believed it to be gold.

"You know," she says, her forehead creasing. "I think...I think I would. If I were able."

"And why aren't you?"

"Because"—her other hand comes up to brush back some of my hair, and my heart stutters, such a soft touch from a woman forged from stone. "You'd probably have to kill me."

I snort a laugh, about to tell her she's reached a new level in dramatics, when I find her eyes have closed, her breathing growing shallow as her hand falls to my neck. Asleep.

Just like that.

I glance to the almost empty bottle that's tucked into her chest and, moving it away, return my attention to her, our hands still clasped. Thick lashes fan against her flush cheeks, the red of her hair a sunset of colors under the low lighting of our room, spilling above and around her like she's floating in water. I take a piece, playing with the soft end, knowing I most likely will never get a moment like this again, before sitting up and tucking her into bed.

Standing, I look down at her, a protective shadow, and then because I must, I lay a kiss to the top of her forehead.

Seeing her walk in tonight, drunk, volatile, and...so open, I would never have guessed this is how our night would have ended. But with her, I should know better than to try to predict such things.

With a sigh, I run a hand through my hair and take a step back, allowing myself another moment to study Nashville's sleeping form, her rare moment of peace, before preparing myself to do something I hope I won't regret later.

I search for her shoes.

CHAPTER 47

Nashville

She walks back and forth in front of me, her blue dress fluttering by her ankles, and I giggle as I try to snag it from my spot on the floor. She clicks her tongue in fake disapproval, the edge of a smile present as she goes from the kitchen to our small dining table, setting down plates. The warm smell of biscuits and eggs heats our home, the tang of orange juice, and I decide this is my favorite time of day—morning. For she looks her best in this light, my mother.

No longer is she blurred, blown out, but crystal clear in focus, and I hungrily study her every inch. Green eyes, red wild hair, and a speckling of freckles cover her face, as if an angel stood in front of her and blew stardust from his palm.

She's everything I want to be.

We are alone in this moment, she and I, but I feel the en-

ergy of his return, and I bounce in excitement, crawling to the door just as it opens. A dark, strong man stands in the frame. He smells of earth, sunshine—my papa. His blue eyes crinkle with his wide smile. "Mi pequeña rosa," he coos as he scoops me into his arms. "Te he extrañado." I've missed you.

I hold my tiny hands to his cheeks, feeling the fibers of his beard, and he turns his head to nibble on my fingers. Laughing, I pull them away, but his affections don't stop. He kisses and buries his face into mine until my belly hurts from my giggles. My papa is silly. My papa is home.

My papa is Manuel Mendoza, but that name means nothing but happiness to me here, in my dreams.

My head aches something fierce as I squint from behind my sunglasses, the crisp early mountain air a small remedy for my stupidity last night. I'm not one to do things with half measure, and my hangovers don't either. I knew I'd suffer today, but that's exactly what I was looking for. I needed my body to match my mind for once, needed it to hate itself. So while I'm in pain, I'm not pissed about it.

The memories of being with Carter last night, however, the things I did, said, and enjoyed feeling...

My left hand flutters at my side, trying to shake away the phantom sensation of his strong fingers entwined with mine, the comfort in it.

"What have you bought me so far?" Ceci answers on the second ring as I hold my phone to my ear.

"How'd you know it was me?" I ask with a frown, watching

Carter walk into a small café across the square to get us some breakfast. We're about to set out for the jungle, to take Jules and Akoni back to the lake where we found the drugs, and I took this rare moment of solitude to phone her.

"You're the only person that calls me from an unlisted number," Ceci says. "At this point, it's hardly a mystery. The phone people might as well rename it Nashville."

For the first time in what feels like an eternity, I sense a genuine smile forming. "How's life?"

"Aw, you actually remembered to ask about me for once."

"It appears people can change."

"Well, look at that. The world *does* have hope."

Hope.

"I'm good," Ceci goes on. "I got promoted to head waiter. Got a raise and everything."

"Ceci, that's great."

"Yeah." She sighs. "Now I just need to decide which Rolls I want."

"The black one," I say. "With tan leather interior. Always go classic before you go eclectic."

"Mmm, sound advice."

"Thanks."

"So what's going on with you? Is the job almost over? Will I get to see your pretty little face soon?"

"Hopefully." An older gentleman passes by, pulling a cart full of coffee bags with *Viento del Este Plantación* stamped across them. "Listen, Ceci. I need you to do something for me."

"Will you pay me in a beautiful Mexican tapestry?"

"Sure."

"Then of course, what can I do you for?"

"I need you to search the name Isabelle in the Vanderbilt University database. Make a list of all of the ones that attended between 1985 and 1995."

Normally I'd ask Akoni for something like this, but...

"Okay..." I hear her tearing off a piece of paper and scribbling something down. "Can I ask why you want me to do this?"

The answer hits against the front of my mouth, wanting to escape, and I stand there, staring out at the slowly rising sun creeping along the terra-cotta roofs. A new day.

"I think...I think I might have found my mother."

It's like a pound of flesh has fallen around my feet from the admission, a snake shedding. Truth, something I rarely indulge in and yet have recently done with more than just my oldest friend. My eyes travel back to the store where Carter slipped into, and there's a beat of silence before—

"Oh my God!" Ceci shrieks, and I wince away from my cell. "Nashville, are you *serious*? You should've started with that! *How*?"

Just then my K-Op partner emerges from the café, a small bag and holder of coffee in hand. He flashes a handsome grin as he finds me still waiting, and begins to make his way over, his tall form sporting a light-gray zippy over jeans, and sneakers. He has yet to wear something that doesn't flatter him.

"I can't get into the details right now," I say. "But I promise I will soon. When...I'm home."

"But—"

"I have to go." I watch Carter getting closer. "When you find it, email it to yourself."

"Well, thanks for letting me know I need a harder password."

"*Ceci*," I say quickly as Carter's brows crinkle, seeing me on the phone.

"Yes, yes, of course I'll do it."

"Thank you."

"Man, this is...just..."

"I know, but I really have to go. I'll call you later."

"Okay. Love you, Nash."

"You too." And with a swipe, I hang up just as Carter reaches my side.

"Who were you talking to?" He hands me my coffee

"Ceci," I say.

No use lying any more than I'm about to.

CHAPTER 48

3

Thirty minutes outside Cuetzalan, Mexico: 0720 hours

I'm an adaptable creature. If I were to be thrown into below-zero temperatures, it would take my body less than five minutes to equalize itself, self-heat so the threat of freezing was never a possibility. If I were dropped into the Sahara Desert at high noon, my body, as pale as it is, would secrete a coating of carbon-based sweat that would absorb UV rays so my skin wouldn't burn. I know this because SI6 tested it. I'm an anomaly, all A+ are.

So while the shock and devastation of my father existing and then turning out to be the leader of the Oculto most assuredly did a number on my mind and body, taking me out of my abilities for a good twenty-four hours, I've been able to recollect myself with unsurprising speed. A characteristic that has thankfully allowed me to smoothly return to playing my part as the K-Op who first came to Mexico, who has always existed.

In the days that follow my meeting with Mendoza, I have traveled with my team to the lake, searching the area again with just as much interest as Carter. I have scouted other locales in the mountains with Akoni and Jules, even suggested driving around the land between Viento del Este and Cuetzalan in the chance we overlooked a detail, all the while keeping eyes peeled for something else, something specific, something that I eventually find on the third day.

With the excuse that I was going for a run, I left Carter in our hotel early this morning to make my way here, to a sprawling field covered in three-feet-tall flowers, their orange, red, and yellow petals dancing softly in the breeze. They are called cosmos, a native flower to Mexico that favor meadowlands. They also have a singular distinct scent—vanilla. Since Cuetzalan and the surrounding territory is mainly a mountainous range, there were only so many meadowlands with this particular flora. Ramie and Mendoza might have knocked me out to bring me to and from their little hovel, but they underestimated my abilities. The aroma that clung to my clothes while I sat in that underground room surrounds me now, and it happens to only be thirty miles out, smack in the middle between Cuetzalan and Viento del Este.

Those sneaky bastards.

With the sun a yellow yawn in the sky, parting the drapes of clouds that float past, I peer across the multicolored field, the buzzing of insects in the grass flooding my ears. This meadowland is southeast from town, hidden behind a tangle of dense trees, and if there really is a bunker here, it must be deeper in, for despite the small road I took here, I see no evidence of tire marks pointing to anyone driving farther out.

Stepping forward away from my car that I "borrowed" from a local villager, I move through the tall stalks, brushing my hand over the soft buds. A foreign sensation of guilt twists in my gut for being here without Carter, without my team, but as adaptable as my body may be, my will is a different beast. And years of doing things alone, separate, is a marble habit hard to break. Plus, despite recent behavior, sharing has never been my strong suit. Especially when telling the truth would lead to my ultimate demise. *Double agent indeed.* Even though a quiet, newer part of me whispers that out of anyone, Carter would understand, would dismiss in a minute this notion Ramie fed me. Akoni too couldn't possibly question where my loyalties lie, not after everything, not after Santiago...but still, I know the brutal business I'm in. How at the end of the day, we're all just numbers to SI6, to COA. Despite how spotless an operative's record, we are merely tools to wield, and when made dull, proficiencies questioned, we're simply replaced—quietly. My greater instincts to survive won't allow this, won't risk it, which is why I find myself here, now, alone.

I have questions I need answered. Things to double-check, lies to craft before I can share the safer parts of this with anyone.

Cresting a small hill, I plunge farther into the thick mess of petals and bugs, happy to be wearing my durable work-out clothes. Studying the surrounding area, I search for a spec of something amiss, but there's nothing but quiet trees in the distance and an empty field. You'd almost believe that humans have yet to touch this land, a sin-free spot in the world.

Yet I can smell it, something...industrial, metal sitting among all this nature. A hum of electricity, of activity directly below me.

But where's the entrance?

Snapping a flower free, I twirl the stalk between my fingers, telling myself that once I find a door, a small shred of proof that this is indeed where the underground facility lies, I'll head straight back to town, make up some excuse for my team to visit, later, together. It's the only way of turning this arou—

A churning of gears and a deep rumble has my head whipping to the left as a slope of land shifts nearby. I crouch below the flowers' tops, the knives strapped to me digging into my spine and thighs as I watch a section lift up. Like a plane's wing, it tears from the ground, rising on an angle, a greater-than symbol, a hiss of air releasing as it comes to a stop. Peering around, I glance back to the now risen plot of dirt, fingers curling into the soil by my feet as I take it all in. The wildflowers on top of the opening sway in the breeze, Mother Nature's camouflage, as a short passageway is revealed in the mouth's opening, a wide titanium door at the back. It's large enough to fit a tractor-trailer, and a second later the ground in front shudders and splits down the middle, the flowers shaking as they retract to either side, gathering together like an accordion to uncover a tar road underneath. It goes into the forest trees in the distance for a good one hundred yards. My heart pounds. That's why I couldn't see any car marks. They are covered up.

Such technology, such precaution. The Oculto couldn't live up to their name anymore.

I peer behind me, back to my little brown car in the distance, wondering if I could run to it fast enough without being seen, but then the scent of copper, of another like me, hits me from the side.

Ramie.

Turning back to the newly revealed bunker, I watch as the

metal doors at the base huff and then open a fraction, letting a tall, well-dressed man in a finely tailored black suit step through.

He walks up and out, his confident footsteps treading softly on the smooth road, and stops where the canopy of the parted ground ends. With one hand, he shields his eyes from the sun that swaths across his tan skin and gazes around. He sniffs the air once, twice. There's a quick patter of his annoyingly calm heart, before a pleased energy floats to me, and his head slowly turns in my direction. I remain crouched, hidden behind the flowers, a lioness in the grass, but I know I might as well be standing right in front of him.

Ramie remains there for a full minute, staring, before a grin presses into the corner of his mouth, and without a word, he turns, stepping back into the slip of dark between the bunker's doors.

As he disappears, the opening remains, an invitation, and I take one last glance to my car, my lifeline now so far away, as the decision that will push me one way or another flaps like a flag in the breeze. With lips set in a hard line, I stand to my full height and, like so many times before, let the black spot remain my focal point as I walk forward.

CHAPTER 49

Carter
Thirty minutes outside Cuetzalan, Mexico: 0815 hours

The car is empty as I drive up beside it, coming to a stop. It's a brown beat-up little Chevrolet Corsa, and I understand why she grabbed it. It's an unassuming lemon, so broken down your eye hardly registers its scrap of metal before moving on to something else.

Glancing out my windshield to the far-stretching meadow in front of me, the orange and yellow wildflowers bowing and arching with the breeze, I search for a red that's more vibrant than the rest, but there's nothing. Only the surrounding ring of green forest in the distance and the thin, dusty trail behind me that returns me to the road in the mountains from which I came.

Looking down at the tracker in my hand, I study the white dot on the screen as it pulses. She's here, right here, yet I can't see her.

I didn't want to be right, didn't want for my instincts that told me to put those tracker pins into her shoes to prove worthy, not after what was said, shared.

She and I...it felt like we'd finally broken through to something, something new that could be healing rather than the usual destruction we've wielded for too long. Despite her drinking, I knew she was lucid enough to remember everything—saw it in her eyes the following morning. The quick blush to her cheeks. It had me hoping that perhaps we could actually start working together without fighting first.

But after she told me she was going for a run, and then seeing that she turned off her phone's GPS—again, my stomach plummeted.

I waited a good ten minutes, still stuck in my naive denial, before switching on my planted trackers to find her heading away from town at a quick pace. Too fast for her to run unless she was in distress or chasing something or in a car.

Sprinting down to find our own vehicle parked, untouched, and in its usual spot, I didn't hesitate to climb in and follow. I had no idea if she was alone, but while this didn't feel right, it didn't feel like she was in trouble either. I know Nashville is more than capable of taking care of herself, and that might be the problem. This had lying, hiding, written all over it. Especially after her out-of-character behavior with the tequila. She wouldn't do such a thing without good reason. She looked spooked, shaken, and what could cause such a reaction from her is what had my grip tightening on the wheel as I drove.

I kept a good distance away, not wanting for her, or them, to sense me, sense anyone chasing. Which is what has me sitting here still, trapped in my car, unable to get out and search further for fear my scent will stick to this spot for her to pick up later. My tire tracks will be spotted, but at least she won't know who drove past when she returns. And I know she'll return.

What are you doing, Nashville?

Though she seemed her usual quick-tongued self this morning, she's proved time and time again how easily she can slip into her different personas. Who she really is, what she's really doing. I hate to admit I still don't know completely. Though a stupid part of me really, *really* wants to.

The Carter I was before I met her is a dimming ghost, being replaced by this new me, this man who *feels*. When this started happening, I can't say, but it's one hundred percent because of her. She shook me out of my stagnant bubble, punched me out of my mirage of being content with what I had. Which brings me here—worried. Actually fucking *worried* about someone besides myself.

That hasn't happened since...

"Goddammit." I punch the seat cushion beside me. It's taking all my strength to stay in this metal cage and not search the car beside me, the field in front, everything appearing calm, peaceful, while I feel anything but.

I should call Akoni and Jules, tell them what's going on, but something has me resisting, wanting *her* to explain first, tell the truth before I do something that will leave us more divided.

The old me is laughing in my face right now.

Who are you? he's sneering. *Why are you risking your record when she obviously doesn't care one sniveling snot about you? She wouldn't hesitate to call Ploom or Axel if the roles were reversed.*

He's right, of course. Why should I give her a chance? Why? Why? Why?

She saved my ass that night. Akoni's words from so many weeks ago come back to me now. *And as hard as it might be to believe, I think she'd save yours too.*

This is why. Because I believe this now. Truly.

Stupidly.

Even after she's obviously been lying to me about something. I have to believe it's for a good reason.

So after sitting for another ten minutes, the meadowland remaining empty and my anger subsiding to a simmer, a stand-by, I switch my car into reverse and head back to town. Every so often I glance to the white dot that stays blinking on my screen, unmoving, and hope to all that is holy that I'm not making a huge, job-ending mistake.

She'll come back, I find myself repeating in my mind. *She has to.*

And when she does, I'll be waiting.

CHAPTER 50

3

Thirty minutes outside Cuetzalan, Mexico: 0745 hours

It takes one and a half seconds for my vision to adjust to the dim lighting as I step through the bunker's doors. It takes ten seconds for me to be stripped of my knives by the four guards who greet me, each carrying MK 16s. Even the small set of syringes, hidden at the base of my neck, under my shirt's collar, are found and taken, Ramie more than thorough with his gifts to sniff things out, though he and I both know I don't need weapons to be deadly.

I keep my hands raised, posturing that I won't be causing trouble, while taking in the tunnel before me. White strips of light run down either side of the cement walls, leading to two black SUVs parked at the back by a large, metal-caged elevator.

"Yes, that's where we'll be going next," Ramie says, seeing where my attention drifts, his deep Spanish words floating around me in a whispered purr. "We weren't expecting your return so soon, but it's no matter. Manuel is pleased that you have come."

"He's happy that I know where he's been hiding?" I raise a brow in skepticism.

"You came alone," Ramie says, pulling a thick black band from his pocket. "Which makes him very happy. May I?" He holds out rubber handcuffs.

Because I know I won't be moving an inch if I don't, I allow him to suction the rubber material to my wrists, binding them together, and I give a testing tug. I'm unable to twist even a centimeter in them and instantly know these are made with the same material that bound me before. How SI6 has not yet come across this, I have no idea. Considering how immobile they render me, maybe it's better if they didn't.

My mind stutters at this last thought. *Whose side are you on?*

The guards circle us as Ramie guides me to the elevator. "I have to ask," he says, swiping a card he removes from his pocket before announcing "Level five." A green dot lights up above the doors, and we begin to ascend. "What led you here?"

I can feel his dark gaze on me as I watch the ground rush up between the mesh walls. *Level five.* So this facility runs deep, deeper than any of us had previously guessed, and this flooding of information sets my hands to fist. It's been a while since I've been around another A+, and I forgot how exhausting it is trying to control not only my outward appearance but my internal one as well.

"Vanilla," I say to Ramie's question. "The flowers, cosmos, in the field. They only grow in a few places around Cuetzalan."

His nostrils flare once, a gentle inhale, and I watch as the meaning of this clicks into place, the scent all over my clothes, all over his.

"And here I've worked so tirelessly to mask smells." His grin is a clever curve.

"You haven't today. Didn't in Mendoza's office."

His smile deepens. "It's not the best idea to smoke in this facility."

A simple sentence filled with all I need to know. His cigarettes, that pungent fragrance...are able to cloak him.

More surprises, more technology SI6 has yet to explore.

And all to do with A+ abilities...

"How?" I ask.

"How is anything with our kind accomplished?" He shrugs. "Science."

With a gentle shudder, the elevator slows and then stops, the cage doors sliding away, and with a hand to my back, Ramie guides me out.

My spine stiffens from his touch, and I step away, coming to stand on a balcony that wraps around a space two floors in height. Below an extensive lab is rolled out, equipped with a Clean Room in the middle and, as far as I can see, five employees in white lab coats. The air is fresh down here, oddly so given how deep underground we are, and I find eight large vents protruding from the ceiling. *If there are vents, there are air ducts, and if there are air ducts, there's a channel to the outside.*

My chest hums, taking in every detail, every support beam, light, object on the tables below, committing it all to memory as Ramie nods for us to keep moving.

Descending metal stairs to the ground floor, I'm not surprised to see who waits for us. I smelled him before I saw him, sensed his energy as soon as we stepped off the elevator. So when his blue eyes meet mine, a gentle smile on his lips, I'm able to keep my heart at its normal murmur, stop my skin from breaking out in a cold sweat as I study Manuel Mendoza studying me.

My father.

His beard is trimmed today, his dark hair with wisps of gray outlining his face. He's in a burgundy sweater with jeans and boots. And besides the vicious gash of a scar on his neck, he looks...kind, pleased to see me, and so like the father from my dreams that my throat dries to an ache at the thought.

But with one quick sweep of the room, this hidden facility, the armed guards, I remember that's all that they are, dreams.

"*Bienvenido,*" Mendoza says, *welcome*, as if I've come for tea and a tour. "When Ramie told me you were spotted above," he continues in Spanish, "I was not surprised. Leave it to my daughter to find her way home."

Daughter. Home.

Words carefully played, picked for whatever game he has begun.

"A home that keeps me tied up, it seems." I glance to my bound wrists.

"Ah." Mendoza nods. "A precaution Ramie seems set on, but now seeing you like this, it won't do. Ramie?"

My A+ brethren stands rigid, eyes sharp as he shakes his head no.

The two men have a silent standoff, Mendoza seeming to grow taller in this moment, bigger, consuming, a master with a demand, and with Ramie's teeth clamping down in silent frustration, he eventually concedes. Pulling out a small device that looks like a lighter, he zaps the rubber material, causing it to grow slack, and I slip my hands out.

I follow the special handcuffs as they are passed to another guard, who tucks them into his belt.

"Amazing, isn't it?" Mendoza says, stepping near, close enough that I could easily grab his head and smash his temple into the corner of the nearest table. His life ended, just like that.

But he seems to be aware of this, knows how easily I could kill him, and yet he removed my binds.

Why?

"Why are you being nice to me?"

"You are my daughter," he explains easily. "How else should you be treated?"

A pawn moving across a chessboard.

"Like the assassin that's been sent to kill you."

His bark of laughter causes me to stiffen, the sound odd but familiar. It echoes in the giant underground room, causing a few scientists to glance our way.

"You're very direct, aren't you? I like that." His attention rests steadily on mine. "If you were going to kill me, you would have done it already. Now come, my little assassin." His mouth twitches from suppressing a grin. "Walk with me."

My stomach twists at his words, more confusion dripping into my pool of uncertainty. He's right, of course…if he was any other man, I would have ended his life the second he entered my eyeline. But he's not, and I didn't.

My hands curl into fists at my side. I'm growing tired of things no longer having a clear path. I'm losing sight of my purpose here, who is meant to be standing in this bunker versus outside.

Swallowing down the uneasy bile that's crept its way up my throat, I follow Mendoza down the center aisle of the lab. Ramie is tight on my heels, no doubt sensing the constantly shifting mood of my energy, not trusting one of my steps from the next. And I don't blame him, for neither do I.

As we pass through the lab, I catalogue everything. The tables are covered with mostly standard equipment of microscopes, computers, vials, and freezer bins. From the few images lighting up screens and tablets, it all looks like gene mapping and DNA studies. A similar setup to the SI6 laboratory. Flicking my gaze to the rest of the space, I find eight metal doors set into the walls under the wrapping balcony, four on either side and each with a small glass window. As we walk by, I pick up the quiet thump of heartbeats in a few, and the hairs on the back of my neck stand on end. *Prisoners?* Taking in a titanium contraption at the end of our path, sized for a body, with the durable rubber straps, I retract that thought.

Human lab rats.

Suddenly everything up until this moment floods me—Ramie being able to cloak his A+ scent, the binds that held me, *specifically made for creatures like me.*

"You're studying my kind?" The question comes out loud in the cavernous space.

Mendoza's chest swells as he turns to face me, a sign of pride that has my lips pursing in displeasure. "Such a quick learner, you are. But we are doing a bit more than studying."

My gaze darts back to the closed doors, the humans locked inside, to Ramie.

"Still can't put it together?" Mendoza asks.

I stay silent.

"It's magnificent," he says. "Seeing you working through this. Your kind is endlessly fascinating. Not only stronger, but smarter. I saw it with Ramie, even so young when I found him. I saw it, which is why I forgave him this." Mendoza touches the ugly scar on his neck, the mutilated skin that twists against his otherwise smooth tan complexion. "I saw you glance at it earlier. Would you like to know what happened?"

Ramie stiffens, his energy shifting to discomfort.

"Ramie attacked you," I say, watching Mendoza's eyes spark, pleased.

"Very good, *mi pequeña rosa*. He did indeed."

A soft compassion fills Mendoza's blue gaze as he looks to the man standing behind me, and something strange and dark twists in my gut. A jealousy, but for what, I'm uncertain.

"Vincente had heard of a boy being born as a *Portafuego* but kept a secret for ten years by his parents. While their deaths were quick, their son was not found in their home, so a manhunt was set in play. I was lucky enough to come across Ramie first, hiding in an abandoned shed in our village. He thought I was there to kill him, so naturally fought me. Bit a good chunk away." Mendoza lightly touches his neck. "But I was able to calm him enough for him to stop, to convince him I was his friend and not there to harm. I wanted to protect him. Which I did. I hid him further in the jungle. Told him to keep quiet and wait for my return while I went to my father and Vincente, telling them I had killed *Los Portafuego*. I kept him a secret until the day I took over the Oculto."

"But how did you explain your wound?" I ask after a moment. "What body did you present Vincente?"

The Oculto would demand such proof.

"I gave them one," Mendoza says, eyes hardening at the memory.

My heart becomes stone. "You murdered an innocent boy."

"I killed for the greater good of our future, a life for a movement," Mendoza says evenly. "Is that not what you do?"

"I *do not* kill innocents or children," I bite out.

"Perhaps you don't," he says, "or perhaps you haven't been placed into a position where you must."

I glance behind me to Ramie, to his finely woven suit, his glossy black hair, the fugitive child made dark prince of the Oculto. No wonder he has such loyalty to Mendoza.

"What do you mean movement?" My eyes narrow back on Mendoza just as a fist smacks into a glass pane of one of the metal doors. We all turn toward it, a nearby scientists mumbling "Not again" in Spanish as she walks over.

"Carlos," Ramie whispers to his master. "He's been having more fits."

"Mmm," Mendoza grunts. "He needs some time in the yard."

"He's been allowed there a lot more than the others."

"Yes, but we are not all the same, are we?" Mendoza raises his brows. "They must be treated like the individuals they are."

I listen to all of this as I keep my eyes glued on the black hand now splayed across the pane, a dark face with a shaved head and light-brown eyes peering out. As he meets my gaze, he gnashes his canines, a wild creature, as a shimmering gold aura surrounds him.

Like a tidal wave, it hits me.

"You're creating A plus?" My voice is a rumble of a barely contained freak-out. "Are you mad?" I take a step closer to the cell that keeps Carlos, before four guards stand to block my path. I bare my teeth, just like the man they are imprisoning, but they merely hold their guns higher, fingers moving to triggers.

They are familiar with my kind and aren't intimidated. *First mistake.*

"Calm yourself, *mi rosa*," Mendoza says behind me while Ramie steps within striking distance. "Let's have your visit stay peaceful, yes? I'd hate to see you in those binds again."

I stand on the balls of my feet, weighing my options. I have a few things Ramie didn't take tucked into my outfit. I could easily remove these thick-headed soldiers in front of me, but then what? I'm deep underground with at least one A+ loose and who knows how many other guards around corners. What would be the result of acting now? Nothing to my benefit.

Shoving my hands into my pants pockets, as if in a silent huff of displeasure, I curl my fingers around the slip of plastic I need.

"I'm glad you can see reason," Mendoza says as I watch the scientist press a button on the side of Carlos's cell, a rush of smoke filtering into the room. The large man standing behind the door keeps his eyes locked on mine before they roll back in his head, and he collapses with a muffled *thud*, disappearing from view.

"Where have you stolen these people from?" I turn back to Mendoza, pulling my hands from my pockets and placing one on the edge of a nearby table, as if to steady myself.

"*Stole?*" His dark brows rise. "These are our guests. They have come willingly and signed their consent. Most were sick or dying, abused by this world. They understand the risks and what they are contributing to, what they are helping to create."

I shake my head, trying to block out his words. "You have no idea what you're messing with."

"I disagree." He indicates for us to walk on. "I've been work-ing on this for years. With the help of Ramie and these guests, I now know the genetic makeup of *Portafuegos* down to the last cell, the difference in your immune system versus mine, that your epidermis, dermis, and hypodermis each have an extra layer, making your skin three times stronger. I know it all, and understand tha—"

"I'm not talking about the science," I say. "Every government with an A+ operative or prisoner knows the science. I'm talking about actually *being* one of us." I level a glare on him. "You think I'm able to stand here, calmly, and not give in to my basic in-stinct to rip through every threat in this compound without using all my control not to? Control that has taken me years to hone, to acquire and suffer through. I've had two decades to learn how to break apart, separate, and subdue the noise in this world. Your heartbeat, his"—I nod to Ramie—"all these guards, the electricity flowing in the lights, the air pumping through vents. And don't get me started on the smells," I scoff. "It's enough to drive some-one mad, which is probably why most of us turn out that way. Do you have any idea the stress and shock you are throwing on these *guests* of yours? Our abilities will eat them alive before you see any progress. Why haven't you warned him of this?" I turn to Ramie with a scowl. "You must see the truth in what I'm saying."

"Of course," Ramie says, chin lifting. "And their rooms have all been acclimated to their different stages of onboarding, slowly introducing sounds and scents. They have been given a much better beginning than mostly all of our kind, than you or I."

"But this thinking and level of understanding is exactly why we need you." Mendoza stops at the beginning of a new hall.

Turning toward me, the silver in his hair winks under the fluorescent floodlights. "By working together, we can assure this is done to the best of our abilities."

I stand there, speechless for a moment, everything that I've just seen, heard, coming back to me in waves, ice-filled waves. This is *not* what I had thought I would find, not the weapon that was to be sold on the black market. "But..." I hear myself saying. "Why would you put this in the hands of criminals? Of countries to wage war?"

"Ah." Mendoza clasps his hands in front of himself. "I can see why you'd be concerned now. But don't worry. All this"—he gestures to the general facility—"Chenglei had no knowledge or dealings in. Like most advancements in science, it comes with a price tag, and drugs can only pay for so much."

He says it like I should find this funny, but nothing about this amuses me.

"We created a simple booster serum for soldiers based off of our research," he explains. "It advances abilities during combat but wears off after twenty-four hours."

"Like steroids?"

"Better than steroids and with no side effects, well besides a bit of jitteriness the next day and perhaps a bit of depression."

"I still don't understand...why do any of this to begin with?"

"Don't you see, *mi rosa*? If only I had your abilities the day my family came for me, for you and Isabelle. Had you been older and known what you were, we could have saved everything. We'd be together. *All* of us."

Three smiling faces under the Tennessee sun.

"I will *never* again let those take away what I hold dear. And now that you're alive..." He takes a step closer, and it's a testament to my strength that I don't step back. "*Mi pequeña rosa*, back from the dead..." He shakes his head, almost in wonder. "Let the world have their drugs and hopped-up soldiers, but we will be safe in our new family. We will protect what's ours and be able to live without fear. All Los Portafuegos will be welcome here. And once we have the numbers, enough to be left alone or have those that try to stop us suffer the consequences, we will break to the surface, and Los Portafuegos can finally live without governments stepping in to claim them as their own, to use as their little tools, to control."

"No, because you'll do that."

"Mi rosa." A frown puckers his brows. "I would never try to control you," he says, placing a large hand on my shoulder. Every cell jumps at the contact, the feel of his palm seeping into my clothes like flames. "Especially not when I have done all this so I can become one of you."

CHAPTER 51

Carter
Cuetzalan, Mexico: 1018 hours

She walks into our room and heads straight for the shower. I silently track her movements as I sit on the small couch tucked along the wall by the balcony. The water turns on, and I drum my fingers against the book in my lap. I've been pretending to read it for the past hour, and neither Consuela's nor Rodrigo's heavy petting were enough to distract me from this moment.

Wrapped in a towel, her skin still dewed with a few droplets of water from her shower and hair tied in a messy bun, Nashville steps from the bathroom, digging through her drawers for clothes.

"That was a long run," I say from my corner.

"I decided to go further than normal," she explains without turning around.

"Thirty minutes outside of town further?"

Her back stiffens, her hands slowing in their work.

I stand, readying for any number of reactions, thankful I removed the Glock 17 she stores in that top dresser. I know she can hear my quickly beating heart, the sound of my tense breathing, the pheromones I give off, and God knows what else in such a moment, but I don't give a damn.

Let her know I'm on to her, I think. *Let her panic.*

A dog's bark comes through the open window, the squeal of a child, and even though I can't see her face, I can sense Nashville's gaze darting to the balcony, the door, her fight or flight kicking in.

Too bad for her I know which one she's more prone to act upon, so with my muscles tensing, I shift to block her from running to either.

"Be very careful," I say, voice low, "with what you do next, Nashville."

"Don't call me—"

"*That's who I need right now*." I cut her off like a blade through the air. "Talk to me as her, like a *human*."

Her head turns, hot blue eyes finding mine over her bare shoulder.

"Don't make me regret giving you this chance."

"*Chance*?" She raises a mocking brow.

"Tell me where you were," I demand. "Or do I need to drag you back to that field for you to show me?"

The room becomes enveloped in shadow as I sense her taking in my words, the moment suspended, gravity lifting before it slams down.

"You *followed me*!" She spins around, gripping her towel.

"Fuck *yes* I followed you. You've been lying to me!"

Her lips pinch together as her eyes dart to her side of the bed.

"All your stashes are empty." My voice remains hard. "It's just you and me."

Her fingers twist into her towel more.

"Please," I say gentler, taking a step closer, which she compensates with a step back, bumping into the dresser. "I don't want to fight. Give me a reason not to. Tell me what's going on."

She presses her lips together as if two people are struggling inside her for control, fighting for what she should do next. Her toned arms stand rigid, her eyes growing wide, desperate. She looks like she's about to burst, but which way, I'm still uncertain.

"We're supposed to be a *team*." I'm trying to push her to my side. "We can't do this separately. It will take *both* of us, or have you forgotten how you reacted when I tried to go solo?"

She remains silent, and I let out a frustrated grunt, fists white knuckled at my side. "I swear to God, Nashville—don't make me regret not going directly to the agencies about this."

"You haven't told them?" she says, blinking back surprise.

"Of course not." I throw out a hand. "I want to *trust you*. Even though only Satan knows why, since you're making it damn near impossible!"

Her teeth work over her bottom lip, her brows furrowing in thought, and if I wasn't preparing for it, I'd have missed grabbing her as she dove for the picture on the wall, the one directly to her left with the watercolor of a flowered meadow.

Shit. I hadn't checked that one.

Getting a good grip on her, I spin her away, the frame flying out of her grasp to smash onto the tiled floor, the knife hidden behind it skidding across the ground. "*Really*?" I growl just as she elbows my arm, breaking my hold and skipping over the bed. I snatch her ankle and drag her back, her towel twisting against the bedsheet, exposing more skin. "You're really going to do this naked?"

She answers by trying to kick free, but I throw all my weight on her, pinning her below me as I grip the mattress. Her coconut bodywash surrounds me just as I feel her teeth cut into my shoulder. I curse and buck off. "*Fuck*," I seethe, dabbing a hand to the broken skin. She wipes a bit of my blood from her lips as she scoots away, a retreating animal.

We stand on either side of the bed now, me by the bathroom, her by the open balcony. Breathing heavy, she fixes her towel, tying it tighter around her chest as her long, toned legs stretch out of the bottom, the morning light filtering a halo around her red hair.

She's three feet from being able to escape. Naked or not, I know it doesn't matter to her, and I hate that I admire her for that. Admire her in the same moment she's shredding me, shattering what little faith I had left for any of this, for us.

"Go." I growl, whipping a hand toward the balcony behind her. "I won't try to stop you anymore. If you really want to sabotage thi—"

"My father." Her gasping the words cuts me off.

"What?"

"Manuel Mendoza...he's...he's my father."

The room tilts, and I actually have to grab the bedpost to steady myself.

"*What*?"

"But I didn't know he was," Nashville quickly goes on, barreling through my question. "I just found out, only four days ago, and I...I didn't know what to do. I knew how it looked. The man we were sent to find and kill ending up being my..." She can't seem to say the word again. "And us not making any progress. All those fucking dead ends, but it wasn't because of me. You have to believe me!" Her gaze is wild, desperate. So unlike her. "I wanted to tell you," she says, the words continuing to tumble, a criminal confessing. "I really did, but I just...I had too many questions. I needed more time, and if anyone found out, I'd be taken off the assignment...or worse." Her gaze drifts away for a moment before snapping back to mine. "I'm *not* a double agent, Carter. *I'm not.* You have to believe me. I had no idea—"

I hold up a hand for her to stop, the silence of the room filling my head with a low ringing as I piece the cut-up ramble she just spouted together.

The most important info to gather at the top.

"You found your father?" The question comes out unbelieving.

She blinks for a second, confused, before answering with a head nod.

"And it's *Manuel Mendoza*?"

A swallow before another nod.

"You're sure?"

"I was shown a DNA test that proved it."

A soft breeze filters into our room, the bed's sheer canopy stirring.

"Oh, Nashville," I breathe out. "I'm so sorry."

I'm not sure if it's the sad tone in which I say it, or if it's from the compassion she sees in my eyes, *or* if my words were the last thing she thought I'd say, but it all appears to finally be too much. For the woman who has stood unmoving in the face of death, strong when outnumbered, finally breaks, splinters before my eyes, and with hands covering her face, she bends forward and cries.

My heart drowns at the sight.

Without another thought, I stride to her side, pulling her into my chest. Her muscles tense for a second, unsure, before she gives in to yet another thing and lets me hold her.

And it's like every one of my nerves settles at the contact, calms, as I brush my fingers through her hair, down her smooth back, over and over again.

"You...you believe me?" She brushes away her tears with an annoyed swipe, and I have a feeling this show of vulnerability will be a one-time-only performance.

"Why on earth would you make this up?"

Her brows furrow. "Yes, but—"

"You're a good actress, but you're not *that* good or that masochistic."

She shakes her head, baffled. "Don't you want to know how I found out?"

I snort. "I want to know a lot more than that, and you'll certainly tell me, but what you just did...have been going through. Fuck." My grip tightens around her. "I'm so sorry. I can't even imagine...your father...Jesus." I'm less than eloquent in this moment, but who can blame me? "How are you really?"

She takes in a stuttering breath, her back muscles loosening under my fingers. "I'm tired," she says. "And...confused."

"Understandably so."

She presses her lips together. "I mean, can life be any more of a bitch?"

I can't help the small smile that forms as I pull her in closer, reveling in the fact that she lets me as the reality of what just transpired, what she just risked, sinks in further. "Thank you."

She leans back. "For what?"

"For telling me. I knew you were hiding something but had no idea it was something like this. No wonder getting it out of you damn near got us both killed," I say. "I would have bit me too," I finish with a grunt. "So while yes, we'll get to all the details of the hows, whys, and what's next soon, let's give ourselves a second, okay? Life may be a bitch, but she can afford us at least that much."

Nashville blinks up to me, blue eyes regarding me with slight wonder, even a bit of confusion, before she does another thing that takes me by complete surprise. Standing on tiptoes, she leans forward and kisses me.

My arms tense around her in shock, confused for a hairsbreadth, before my brain connects what's happening.

Nashville is kissing me.

On purpose.

And as her body presses deeper into mine, the heat of her skin through her thin towel seeps into my clothes, wrapping around my everything and slowly piecing together what was so quickly breaking, I let out a small moan and kiss her back.

CHAPTER 52

Nashville

My world is a wash of sensations, a spinning of colors behind my eyelids as my heart pounds against my rib cage. *Let me fly*, it demands. *Let me soar.*

And I let it.

I let us.

With strong hands sliding down to my thighs, Carter lifts me up to wrap my legs around his waist, carrying me the short distance to the bed.

I'm kissing Carter.

Carter is kissing me.

And I don't want either of us to stop. Not for a long, long time.

I've officially lost my mind, but for once I don't care. Let me lose it. Let it crash and burn around us.

It's been exhausting trying to hold myself together these past few days, and I need a break. Need to collapse and let go. Disappear into someone else, someone who isn't just another version of myself.

I need *him*, and perhaps he knows it, because with a gentleness I'm unused to, Carter lowers me to the cool sheets before draping his body over mine, not giving me a second to think, breathe, as his lips collide with mine, lick their way down my neck, fingers digging into my thighs to pull them around his back. He's all hard muscle and cinnamon, touches of desperation and desire, and I'm a similar greedy beast.

Since that night at Viento del Este and even before that, if I was being honest, I have wanted something, something I was unable to clearly see or admit to needing, afraid it would make me weak, at risk. But feeling the weight of this man on top of me, recalling the trust in his eyes at my words, to feel safe while being so vulnerable, was enough to let my walls weaken just a fraction and let him in.

I feel understood for the first time since meeting Ceci, and though it terrifies me, I can't stop grabbing handfuls of the sensation.

Carter has met me head for head every time, unafraid, and it's been stirring a fire in me that has nothing to do with anger but everything to do with respect.

With a growl, I flip Carter to lie beneath me, my legs straddling his waist. Nothing but his jeans separate him from me, my towel a mere curtain easily ripped to the side. His green eyes spark with a darkness gazing up at my body as he slowly removes his gray T-shirt, baring his toned chest and abs, his tan skin peppered with slashes of scars, and I run my hands over every one of them.

His muscles grow taut under my touch, and his fingers knead my thighs, an attempt to keep himself in control, to let me have my way, if only for a few seconds. But we wouldn't be us if there wasn't a constant give and take, a tug of dominance. And while I appreciate his discipline, I want none of it, so bringing one hand to the knot of my towel, I give a decisive tug and let the white material fall free.

"*Good Lord,*" Carter groans, taking me in.

My nipples tighten as a soft breeze whispers through the open balcony, an invisible finger trailing down my spine as I sit there, straddling him, until he's pulling himself up, wrapping his arms around my waist to kiss my breasts.

I throw my head back on a gasp, feeling his arousal, his teeth, his fingers on my back, and then lower.

With the sound of deep pleasure emanating from his throat, he spins me to lie under him, pinning my hands on either side of my head and grinding into me. He's in control, and I willingly accept this...for now.

He goes after my mouth again, and I pull my fingers free to dig into his thick hair, yanking a portion back so I can nip and bite his throat. We are animals, tumbling, claiming, and with a tug of his jeans, down and then off, we become pressed together, skin to skin. My senses lap in every hard inch of him, a crooning purr as I feel what's waiting for me.

Fumbling for his nightstand with one hand, Carter continues to lick and kiss, holding me in place beneath him. But when he pulls out a package of condoms, I can't help the bark of laughter that escapes me.

"Please tell me you didn't bring those for me."

He answers by shooting me a devilish grin. "We'll never know," he says before cutting off my next words with a kiss. A kiss that curls my toes, for it's a slow massage at midnight, a nap under the sun, and I decide I could do this for the rest of my life, before he rises above me again. Resting on his knees, his broad shoulders and rippling body stretches above, green eyes darkening to shaded moss as he peers down. He rolls on the condom, slowly, and I let out a pant.

The corner of his mouth curls at the side, taking me in, my apparent hunger, and he waits right at the edge, at the beginning until I let out a soft growl.

With the sound, his eyes dilate, a man becoming possessed, and I hold my breath as he slides in.

"Jesus," he groans, grasping my hips.

"No, Nashville," I say teasingly, before my eyes flutter back on a gasp as he thrusts in again. *Hard.*

"If you can make jokes right now," he breathes, teeth clenched, "I'm not doing a good enough job."

Pulling my legs to rest against his shoulders, his hand dips perfectly between them, and all my ability to speak is lost as he works me like the man he has flaunted for so many weeks to be. And my God, does he have reason. He plays me precisely, teasingly, skillfully, sending me spinning up until the minute I'll explode, before pulling back, only to do it over and over and over, a torture. Every inch of the room becomes ours to throw the other upon, the walls for him to press me against as he pumps into me, the stone floor for me to ride him into ecstasy, the posts on the bed for me to grasp as his muscles bulge under his movements, his abs to tense as my moans and his grunts fill the air for an endless ticking of time.

Even in our pleasure we compete, neither of us ready for this to end even in our race to get there quicker. I have no idea what will be on the other side once this is done. My brain won't think that far. It can only handle so much stimulation at once, can only allow Carter's intoxicating pheromones to coat my skin, to take in the beauty of his sweat dewing under my fingers and his gloriously concentrated expression as he hovers over me.

This man whom I had hated, despised the very moment I met him, is claiming every inch of me and I him. A shiver runs the length of me because I like it. I like him, more than I want to or probably should. We both seem to be thinking this, for our tornado only picks up speed, our fight for position above the other a constant twirl. It's a combat I've never played before, but with him I'll gladly do again and again.

Let's give ourselves a second, he'd said, and that's just want we do. We give ourselves many seconds, seconds that turn into hours. And it isn't until the sun turns a lazy orange, lowering in the sky, that I find myself on all fours on the bed, Carter behind me, hands and angles right where they need to be as we finally, violently, burst apart only to collapse as one.

His fingers trail a slow path down my arm as I lie tucked into him, his chest warm at my back, and I stare out at the darkened courtyard beyond our balcony. I just finished telling him everything, all of it, and my throat burns from the unnatural act of confiding in someone. But he didn't say a word as I went on, only listened, waited, until I squeezed out the last drop, a towel wrung through.

"We should probably check out of this hotel," Carter says after a moment. "If they know who you are, they know who we *all* are and where we've been staying."

"I thought about that, but if we leave, I think it would draw suspicion. They haven't indicated that they'd attack, nor have I felt anyone watching our hotel. I've been doing sweeps of our room for bugs, but it's been empty. Mendoza seems sincere in his hope that I'll join him and is giving me time to gather myself before making any moves. If we disappear now, it will only make him do the same."

"So we have to play the sitting duck?"

"Unfortunately. But I think that could be to our benefit."

"Mmm." Carter seems to agree, and I turn to find him looking up at our bed's canopy, his full lips and sharp jaw making up his gorgeous profile. *Yes*, I'm admitting that Carter is gorgeous.

"He's put a lot of faith in you," he says. "To keep his secret."

"He knows what I'm risking if I tell."

Green eyes slide to me. "Yes, I suppose he does."

The way he says it, with his gaze steady, makes me realize we aren't just talking about Mendoza.

For some reason this moment, with his fingers playing across my skin, his attention never wavering from mine, becomes more intimate than everything we just did, with lips and limbs locked together, and I shift under the sheets.

"No you don't." Carter brings me in closer just as my muscles tense. "Stop it, Nashville."

"I'm not doing anything."

"Yes you are. You're thinking about what we just did, what this means for us. Internally talking yourself onto a ledge of a freak-out, and I have no patience for that. Now or ever," he adds.

"Well, how are *you* not freaking out?"

"Because I'm obviously more mature than you."

I elbow him in the side, and he laughs through his *oof*.

"I'm being serious," I say.

"When are you ever not?"

"*Carter*."

"I love it when you say my name."

A frustrated growl leaves me as I push away, but he merely chuckles and pulls me back.

"Fine," he says. "You really want to know why I'm not sitting in a corner sucking my thumb right now?"

I nod.

"Because nothing in me is saying this is wrong."

I wait for him to elaborate.

"Listen. Everything we do, you and I, is with our gut, our instincts. I've let it guide me through the army, my brother's death, then my parents, and every assignment I've had. It's served me well with this job and even how to handle you."

"*Handle me?*"

"Like right now it's telling me that it's in my best interest not to answer that, but do something ridiculous instead like..." He lifts my arm and blows a raspberry against it, eliciting a farting sound.

"That's disgusting." I pull away with a scowl.

"Extremely," he agrees. "But back to my perfect instincts," he says, and I realize his odd distraction worked, my earlier flare of annoyance gone.

Shit.

"It's so far never led me astray. My interpretations of what it's trying to tell me might have been off at times, but that's my own fault. I've learned to trust it, listen to it, and while a part of me is definitely wondering how the hell I can be lying in bed with possibly the most dangerous person I've ever met and not have seven knives hidden under my pillow, I don't have any more stashed weapons because it's telling me I no longer need them."

"Are you sure?" I ask, twisting a serpent's grin onto my lips. "It does seem rather precarious of you."

"Aw, you're cute," he says and bops me on the nose with his

finger.

My eyes go wide. I've *never* been called cute, especially not when it comes to my threats. *Oh, this won't do.* But before I can make an example out of such behavior, Carter cuts me off.

"I've been running for a very long time from a lot of things," he says. "And I can't tell you that I no longer have issues about my past, because I do. I'm still terrified of...losing like that again. It's not an emotion that's going to go away overnight. Especially not in our line of work, but..." His gaze slides back to mine. "I've finally found something that has me wanting to risk it despite that. And my instincts"—he brings the back of my hand to his lips—"are telling me that's okay."

I swallow against the tightness that's formed in my throat, not knowing how to respond. I can feel myself understanding his words, even agreeing with them, but I have yet to find such a voice to utter similar sentiments. This *does* feel right, but in its rightness, it feels extremely wrong. I've never known such intimacy, don't know what comes next, and can't draw on my friendship with Ceci to break apart what's happening to me right now. This is so different. It's creating things in me that have never existed before. I can sense my cells testing Carter's and bending, remolding to allow him to fit beside me, a worthy ally. It's exciting just as it's terrifying. For so long I've been alone with this side of my life and have been okay with that. It was less messy, but now...picturing myself returning to my old ways feels colder somehow, *more* alone. How do I explain this to him when I've never been good with words, especially the emotional kind?

Meeting his gaze, I decide to answer him the only way I know best—physically.

Leaning forward I press my mouth to his, drawing him in

for a deep kiss, and he allows it, understands its purpose as he moves his lips with mine.

With fingers combing through his hair, I pull him more securely against me, and a deep rumble of pleasure sounds in his chest. *Take your time*, he seems to say. *All the time you need.* And I do. I keep us pressed together until he's above me and then between me, spreading my legs.

We're not as havocked this time, not as greedy, but we still demand the most from each other, always, as we ride another crest of pleasure, of him showing his dominance before I show mine. Two independent partners finally acting as one, and after we finish, just as out of breath and wrung dry as the first time, I rest my head back on my pillow.

Carter is right there with me, the soft yellow light of our bedside lamps cutting the planes of his angular features with a warm shadow. Though I've studied him many times, he looks different now, more...*him*, and I wonder if he feels the same about me.

Cuddling closer, yes, actually friggin' *cuddling*, I allow myself to breathe in the rare quiet of this moment, where the world seems to have paused just for him and me.

But like all things in my life, the darkness that waits like a predator beyond our door knocks, and everything about the Oculto, Mendoza's true plan, and our mission comes back in a dark wave.

"They can't know," I eventually find myself saying. "That he's my father."

"No," Carter agrees. "They can't."

"And the weapons, what Mendoza made for himself and the armies. We can't hand over either." My voice is firm. "That science...I don't care what Ploom and Axel think. It's not safe with anyone, not even our own government."

He doesn't answer right away, his gaze pinned to some nondescript spot on the bed's canopy, and I've never cared more about what someone will say than I do in this moment. I'm asking him to go against our orders, something that, if anyone finds out, would put a mark on both our heads. His answer could end us, right here, now, after so much, and yet before anything has really begun.

"No," he eventually says, his arms tightening. "It's not safe with anyone."

I let out a soft breath, a swell of a strange hope. "You'll keep this a secret, after it's all done?"

His face turns to mine, green eyes boring into my blue. "Beyond my death," he says, and I don't know how, but I can tell he means it. I'm not sure why either of us has found such shelter in the person each believed to have hated, but we have, and it has set a strange chain in motion.

So much to plan, take care of, and then there's my father...

"What am I going to do?" I play with a bit of sheet in my hands.

"I'm not sure," Carter answers, moving my fingers to lie still in his. "But we will figure it out."

Hooking an arm under my head, he brings me closer, and as I lie on his chest, his heart a steady rhythm in my ears, I replay the only word he spoke that truly matters.

That's all the difference.

We.

CHAPTER 53

Carter
Undisclosed location
Puebla City, Mexico: 1245 hours

Lying shouldn't be this easy, especially not when it's at the expense of your team that's worked so tirelessly beside you to get to this point. But it turns out it is.

Everything we do is built on lies anyway, right? What's a few more. Plus, what they don't know can't get us killed, or however that phrase goes.

Sitting in a windowless gray conference room in one of COA's outposts in Puebla City, a metropolis between Cuetzalan and Mexico City where our larger unit has been standing by, Nashville and I finish sharing our well-crafted story to Akoni, Jules, and two large TV screens that frame David Axel's and Anthony Ploom's heads. In the span of an hour, the two of us recount finding Manuel Mendoza's hideout on a side drive we took searching the land south of Viento del Este. Learning soon after, through various torture methods placed on one of his scientists that we snagged on their shift change, that the biochemical weapon is a serum that temporarily creates superhuman soldiers. We made sure, of course, to leave out such tediously boring things like how Mendoza turned out to be Nashville's long-lost father and his bigger threat of creating an effective DNA mutation method that allows regular humans to become A+. These remain locked between us, two children sharing a pinky swear in the middle of the night.

"This place is huge," Akoni says, the hovering 3-D map of Mendoza's bunker reflecting in his glasses as he studies it, twirling in the center of the room. He's paused in peeling apart an orange, wearing one of my favorite T-shirts of his. It's black with white lettering that reads *You Have to Be Odd to Be Number One.*

Nashville just clicked on schematics that, thanks to her quick thinking when in Mendoza's compound, she was able to obtain by sticking an Echo Mapper to the underside of one of the lab's tables. She explained to me earlier that if Ramie was in the premises, there was a slight risk in activating it since it gives off a pulsed energy. But because it's set to dissolve once used, even if he searched for the source, there would hopefully be nothing but tiny bits of dust on the ground under where it was placed. Our story to our team was different of course, explaining we got the Echo Mapper there under different circumstances involving fancy assassin things like air vents and Nashville's ability to squeeze through tight corners to drop the bug.

So far no one has questioned anything, and the adrenaline

pumping through my veins is similar to the feeling I get when a target steps into Minnie's line of sight.

"There are five levels," Nashville says while tapping a button on her tablet, causing the blueprints to separate into five sections. "The bottom level seems to be the main lab and offices. Three and four, dormitory and living space for staff and soldiers. Level two is electrical and mechanical, the engine of the place, while one looks like it's for vehicle and weapon storage."

I watch Nashville go through our report, while studying her hair that's pulled back into a tight ponytail, her black leather jacket resting over a white tee and black jeans tucked into boots. It's all similar to what I'm wearing, and when we regarded each other this morning, caused me to smile and her to frown. She's 3 today, poised, hard around the edges, and a scowl a second away from appearing. But while she looks every bit the spy I ran into in China, she'll never be anything but Nashville to me now. Nashville, who earlier this AM let me wash her hair in the shower before spreading my hands over the rest of her supple yet firm body. I shift in my chair, readjusting. If sitting across from her before was difficult, now it's plain torture.

"This is great work," Axel says, his army physique barely fitting into his screen, while Ploom looks like a deflated balloon beside him. "The boards are going to be very pleased, especially since this stamps an approval on the success of our cross-pollination test."

"Yeah." Jules regards Nashville and I with slight skepticism. "You really turned this around quickly while managing not to kill each other."

"There's still time." I shoot my tech assistant a crooked grin.

"Plus..." Nashville leans back in her chair. "We always work well when Carter simply does everything I say."

"Yes." I nod. "Especially when it's to order me to tie her up and slip a dirty sock in her mouth before shoving her into a closet. I can complete our assignment *way* easier that way."

"All right." Jules raises her hands, her blond hair twisting around her shoulders with her headshake. "I didn't mean to ruin this rare second of peace. I'm just impressed is all."

I scoff. "You should be used to that after working with me for so long."

"Ugh." She and Nashville both groan at once, and I glance over to my little redheaded vixen. Her full lips purse in annoyance, and my hand grips my thigh under the table. *Oh, the things I could do to make that mouth of yours relax*, I say to her with my steady gaze.

Her eyes flash once, a hot storm—my favorite—before she straightens and turns away.

This may be more fun than hating each other, I think.

"We have to move fast." Ploom's voice brings me back to the room. "There's a lot to plan and a lot to make sure doesn't go to shit. The Mexican government is giving us free rein on this as long as we keep it clean, quiet, and they can share the credit of the Oculto's downfall. Once Axel and I debrief the board, we'll conference back in for our larger meeting with our full unit. We have to make sure we remember our client's main ask on this one." Ploom's thinning brown hair looks thinner under the fluorescent lighting of his office. "The Oculto have supplied drugs to North and South America for over fifty years, are responsible for countless deaths from territory wars and supplying armament to low-tiered gangs, not to mention the endless list of other sins. So while we're to retrieve a sampling of his serum, when it comes to

Mendoza, it is *not* a capture. It's a termination."

I glance to Nashville, who sits across the table, and look for any sign of what she's thinking in this moment, but there's nothing but her blank mask. We knew this was coming but have been dancing around discussing it. Me not wanting to blow apart the rare openness she's been showing, and her...well, she probably has a list a mile long of excuses, rightfully so. I can't fathom what it's like to be in her position, but I'm determined to help her in any way I can.

I just hope she'll let me.

"This shouldn't be too difficult," Axel adds. "Considering we have two of the best agents in the business on this."

He grins to Nashville, and my lips curl down. *Easy, buddy.*

"We'll need proof, however," he goes on. "And need to decide who will be acting as point."

I'm about to answer that I'll be carrying out the K-order, when Nashville's words cut me off.

"It'll be me," she says, her face cold marble. "I'll kill Mendoza."

CHAPTER 54

Carter
Undisclosed location
Puebla City, Mexico: 2130 hours

I can hear Nashville's soft voice talking to someone on the phone as I walk toward her room in the sleeping quarters of COA's satellite office. It's been two days since our briefing with our full unit, and we are back in Puebla City, finalizing details before we hit Mendoza's bunker tomorrow. Nashville got word to Ramie through the bartender at Búho Oculto that she's ready to meet Mendoza and discuss their future. She didn't tell him an exact date, only that she'll show up when she can find a moment to get away. If there were any more specifics, it would come across as too planned, suspicious, and this way we can ensure Mendoza will be there waiting when we go in.

From studying the Echo Mapper, we've found only two other ways to enter his underground lair besides the main docking gate, and we've planned, and then planned some more. Discussing every possibility, every second of what's to go down and how I'll avoid the cameras they have planted around the meadowland while she enters through the main gate. Nashville and I have organized with our team and without, our own checklist of what must happen just as important, if not more. Nothing can go wrong, *nothing*, and for the first time in a long time, I feel nervous before an assignment.

This of course has nothing to do with the actual mission but everything to do with what I now have riding on it, *who* I have. Glancing down either side of the sterile hallway, finding it just as empty as when I first stepped onto this floor, I stare back at Nashville's door. We're not playing married couple anymore and have been given separate rooms. Little do the agencies know I no longer want a separate room.

"Thank you for gathering that." I can hear Nashville's muffled voice through the dark wood door. "Yes, I know. It's a lot, but this is still really helpful. We can do more when I get home."

Home.

She must be talking to Ceci.

There's a beat of silence before, "I have to go though. Someone's waiting for me."

Shit. Stupid spidey senses.

I grip the take-out bag in my hand tighter as her door swings open, revealing Nashville in pajamas. *Pajamas.* I resist a groan as my skin heats, taking in her little shorts and thermal long-sleeve shirt, her red hair loose around her shoulders. The room behind her is lit in a soft orange glow, and I glance in to see there's a room-service tray on her king-sized bed.

Well, shit again.

"I thought you might want to have dinner with me." I hold up the bag. "But I can see you already—"

She grabs the takeout, peering inside. "Is this really from Cinco Torres?"

"Uh, yeah."

"This is a three-Michelin-starred restaurant," she says, stepping back into her room, allowing me to follow before closing the door with a click.

"It is." I watch her move to her bed, pushing away the old trays before sitting to tear open the new food.

"They don't do takeout."

I shrug. "They did for me."

"Oh yeah?" She raises a brow in my direction. "And how many waitresses did you have to sleep with for that to happen?"

"Just the seven." I flash her a crooked grin as I come to sit beside her, watching as she lays out our meal on her sheets. "You're really still hungry?"

"The food here sucks." She waves a hand at her empty trays. "Plus, I can't turn this down."

"I hope you feel the same way about the other thing I'll be propositioning you for later."

Her blue gaze slides over to meet mine as she bites into a forkful of chicken. "Well," she says after she swallows. "That all depends on how you ask."

She cleans a bit of sauce from her lip with her tongue, and my jeans are suddenly too tight, my white T-shirt too layered.

"It won't be nicely," I say, my voice gruff.

"Good." Her smile is a whip of trouble. "I've never been able to handle *nice*."

The air between us grows thick, as it always does, while my skin hums with every molecule that brushes up against it. We've kept our distance while in public, kept up our personas of two operatives who hate each other, and my strength to keep my hands to myself has worn thin, especially as I find Nashville looking at me like I'm the new meal, looking at me like that while in *pajamas*.

Our food never stood a chance.

One second we're still. The next we're tumbling from the bed to the carpet as we pounce on each other. I hear a tearing as my shirt is ripped from me, Nashville losing no time to get to my skin underneath. She bites her way down my chest to my stomach, nails raking the whole way, and I groan, her body rubbing against my most important part. Hooking my hands under her arms, I pull her up before twirling her below, palming her full breasts as I claim her lips with my own. The coconut of her skin, in her hair, rocks my equilibrium as I breathe, wanting to devour every inch, feeling her muscular smooth thighs wrap around my waist, demanding me to move against her.

God, she's glorious. So wild and strong and...everything.

I curse and drop my head into the crook of her neck.

"What?" she pants.

"I didn't bring a condom."

"Bedside table," she mumbles as she licks the edge of my ear.

"Why, Nashville." I lean up with a grin, taking in her red hair that's fanned around her delicate face, blue eyes darkened to twilight. "I hope you didn't buy those for me?"

"If your name's Rodrigo and mine's Consuela, then yes."

I let out a gasp. "You've been reading my book?"

"If you get that condom, maybe I'll reenact my favorite

scene."

She doesn't have to tell me twice. I'm up before I'm back beside her, but then she's standing and pushing me into a nearby armchair. I go down willingly, not removing my eyes from her as she slips out of her shirt, baring her perfect breasts, so round and heavy, the nipples little strawberry kisses, and my mouth waters.

"Come here."

But she doesn't move, merely gives me a Persephone-slinking-from-Hades grin and slowly pushes her shorts down and then off. She stands there, under the warm glow of the room, naked, confident, her skin a rosy blush under the lights, her apricot hair a shock of delicious color as it spills around her shoulders.

She couldn't look any more like a goddess if she tried.

This time I don't ask as I lean forward and pull her to me. Her legs straddle mine, and I run my hands up her thighs to her backside before grabbing both her wrists and bringing them behind her with a tug. Her breasts jut forward, just where I want them, and I lick and taste and lay claim to each one. She moans under my attention, trying to twist free, but I merely grip tighter with one hand while bringing the other to unbuckle my jeans. Each of her excited pants brings her chest closer, and I feel like I'm already ready to explode as I roll on the condom, positioning her over me.

Her stormy blue eyes gaze down, watching, waiting, a lightning strike in the distant sky, and as I push into her we both let out sighs of relief. We're two addicts getting our fix, and as I let go of Nashville's hands, she brings them to my shoulders and consumes me, rides me with a passion that's dizzying to witness. She stopped my pulse the moment I saw her across the room at the gala and completely lays waste to me now.

I should be terrified, running and getting as far away from this woman as I can, for she vibrates with future heartache. No man can claim this creature, but I understand this and would never try. I merely want to hunt beside her, be gifted the chance to lie in her bed and soak in the endless energy that radiates around her. I want her presence as well as her heart, and as I realize this, with her looming above me, my hands tighten around her waist, following her movements up and down, up and down, a shudder running the length of me. My heart has regrown, been recovered from where it was buried six feet under, and despite clutching it tightly to my chest, a protective wrapping, I've found a person I want to give a part of it to.

The question is, will she break off a piece of her own in return?

CHAPTER 55

Nashville

We sit cross-legged on my bed, draped in our separate bath-robes, finally digging into the food Carter brought. Our previous activity built up a ravenous appetite for me to eat, and I enjoy the quiet of the moment. That is, until he ruins it.

"Are you ready for tomorrow?" Carter asks, handing me a piece of bread.

I take it and dip into the leftover sauce on his plate. "Of course."

A beat of silence.

"Nashville."

He doesn't call me 3 anymore.

"Nashville, look at me."

"I'm good." I turn to pick through the dessert bag, but his hand curling around my wrist stops me.

This time I don't fight my eyes as they meet his green gaze. His dark hair is mussed, and his sharp jaw is shadowed with the beginning of scruff. "I said I'm *good*," I repeat, twisting out of his grip. "We've gone over everything a hundred times. I've taken the explosives we need from the Weapons Depot, we're packed to the gills with KO and TML spray, and I know when to expect—"

"That's not what I'm asking about."

"Of course you aren't." I return to perusing through the desserts, selecting a brownie.

We haven't discussed what I volunteered to do, and this has been intentional on my part. The less I have think about it, the better. I need to remain switched off, detached. He's not a person, merely a name with a check-box next to it.

"I think we should talk about this."

Carter ignores my blatant body language that says *I don't*.

"He's your fath—"

"He's a murderous drug lord." I fist my hand in my lap. "He is *not* the man that was my father."

Was, not is.

Is, is Manuel Mendoza. *Was*, was the man I lost when my mother ran.

Carter's angular features search mine. "Yes, but still. If you need me to—"

"I don't."

Tense silence suffocates the room.

"Don't take this the wrong way." His voice becomes carefully flat. "But I'm having a bit of trouble agreeing that you should be the one to do this. There will be a tomorrow for you after it's done."

I understand. A tomorrow that *I'll* have to live with, have to always remember.

Consequences for actions.

But isn't that always the case?

The weight of it shouldn't change because the person has. I wouldn't be the best at my job if it did. Because that would mean he'd have taken away another thing from my life, the one thing that I built without him, without *them*, leaving me with nothing left to control, to have all my own.

"And there will be a tomorrow for you too," I say, wiping my hands on a napkin.

"Yes." Carter nods. "But I'm not sacrificing nearly as much."

"And who says I am? To sacrifice you have to be losing something. My father has been gone for the past twenty years."

"Gone is different from dead."

"Not to me."

If I say it, think it enough, it will be true.

"Okay…" He says after a moment. "But know that I'm here, Nashville. As difficult as that is for you to accept, I'm here, and though I know you never need me to, I *can* help. I want to," he adds, tipping his head so I look at him again.

An earlier me would have sneered at that, told him to take his disconcerting words and shove them up his bum, but as I hold Carter's gaze, seeing nothing but genuine truth, respect, and concern, I find myself swallowing back my cutting remarks.

I know what it's like to want to protect someone. All too well. And if the roles were reversed, I'd burn down the world before I allowed someone to hurt him.

This realization has me blinking away from Carter's stare, has my heart pulsing a beat faster. *Oh God*. This can't be happening. Not now. Not before what we're about to do.

With a swallow, I manage to suppress acknowledging the feelings that are suddenly rushing through my veins, a dam set free, and instead force myself to say something a bit simpler but no less powerful. "Thank you."

Thank you for not doubting my strength while extending your own.

Carter's responding smile is soft, a gentle press to the corner of his mouth. "Of course."

There will be a tomorrow for you. Carter's earlier words spin a new meaning in my head, my chest tightening with these unfamiliar emotions as, perhaps for the first time in my life, I find myself hoping there won't be one only for me, but for us.

CHAPTER 56

3

The Oculto Compound
Mexico: 1105 hours

Ramie greets me with the same six guards as my first visit when I walk into the mouth of the Oculto's underground bunker. Dressed in black military fatigues, he matches the soldiers down to their boots, except where they have MK 16s, he has a standard handgun, Beretta M9, strapped to his thigh. My senses triple in awareness as I glance around, trying to maintain my heart's steady rhythm.

Why would you need this? Why now?

I'm in my unassuming casual clothes, with no weapons in sight—dark jeans, boots, and a long-sleeved charcoal shirt that feels and looks like cotton, but is more protective than Kevlar.

Like some ancient mechanical animal lying down, the entrance behind me locks back into place, eliciting a metal groan as it cuts off the sun and the soft scent of vanilla that chased me in from the outside. The ground above now resumes its undisturbed visual of a rolling meadowland as nothing but white floodlights, cement walls, and armed cartel stand around me below.

"Check her mouth too," Ramie says in Spanish as a few move in for a frisk. The smell of his A+ abilities swirl around him like shimmering dust, and with his arms crossed over his large chest, his dark gaze watches me like I'm a thief entering a royal wedding.

"You could always give me a kiss and check it yourself." I slide him a sharpened grin, pleased as the guard who stepped up to do the job hesitates at my words, glancing back to his prince.

"Cute," Ramie says. "But you wouldn't remember how to put one foot in front of the other after I did something like that, and then what good would you be? Come on." He turns once the inspection's done, not allowing me a response.

Passing the black SUVs parked in the tunnel, we enter the large service elevator in the back, following the same path as before. Down to level five, descending the metal stairs from the wraparound balcony to the main floor. The scientists barely turn my way as they rush to and from their tables, their white lab coats fluttering as they place their materials into metal storage containers, packing up. My nerves buzz as my gaze swings to the cells along the wall. All remain closed except one.

"Where's Carlos?" I ask Ramie, who's kept step beside me.

"Not here."

"Where'd he—"

"It doesn't concern you."

I raise my brows. "Since I'm about to join you, I think it

does."

Ramie's footsteps halt, causing our circle of guards to stop as well. The energy that surrounds him shifts from bored, closed off, to a spark of annoyance.

"Let's get something straight," he says, his shoulders seeming to grow wider, his shadow larger, as he pins me with his brown gaze, a gorilla baring his chest. "You might be his daughter by birth, but *I* am his *son* by choice."

A flare of heat erupts in my chest, a lashing of jealousy that rocks me back, confused.

"I've been with him and built this by his side." Ramie's voice is a dark storm. "I will *not* have you waltzing in here thinking you're the new little princess. I don't trust you. *He* doesn't trust you, despite what he might say. And before you get *any* privileges, you will need to prove yourself *to me*. You might have a DNA test linking him to you, but I have his loyalty."

A hiss escapes me, teeth flashing, some deep-rooted instinct flaring at his words. Words that cut deeper than I knew could. How dare Ramie take the father who was mine and claim him as his own. How dare he throw a loss that I had no control over in my face.

He's my father! The monster in me growls. *Mine!*

With a snarl, I find myself flying toward the dark spot in front of me, and Ramie meets me head on, his A+ abilities a brick wall as I slam into him. But I've fought bigger mutants than him and know my strength lies in quickness and flexibility. As his vice grips tears me from him, throwing me into a nearby table like a rag doll, I collide into lab equipment, the glass shattering against the ground. But in the last second I spin with the move and am up on my feet, grabbing a nearby metal chair. Pushing the legs in, I crumble it into a ball before launching it at Ramie's head. He dodges it a hairsbreadth before it slices through his cheek, crashing into a computer behind him.

"Children, please!" Mendoza's deep voice booms through the air, and it's a testament to my haze of rage that I didn't notice him approach.

Blinking back to the half-destroyed underground lab, I glance to Mendoza, who stands surprisingly calm regarding us. The scent of our bond makes my head spin further, my hackles rise more as I return my attention to Ramie, who's locked in a similar position as me. Feet apart, hands balled into fists, and nostrils flaring. His eyes flash once, running the length of me before he stands, readjusting himself.

And then he says something that freezes my blood. "Welcome home, Sister."

What the—

"Are you two feeling better now?" Mendoza asks, his blue eyes twinkling with hidden amusement. "We'll need to find a more secure space for you two to work through your differences in the future."

Future.

I feel dizzy. *What just happened?* Did I really just lose my temper over this man? Get jealous over him being more of a father to Ramie than me?

And Ramie, was he looking for that?

Taking in a shallow breath, I force myself into a calm, scrambling to remember my true purpose here.

"I have to use the bathroom," I say. "I need a...second."

"Of course." Mendoza's eyes soften as he looks upon what must appear like a woman flustered.

Good, I think. *Drink it in.*

"Gabriel." He turns to one of the armed guards. "Please show my daughter to the restroom."

Daughter. Father. Sister.

"I'll take her," Ramie says, stepping forward. "Follow me."

I hesitate for a second, glancing back to Mendoza, looking for his approval, which seems to please him further, for a warm energy radiates forward with his head nod.

Ramie shows me down a short gray passageway, the walls covered with pipes and metal plates. He stops in front of a door marked WC. "I'll wait out here."

"Of course you will," I grumble as I push inside before slamming the door shut. As the bolt clicks into place, I turn to regard myself in the mirror that's over a small sink. My hair, which is braided to one side, has wisps of red coming loose from our fight, my cheeks a rosy pink as my blue eyes blink wide.

Staring at my reflection, I allow my shoulders to droop once, my muscles to grow weary for only a second before I tip my head back and steel my spine.

I am 3.

I am 3.

I am 3.

With each repeat, my emotions drain, a plug lifted, and I watch as my gaze regains its sharpness. My mouth flattens, and my features harden into planes of stone.

It's time.

The bathroom is small, simple, and empty of any flourishment. A single light fixture is hooked into the wall, and seeing it, I get to business. Untucking my shirt, I lift up the underwire of my bra and snap off two wiretaps. They are gray squares, no bigger than my pinky nail, and silently standing on the toilet, I unhook the back of the light fixture, exposing wires running into the cement wall. Using my teeth, I fray the rubber around one before clipping in the small devices. It'll be a weak signal, but Akoni and Jules should be able to hack into the electrical from here.

Returning everything to the way it was, I sit down to pee (Ramie's listening after all) while taking out the last thing from the underwire of my bra.

It's a thin flexible syringe, and testing the retractable needle, I gaze at the clear liquid inside.

Innocuous as water, more deadly than a bite from a blue krait snake.

Taking off the extra hair tie wrapped around my braid, I slip it onto my wrist and, flipping out two sections on the syringe, snap it into place. The poison now sits like a dart, tucked into the sleeve of my shirt, ready to be launched.

Flushing the toilet, I pull back up my pants and take one last glance at my reflection in the sink as I wash my hands, the hard-blue eyes that stare out, before exiting the bathroom.

Ramie's just where he said he'd be, leaning against the opposite wall, waiting, and the syringe sits cool against my skin as he leads me to Mendoza's office on the other side of the lab.

As I stand in the doorframe, I find my father sitting behind his old wooden desk, bookcase to one side, grandfather clock to the other, looking at a laptop. He's wearing similar military fatigues as Ramie, the black material hugging his broad shoulders, a man used to combat, as his hair winks with more gray than the last time I saw him under the low lighting. The twisted scar on his neck that leads into his beard stretches as he glances up, eyes the same shade as mine pinning me in place.

"Come in, *mi rosa*," he says. "We have much to plan and not a lot of time to do it."

And so, with my chin tipped up, I force myself to step in and return to the space where I found my father, only to have to kill him.

CHAPTER 57

Carter
The Oculto Compound
Mexico: 1115 hours

The air is freezing even though sweat has begun to soak into my black protective gear. I hate small spaces, so crawling through an air vent no wider or taller than myself is my very definition of a horrible time. The breathing mask around my face and eyes only heightens my claustrophobia, and I let out a thankful sigh seeing the slits of light coming through a grate at the end of my path. My exit.

"Reaching my stop on level two," I say.

"We see you." Jules speaks into my ear, obviously watching the small dot that I come up as on their screens.

After much deliberation between a sewage tunnel and HVAC system, my team finally, *thankfully*, agreed with me that

I should enter through the main air duct that brings in fresh oxygen. It sits tucked away in the jungle, covered by a forgotten Viento del Este storage facility.

Nashville ended up being right about the owner, Rodrigo. He was hiding something, just not officially on his land. After mirror-scrambling the security cams that watched the dilapidated shack, I slid into one of the large ducts that sat a good distance away from Mendoza's compound, only to twist, turn, and mutter curses through smaller and smaller shafts to end up here.

"One of their control rooms should be directly below you." Akoni's deep voice swaps in for Jules's. Our two tech Ops sit five miles away in the jungle in an unmarked van, acting as my GPS guides to get me to this point. Our remaining unit waits in military helicopters to be called in to retrieve whatever they can grab from the compound. Once I reached this point, it's only supposed to take Nashville and I thirty minutes to complete our tasks and meet them outside.

Besides the bare essentials to carry out the K-order, Nashville had to go in wireless and weaponless, and my heart beats a faster rhythm hoping everything is going according to plan.

Peering through the small gaps in the vent, I count two men and one woman manning the closed control room below, their conversation jumbled by the whoosh of air pumping through the space I lie. Gazing around the rest of the room, I take in the screens and computers set up on tables and inlaid into a far wall, seeing no other guards. My neck aches from holding it at an odd angle for so long, and I'm more than ready to get out of this metal container.

"Setting sleepers," I whisper to my team as I remove two small canisters that are strapped to my wrists. Angling them to the edge of the vent, I twist them open.

A barely audible hiss escapes, releasing an invisible cloud of gas that flows into the room.

Ten seconds.

Twenty.

The sound of one body dropping before—

Thunk. Thunk.

The other two go down.

Punching out the grate, I slide and flip out, landing with a crouch on the cement floor before standing.

Stretching my neck, back, and arms, I let out a groan before walking the small distance to the monitors. "Jules, make a note that the agency will be paying for my next massage."

"I'm your tech Op, not your assistant, jackass."

"Po-tatoes, pa-tatoes," I say, studying the cameras that watch every inch of this place. There are a handful of guards eating in the mess hall, in their barracks, walking in twos around the compound, and loading crates into vehicles on the upper level. The scientists are similarly packing things away, and I cock my head to the side.

Where are you going, little ants?

"We just got control of the electrical," Jules says.

Good girl, Nashville, I think with a small grin. "OK, start shutting down sections of level two. I'll call a crew to come and take a look at the malfunction."

Snapping up one of the unconscious guard's radios, I quickly repeat myself in Spanish, hoping it reaches the ear of one man in particular before sliding to the door of the control room. Peering into the hall through the small glass window, I watch two nearby soldiers turn to walk my way, hearing my request on their transmitters.

Popping against the wall, I wait for them to make their way in, and before they can register their comrades on the ground, I slither up behind them and slam their heads together. They go down just as the lights in the room begin to flicker.

"Good, Jules. It's working," I say as I step into the now empty hallway.

My blood pumps an excited rhythm as the electricity continues to flash before going dark, everything drowning in black before red emergency lights turn on, lighting the length of the hall. My actions are illuminated in shadowed crimson as I detach two more canisters from my ankles, opening them before rolling them down the long passageway to smack up against the elevator that rests at the end.

I wait five minutes, leaning against the wall while rubbing a spot of dirt from Minnie's handle. "Sorry about that, old girl. That vent hadn't been cleaned in ages."

"Carter." Jules's dry voice comes through my ear. "Are you talking to your gun again?"

I'm cut off from responding with a *duh* by the sound of the elevator bay moving, the car traveling up.

"Got company," I say, rechecking that my breathing mask's in place, my silencer attached, as the elevator stops and then opens at my level.

The first two guards barely get a foot out before they collapse to the ground.

Knockout gas is a bitch like that.

The remaining three get two rounds off, causing me to scoot back into the control room's doorframe, before they go down as well. Stepping out, I regard the one large, very pissed-off man remaining.

Ramie glares at me, murder in his dark eyes as a small breathing mask is placed over his nose and mouth. He must have smelled the beginnings of the gas on the way up and thought fast. A+ are smart like that. He's bigger than I remember, dark hair, tan skin, black military fatigues. Basically a looming shadow of death under the red lights, and while his presence is more than intimidating, he's the one man I needed to see, needed to draw up. If he's here that means Nashville's alone.

Alone with Mendoza.

Like an angry god, an earthquake of a growl comes from his end of the hall as he barrels toward me, and I raise Minnie, getting out three shots. Like snapping lightning, he dodges them all, and I internally curse his superhuman speed just as he throws a fist that would shatter my skull in two.

I dodge it just in time, dropping into a roll and popping up a few feet down the corridor. Ramie turns, charging again, and before I can do much of anything, his hand is around my throat and he's lifting me off my feet and slamming me against the wall.

I can feel my larynx, esophagus, and every other body part that's between his grasp being squeezed to their limit, my eyes bulging as my hand flails at my side. My dimming brain barely registers what I'm looking for before my fingers curl around it, and on my last mortal gasp, I hook my legs around Ramie's torso, bringing him closer before shoving the canister up and into his mask, and spray.

I spray even when he releases his grip, and I'm gasping and gagging while remaining locked to the mountain of a man.

With a grizzly bear shove, he finally gets me loose, and I slide across the cement floor, watching him flailing to remove his face cover as I hold my bruised throat.

Finally ripping it off, he takes in a lungful of air, wiping against his mouth, nose, as his eyes suddenly blink to a blankness, his gaze swinging around in confusion before it locks back to mine. And then, because of the other gas still circling the air, he collapses to the ground, unconscious.

I glance to the canister still curled in my hand, to the TML stamped across the side.

Temporary memory loss.

Standing up, I straighten my clothes and take one last look at the sleeping Ramie, to the pile of knocked-out guards, telling myself to never get sprayed with any of this stuff.

And then I turn, making my way to plant some bombs.

CHAPTER 58

3
The Oculto Compound
Mexico: 1122 hours

My father just finished explaining that we're to leave in an hour, this compound having run its course of use, before Ramie was called away to check on an issue with the electrical on level two.

He was less than pleased to leave Mendoza and I alone, but after stationing two guards by the open door, saying that if I moved even an inch the wrong way, to shoot me with a tranquilizer, he left.

"He's a bit protective," Mendoza says with a smile.

"Why wouldn't a son be for his father?"

A steady blue gaze regards me as he leans back in his chair. "Yes," Mendoza says. "Ramie has become a son to me, but I don't want you to think there isn't space for you by my side as well. Even when I thought you were dead, that spot was never to be filled."

I swallow against the tightness in my throat, sensing the truth in his words. "Why do you trust me with your secrets? When you found me, I was the enemy."

"Was," he says. "That's a very significant difference. And we all have reasons for doing things. You and I definitely have a long path to travel, time to make up for, and while we both might be many things in this world, can we not first be a father and a daughter merely hoping to regain what we lost?"

I take in his searching eyes, dark beard covering a face that's seen so much blood, has been the cause of so much suffering for so many people, while still taking on the mask of the man I remembered from so many years ago. His gentle touch.

"I guess we'll see." I rest my hands on the arms of my chair where I sit in front of him, hesitating to turn one of them over. His words always seem to bring forth a barrel of confusion, shining a light on my hidden desires, wishes that could be. And this is why I find myself prolonging what I must do. *Maybe there's another way?* A voice inside me whispers. *A different end.*

"When will you undergo the change?" I find myself asking.

"When we reach our next location," he says, sitting up and clicking something on his computer that faces away from me. "It takes about a month to complete the transfer, and there are a few things I need to make sure are in order before I step aside for that amount of time."

"Like me," I say.

"Yes." Sharp blue eyes return to me. "Like you. Now tell me, mi rosa." Mendoza interlocks his fingers on his desk. "Why did *you* decide to abandon your people to come here today?"

"They were never my people," I say, my voice flat.

"No?" He cocks a brow. "And why's that? Did they not raise you, make you into what you are today?"

"Which is exactly why they hold none of my loyalty. Do you think I've enjoyed being their little errand girl for all these years? Forced to end lives with the ring of my phone?"

"But you told me yourself that those lives were deserving of their end, that they were never *children* or *innocents*." He quotes my earlier words. "You and I have seen what happens to your kind without a stroke of luck stepping in. You might have been sculpted into an assassin, but you could have run wild as a murderer without your agency. Do you feel no affinity to them, no gratitude?"

Gratitude.

The syringe grows hot against my wrist, a boiling kettle ready to sing. I've been waiting for this. The part where I'm meant to convince this man of my intentions, why a woman like me might step over to stand beside a man like him despite our differences or common blood.

Ignoring the guards at my back and the task that's ticking down, I pull forward the words that sit on the edge of truth and lies. "Ever since I was brought to Bell Buckle Orphanage, I was forced by the caretakers to believe that me being parent-less wasn't my fault. That my life *was* wanted, despite present circumstances, and it would be again. When the agency found me, brought me in, I first thought it was because they saw me as a little girl worth having, a little *normal* girl. I quickly learned that wasn't true. It was my genes they wanted, saw value in. It wasn't because my favorite color was green or that I had a knack for making paper airplanes or enjoyed eating outside. There was no *me* in their minds, just an A plus they could own, mold. I saw this and realized that everyone has their prerogatives, things that, if they owned it, would put them above others. Everyone is just looking for their one-up in this world, and so I accepted this, decided if that's where my value lay, then I'd be the best operative they had. If someone couldn't appreciate me for me, I'd just become what they *could* appreciate." I lower my hands into my lap, stalling more. "But then you came back." I glance to my father. "And it was the first time I had ever experienced someone looking at me, not for what I could do but for who I was. I could see that for you, I wasn't just an A plus, but a girl that was capable of being a daughter too."

Mendoza takes me in with a look that sends a weird flutter through my chest. Its pride mixed with a million other things, and as I sit there, under his scrutiny, I feel something that terrifies me down to the edge of my blackened soul.

I feel guilty.

And sad.

And angry.

For life is a terribly unfair thing to force me here, to do what I must.

"Oh, *mi rosa*," he says, "that's—"

Something happening on Mendoza's computer draws his attention away, and I watch as his features fall into a scowl before they drop into a neutral mask.

His eyes collide back with mine, my heart pumping a quick beat as I take in the energy shifting around him. *Something's happened.* And I silently curse, knowing what it is.

Shit. Shit. Shit. I should have been done by now.

A long moment stretches before us, one where I run through

all my options, trying to measure the quickness of the guards drawing their weapons behind me with me lifting my wrist. I could do it. I could do it quicker than any of them and be on the floor in half a second.

Yet I don't. I sit there, frozen. Denying what must be done—again—what I said I alone *had* to do. All because of what? My deluded selfishness to finish something I thought I was responsible for? To prove to myself that I could still do what needed to be done, no matter who was on the other side of my gun?

"Those were beautiful words," Mendoza says, his voice shifting to something distant, no longer warm as he opens a drawer by his side. "But there is one thing I have *never* tolerated, by *anyone*, in all the years I have led the Oculto. Being lied to." And then with a simple lift of his hand, he goes from my father back to a drug lord as he points a shiny Glock 22 straight at me.

CHAPTER 59

Nashville

Mendoza holds the gun steady as the syringe screams against my wrist to be set free, but my heart combusting in my chest continues to keep me paralyzed to my spot.

The world around me rocks with uncertainty.

In all the circumstances I ran through, this wasn't even on the list of possibilities. Mendoza gave off nothing but desperate hope to be reconnected with his resurrected daughter. He had created this whole godforsaken facility because of the very heartache of me and my mother's deaths. It was unthinkable that he could be sitting here now, ready to pull the trigger on one of them.

How arrogant could I be?

How stupid to doubt this man's capability to do the very thing I was planning.

We share the same toxic blood, after all, the long lineage of sinners.

Stupid. Stupid. Stupid.

I open my mouth to respond, to say something, but everything stays locked in, stuck in my throat. My two selves fight for dominance, one ready to act while the other mourns this moment, the loss of the father a part of me was desperate to believe was real, possible.

"You have disappointed me more than you know," Mendoza says, standing with ice in his eyes, the same hard eyes that were captured in his profile picture. The father he let me see is no longer here. Like a coin flip, he all too easily became another man. Two people in one body.

Just like me.

A shudder runs down my spine as I feel the guards at my back tensing, these next seconds everything, and I block out all but what's in this room. "When I found you, you have no idea the joy I felt in that moment." He rounds his desk. "I could have given you the *world*," he hisses. "We could have been a family again."

"We still can be," I force out, trying to buy myself more time from what I have already wasted.

"Don't insult me more than you already have," he sneers. Twirling his laptop around, he shows me an image of what I feared as well as hoped—security footage of collapsed guards in a hall.

Carter.

"You have been disloyal since the moment we met, haven't you?" He holds his gun firmer, a dash of rage mixed with hurt in his eyes. "Even when I've shown you nothing but truth and compassion. I've never lied about who I was. Never spoke false words about what you'd be here. Gave you time to process just as I had. I could easily have stopped your little mission, ended your friends' lives with a snap of my fingers. *I still can*," he rumbles. "Do you understand the restraint I have granted you? The trust you have just thrown—"

"*I* was left to fend for myself." The words barrel out with a growl, my chest filling with a familiar fire. "*I* have been forced to survive over and over. Forced to end a life at too young an age all because of *your* sins. You might not have lied to me, but what about my mother?"

Mendoza's head juts back as if I've slapped him.

"Did you not wrap her in a false sense of safety? Paint her an innocent past to keep her heart? And then when I was born, when you knew what I was, why did you not run right away? Hide us before your family had a chance to find us?" Tears burn a path down my cheeks, and I curse their existence. *I am not a creature prone to crying.* "You damned us all with your lies. So you don't get to stand here offended by what I am, what I turned out to be, when I'm more *your* daughter now than either of us are proud to admit."

We hold each other's gaze, two opposing mountains as my words hang in the air, my chest pumping with my rapid breaths.

"You're right," Mendoza says after a moment. "You're very much my daughter, and it saddens me that I'm not proud of that."

My skin erupts with a chill of pain, of loss, at the same second my senses clear. Whatever delusion I was sitting in lifts, allowing me to barrel back to my surroundings, do the math of my chances to move versus getting hit by his bullet, of getting my shot off before he gets his.

All this runs through my mind just as every action I've ever taken in my life leads me to this very second, sitting here looking down the barrel of a gun that my father holds. Like an anvil, it all bores down on my shoulders, and I grow weary.

I've done extremely heinous things in my short time on this planet, but am I really ready to add on patricide?

It's too much, my shriveled soul yells. *Too much.*

I thought I could come here, prove to myself, and even Carter, that I could kill this man with one flick of my wrist. That his existence didn't change the woman I had always believed myself to be, was proud to have created. But as I look into the hard eyes of one of the people responsible for bringing me into this world, I realize I can't.

Even though I barely know him, have been made to survive at all costs, this is one sin I cannot bear.

And one I see Mendoza, my father, can all too easily.

This, I decide, is all the difference. What, in the end, will separate me from the monster.

My wickedness has a limit.

So with vision blurring, more tears trying to fall free, I ignore the prick of death hidden up my sleeve and say, "Do it."

Mendoza blinks, a snap of surprise behind his stone features, and for a tiny sliver of a moment I see the lucidness of my father again. With a frown, his gaze goes from me to the gun in his hand, and my heart pumps wildly in my chest, seeing it lower a fraction.

His mouth opens, words about to be spoken, but they never make it out, for muffled shots fill the air, and Mendoza's head snaps back. A perfect bloody hole straight between his eyes as he collapses against his desk.

It's only an instant, but just like that, he goes from alive to dead.

A gasp has me lurching forward as I'm doused in frostbite.

No!

My hands flutter over his slack body, watching crimson pool beneath his head, soaking his desk.

Dead. He's Dead.

As he was supposed to be, a voice whispers in my mind.

As *I* was meant to make happen.

Spinning around, I take in the man who fills the doorway.

Carter stands, the two other guards unmoving at his feet, with his gun still aimed at the spot Mendoza once stood.

Before he killed him.

CHAPTER 60

Carter
The Oculto Compound
Mexico: 1128 hours

She silently watches as I take a quick video and picture of the lifeless body of Manuel Mendoza, his eyes staring unseeing as I zero in on the hole in his skull, the blood dripping an artful path across his forehead to paint the oak desk ruby.

"Nashville." I try getting her attention again as I dip my head from the office, checking that no other guards are making their way over. "We have fifteen minutes to get out of here."

I look back to find her still regarding Mendoza. His arm is thrown at an odd angle under his neck, his legs half draped over the ledge of the desk to the floor. I have no idea what she's thinking, no clue the emotions filling her to see her father in such a state, that I was the man who put him there, but this is not the time to process it. We can do that and more when we're out, when she's safe.

I didn't hesitate when I saw Mendoza pointing his gun at her. It merely cemented my resolve further. Even with her current bleached complexion and silent vigil, I would pull the trigger again if given a second chance.

I was hiding behind a corner down the hall, and with the two guards' attention pinned to what was taking place in the office, I ran.

The soldiers went down a millisecond before I took out Mendoza.

What would have cost Nashville a lot more than she cares to admit, took me no pain to complete.

Her not being able to kill her father doesn't make her weak. It makes her human. It makes her have a chance in this fucked-up world we live in.

"Nashville." I try again, this time getting a response as she turns, wiping at the tracks of tears running down her cheeks. My rage floods higher seeing her like this, and I want to wrap her in my arms, but we both know this is not the time. "We have to go," I say more gently. "Guards will be here soon."

She merely nods as I hand her my extra gun, remains silent as she follows me out, and doesn't so much as glance back to the room that is now her father's tomb.

The scientists scurry away as they see us running through the lab, one brave enough to pick up a discarded gun, but Nashville has woken up 3, for she doesn't even blink as she puts down the woman with a clear shot to her temple.

"We need to grab someone to control the elevator," she says just as I finished telling Jules and Akoni that I've regrouped with

Nashville and we've taken out the target.

"Get samples of the serum!" Ploom's voice comes through my ear, a silent ghost on the line until now. "You can't leave until you've acquired that."

"They've set a self-destruct mechanism," I say to him as Nashville spins to scoop up a cowering man in a lab coat, hiding behind a desk. "We need to get out before this place blows."

"Get the serum!" Ploom repeats. "Any amount will do." But I ignore his order as we run up the metal stairs to the wraparound balcony leading to the elevator.

Nashville has no issue taking the doctor with her, a child dragging a stuffed animal.

"Carter?" Ploom's annoying voice echoes in my head again. "Did you hear—" I tear off the earpiece and throw it behind me as we skid to a stop, calling the elevator.

A group of guards enter the downstairs lab, and seeing us, start shooting. We dip behind a column as cement debris explodes near our heads. I swivel around and put down two soldiers just as the elevator opens, revealing four more.

Shit.

The alarm must have sounded, for not only are they in full gear, but they are not surprised to see us as they charge our way.

Nashville throws the scientist into my arms as she pounces forward.

Like a possessed demon, she kicks up onto the wall to run and drop behind the group. With a burst of her gun, two are shot in the back of the head, falling with a *thunk*, before she kicks the remaining guards in the back of the knees, messing up each man's aim, which was pointed my way. Their rounds of bullets puncture the piped ceiling, setting off wheezes of steam.

With barely trackable reflexes, she pulls a knife sheathed at one of their thighs, and with a *whoosh*, *whoosh* cuts each of their throats before they realize what's happening. Blood covers the metal-meshed floor, dripping to the ground below as they gurgle their last breaths.

The man in my hands sobs at the sight while I shove our way into the awaiting car. Pressing the scientist's head to the voice command screen, I swipe his key card, demanding. "Say *level one*."

He squeaks and shivers under my grasp.

"*Level one!*" I order again in Spanish as the second group of guards below make their way up the metal stairs. Nashville hits everyone she aims at, but she only has so many bullets left.

"Carter!" she yells.

"If you cooperate," I whisper to the man, "I'll tell her to let you live."

"*Nivel uno!*" he says in the next instant, and I let out a relieving sigh as the car doors close and we make our way up, a spray of bullets *thunking* against the outside of our metal cage.

"Please, please," pleads the lab rat under my grip. "I have a family. I'll do whatever you say. Just don't kill me."

Nashville and I glance to one another.

"They always have families."

"Death seems to bring that out in people," she mumbles as she checks the remaining rounds in her gun.

I watch her for a moment, her braided red hair sitting calmly over one shoulder as her features are cut into their usual stone mask of 3. I know she's back to being that woman right now, needs to be to get through this last leg of our journey. So even though I want to say a thousand things, I bite the inside of my cheek and remain quiet.

Later. We'll say it all later.

Soon the elevator shudders to a stop as the doors open on level one. Cautiously stepping out, we take in the quiet tunnel before us. The guards usually stationed here must have been ordered belowground when the alarm was sounded, leaving our exit unmanned.

Five black SUVs sit idle to one side of the tar road, boxes and crates, waiting to be packed, against a wall. The rest of the space pinches away in the distance as the roof remains closed at the far end.

"How do we open the tunnel?" I ask the man.

"I...I don't know." He glances around. "That's never been shared with us."

I'm about to trade him some pain for a better answer, when Nashville stops me.

"He's telling the truth," she says, running to a side panel set in the wall.

I check my watch. "Well, what do you suggest we do? We have eight minutes."

"Hotwire one of the cars. I'll work on this."

Pulling the man with me to the vehicles, I check the driver's-side door, smiling when it opens easily. As I glance inside, my grin grows wider. "No need," I call back to her. "The keys are in the ignition."

The last of my words are drowned out by the cover above us lifting, the hidden top of the bunker opening to streak in beams of daylight as Nashville runs toward me.

"And I found out how to open it."

Relief barrels into my chest as I open the backseat passenger side and shove the scientist in. "This facility is about to be wiped out." I continue to talk in Spanish. "Burned to a crisp, devoured into hell, understand? So if you truly want to live to see your family, I suggest you sit here and don't move a goddamn muscle."

Slamming the door on his panicked squeak, I sprint to the trunk, and with Nashville's help, dump out crates that were loaded in. If we're going to disobey orders, we're going to disobey orders properly. None of this will make its way out.

With the last box hitting the ground, I shut the back and slip into the driver's seat just as Nashville hops in beside me.

"We can't bring him." She points to the mouse of man in the back.

"We'll drop him when we're out."

Revving the engine, I'm ready to haul ass when Nashville's door suddenly swings open and she gets pulled out by her hair.

"*Nashville!*" I twist in my seat, pumping the brakes with a screech.

Ramie stands like a resurrected zombie, holding Nashville in a vice grip, her head squeezed between the crook of his arm and his chest.

What the—

He's supposed to be reenacting sleeping beauty two levels down.

Stupid A+ and their advanced healing.

With a two-fisted punch to each of his eye sockets, Nashville is able to twist out of his grip, only to find herself defending again. Ramie's a looming force of destruction as he holds her back, his hair a tattered mess, his black clothes marked with grime, as if he's been crawling through—

I glance beyond the two of them to the wall near the elevator bay, seeing a kicked-out ventilation grate in the corner.

"*Son of a bitch.*" Whipping up Minnie, I aim for Ramie's head, but they are tossing around like two superhumans out for blood, leaving me without a clear shot. "*Fuck.*"

"Go!" Nashville yells to me just as I glance at my watch. Two minutes.

"Yes, go!" the scientist says behind me.

"Shut up," I growl just as Ramie bellows, "*You killed him!*"

He swings a fist like a possessed Frankenstein's monster, and I'm not even sure how she does it, but with blurred speed, she's up and around his shoulders, a spider monkey holding tight.

"I'm sorry," I hear her say before she flicks her wrist, and a tiny dart lodges into his neck.

Ramie palms it, ripping it from his skin, but it's too late. The toxin that was meant for another's end all too rapidly becomes his own. His mouth foams with his gurgle, his eyes rolling back in his head as he stands, swaying, a majestic skyscraper, before he topples to the ground with a *thud*.

Dead.

Nashville nimbly lands on her feet beside him, a quick flash of pain in her eyes. But then she shakes away the expression and runs back to the car.

"Go!" she yells as she hops in, and she doesn't have to tell me twice before I'm flooring it, the final seconds counting down just as we crest the lip of the bunker, soaring through the peaceful sun-soaked meadow before it all erupts behind us in flames.

CHAPTER 61

Carter
Undisclosed Location
Mexico City, Mexico: 1430 hours

The questions are endless, and they come from everyone.

Did you get any of the serum? Any files from computers? What about employees, soldiers? Any make it out alive?

No. No. And *no.*

We dropped the scientist in the jungle before the helicopters came to pick us up. Explained that if he wanted to stay alive, he needed to forget everything, or we'd come back to permanently help him with the amnesia. I wanted to shoot him to eliminate any risk, but Nashville stopped me by saying that was enough death for today, and coming from her, that's saying something.

I held her gaze for a long moment, hating the shadows I saw there, and nodded. If any other employees got out, we have yet to know as we sit back in Mexico City, going through our debrief in the darkened conference room.

Nashville is quiet beside me. Jules and Akoni sit across the table, while Ploom's and Axel's heads fill the two screens at the front.

We were flown directly here from the Oculto's compound and, after being checked for wounds, fed, and allowed a quick shower, were called to regroup for the usual debrief after a mission. Once done, we're scheduled to travel back to the States later tonight.

Just like that, mission complete. Pack up and go home.

And though I've wanted to hear those words every day since starting this assignment, I now find myself digging my heels in to pump the brakes.

The idea of stepping back on US soil seems to mark the end of more than just our mission.

Nashville and I have yet to talk about what happened back at the compound. We've been constantly surrounded by doctors, guards, and team members since stepping into the building, and my leg bounces under the table with my impatience. Now that she's safe, we're safe, and it's all done, I want to ask her how she is, what's barreling through her mind as she sits beside me with her blue gaze pinned to the center of the table. Is she mad at me for Mendoza? Is she mad at herself?

Wearing a soft cream sweater over jeans, her hair up in a messy bun, she answers all the questions directed at her, but otherwise remains closed mouthed. Her mind, no doubt, preoccupied with thoughts that most of the room has no idea about.

My hands grip my chair's armrests as I glance her way, fighting the urge to wrap her in my arms and take both of us far from here. I want to be who we are when we're alone, see who we become when we're not on a mission. I want to go back to waking up next to her every day, but this time be able to roll over and touch her, stay there until nightfall. Over and over again.

Even though it goes against everything the two of us have worked toward, or more accurately, away from, I want there to be an *us*, and I want *us* to work together on learning what that's like.

And I want to tell her all this.

"Well, at least you got proof of Mendoza's death," Axel says from his screen, his blond hair perfectly swept to one side as his military physique fills out his white oxford. Ploom sits on the TV beside him like no creature meant for hi-def. Mousy brown hair thinly covering a pasty complexion. The man desperately needs time in the sun and some multivitamins.

"Yeah," Ploom says sourly. "Especially since the compound is now a charred hazard-suit mess. We wouldn't be able to identify one body from the next even if we wanted to."

Arial footage of a blackened, sizzling hole in the middle of the meadowlands hovers in the center of our conference table, while pictures of Mendoza's lifeless eyes are stacked beside it, bloody hole in the center of his head. My work, my pictures.

I glance to Nashville, my lips set in a hard line, but if she feels anything from seeing her father again, she's hiding it well. She stares unblinking at the man who fills the room, and besides her fingers curling into her bicep as she sits with her arms crossed over her chest, she doesn't so much as move an inch.

"Still," Axel adds. "This has been a successful mission despite the loss of part of our assignment. The cross-pollination of the agencies has been marked a success, and the boards have already begun rolling out assignments for other Ops. Any repercussions from not obtaining the serum along with cleaning up this mess for Mexico, Ploom and I will handle. Right, Ploom?" He asks as if he's speaking to a pouting child.

"Yeah," Ploom grumbles.

"Great." Axel grins. "Again, good job, team. We'll look forward to seeing you back in the States. And, 3"—he glances to the woman beside me—"book that vacation now."

She gives him a halfhearted grin before their screens click off and the lights come back on. Meeting adjourned.

"Can we talk?" I turn to Nashville.

Her red hair shines apricot as she twists in her seat, blue eyes finding mine. "Not right now."

"Yes, now," I say in a forced whisper, standing when she does. "We have to talk about—"

"Carter." The steel in her voice cuts me off, her gaze sweeping the room. "Not here."

"Come walk with me then. We'll find a place outside."

"No, listen. I..." Her features grow distant once more, and I hate it. "I still need some time," she says. "It's been a long twenty-four hours, and I need some time."

I frown. "Okay, but—"

"Please," she says softer, her unfamiliar plea opening a fissure in my chest.

I want to reach for her, pull her to me like she let me once before, but I can't because we stand here now, not alone, and I can feel a chasm opening by our feet. Are we back to being strangers? Two operatives on opposite sides?

No, I won't let that happen.

I'm about to force the barrier to break, when a person clearing her throat sounds at my back.

Glancing behind me, I find Jules and Akoni waiting for us in an otherwise empty room. Jules is in her usual business outfit of gray pantsuit, with blond hair pulled into a tight bun, while Akoni is rocking a sweatshirt that reads *Byte Me!*

"We know about the explosives." Jules's hushed voice cuts into the quiet.

"Uh...yeah, they went off at the compound," I say, turning back to Nashville.

"No," Akoni says. "We know that *you guys* took them from the Depot."

My gaze collides with Nashville's, each of our jaws clenching as I face our tech Ops again.

"And..." I raise a brow.

"And we understand why," Jules says.

I remain silent.

"It wasn't safe with anyone, the serum," Akoni clarifies, pushing his black-rimmed glasses up his nose. "We both knew the moment you explained its use."

I regard the large man. "Okay..."

"But you left a trail back to the weaponry," he goes on. "We saw it when we were collecting material for our unit. There was a hole in the inventory list."

"But we covered it up," Jules adds.

I glance between our two tech Ops, realizing what an odd little family the four of us have become over the span of this assignment. Though Jules and Akoni don't know everything, I believe, if given the opportunity, they'd honor our secrets. Maybe one day...

"Thank you," I say. "That...means a lot."

"It's the least we could do." Akoni slaps me on the shoulder.

"Yeah, especially since you didn't annoy me half as much as you usually do on assignments." Jules shoots me a sly grin.

"And nice moment ruined." I return her smile while glancing over my shoulder to Nashville, but it quickly drops when I see she's no longer there, the door beyond just starting to close.

Without another word to Jules or Akoni, I run to it and step into the hall, but just as I feared, the carpeted tunnel is void of a redheaded woman.

CHAPTER 62

Nashville

I stare at the plane ticket in my hand, its return date left empty as the surrounding airport vibrates with noise. Cell phones ring, kids cry, parents yell, people crunch and sip their food, while plane engines rev and TSA agents chatter among themselves.

Yet I ignore it all as I study the arrival location printed across my slip of paper. It took me longer than I thought it would to finally book this trip, my mind a scattered mess since Mexico, but after a few days of procrastination, and with the help of Ceci, I finally took the plunge.

"Now boarding first class." The flight attendant's voice echoes through the terminal speakers.

Grabbing my small carry-on, I hand the man my ticket to scan, and walk on board, taking my seat at the front. Leaning my head on the headrest, I stare out the window to the tarmac below, watching the bag carts weave through ground staff.

I still feel numb, distant from myself, and it's at odds with the usual simmering rage that has always sung through my veins. It's as if Carter's bullet killed more than one thing that day, or at least forced it into slumber. Causing a part of me to become docile until I can piece together this new reality of mine.

Thinking of my K-Op partner, of the man who has grown to mean so much more than I wanted anyone to in my life, I glance to the empty seat beside me. He should be here, taking this trip, and maybe one day he will, but for now I remain alone.

Because I need to.

CHAPTER 63

Carter
Chicago, Illinois
Two weeks and three days since Mexico

I've been banging on the door for a good twenty minutes.

I know this is her apartment, since I had to purchase an obscene amount of tech toys for Akoni to finally hand over its location. Obtaining an operative's home address is harder than hacking into the FBI director's browser history, and Akoni was quick to say he would deny any involvement if she, or anyone else, came for his head.

I've tried to give Nashville the space she needs, but time's up. We need to talk, not just about Mexico, but about everything. Despite what happened with her father, the assignment, her default action to run, there *will* be a her and me. We didn't just go through all that, each shedding armor we've held up for so many years, for there not to be.

"I have Mace." A woman's voice stops me from pulling the lockpick from my jeans. "And my thumb's ready to hit 911!"

Glancing to my right, I find a very cute girl with wavy brown hair, dark skin, and a chic gray pencil skirt and blouse, standing with both arms raised, holding those two exact things. Her startling gray eyes narrow as she stares my way, her leather purse hanging from the crook of her elbow.

"I'm a great multitasker," she warns. "So I can do both at once if you don't explain, *right now*, why you're standing outside my door looking like you're about to break in."

"You live here?" I frown, nodding to the apartment in question.

"Asks the murderer to his victim." Her thumb pulses to press Call.

"Wait!" I hold up a hand. "Wait, that means...are you Ceci?"

I take a more thorough study of the woman who's gained the trust of such a creature as Nashville.

Under my scrutiny her shoulders stiffen further. "Depends. Who's asking?"

"Sorry," I say, slowly extending a handshake. "I'm Carter. I work with Nashville. Is she home?"

"Carter?" She blinks before understanding flows over her features. "Carter Smith?" she says again as her eyes travel the length of me. "Yes," she tuts, "you most certainly *are*."

"Um..."

"It's so nice to meet you." She lowers her weapons to take my hand, her demeanor quickly going from attack dog to friendly neighbor. "I've heard *many* things about you, Carter Smith."

"You have?" My brows creep up in surprise. "Well, I hope

they were good things."

"Hardly any," she says with a grin. "And I'm sorry, but Nashville isn't here."

Disappointment constricts my chest. "When will she be back?"

"I never really know those things," she says with a shrug. "Sometimes it's days. Sometimes weeks or months. She was only here for a few days after Mexico before she was off again. She lets me squat to make sure her rubber plants don't die."

"Oh." I glance to their closed apartment door. "Did she say where she was going?"

I know for a fact she's not on another assignment, given what Ploom recently emailed me, information I was hoping to talk to her about in person. I tried asking Axel if she took her long-awaited vacation, but he seemed even less inclined to share personal facts regarding his favorite operative than Akoni was to be bribed into giving me her address.

"I don't know *precisely* where she went," Ceci says, a slight hesitancy in her eyes. "But..." She bites her bottom lip in thought before a resigned huff escapes her. "She'll probably kill me for this, but in all the years I've known Nash, I've never heard her talk about a man the way she talks about you, nor have I seen one actually come here looking for her. With good intentions, at least."

My blood pumps wildly hearing her words.

I've never heard her talk about a man the way she talks about you.

"You *do* have good intentions, right?" Ceci studies me again, from my booted feet up to my hairline.

"Only the very best."

"Hmm, and you promise not to hurt her?"

"Like anyone could."

"You'd be surprised," she says, an edge of sadness in her voice that has us sharing a look.

"I promise not to hurt her." I keep my eyes level to hers.

"Okay." Ceci eventually nods. "I can't give you anything besides a name. But you guys are private investigators..." She waves a hand as I cock a brow.

Private investigators?

"So you can do whatever fancy things you do to get more info from here." Taking out a pen from her bag, she tears off a piece of paper from the junk mail she was carrying and scribbles something down.

"This is all Nashville had to go on." She hands me the slip. "But I'm pretty certain whatever's at the end of it is where she'll be."

"Thank you."

"Good luck." Ceci opens her apartment. "I hope next time I see you it'll be when you're picking up our lady on a proper date."

"Me too," I say with an edge of a grin.

Me too.

With a click of the door, Ceci leaves me alone in the hall to peer down at a single name grasped between my fingers.

Isabelle MacClery.

CHAPTER 64

Nashville

The sun is warm against my skin as I tip my head up and enjoy the cloudless sky. Sounds of squirrels skittering in a nearby oak tree dust across my ears as the low murmuring of voices inside a house float forward. A light breeze carries the sweet smells of the beginnings of a Tennessee autumn, while the temperature still feels very much like summer. It's been ages since I took a vacation, and while this is the last place I thought I would be enjoying one, it's proved more therapeutic than any sandy beach to calm my frayed soul. And even after everything that happened in Mexico, it turns out I still had one worth fixing.

My mind continues to drift aimlessly under the blue sky, as it's done in the past two days, just as a husky but light voice brings my attention back to a small white farmhouse a few yards away, a flowerbed of yellow and red perennials lining its edge.

"Nashville, you have a visitor," an older woman calls through a half-opened screen door.

I shield my eyes, taking in her short gray hair, worn jeans, and T-shirt.

"Thank you," I say to my grandmother with a smile, my skin pricking, sensing what fills the space behind her.

In the next moment, a tall man with dark-brown hair and devastating green eyes walks out. His defined jaw is made shaper with his clean shave, while the rest of him is in his usual gray T-shirt, black jeans, and boots.

Carter doesn't seem very happy as he makes his way over. In fact, his frown deepens just as his pulse kicks into a faster rhythm.

He stops at the edge of my lounge chair, blocking a bit of the sun with his broad shoulders and height. I lie in jean shorts and a green tank top, hair braided to one side. We regard each other, his cinnamon and male scent taking over the fresh-cut grass, and I forgot how much his presence effortlessly affects my body, the way it heats, almost unbearably so.

Setting my Scrabble game aside, I gesture to the second chair. "Join me?"

He glances to it before sitting on the edge of my own instead, forcing me to move my legs to rest against his lower back. A chirping sparrow soars across the sky behind him, its small brown wings fluttering rapidly toward the distant field.

While I've learned that my grandparents' farm hasn't been working in ages, my grandfather still manages to keep the surrounding area trimmed and usable for any future landowners.

"They seem nice." Carter's deep voice floats over on the soft buzz of insects as he nods toward the house he just came from.

"They are."

"She showed me the picture you brought them." His gaze moves to the distant woods that butts up against the property. "Of you and your parents."

"They believed who I was before I even showed them that."

"Why wouldn't they?" His green eyes swing back to mine. "You look just like her."

My stomach tightens.

There's so much of her in you.

My father's voice floats forward from a dark haze, and I swallow against the lump that forms in my throat. I left my tears in Mexico.

"Yes," I say. "I do."

When meeting my grandparents, I was surprised to learn that they knew Isabelle had a child and had even met me a handful of times, but I guess in my mother's quick moment of fleeing, and fear of leading the Oculto back to them, she felt I was safer alone, for the authorities to find. My grandparents had thought I'd died along with their daughter, or at the very least had been taken by my father, who'd disappeared.

But of course, my life's path was neither of those things, and over an emotion-filled evening, I told them the surface version of my upbringing, the one meant for the rest of the world.

I barely finished talking before they stood as one and wrapped me in their arms, saying that I could stay as long as I wished. And as strange as it was to accept another's kindness and charity, I did just that.

Away from what awaited me in Chicago, what I left in Mexico, I stayed and spent time with a family I thought I'd never find. Never deserved to have. And over the course of the weeks, I finally got to see what those lucky enough to be born into a loving household experience. I made dinner with my grandmother, pulled weeds out back with my grandfather, drove to the local store to get groceries in their beat-up pickup truck, and let the wind stream through my open window to dance in my red hair, tapping my fingers on the steering wheel to the rhythm of the radio as I went.

I felt free, and different, and...happy.

Whatever piece of me that got shot, left to die in that office, was slowly replaced by something else. Something good. Something that caused me to stop looking at my past for how I should be and start thinking about my future and what I want to become.

All of this is why I'm able to take in the man before me with a lightness I've never felt before. If he hadn't come today, I had already planned to leave to find him tomorrow.

"I'm glad you're here," I say.

"I've been looking for you for a long time." His gaze remains steady to mine, and I understand his words mean more than just finding me in Tennessee.

"I'm sorry I left like that."

He shakes his head. "I understand why you did."

Silence fills our moment as I allow his presence to wash over me again, to take in the planes of his face, small bump in his nose.

"About...your father." Carter eventually fills the quiet.

"We knew what needed to happen."

"I'm still sorry."

I look down at my lap. "Me too."

"And I want you to know," he goes on, "if I could have

changed what I had to do—"

Leaning up, I stop his words by curling my fingers into his that rest across his knee.

"I'm not mad at you, Carter," I say, squeezing his hand. "You were right. About there being a tomorrow for me. I realized, in that moment of deciding between him and me, that I wouldn't have much of one if I let that syringe go. You saved my life by doing what you did. More than you realize." I study our entwined fingers. "And while I don't think Mendoza was a good man, I don't think he was pure evil either. People don't work like that. We're more nuanced and have the capability to be many things at once. I mean, look at us and what we do for a living." I meet his gaze. "But in the end, my father and I...we would never have been the people we wanted each other to be, and family...well, I learned a long time ago that it has nothing to do with sharing someone's blood."

The buzzing of insects in the distant field fill the air, my words soaking into the sun's rays.

"So...you don't want to kill me?" Carter's green gaze dances as it holds mine.

I give him a small smile. "Not today at least."

Carter searches my features one last time, running his eyes down my body and up again right before he tugs me forward into a kiss.

My heart flutters like the bees' wings in the flowerbeds, my skin warming as his lips slowly play with mine, lazily, like the rolling land around us. With his free hand curling around the back of my neck, he brings me closer, a small moan escaping me as I press into his hard chest. We're two teenagers stealing a moment in the backyard, adolescent pheromones coating the air.

And after an indecent amount of time, given that my grandparents could be watching, we gently separate, grinning like idiots.

"I want you to know," Carter says, his voice coming out a husky rumble. "I don't hate you anymore, Nashville Brown."

I throw my head back with a laugh, a genuine, belly-shaking laugh, and when I glance back to Carter, he appears as if he's glowing like an A+.

"I don't hate you either, Carter Smith."

We could say it, the three words that hide under each of our declarations, but I know we won't, not because we're scared but because we don't need to. That wouldn't be us.

Our actions have always spoken louder.

"Ours won't be a normal kind of relationship, will it?" Carter asks as he shifts me around so I lean against him in the lounge chair, tucked between his legs, my back resting on his chest.

"God, I hope not," I mutter, causing him to chuckle as he rests his chin on the top of my head.

"They want us to partner up again, you know," he says after a moment, each of our gazes resting on the white farmhouse across the yard. It sits like a slumbering pet under the sun, peaceful.

"Of course they do."

"And we'll agree?"

"On occasion."

Another rumble of his laughter plays across my back, warming my heart. "Yes, we'll need to keep them working for it."

"But for right now we'll stay here."

Carter's arms tighten around me. "We'll stay here for as long as you like."

And we do. We stay lying under the Tennessee sun together, until it lowers in the sky, and a smile paints its way across my face, as I finally settle into the girl my name was always meant for.

ACKNOWLEDGMENTS

The character of Nashville (a.k.a 3) came to me hard and fast, like one of her punches. I was in the midst of writing The Destined, my third book in The Dreamland Series, when she kicked open my door, vying for my attention. While I forced her to wait until I was done with my trilogy, Nashville's energy only got stronger, 3's nearly overwhelming. So much so that by the time I was able to properly explore who this woman was, she pulled me into a half-possessed state of writing and plotting and more writing until her story was complete. I love her dearly, envy her superhuman strength, and have never had so much fun getting to know characters as I have with her and Carter. They, in a delightfully twisted way, are my spirit animals, and I know without a doubt I wouldn't have thought them up if it wasn't for my friendship with a certain real-life badass redhead Alicia Heckler, a.k.a Joy, to whom this book is dedicated.

So to her I say thank you. Thank you for going to archery lessons with me, self-defense classes, every action film, and for being an all-around ninja. I'm grateful and lucky to have you in my life.

A big thank you to my family, who are responsible for raising me in an environment where thinking up at least one imaginary thing a day is a mandatory.

To my book-club and bottles-of-wine sisters, Nicky, Jess, Lauren D., Erin, Meg, Giselle, Jillian, and Lauren M.—thank you for being the best supportive team any woman could ask for. You make me laugh when I need to most.

A special call-out of appreciation to Erin Asquith from

Verus Therapy for her notes on the mental health of characters such as Nashville and Carter, specifically the trauma and subsequent behavior one might face from being abandoned at a young age. I thank you for lending me your experience and guidance.

To Dan, my partner in crime, my steady guide in my often spiraling ways—thank you for always cheering me on and for giving me your endless support. I love you.

To my superhero of an editor, Dori Harrell—this book would be a sight for sore eyes without your thoughtful notes, meticulous editing, and constant encouragement. I think part of me is continuing to write just so I can keep you in my life. Thank you. Thank you. Thank you!

To Natasha Minoso—I'm so glad you decided to do such a silly thing as run a half marathon for us to meet. My days are brighter, my TBR pile higher, and my PJ collection larger. Thank you for being a powerhouse of awesome. I love you forever and always. Now stop reading this and come over already!

To Google and the US government, who might stumble upon my web-browsing history—I swear all those searches for poisons, weapons, and how to kill someone without leaving a trace were purely for fictional purposes. Please don't arrest me.

To my Mellow Misfits, Mellow Mob, and the rest of my friends and family, who, for the sake of length, I can't name individually, I am giving you a big hug of love. I've said it before, but I'll say it again—I couldn't have come this far without each of you in my life. I am eternally gratefully.

To my readers—there are no succinct words to describe

how humbled and appreciative I am for you to continue with me on these journeys. I write thinking of you, for you, and with you. I love you dearly, and I hope to travel many more worlds together.

ABOUT THE AUTHOR

 E.J. Mellow is the Award-Winning author behind the NA Contemporary Fantasy trilogy The Dreamland Series and The Animal Under The Fur. With a bachelor's degree in Fine Arts, E.J. Mellow splits her time between her two loves – visual design and writing. Residing in NYC, E.J. is a member of Romance Writers of America and their Fantasy, Futuristic & Paranormal Chapter. She has no animals but loves those who do.

STAY CONNECTED

Website: www.ejmellow.com
Instagram: www.instagram.com/ejmellow
Twitter: www.twitter.com/ej_mellow
Facebook: www.facebook.com/ejmellow

CPSIA information can be obtained
at www.ICGtesting.com
Printed in the USA
LVOW10s1520150517
534580LV00001B/431/P